William Meisters

Thomas Carlyle

William Meisters

Thomas Carlyle

ISBN/EAN: 9783744645416

Printed in Europe, USA, Canada, Australia, Japan

Cover: Foto ©Raphael Reischuk / pixelio.de

More available books at **www.hansebooks.com**

THOMAS CARLYLE

TRANSLATED FROM THE
GERMAN OF GOETHE

IN TWO VOLUMES

VOLUME II

CHAPMAN AND HALL
LIMITED

Originally published 1824

CONTENTS OF VOLUME II

LIST OF PLATES

Goethe – from the statue at Franckfort

"Today at least you are not wrong," replied the other, taking off his hat and showing him the tonsure   "Where is your company gone ? Did you stay long with them ?"

"Longer than was good   on looking back upon the period which I passed in their society, it seems as if I looked into an endless void , nothing of it has remained with me "

"Here you are mistaken," said the stranger, "everything that happens to us leaves some trace behind it, everything contributes imperceptibly to form us   Yet often it is dangerous to take a strict account of that   For either we grow proud and negligent, or downcast and dispirited , and both are equally injurious in their consequences.   The safe plan is, always simply to do the task that lies nearest us , and this in the present case," added he with a smile, " is to hasten to our quarters "

Wilhelm asked how far Lothario's house was distant, the stranger answered that it lay behind the hill   "Perhaps I shall meet you there," continued he , " I have merely a small affair to manage in the neighbourhood   Farewell till then ! " And with this, he struck into a steep path, that seemed to lead ore speedily across the hill

"Yes, the man is right ! " said Wilhelm to himself as he proceeded , " we should think of what is nearest   and for me at present there is nothing nearer than the mournful errand I have come to do   Let me see whether I can still repeat the speech, which is to put that cruel man to shame "

He then began reciting to himself this piece of oratory not a syllable was wanting , and the more his recollection served him, the higher grew his passion and his courage Aurelia's sorrows and her death were vividly present to his soul

"Spirit of my friend ! " exclaimed he , " hover round me , and if thou canst, give some sign to me that thou art softened, art appeased ! "

Amid such words and meditations, he had reached the summit of the hill , and near the foot of its declivity, he now vexed and out of tune, when at last a handsome man, in boots and light surtout, stept in from a side-door " What good news have you for me ? " said he to Wilhelm, with a friendly voice , " pardon me, that I have made you wait "

So speaking, he kept folding a letter, which he held in his hand   Wilhelm, not without embarrassment, delivered him Aurelia's paper, and replied " I bring you the last words of a friend, which you will not read without emotion "

Lothario took it, and returned to his chamber with it , where, as Wilhelm through the open door could very easily observe, he addressed and sealed some letters, before opening Aurelia's   He appeared to have perused it once or twice, and Wilhelm, though his feelings signified that the pathetic speech would sort but ill with such a cool reception, girded up his mind, went forward to the threshold, and was just about beginning his address, when a tapestry door of the cabinet opened, and the clergyman came in

" I have got the strangest message you can think of," cried Lothario to him   " Pardon me," continued he, addressing Wilhelm, " if I am not in a mood for speaking farther with you at this moment   You remain with us tonight   you, Abbé, see the stranger properly attended to "

With these words, he made his guest a bow   the clergyman took Wilhelm by the hand, who followed, not without reluctance

They walked along some curious passages, in silence, and at last reached a very pretty chamber   The Abbé led him in , then left him, making no excuses   Ere long, an active boy appeared , he introduced himself as Wilhelm's valet, and brought up his supper   In waiting, he had much to say about the order of the house, about their breakfasting and dining, labours and amusements, interspersing many things in commendation of Lothario

Pleasant as the boy was, Wilhelm endeavoured to get rid of him as soon as possible   He wished to be alone , for he felt exceedingly oppressed and straitened, in his new position

He reproached himself with having executed his intentions so ill, with having done his errand only half   One moment, he proposed to overtake next morning what he had neglected tonight, the next, he saw that by Lothario's presence he would be attuned to quite a different set of feelings   The house, too, where he was, seemed very strange to him   he could not be at home in his position   Intending to undress, he opened his travelling-bag   with his night-clothes, he took out the Spirit's veil, which Mignon had packed in along with them   The sight of it increased the sadness of his humour. " Fly ! youth, fly !" cried he   " What means this mystic word ? What am I to fly, or whither ?   It were better had the Spirit called to me   Return to thyself !"   He cast his eyes on some English copperplates, hung round the room in frames, most of them he looked at with indifference   at last he met with one, in which a ship was represented sinking in a tempest, a father with his lovely daughters was awaiting death from the intrusive billows   One of the maidens had a kind of likeness to the Amazon   an indescribable compassion seized our friend, he felt an irresistible necessity to vent his feelings, tears filled his eyes, he wept, and did not recover his composure, till slumber overpowered him

Strange dreams arose upon him towards morning   He was in a garden, which in boyhood he had often visited, he looked with pleasure at the well-known alleys, hedges, flower-beds Mariana met him, he spoke to her with love and tenderness, recollecting nothing of any bygone grievance   Ere long his father joined them, in his week-day dress, with a look of frankness that was rare in him, he bade his son fetch two seats from the garden-house, then took Mariana by the hand, and led her into a grove

Wilhelm hastened to the garden-house, but found it altogether empty, only at a window in the farther side he saw Aurelia standing   He went forward and addressed her, but she turned not round, and though he placed himself beside her, he could never see her face. He looked out from the

window, in an unknown garden, there were several people,
some of whom he recognised Frau Melina, seated under a
tree, was playing with a rose which she had in her hand,
Laertes stood beside her, counting money from the one hand
to the other   Mignon and Felix were lying on the grass, the
former on her back, the latter on his face Philina came and
clapped her hands above the children, Mignon lay unmoved,
Felix started up and fled   At first he laughed while running,
as Philina followed but he screamed in terror, when he saw
the Harper coming after him with large, slow steps Felix
ran directly to a pond, Wilhelm hastened after him too late,
the child was lying in the water! Wilhelm stood as if rooted
to the spot   The fair Amazon appeared on the other side of
the pond, she stretched her right hand towards the child, and
walked along the shore   The child came through the water,
by the course her finger pointed to, he followed her as she
went round, at last she reached her hand to him, and pulled
him out   Wilhelm had come nearer   the child was all in
flames, fiery drops were falling from his body Wilhelm's
agony was greater than ever, but instantly the Amazon took
a white veil from her head, and covered up the child with it
The fire was at once quenched But when she lifted up the
veil, two boys sprang out from under it, and frolicsomely
sported to and fro, while Wilhelm and the Amazon proceeded
hand in hand across the garden; and noticed in the distance
Mariana and his father walking in an alley, which was formed
of lofty trees, and seemed to go quite round the garden He
turned his steps to them, and with his beautiful attendant was
moving through the garden, when suddenly the fair-haired
Friedrich came across their path, and kept them back with
loud laughter and a thousand tricks Still, however, they
insisted on proceeding, and Friedrich hastened off, running
towards Mariana and the father These seemed to fly before
him, he pursued the faster, till Wilhelm saw them hovering
down the alley almost as on wings Nature and inclination
called on him to go, and help them, but the hand of the

Amazon detained him How gladly did he let himself be held! With this mingled feeling he awoke, and found his chamber shining with the morning beams

CHAPTER II

Our friend was called to breakfast by the boy he found the Abbé waiting in the hall, Lothario, it appeared, had ridden out The Abbé was not very talkative, but rather wore a thoughtful look, he inquired about Aurelia's death, and listened to our friend's recital of it, with apparent sympathy "Ah!" cried he, "the man that discerns, with lively clearness, what infinite operations art and nature must have joined in, before a cultivated human being can be formed, the man that himself as much as possible takes interest in the culture of his fellowmen, is ready to despair when he sees how lightly mortals will destroy themselves, will blamelessly or blameably expose themselves to be destroyed When I think of these things, life itself appears to me so uncertain a gift, that I could praise the man who does not value it beyond its worth."

Scarcely had he spoken, when the door flew violently up, a young lady came rushing in, she pushed away the old servant who attempted to restrain her She made right to the Abbé, and seized him by the arm, her tears and sobs would hardly let her speak these words "Where is he? Where have you put him? 'Tis a frightful treachery! Confess it now! I know what you are doing I will after him, will know where you have sent him!"

"Be calm, my child," replied the Abbé, with assumed composure, "come with me to your room, you shall know it all, only you must have the strength to listen, if you ask me to relate" He offered her his hand, as if he meant to lead her out. "I will not return to my room," cried she "I hate the walls where you have kept me prisoner so long I know it all already the Colonel has challenged him, he is gone to meet his enemy, perhaps this very moment he—Once or twice I thought I heard the sound of shots! I tell you, order out a coach, and come along with me, or I will fill the house and all the village with my screaming"

Weeping bitterly, she hastened to the window, the Abbé held her back, and sought in vain to soothe her

They heard a sound of wheels she threw up the window, exclaiming "He is dead! They are bringing home his body" "He is coming out," replied the Abbé, "you perceive he lives" "He is wounded," said she wildly, "else he would have come on horseback They are holding him! The wound is dangerous!" She ran to the door, and down the stairs the Abbé hastened after her, and Wilhelm following, observed the fair one meet her lover, who had now dismounted

Lothario leaned on his attendant, whom Wilhelm at once knew as his ancient patron Jarno The wounded man spoke very tenderly and kindly to the tearful damsel, he rested on her shoulder, and came slowly up the steps, saluted Wilhelm as he passed, and was conducted to his cabinet

Jarno soon returned, and going up to Wilhelm, "It appears," said he, " you are predestined everywhere to find a theatre and actors We have here commenced a play which is not altogether pleasant "

"I rejoice to find you," answered Wilhelm, "in so strange an hour I am astonished, frightened, and your presence already quiets my mind Tell me, is there danger? Is the Baron badly wounded?" "I imagine not," said Jarno

It was not long till the young surgeon entered from the cabinet "Now what say you?" cried Jarno to him "That it is a dangerous piece of work," replied the other, putting several instruments into his leathern pouch Wilhelm looked at the band, which was hanging from the pouch, he fancied he knew it Bright contrary colours, a curious pattern, gold and silver wrought in singular figures, marked this band from all the bands in the world Wilhelm was convinced he beheld

the very pouch of the ancient surgeon, who had dressed his
wounds in the green of the forest, and the hope, so long
deferred, of again finding traces of the lovely Amazon, struck
like a flame through all his soul

"Where did you get that pouch?" cried he "To whom
did it belong before you? I beg of you, tell me" "I bought
it at an auction," said the other "what is it to me, whom it
belonged to?" So speaking, he went out, and Jarno said
"If there would come but one word of truth from our young
Doctor's mouth!" "Then he did not buy the pouch?" said
Wilhelm "Just as little as Lothario is in danger," said the
other

Wilhelm stood immersed in many reflections, Jarno asked
how he had fared of late Wilhelm sketched an outline of his
history, and when he at last came to speak of Aurelia's death,
and his message to the place, his auditor exclaimed "Well!
it is strange, most strange!"

The Abbé entered from Lothario's chamber, beckoned
Jarno to go in instead of him, and said to Wilhelm "The
Baron bids me ask you to remain with us a day or two, to
share his hospitality, and, in the present circumstances, contri-
¹ ute to his solacement If you need to give any notice to
your people, your letter shall be instantly despatched Meanwhile, to make you understand this curious incident, of which
you have been witness, I must tell you something, which indeed
is no secret The Baron had a small adventure with a lady,
which excited more than usual attention, the lady having
taken him from a rival, and wishing to enjoy her victory too
ostentatiously After a time, he no longer found the same
delight in her society, which he of course forsook but being
of a violent temper, she could not bear her fate with patience
Meeting at a ball, they had an open quarrel. she thought
herself irreparably injured, and would be revenged No
knight stept forth to do battle for her, till her husband,
whom for years she had not lived with, heard of the affair
and took it up He challenged the Baron, and today he has

wounded him, yet, as I hear, the gallant Colonel has himself
come still worse off"

From this hour, our friend was treated in the house as if he
had belonged to it

CHAPTER III

AT times they had read a little to the patient, Wilhelm
joyfully performed this service   Lydia stirred not from
Lothario's bed, her care for him absorbed her whole attention
But today the patient himself seemed occupied with thought
he bade them lay aside their book   "Today," said he, "I feel
through my whole heart how foolishly we let our time pass on
How many things have I proposed to do, how many have I
planned, yet how we loiter in our noblest purposes'   I have
just read over the scheme of the changes which I mean to
make in my estates   and it is chiefly, I may say, on their
account that I rejoice at the bullet's not having gone a deadlier
road "

Lydia looked at him with tenderness, with tears in her eyes,
as if to ask if *she*, if his friends could not pretend to any
interest in his wish to live   Jarno answered   " Changes, such
as you project, require to be considered well on every side,
before they are resolved on "

"Long considerations," said Lothario, "are commonly a
proof that we have not the point to be determined clearly in
our eye, precipitate proceedings, that we do not know it   I
see distinctly that in managing my property, there are several
particulars, in which the services of my dependants cannot be
remitted, certain rights which I must rigidly insist on   but I
also see that there are other articles, advantageous to e, but
by no means indispensable, which might admit of relaxation
Do I not profit by my lands far better than my father did ?
Is not my income still increasing ?   And shall I alone enjoy
this growing benefit ?   Shall not those who labour with and

for me partake, in their degree, of the advantages which expanding knowledge, which a period of improvement are procuring for us ? "

" 'Tis human nature ! " cried Jarno " I do not blame myself when I detect this selfish quality among the rest Every man desires to gather all things round him, to shape and manage them according to his own pleasure the money which he himself does not expend, he seldom reckons well expended "

" Certainly," observed Lothario, " much of the capital might be abated, if we consumed the interest less capriciously "

" The only thing I shall mention," said the other, " the only reason I can urge against your now proceeding with those alterations, which, for a time at least, must cause you loss, is, that you yourself are still in debt, and that the payment presses hard on you My advice is, therefore, to postpone your plan till you are altogether free '

" And in the mean while leave it at the mercy of a bullet, or the fall of a tile, to annihilate the whole result of my existence and activity ! O my friend ! it is ever thus , it is ever the besetting fault of cultivated men, that they wish to spend their whole resources on some idea, scarcely any part of them on tangible existing objects Why was it that I contracted debts, that I quarrelled with my uncle, that I left my sisters to themselves so long ? Purely for the sake of an idea In America, I fancied I might accomplish something , over seas, I hoped to become useful and essential if any task was not begun with a thousand dangers, I considered it trivial, unworthy of me How differently do matters now appear ! How precious, how important seems the duty which is nearest me, whatever it may be ! "

" I recollect the letter which you sent me from the Western world," said Jarno " it contained the words ' I will return, and in my house, amid my fields, among my people, I will say *Here or nowhere is America !* ' "

" Yes, my friend ! and I am still repeating it, and still

repining at myself that I am not so busy here as I was there
For certain equable, continuous modes of life, there is nothing
more than judgment necessary, and we study to attain nothing
more, so that we become unable to discern what extraordinary
services each vulgar day requires of us, or if we do discern
them, we find abundance of excuses for not doing them   A
judicious man is valuable to himself, but of little value for
the general whole "

"We will not," said Jarno, " bear too hard upon judgment
let us grant that whenever extraordinary things are done, they
are generally foolish "

"Yes! and just because they are not done according to
the proper plan   My brother-in-law, you see, is giving up
his fortune, so far as in his power, to the Community of
Herrnhut   he reckons that by doing so, he is advancing the
salvation of his soul   Had he sacrificed a small portion of his
revenue, he might have rendered many people happy, might
have made for them and for himself a heaven upon earth
Our sacrifices are rarely of an active kind, we, as it were,
abandon what we give away   It is not from resolution but
despair, that we renounce our property   In these days, I
confess it, the image of the Count is hovering constantly
before me, I have firmly resolved on doing from conviction,
what a crazy fear is forcing upon him   I will not wait for
being cured   Here are the papers   they require only to be
properly drawn out   Take the lawyer with you, our guest
will help   what I want, you know as well as I, recovering
or dying I will stand by it, and say   *Here or nowhere is
Herrnhut!*"

When he mentioned dying, Lydia sank before his bed, she
hung upon his arm, and wept bitterly   The surgeon entered,
Jarno gave our friend the papers, and made Lydia leave the
room

"For Heaven's sake! what is this about the Count?" cried
Wilhelm, when they reached the hall and were alone   "What
Count is it that means to join the Herrnhuters?"

"One whom you know very well," said Jarno "You your-self are the ghost who have frightened the unhappy wiseacre into piety, you are the villain who have brought his pretty wife to such a state, that she inclines accompanying him "

"And she is Lothario's sister ? " cried our friend

"No other ! "—"And Lothario knows— ?"

"The whole "

"O let me fly ! " cried Wilhelm "How shall I appear before him ? What can he say to me ?"

"That no man should cast a stone at his brother, that when one composes long speeches, with a view to shame his neighbours, he should speak them to a looking-glass "

"Do you know that too ?"

"And many things beside," said Jarno with a smile "But in the present case," continued he, "you shall not get away from me so easily as you did last time You need not now be apprehensive of my bounty-money, I have ceased to be a soldier, when I was one, you might have thought more charitably of me Since you saw me, many things have altered My Prince, my only friend and benefactor, being dead, I have now withdrawn from busy life and its concerns I used to have a pleasure in advancing what was reasonable, when I met with any despicable thing, I hesitated not to call it so and men had never done with talking of my restless head and wicked tongue The herd of people dread sound understanding more than anything; they ought to dread stupidity, if they had any notion what was really dreadful Understanding is unpleasant, they must have it pushed aside, stupidity is but pernicious, they can let it stay Well, be it so ! I need to live, I will by and by communicate my plans to you, if you incline, you shall partake in them But tell me first how things have gone with you I see, I feel that you are changed How is it with your ancient maggot of producing something beautiful and good in the society of gypsies ?"

"Do not speak of it ! " cried Wilhelm "I have been

already punished for it People talk about the stage, but none, that has not been upon it personally, can form the smallest notion of it How utterly these men are unacquainted with themselves, how thoughtlessly they carry on their trade, how boundless their pretensions are, no mortal can conceive Each not only would be first, but sole, each wishes to exclude the rest, and does not see that even with them, he can scarcely accomplish anything Each thinks himself a man of marvellous originality, yet with a ravening appetite for novelty, he cannot walk a footstep from the beaten track How vehemently they counterwork each other! It is only the pitifulest self-love, the narrowest views of interest, that unite them Of reciprocal accommodation they have no idea, backbiting and hidden spitefulness maintain a constant jealousy among them In their lives they are either rakes or simpletons Each claims the loftiest respect, each writhes under the slightest blame 'All this he knew already,' he will tell you! Why then did he not do it? Ever needy, ever unconfiding, they seem as if their greatest fear were reason and good taste, their highest care were to secure the majesty of their self-will"

Wilhelm drew breath, intending to proceed with his eulogium, when an immoderate laugh from Jarno interrupted him "Poor actors!" cried he, threw himself into a chair, and laughed away "Poor dear actors! Do you know, my friend," continued he, recovering from his fit, "that you have been describing not the playhouse, but the world, that out of all ranks I could find you characters and doings in abundance, to suit your cruel pencil? Pardon me, it makes me laugh again, that you should think these amiable qualities existed on the boards alone"

Wilhelm checked his feelings Jarno's extravagant, untimely laughter had in truth offended him "It is scarcely hiding your misanthropy," said he, "when you maintain that faults like these are universal"

"And it shows your unacquaintance with the world, when

you impute them to the theatre in such a heinous light I pardon in the player every fault that springs from self-deception and the desire to please If he seem not something to himself and others, he is nothing To seem is his vocation, he must prize his moment of applause, for he gets no other recompense, he must try to glitter, he is there to do so "

"You will give me leave at least to smile, in my turn," answered Wilhelm "I should never have believed that you could be so merciful, so tolerant "

"I swear to you I am serious, fully and deliberately serious All faults of the man I can pardon in the player, no fault of the player can I pardon in the man Do not set me upon chanting my lament about the latter it might have a sharper sound than yours "

The Surgeon entered from the cabinet, and to the question how his patient was, he answered with a lively air of complaisance "Extremely well indeed, I hope soon to see him quite recovered " He hastened through the hall, not waiting Wilhelm's speech, who was preparing to inquire again with greater importunity about the leathern case His anxiety to gain some tidings of his Amazon inspired him with confidence in Jarno he disclosed his case to him, and begged his help "You that know so many things," said he, "can you not discover this ? "

Jarno reflected for a moment, then turning to his friend "Be calm," said he, "give no one any hint of it we shall come upon the fair one's footsteps, never fear At present, I am anxious only for Lothario the case is dangerous, the kindliness and comfortable talking of the Doctor tells me so We should be quit of Lydia, for here she does no good · but how to set about the task, I know not Tonight I am looking for our old Physician, we shall then take farther counsel "

CHAPTER IV

THE Physician came it was the good, old, little Doctor whom we know already, and to whom we were obliged for the communication of the pious Manuscript First of all, he visited the wounded man , with whose condition he appeared to be by no means satisfied He had next a long interview with Jarno but they made no allusion to the subject of it when they came to supper

Wilhelm saluted him in the kindest manner, and inquired about the Harper. "We have still hopes of bringing round the hapless creature," answered the Physician "He formed a dreary item in your limited and singular way of life," said Jarno "How has it fared with him ? Tell me "

Having satisfied Jarno's curiosity, the Physician thus proceeded "I have never seen another man so strangely circumstanced For many years, he has not felt the smallest interest in anything without him, scarcely paid the smallest notice to it. wrapped up in himself, he has looked at nothing but his own hollow empty Me, which seemed to him like an immeasurable abyss It was really touching, when he spoke to us of this mournful state 'Before me,' cried he, 'I see nothing , behind me nothing but an endless night, in which I live in the most horrid solitude There is no feeling in me, but the feeling of my guilt and this appears but like a dim formless spirit, far before me Yet here there is no height, no depth, no forwards, no backwards , no words can express this never-changing state Often in the agony of this sameness, I exclaim with violence Forever ! forever and this dark incomprehensible word is clear and plain to the gloom of my condition No ray of a Divinity illuminates this night , I shed all my tears by myself and for myself Nothing is more horrible to me than friendship and love , for they alone excite in me the wish that the Apparitions which surround me might be real

But these two Spectres also have arisen from the abyss to plague me, and at length to tear from me the precious consciousness of my existence, unearthly though it be.'

"You should hear him speak," continued the Physician, "when in hours of confidence he thus alleviates his heart I have listened to him often with the deepest feelings When pressed by anything, and as it were compelled for an instant to confess that a space of time has passed, he looks astounded, then again refers the alteration to the things about him, considering it as an appearance of appearances, and so rejecting the idea of progress in duration One night he sung a song about his grey hairs we all sat round him weeping"

" O get it for me !" cried Wilhelm

"But have you not discovered any trace of what he calls his crime?" inquired Jarno "nor found out the reason of his wearing such a singular garb, of his conduct at the burning of the house, of his rage against the child ?"

"It is only by conjectures that we can approximate to any knowledge of his fate to question him directly, contradicts our principle Observing easily that he was of the Catholic religion, we thought perhaps confession might afford him some assuagement, but he shrinks away, with the strangest gestures, every time we try to introduce the priest to him However, not to leave your curiosity respecting him entirely unsatisfied, I may communicate our suppositions on the subject In his youth, we think, he must have been a clergyman hence probably his wish to keep his beard and long cloak The joys of love appear to have remained for many years unknown to him Late in life, as we conceive, some aberration with a lady very nearly related to him, then her death, the consequence of an unlucky creature's birth, have altogether crazed his brain

"His chief delusion is a fancy that he brings misfortune everywhere along with him, and that death, to be unwittingly occasioned by a boy, is constantly impending over him At first he was afraid of Mignon, not knowing that she was a girl, then Felix frightened him, and as, with all his misery, he has a boundless love of life, this may perhaps have been the origin of his aversion to the child "

" What hopes have you of his recovery ? " inquired our friend

" It advances slowly," answered the Physician , " yet it does advance   He continues his appointed occupations   we have now accustomed him to read the newspapers , he always looks for them with eagerness "

" I am curious about his songs," said Jarno

" Of these I can engage to get you several," replied the Doctor   " Our parson's eldest son, who frequently writes down his father's sermons, has, unnoticed by the Harper, marked on paper many stanzas of his singing , out of which some songs have gradually been pieced together "

Next morning Jarno met our friend, and said to him   " We have to ask a kindness of you   Lydia must, for some time, be removed   her violent unreasonable love and passionateness hinders the Baron's recovery   His wound requires rest and calmness, though with his healthy temperament it is not dangerous   You see how Lydia tortures him with her tempestuous anxieties, her ungovernable terrors, her never-drying tears, and—Enough ! " he added with a smile, after pausing for a moment, " our Doctor expressly requires that she must quit us for a while   We have got her to believe that a lady, one of her most intimate friends, is at present in the neighbourhood, wishing and expecting instantly to see her   She has been prevailed upon to undertake a journey to our lawyer's, which is but two leagues off   This man is in the secret   he will wofully lament that Fräulein Theresa should just have left him again , he will seem to think she may still be overtaken   Lydia will hasten after her , and if you prosper, will be led from place to place   At last, if she insist on turning back, you must not contradict her , but the night will help you , the coachman is a cunning knave, and we shall speak with him before he goes   You are to travel with her in the coach, to talk to her, and manage the adventure "

" It is a strange and dubious commission that you give me," answered Wilhelm " How painful is the sight of true love injured ! And am I to be the instrument of injuring it ? I have never cheated any person so , for it has always seemed to me that if we once begin deceiving with a view to good and useful purposes, we run the risk of carrying it to excess "

" Yet you cannot manage children otherwise," said Jarno

" With children it may do," said Wilhelm , " for we love them tenderly, and take an open charge of them   But with our equals, in behalf of whom our heart is not so sure to call upon us for forbearance, it might frequently be dangerous Yet do not think," he added, after pausing for a moment, " that I intend to decline the task on this account   Honouring your judgment, as I do, feeling such attachment to your noble friend, such eagerness to forward his recovery by whatever means, I willingly forget myself and my opinions 'It is not enough that we can risk our life to serve a friend , in the hour of need we should also yield him our convictions   Our dearest passions, our best wishes we are bound to sacrifice in helping him   I undertake the charge , though it is easy to foresee the pain I shall have to suffer from the tears, from the despair of Lydia "

" And for this, no small reward awaits you," answered Jarno   " Fraulein Theresa, whom you get acquainted with, is a lady such as you will rarely see   She puts many a man to shame   I may say, she is a genuine Amazon , while others are but pretty counterfeits, that wander up and down the world in that ambiguous dress "

Wilhelm was struck   he almost fancied that in Theresa he would find his Amazon again , especially as Jarno, whom he importuned to tell him more, broke off abruptly, and went away

The new, near hope of once more seeing that beloved and honoured being, awoke a thousand feelings in his heart.   He now looked upon the task, which had been given him, as the intervention of a special Providence , the thought that he

was minded treacherously to carry off a helpless girl frc
the object of her sincerest warmest love, dwelt but a momer.
in his mind, as the shadow of a bird flits over the sunshiny
earth.

The coach was at the door, Lydia lingered for a moment,
as she was about to mount "Salute your lord again for me,"
said she to the old servant, "tell him that I shall be home
before night" Tears were standing in her eyes, as she again
looked back when the carriage started She then turned round
to Wilhelm, made an effort to compose herself, and said
"In Fraulein Theresa you will find a very interesting person
I wonder what it is that brings her hither for, you must know,
Lothario and she once passionately loved each other In spite
of the distance, he often used to visit her I was staying with
her then, I thought they would have lived and died for one
another But all at once it went to wreck, no creature could
discover why He had seen me, and I must confess that I
was envious of Theresa's fortune, that I scarcely hid my love
from him, that when he suddenly appeared to choose me in
her stead, I could not but accept of him She behaved to
me beyond my wishes, though it almost seemed as if I had
robbed her of this precious lover But ah, how many thousand
tears and pains that love of his has cost me! At first we met
only now and then, and by stealth, at some appointed place;
but I could not long endure that kind of life in his presence
only was I happy, wholly happy! Far from him, my eyes
were never dry, my pulse was never calm Once he stayed
away for several days I was altogether in despair, I ordered
out my carriage, and surprised him here He received me
tenderly, and had not this unlucky quarrel happened, I
should have led a heavenly life with him But since the
time when he began to be in danger and in pain, I shall
not say what I have suffered at this moment I am bitterly
reproaching myself, that I could leave him for a single day"

Wilhelm was proceeding to inquire about Theresa, when
they reached the lawyer's house This gentleman came

forward to the coach, lamenting wofully that Fraulein Theresa
was already gone   He invited them to breakfast, signifying,
however, that the lady might be overtaken in the nearest
village   They determined upon following her   the coachman
did not loiter, they had soon passed several villages, and yet
come up with nobody   Lydia now gave orders for returning,
the coachman drove along, as if he did not understand her
As she insisted with redoubled vehemence, Wilhelm called to
him, and gave the promised token   The coachman answered,
that it was not necessary to go back by the same road, he
knew a shorter, and at the same time greatly easier one   He
now turned aside across a wood, and over large commons   At
last, no object they could recognise appearing, he confessed
that unfortunately he had lost his way, declaring at the
same time that he would soon get right again, as he saw a
little town before him   Night came on, the coachman
managed so discreetly that he asked everywhere, and nowhere
waited for an answer   He drove along all night   Lydia
never closed an eye, in the moonshine she was constantly
detecting similarities, which as constantly turned out to be
dissimilar   In the morning, things around seemed known to
her, and but more strange on that account   The coach drew
up before a neat little country-house, a young lady stepped
out, and opened the carriage-door   Lydia looked at her with
a stare of wonder, looked round, looked at her again, and
fainted in the arms of Wilhelm

CHAPTER V

WILHELM was conducted to a little upper-room   the house
was new, as small nearly as it could be, and extremely orderly
and clean   In Theresa, who had welcomed him and Lydia at
the coach, he had not found his Amazon   she was another
and an altogether different woman   Handsome, and but of
middle stature, she moved about with great alertness, and

it seemed as if her clear blue open eyes let nothing that occurred escape them

She entered Wilhelm's room, inquiring if he wanted anything "Pardon me," said she, "for having lodged you in a chamber which the smell of paint still renders disagreeable. my little dwelling is but just made ready, you are handselling this room, which is appointed for my guests Would that you had come on some more pleasant errand! Poor Lydia is like to be a dull companion, in other points also, you will have much to pardon My cook has run away from me, at this unseasonable time, and a serving-man has bruised his hand The case might happen I had to manage everything myself, and if it were so, why then we should just put up with it One is plagued so with nobody as with one's servants, none of them will serve you, scarcely even serve himself"

She said a good deal more on different matters, in general she seemed to like speaking Wilhelm inquired for Lydia, if he might not see her, and endeavour to excuse himself.

"It will have no effect at present," said Theresa, "time excuses, as it comforts Words, in both cases, are of little effect Lydia will not see you 'Keep him from my sight,' she cried, when I was leaving her, 'I could almost despair of human nature Such an honourable countenance, so frank a manner, and this secret guile!' Lothario she has quite forgiven in a letter to the poor girl he declares 'My friends persuaded me, my friends compelled me!' Among these she reckons you, and she condemns you with the rest"

"She does me too much honour in so blaming me," said Wilhelm "I have no pretension to the friendship of that noble gentleman, on this occasion, I am but a guiltless instrument I will not praise what I have done, it is enough that I could do it It concerned the health, it concerned the life of a man, whom I value more than any one I ever knew before O what a man is he, Fraulein, and what men are they that live about him! In their society I for the first

time, I may well say, carried on a conversation, for the first
time, was the inmost sense of my words returned to me, more
rich, more full, more comprehensive, from another's mouth,
what I had been groping for, was rendered clear to me, what
I had been thinking, I was taught to see   Unfortunately
this enjoyment was disturbed, at first by numerous anxieties
and whims, and then by this unpleasant task   I undertook
it with submission, for I reckoned it my duty, even though
I sacrificed my feelings, to comply with the request of this
gifted company of men "

While he spoke, Theresa had been looking at him with a
very friendly air   " O how sweet is it, to hear one's own
opinion uttered by a stranger tongue !   We are never properly
ourselves until another thinks entirely as we do   My own
opinion of Lothario is perfectly the same as yours: it is not
every one that does him justice, and therefore all that know
him better are enthusiastic in esteem of him   The painful
sentiment that mingles with the memory of him in my heart,
cannot hinder me from thinking of him daily "   A sigh heaved
her bosom as she spoke thus, and a lovely tear glittered in
her right eye   " Think not," continued she, " that I am so
weak, so easy to be moved   It is but the eye that weeps
There was a little wart upon the under eyelid, they have
happily removed it, but the eye has been weak ever since,
the smallest cause brings a tear into it   Here sat the little
wart   you cannot see a vestige of it now "

He saw no vestige, but he saw into her eye, it was clear
as crystal, he almost imagined he could see to the very
bottom of her soul

" We have now," said she, " pronounced the watchword of
our friendship   let us get entirely acquainted as fast as
possible   The history of every person paints his character
I will tell you what my life has been   do you too place a
little trust in me, and let us be united even when distance
parts us   The world is so waste and empty, when we figure
only towns and hills and rivers in it, but to know of some

one here and there whom we accord with, who is living on with us even in lence, this makes our earthly ball a peopled garden "

She hastened off, engaging soon to take him out to walk Her presence had affected him agreeably he wished to be informed of her relation to Lothario He was called, she came to meet him from her room While they descended, necessarily one by one, the strait and even steepish stairs, she said "All this might have been larger and grander, had I chosen to accept the offers of your generous friend but to continue worthy of him, I must study to retain the qualities which gave me merit in his eyes —Where is the steward?" asked she, stepping from the bottom of the stairs "You must not think," continued she, "that I am rich enough to need a steward the few acres of my own little property I myself can manage well enough The steward is my new neighbour's, who has bought a fine estate beside us, every point of which I am acquainted with The good old gentleman is lying ill of gout, his men are strangers here, I willingly assist in settling them "

They took a walk through fields, meadows and some orchards Everywhere Theresa kept instructing the steward, nothing so minute but she could give account of it, and Wilhelm had reason to wonder at her knowledge, her precision, the prompt dexterity with which she suggested means for ends She loitered nowhere, always hastened to the leading points, and thus her task was quickly over "Salute your master,' said she, as she sent away the man, "I mean to visit him as soon as possible, and wish him a complete recovery —There now," she added with a smile, as soon as he was gone, 'I might soon be rich my good neighbour, I believe, would not be disinclined to offer me his hand "

"The old man with the gout?" cried Wilhelm "I know not how, at your years, you could bring yourself to make so desperate a determination " "Nor am I tempted to it!" said Theresa "Whoever can administer what he possesses has enough, and to be wealthy is a burdensome affair, unless you understand it "

Wilhelm testified his admiration at her skill in husbandry concerns "Decided inclination, early opportunity, external impulse, and continued occupation in a useful business," said she, "make many things, which were at first far harder, possible in life   When you have learned what causes stimulated me in this pursuit, you will cease to wonder at the talent you now think strange '

On returning home, she sent him to her little garden Here he could scarcely turn himself, so narrow were the walks, so thickly was it sown and planted   On looking over to the court, he could not help smiling   the firewood was lying there, as accurately sawed, split and piled, as if it had been part of the building, and had been intended to continue permanently there   The tubs and implements, all clean, were standing in their places   the house was painted white and red , it was really pleasant to behold   Whatever can be done by handicraft, which knows not beautiful proportions, but labours for convenience, cheerfulness and durability, appeared united in this spot   They served him up dinner in his own room , he had time enough for meditating   Especially it struck him, that he should have got acquainted with another person of so interesting a character, who had been so closely related to Lothario   "It is just," said he to himself, "that a man so gifted should attract round him gifted women   How far the influence of manliness and dignity extends !   Would that others did not come so wofully short, compared with him !   Yes, confess thy fear When thou meetest with thy Amazon, this woman of women, in spite of all thy hopes and dreaming, thou wilt find her, in the end, to thy humiliation and thy shame,—his bride "

CHAPTER VI

WILHELM had passed a restless afternoon, not altogether without tedium, when towards evening his door opened, and a handsome hunter-boy stept forward with a bow "Shall we have a walk?" said the youth, and in the instant Wilhelm recognised Theresa by her lovely eyes

"Pardon me this masquerade," said she, "for now, alas, it is nothing more   But as I am going to tell you of the time when I so enjoyed the world, I will recall those days, by every method, to my fancy   Come along!   Even the place, where we have rested so often from our hunts and promenades, shall help me"

They went accordingly   On the way, Theresa said to her attendant   "It is not fair that I alone should speak   you already know enough of me, I nothing about you   Tell me in the mean while something of yourself, that I may gather courage to submit to you my history and situation"   "Alas!" said Wilhelm, "I have nothing to relate but error on the back of error, deviation following deviation   and I know none from whom I would more gladly hide my present and my past embarrassments than from yourself   Your look, the scene you move in, your whole temperament and manner, prove to me that you have reason to rejoice in your bygone life, that you have travelled by a fair, clear path, in constant progress, that you have lost no time, that you have nothing to reproach yourself withal"

Theresa answered with a smile   "Let us see if you will think so, after you have heard my history"   They walked along   among some general remarks, Theresa asked him "Are you free?"   "I think I am," said he, "and yet I do not wish it"   "Good!" said she   "that indicates a complicated story, you also will have something to relate"

Conversing thus, they ascended the hill, and placed themselves beside a lofty oak, which spread its shade far out on

every side " Here," said she, " beneath this German tree,
will I disclose to you the history of a German maiden listen
to me patiently

" My father was a wealthy nobleman of this province, a
cheerful, clear-sighted, active, able man , a tender father, an
upright friend, an excellent economist I knew but one fault
in him , he was too compliant to a wife who did not know his
worth. Alas, that I should have to say so of my mother!
Her nature was the opposite of his She was quick and
changeful, without affection either for her home, or for me
her only child , extravagant, but beautiful, sprightly, full of
talent, the delight of a circle she had gathered round her
Her society in truth was never large , nor did it long continue
the same It consisted principally of men , for no woman
could like to be near her, still less could *she* endure the merit
or the praise of any woman I resembled my father, both in
form and dispositions As the duckling, with its first footsteps, seeks the water , so, from my earliest youth, the kitchen,
the store-room, the granaries, the fields, were my selected
element Cleanliness and order in the house, seemed, even
while I was playing in it, to be my peculiar instinct, my
peculiar object This tendency gave my father pleasure , and
he directed, step by step, my childish endeavour into the suit-
ablest employments On the contrary, my mother did not
like me, and she never for a moment hid it

" I waxed in statue with my years, increased my turn for
occupation and my father's love to me When we were by
ourselves, when walking through the fields, when I was helping
to examine his accounts, it was then I could see how glad he
was While gazing on his eyes, I felt as if I had been looking
in upon myself for it was in the eyes that I completely resembled him But in the presence of my mother, he lost this
energy, this aspect he excused me mildly, when she blamed me
unjustly and violently , he took my part, not as if he would
protect me, but as if he would extenuate the demerit of my
good qualities To none of her caprices did he set himself in

opposition   She began to be immensely taken with a passion for the stage , a theatre was soon got up , of men of all shapes and ages, crowding to display themselves along with her upon her boards, she had abundance , of women, on the other hand, there was often a scarcity   Lydia, a pretty girl, who had been brought up with me, and who promised from the first to be extremely beautiful, had to undertake the secondary parts, the mothers and the aunts were represented by an ancient chambermaid , while the leading heroines, lovers, and shepherdesses of every kind, were seized on by my mother   I cannot tell you how ridiculous it seemed to me, to see the people, every one of whom I knew full well, standing on their scaffold, and pretending, after they had dressed themselves in other clothes, to pass for something else than what they were   In my eyes they were never anything but Lydia and my mother, this baron and that secretary, whether they appeared as counts and princes or as peasants   and I could not understand how they meant to make me think that they were sad or happy, that they were indifferent or in love, liberal or avaricious, when I well knew the contrary to be the case   Accordingly, I very seldom stayed among the audience   I always snuffed their candles, that I might not be entirely without employment , I prepared the supper , and next morning before they rose I used to have their wardrobe all sorted, which commonly, the night before, they had left in a chaotic state

"To my mother this activity appeared quite proper , but her love I could not gain   She despised me , and I know for certain that she more than once exclaimed with bitterness 'If the mother could be as uncertain as the father, you would scarcely take this housemaid for my daughter !'   Such treatment, I confess, at length entirely estranged me from her   I viewed her conduct as the conduct of a person unconnected with me , and being used to watch our servants like a falcon (for this, be it said in passing, is the ground of all true housekeeping), the proceedings of my mother and her friends, at the same time, naturally forced themselves upon my observa-

tion   It was easy to perceive that she did not look on all the
men alike   I gave sharper heed, and soon found out that
Lydia was her confidant, and had herself, by this opportunity,
become acquainted with a passion, which from her earliest
youth she had so often represented   I was aware of all their
meetings   but I held my tongue, hinting nothing to my
father, whom I was afraid of troubling   At last, however, I
was obliged to speak   Many of their enterprises could not be
accomplished without corrupting the servants   These now
began to grow refractory, they despised my father's regulations, disregarded my commands   The disorders which arose
from this I could not tolerate, I discovered all, complained of
all to my father

"He listened to me calmly   'Good girl!' replied he with
a smile, 'I know it all. be quiet, bear it patiently, for it is
on thy account alone that I endure it'

"I was not quiet, I had not patience   I in secret
blamed my father, for I did not think that any reason should
induce him to endure such things   I called for regularity
from all the servants, I was bent on driving matters to
extremity

"My mother had been rich before her marriage, yet she
squandered more than she had a right to, and this, as I
observed, occasioned many conferences between my parents
For a long time, the evil was not helped, till at last the
passions of my mother brought it to a head

"Her first gallant became unfaithful in a glaring manner
the house, the neighbourhood, her whole condition grew
offensive to her   She insisted on removing to a different
estate, there she was too solitary   she insisted on removing
to the town, there she felt herself eclipsed among the crowd.
Of much that passed between my father and her I know
nothing   however, he at last determined, under stipulations
which I did not learn, to consent that she should take a
journey, which she had been meditating, to the South of
France

"We were now free, we lived as if in heaven. I do believe, my father could not be a loser, had he purchased her absence by a considerable sum. All our useless domestics were dismissed, and fortune seemed to smile on our undertakings: we had some extremely prosperous years, all things succeeded to our wish. But, alas, this pleasing state was not of long continuance, altogether unexpectedly my father had a shock of palsy, it lamed his right side, and deprived him of the proper use of speech. We had to guess at everything that he required, for he never could pronounce the word that he intended. There were times when this was dreadfully afflicting to us. he would require expressly to be left alone with me, with earnest gestures he would signify that every one should go away, and when we saw ourselves alone, he could not speak the word he meant. His impatience mounted to the highest pitch. his situation touched me to the inmost heart. Thus much seemed certain. he had something which he wished to tell me, which especially concerned my interest. What longing did I feel to know it! At other times, I could discover all things in his eyes. but now it was in vain. Even his eyes no longer spoke. Only this was clear. he wanted nothing, he desired nothing, he was striving to discover something to me, which unhappily I did not learn. His malady revisited him. he grew entirely inactive, incapable of motion, and a short time afterwards he died.

"I know not how it had got rooted in my thoughts that somewhere he had hid a treasure, which he wished at death to leave me rather than my mother. I searched about for traces of it while he lived, but I could meet with none, at his death a seal was put on everything. I wrote to my mother, offering to continue in the house, and manage for her. she refused, and I was obliged to leave the place. A mutual testament was now produced, it gave my mother the possession and the use of all, and I was left, at least throughout her life, dependent on her. It was now that I conceived I rightly understood my father's beckoning. I pitied him for having been so weak, he had let himself be forced to do unjustly to me even after he was dead Certain of my friends maintained, that it was little better than if he had disinherited me they called upon me to attack the will by law, but this I never could resolve on doing I reverenced my father's memory too much, I trusted in destiny, I trusted in myself

"There was a lady in the neighbourhood possessed of large property, with whom I had always been on good terms she gladly received me, I engaged to superintend her household, and ere long the task grew very easy to me She lived regularly, she loved order in everything and I faithfully assisted her in struggling with her steward and domestics I am neither of a niggardly nor grudging temper, but we women are disposed to insist, more earnestly than men, that nothing shall be wasted Embezzlement of all sorts is intolerable to us we require that each enjoy exactly in so far as right entitles him

"Here I was in my element once more, I mourned my father's death in silence My protectress was content with me one small circumstance alone disturbed my peace Lydia returned my mother had been harsh enough to cast the poor girl off, after having altogether spoiled her Lydia had learned with her mistress to consider passions as her occupation, she was wont to curb herself in nothing On her unexpected reappearance, the lady whom I lived with took her in, she wished to help me, but could train herself to nothing

"About this time, the relatives and future heirs of my protectress often visited the house, to recreate themselves with hunting Lothario was frequently among them it was not long till I had noticed, though without the smallest reference to myself, how far he was superior to the rest He was courteous towards all, and Lydia seemed ere long to have attracted his attention to her Constantly engaged in something, I was seldom with the company while he was there I did not talk so much as usual, for I will confess it, lively conversation, from of old, had been to me the finest seasoning of existence   With my father I was wont to talk of everything that happened   What you do not speak of, you will seldom accurately think of   No man had I ever heard with greater pleasure than I did Lothario, when he told us of his travels and campaigns   The world appeared to lie before him clear and open, as to me the district was in which I lived and managed   We were not entertained with marvellous personal adventures, the extravagant half-truths of a shallow traveller, who is always painting out himself, and not the country he has undertaken to describe.   Lothario did not tell us his adventures, he led us to the place itself   I have seldom felt so pure a satisfaction

"But still higher was my pleasure, when I heard him talk, one evening, about women   The subject happened to be introduced, some ladies of the neighbourhood had come to see us, and were speaking, in the common style, about the cultivation of the female mind   Our sex, they said, was treated unjustly, every sort of higher education men insisted on retaining for themselves   they admitted us to no science, they required us either to be dolls or family drudges   To all this Lothario said not much   but when the party was a little thinned, he gave us his opinion more explicitly   'It is very strange,' cried he, 'that men are blamed for their proceeding here   they have placed woman on the highest station she is capable of occupying   And where is there any station higher than the ordering of the house ?   While the husband has to vex himself with outward matters, while he has wealth to gather and secure, while perhaps he takes part in the administration of the state, and everywhere depends on circumstances, ruling nothing, I may say, while he conceives that he is ruling much, compelled to be but politic where he would willingly be reasonable, to dissemble where he would be open, to be false where he would be upright, while thus, for the sake of an object which he never reaches, he must every moment sacrifice the first of objects, harmony with himself,—

a reasonable housewife is actually governing in the interior
of her family, has the comfort and activity of every person in
it to provide for, and make possible What is the highest
happiness of mortals, if not to execute what we consider right
and good, to be really masters of the means conducive to our
aims ? And where should or can our nearest aims be, but
in the interior of our home ? All those indispensable, and
still to be renewed supplies, where do we expect, do we require
to find them, if not in the place where we rise and where
we go to sleep, where kitchen and cellar, and every species of
accommodation for ourselves and ours is to be always ready ?
What unvarying activity is needed to conduct this constantly
recurring series in unbroken living order! How few are the
men, to whom it is given to return regularly like a star,
to command their day as they command their night, to form
for themselves their household instruments, to sow and to
reap, to gain and to expend, and to travel round their circle
with perpetual success and peace and love ! It is when a
woman has attained this inward mastery, that she truly makes
the husband whom she loves a master her attention will
acquire all sorts of knowledge, her activity will turn them
all to profit Thus is she dependent upon no one, and she
procures her husband genuine independence, that which is
interior and domestic whatever he possesses, he beholds
secured, what he earns, well employed, and thus he can
direct his mind to lofty objects, and if fortune favours, he may
act in the state the same character which so well becomes his
wife at home '

"He then described to us the kind of wife he wished I
reddened, for he was describing me as I looked and lived
I silently enjoyed my triumph, and the more, as I perceived, from all the circumstances, that he had not meant
me individually, that indeed he did not know me I cannot
recollect a more delightful feeling in my life than this,
when a man whom I so highly valued gave the preference,
not to my person, but to my inmost nature What a re-

compense did I consider it ! What encouragement did it afford me !

"So soon as they were gone, my worthy benefactress, with a smile, observed to me 'Pity that men often think and speak of what they will never execute, else here were a special match, the exact thing for my dear Theresa !' I made sport of her remark, and added, that indeed men's understanding gave its vote for household wives, but that their heart and imagination longed for other qualities, and that we household people could not stand a rivalry with beautiful and lovely women This was spoken for the ear of Lydia, she did not hide from us that Lothario had made a deep impression on her heart, and in reality, he seemed at each new visit to grow more and more attentive to her She was poor and not of rank, she could not think of marriage but she was unable to resist the dear delight of charming and of being charmed I had never loved, nor did I love at present but though it was unspeakably agreeable to see in what light my turn of mind was viewed, how high it was ranked by such a man, I will confess I still was not altogether satisfied I now wished that he should be acquainted with   e, and should take a personal interest in me This wish arose, without the smallest settled thought of anything that could result from it

"The greatest service I did my benefactress, was in bringing into order the extensive forests which belonged to her In this precious property, whose value time and circumstances were continually increasing, matters still went on according to the old routine, without regularity, without plan no end to theft and fraud Many hills were standing bare, an equal growth was nowhere to be found but in the oldest cuttings I personally visited the whole of them, with an experienced forester I got the woods correctly measured, I set men to hew, to sow, to plant, in a short time, all things were in progress That I might mount more readily on horseback, and also walk on foot with less obstruction, I had a suit of

men s clothes made foi me, I was piesent in many places, I
was feared in all

"Hearing that our young friends with Lothaiio weie pui-
posing to have another hunt, it came into my head, for the
fiist time in my life, to make a figure, or that I may not do
myself injustice, to pass in the eyes of this noble gentleman
for what I was I put on my men's-clothes, took my gun
upon my shoulder, and went forward with our huntei s, to
await the party on our marches They came, Lothario did
not know me a nephew of the lady's introduced me to him,
as a clever foiester, joked about my youth, and cai i ed on
his jesting in my piaise, till at last Lothario recognised me.
The nephew seconded my project, as if we had concocted it
together. He circumstantially and gratefully described what
I had done for the estates of his aunt, and consequently for
himself.

"Lothario listened with attention, he talked with me,
inquii ed concerning all particulars of the estates and distinct
I of course was glad to have such an opportunity of showing
him my knowledge I stood my ordeal veiy well, I submitted
certain projects of i provement to him, which he sanctioned,
telling me of similar examples, and stiengthening my arguments by the connexion which he gave them My satisfaction
grew ore perfect every moment Happily, however, I merely
wished that he should be acquainted with me, not that he
should love me We came home and I obsei ved more cleaily
than before, that the attention he showed to Lydia seemed
expressive of a secret inclination I had reached my object,
yet I was not at rest from that day, he showed a tiue
respect for e, a fine tiust in me, in company he usually
spoke to me, asked my opinion, and appeaied to be persuaded
that, in household matters, nothing was unknown to me
His sympathy excited me extremely even when the conversation was of general finance and political economy, he
used to lead me to take pait in it, and in his absence, I
endeavoured to acquire more knowledge of our provime, nay,

of all the empire The task was easy for me it was but repeating on the great scale what I knew so accurately on the small

"From this period he visited our house oftener We talked, I may say, of everything yet in some degree our conversation always in the end grew economical, if even but in a secondary sense What immense effects a man, by the continuous application of his powers, his time, his money, even by means which seem but small, may bring about, was frequently and largely spoken of

"I did not withstand the tendency which drew me towards him and, alas, I felt too soon how deep, how cordial, how pure and genuine was my love, as I believed it more and more apparent that Lydia and not myself was the occasion of these visits She, at least, was most vividly persuaded so, she made me her confidant, and this, again, in some degree, consoled me For in truth, what she explained so much to her advantage, I reckoned nowise of importance, there was not a trace of any serious lasting union being meditated, but the more distinctly did I see the wish of the impassioned girl to be his at any price

"Thus did matters stand, when the lady of the house surprised me with an unexpected message 'Lothario,' said she, 'offers you his hand, and desires through life to have you ever at his side' She enlarged upon my qualities, and told me, what I liked sufficiently to hear, that in me Lothario was persuaded he had found the person whom he had so long been seeking for

"The height of happiness was now attained for me my hand was asked by a man for whom I had the greatest value; beside whom and along with whom I might expect a full, expanded, free and profitable employment of my inborn tendency, of my talent perfected by practice The sum of my existence seemed to have enlarged itself into infinitude I gave my consent, he himself came, and spoke with me in private, he held out his hand to me, he looked into my eyes, he

clasped me in his arms, and pressed a kiss upon my lips   It
was the first and the last   He confided to me all his circumstances, told me how much his American campaign had cost
him, what debts he had accumulated on his property, that,
on this score, he had in some measure quarrelled with his
granduncle, that the worthy gentleman intended to relieve him,
though truly in his own peculiar way, being minded to provide
him with a rich wife, whereas a man of sense would choose a
household wife at all events, that however, by his sister's
influence, he hoped his noble relative would be persuaded
He set before me the condition of his fortune, his plans, his
prospects, and requested my cooperation   Till his uncle
should consent, our promise was to be a secret

    " Scarcely was he gone, when Lydia asked me, whether he
had spoken of her   I answered no, and tired her with a
long detail of economical affairs   She was restless, out of
humour, and his conduct, when he came again, did not
improve her situation

    ' But the sun, I see, is bending to the place of rest.   Well
for you, my friend '   You would otherwise have had to hear
this story, which I often enough go over by myself, in all its
most minute particulars   Let me hasten   we are coming to
an epoch, on which it is not good to linger

    " By Lothario I was made acquainted with his noble sister,
and she, at a convenient time, contrived to introduce me to
the uncle   I gained the old man, he consented to our wishes,
and I returned, with happy tidings, to my benefactress   The
affair was now no secret in the house   Lydia heard of it,
she thought the thing impossible   When she could no longer
doubt of it, she vanished all at once   we knew not whither
she had gone

    " Our marriage-day was coming near   I had often asked
him for his portrait, just as he was going off, I reminded him
that he had promised it   He said ' You have never given
me the case you want to have it fitted into '   This was true
I had got a present from a female friend, on which I set no

ordinary value   Her name, worked from her own hair, was
fastened on the outer glass, within there was a vacant piece
of ivory, on which her portrait was to have been painted,
when a sudden death snatched her from me   Lothario's love
had cheered me at the time her death lay heavy on my spirits.
and I wished to have the void, which she had left me in her
present, filled by the picture of my friend

"I ran to my chamber, fetched my jewel-box, and opened
it in his presence   Scarcely had he looked into it, when he
noticed a medallion with the portrait of a lady   He took it
in his hand, considered it attentively, and asked me hastily
whose face it was   'My mother's,' answered I   'I could have
sworn,' said he, 'that it was the portrait of a Madame Saint
Alban, whom I met some years ago in Switzerland'   'It is
the same,' replied I, smiling, 'and so you have unwittingly
become acquainted with your mother-in-law   Saint Alban is
the name my mother has assumed for travelling with   she
passes under it in France at present'

"'I am the miserablest man alive!' exclaimed he, as he
threw the portrait back into the box, covered his eyes with his
hand, and hurried from the room   He sprang on horseback,
I ran to the balcony, and called out after him   he turned,
waved his hand to me, went speedily away,—and I have never
seen him more"

The sun went down   Theresa gazed with unaverted looks
upon the splendour; and both her fine eyes filled with tears

Theresa spoke not   she laid her hand upon her new friend's
hands   he kissed it with emotion, she dried her tears, and
rose   "Let us return, and see that all is right," said she

The conversation was not lively by the way   They entered
the garden-door, and noticed Lydia sitting on a bench   she
rose, withdrew before them, and walked in   She had a paper
in her hand, two little girls were by her.   "I see," observed
Theresa, "she is still carrying her only comfort, Lothario's
letter, with her. He promises that she shall live with him
again, so soon as he is well   he begs of her till then to stay

in peace with me   On these words she hangs, with these lines she solaces herself   but with his friends she is extremely angry "

Meanwhile the two children had approached   They courtesied to Theresa, and gave her an account of all that had occurred while she was absent   "You see here another part of my employment," said Theresa   "Lothario's sister and I have made a league   we educate some little ones in common : such promise to be lively serviceable housewives I take charge of, she of such as show a finer and more quiet talent   it is right to provide for the happiness of future husbands both in household and in intellectual matters   When you become acquainted with my noble friend, a new era in your life will open   Her beauty, her goodness, make her worthy of the reverence of the world "   Wilhelm did not venture to confess, that unhappily the lovely Countess was already known to him   that his transient connexion with her would occasion him perpetual sorrow   He was well pleased that Theresa let the conversation drop, that some business called for her within   He was now alone   the intelligence which he had just received, of the young and lovely Countess being driven to replace, by deeds of benevolence, her own lost comfort, made him very sad, he felt that with her it was but a need of self-oblivion, an attempt to supply, by the hopes of happiness to others, the want of a cheerful enjoyment of existence in herself   He thought Theresa happy, since even in that unexpected melancholy alteration which had taken place in her prospects, there was no alteration needed in herself   "How fortunate beyond all others," cried he, "is the man who, in order to adjust himself to fate, is not required to cast away his whole preceding life ! "

Theresa came into his room, and begged pardon for disturbing him   "My whole library," said she, "is in the wall-press here, they are rather books which I do not throw aside, than which I have taken up   Lydia wants a pious book   there are one or two of that sort among them   Persons who throughout the whole twelve months are worldly, think it necessary to be godly at a time of straits all moral and religious matters they regard as physic, which is to be taken, with aversion, when they are unwell in a clergyman, a moralist, they see nothing but a doctor, whom they cannot soon enough get rid of Now, I confess, I look upon religion as a kind of diet, which can only be so when I make a constant practice of it, when throughout the whole twelve months I never lose it out of sight "

She searched among the books, she found some edifying works, as they are called "It was of my mother," said Theresa, "that poor Lydia learned to have recourse to books like these While her gallant continued faithful, plays and novels were her life, his departure brought religious writings once more into credit I, for my share, cannot understand," continued she, " how men have made themselves believe that God speaks to us through books and histories The man, to whom the universe does not reveal directly what relation it has to him, whose heart does not tell him what he owes to himself and others,—that man will scarcely learn it out of books, which generally do little more than give our errors names "

She left our friend alone he passed his evening in examining the little library, it had, in truth, been gathered quite at random

Theresa, for the few days Wilhelm spent with her, continued still the same she related to him, at different times, the consequences of that singular incident with great minuteness Day and hour, place and name, were present to her memory we shall here compress into a word or two, so much of it as will be necessary for the information of our readers

The reason of Lothario's quick departure was unhappily too easy to explain He had met Theresa's mother on her journey her charms attracted him, she was no niggard of them, and this luckless transitory aberration came at length to shut him out from being united to a lady, whom nature seemed to have expressly made for him. As for Theresa, she continued in the pure circle of her duties They learned that

Lydia had been living in the neighbourhood in secret She was happy that the marriage, though for unknown causes, had not been completed She endeavoured to renew her intimacy with Lothario and more, as it seemed, out of desperation than affection, by surprise than with consideration, from tedium than of purpose, he had met her wishes

Theresa was quiet on the subject, she made no pretensions farther to him, and if he had even been her husband, she would probably have had sufficient spirit to endure a matter of this kind, if it had not troubled her domestic order   at least she often used to say, that a wife, who properly conducted her economy, should take no umbrage at such little fancies of her husband, but be always certain that he would return

Ere long, Theresa's mother had deranged her fortune the losses fell upon the daughter, whose share of the effects, in consequence, was small   The old lady, who had been Theresa's benefactress, died, leaving her a little property in land, and a handsome sum by way of legacy Theresa soon contrived to make herself at home in this new narrow circle Lothario offered her a better property. Jarno endeavouring to negotiate the business but she refused it "I will show," said she, "in this little, that I deserved to share the great with him but I keep this before me, that, should accident embarrass me, on my own account or that of others, I will betake myself without the smallest hesitation to my generous friend."

There is nothing less liable to be concealed and unemployed than well-directed practical activity Scarcely had she settled in her little property. when her acquaintance and advice began to be desired by many of her neighbours, and the proprietor of the adjacent lands gave her plainly enough to understand, that it depended on herself alone, whether she would take his hand, and be heiress of the greater part of his estates She had already mentioned the matter to our friend she often jested with him about marriages, suitable and unsuitable

"Nothing," said she once, "gives a greater loose to people's tongues, than when a marriage happens, which they can

denominate unsuitable   and yet the unsuitable are far more
common than the suitable, for, alas, with most marriages, it
is not long till things assume a very piteous look   The confusion of ranks by marriage can be called unsuitable, only
when the one party is unable to participate in the manner of
existence which is native, habitual, and which at length grows
absolutely necessary to the other   The different classes have
different ways of living, which they cannot change or communicate to one another, and this is the reason why connexions
such as these, in general, were better not formed   Yet exceptions, and exceptions of the happiest kind, are possible   Thus
too, the marriage of a young woman with a man advanced in
life is generally unsuitable, yet I have seen some such turn
out extremely well   For me, I know but of one kind of
marriage that would be entirely unsuitable, that in which I
should be called upon to make a show, and manage ceremonies
I had rather give my hand to the son of any honest farmer in
the neighbourhood"

Wilhelm at length made ready for returning   He requested
of Theresa to obtain for him a parting word with Lydia   The
impassioned girl at last consented   he said some kindly things
to her, to which she answered   "The first burst of anguish
I have conquered   Lothario will be ever dear to me   but for
those friends of his, I know them, and it grieves me that they
are about him   The Abbé, for a whim's sake, could leave a
person in extreme need, or even plunge one into it, the Doctor
would have all things go on like clock-work, Jarno has no
heart   and you—at least no force of character ! Just go on,
let these three people use you as their tool, they will have
many an execution to commit to you   For a long time, as I
know well, my presence has been hateful to them   I had not
found out their secret, but I had observed that they had one.
Why these bolted rooms, these strange passages ? Why can
no one ever reach the central tower ? Why did they banish
me, whenever they could, to my own chamber ? I will confess,
jealousy at first incited me to these discoveries   I feared some

lucky rival might be hid there   I have now laid aside that
suspicion   I am well convinced that Lothario loves me, that
he means honourably by me, but I am quite as well convinced
that his false and artful friends betray him   If you would
really do him service, if you would ever be forgiven for the
injury which I have suffered from you, free him from the
hands of these men   But what am I expecting !   Give this
letter to him   repeat what it contains, that I will love him
for ever, that I depend upon his word   Ah !" cried she, rising
and throwing herself with tears upon Theresa's neck   "he is
surrounded by my foes, they will endeavour to persuade him
that I have sacrificed nothing for his sake   O ! Lothario may
well believe that he is worthy of any sacrifice, without needing
to be grateful for it."

Wilhelm's parting with Theresa was more cheerful   she
wished they might soon meet again   "Me you wholly know,"
said she. "I alone have talked while we have been together
It will be your duty, next time, to repay my candour"

During his return, he kept contemplating this new and
bright phenomenon, with the liveliest recollection   What
confidence had she inspired him with !   He thought of
Mignon and Felix, and how happy they might be if under
her direction   then he thought of himself, and felt what
pleasure it would be to live beside a being so entirely serene
and clear   As he approached Lothario's Castle, he observed,
with more than usual interest, the central tower and the many
passages and side-buildings . he resolved to question Jarno or
the Abbé on the subject, by the earliest opportunity.

CHAPTER VII

On arriving at the Castle, Wilhelm found its noble owner
in the way of full recovery   the Doctor and the Abbé had
gone off, Jarno alone was there   It was not long till the
patient now and then could ride, sometimes by himself,

sometimes with his friends His conversation was at once courteous and earnest, instructive and enlivening you could often notice in it traces of a tender sensibility, although he strove to hide it, and almost seemed to blame it, when in spite of him it came to view

One evening while at table he was silent, though his look was very cheerful

"Today," said Jarno, "you have met with an adventure, and a pleasing one?"

"I give you credit for your penetration!" said Lothario. " Yes, I have met with a very pleasing adventure At another time, perhaps I should not have considered it so charming as today, when it came upon me so attractively Towards night, I rode out beyond the river, through the hamlets, by a path which I had often visited in former years My corporeal sufferings must have reduced me more than I supposed I felt weak, but as my strength was re-awakening, I was as it were new-born All objects seemed to wear the hues they had in earlier times, all looked graceful, lovely, charming, as they have not looked to me for many years I easily observed that it was mere debility, yet I continued to enjoy it I rode softly onwards, and could now conceive how men may grow to like diseases, which attune us to those sweet emotions You know, perhaps, what used of old so frequently to lead me that way?"

"If I mistake not," answered Jarno, "it was a little love concern you were engaged in with a farmer's daughter"

"It might be called a great one," said Lothario "for we loved each other deeply, seriously and for a long time Today, it happened, everything combined to represent before me in its liveliest colour the earliest season of our love The boys were again shaking maybugs from the trees, the ashen grove had not grown larger since the day I saw her first It was now long since I had met with Margaret She is married at a distance, and I had heard by chance, that she was come with her children, some weeks ago, to pay a visit to her father."

" This ride, then. was not altogether accidental ? "

" I will not deny," replied Lothario, " that I wished to meet her   On coming near the house, I saw her father sitting at the door , a child of probably a year old was standing by him   As I approached, a female gave a hasty look from an upper window , and a minute afterwards, I heard some person tripping down-stairs   I thought surely it was she   and I will confess, I was flattering myself that she had recognised me, and was hastening to meet me   But what was my surprise and disappointment, when she bounded from the door , seized the child, to which the horses had come pretty close, and took it in !   It gave me a painful twinge   my vanity, however, was a little solaced, when I thought I saw a tint of redness on her neck, and on the ear, which was uncovered

" I drew up, and spoke a little with the father, glancing sideways, in the mean time, over all the windows, to observe if she would not appear at some of them   but no trace of her was visible   Ask I would not , so I rode away   My dis- pleasure was a little mollified by wonder   though I had not seen the face, it appeared to me that she was scarcely changed , and ten years are a pretty space !   Nay, she looked even younger, quite as slim, as light of foot, her neck if possible was lovelier than before , her cheeks as quick at blushing , yet she was the mother of six children, perhaps of more   This apparition suited the enchantment which surrounded me so well, that I rode along with feelings grown still younger   and I did not turn till I was at the forest, when the sun was going down   Strongly as the falling dew, and the prescription of our Doctor, called upon me to proceed direct homewards, I could not help again going round by the farm-house   I observed a woman walking up and down the garden, which is fenced by a light hedge   I rode along the footpath to it, and found myself at no great distance from the person whom I wanted

" Though the evening sun was glancing in my eyes, I saw that she was busy with the hedge, which only slightly covered her   'I thought I recognised my mistress   On coming up, I halted, not without a palpitation at the heart Some high twigs of wild roses, which a soft air was blowing to and fro, made her figure indistinct to me I spoke to her, asked her how she was She answered in an under-tone, 'Quite well.' In the mean time I perceived a child behind the hedge, engaged in plucking roses, and I took the opportunity of asking where her other children were 'It is not my child,' said she 'that were rather early!' And at this moment, it happened that the twigs were blown aside, and her face could be distinctly seen I knew not what to make of the affair It was my mistress, and it was not Almost younger, almost lovelier than she used to be ten years before 'Are not you the farmer's daughter, then?' inquired I, half confused. 'No,' said she 'I am her cousin'

"'You resemble one another wonderfully,' added I

"'Yes, so says every one that knew her half-a-score of years ago'

"I continued putting various questions to her my mistake was pleasant to me, even after I had found it out I could not leave this living image of bygone blessedness, that stood before me The child meanwhile had gone away, it had wandered to the pond in search of flowers She took her leave, and hastened after it

"I had now, however, learned that my former love was really in her father's house while riding forward, I employed myself in guessing whether it had been her cousin or she, that had secured the child from harm I more than once, in thought, repeated all the circumstances of the incident I can remember few things that have affected me more gratefully But I feel that I am still unwell we must ask the Doctor to deliver us from the remains of this pathetic humour "

With confidential narratives of pretty love-adventures, it often happens as with ghost-stories, when the first is told, the others follow of themselves

Our little party, in recalling other times, found numerous passages of this description. Lothario had the most to tell

Jarno's histories were all of one peculiar character   what Wilhelm could disclose we already know   He was apprehensive they might mention his adventure with the Countess, but it was not hinted at, not even in the remotest manner

"It is true," observed Lothario, "there can scarcely any feeling in the world be more agreeable, than when the heart, after a pause of indifference, again opens to love for some new object, yet I would forever have renounced that happiness, had fate been pleased to unite me with Theresa   We are not always youths, we ought not always to be children   To the man, who knows the world, who understands what he should do in it, what he should hope from it, nothing can be more desirable than meeting with a wife who will everywhere co-operate with him, who will everywhere prepare his way for him, whose diligence takes up what his must leave, whose occupation spreads itself on every side, while his must travel forward on its single path   What a heaven had I figured for myself beside Theresa!   Not the heaven of an enthusiastic bliss, but of a sure life on earth   order in prosperity, courage in adversity, care for the smallest, and a spirit capable of comprehending and managing the greatest   O! I saw in her the qualities, which, when developed, make such women as we find in history, whose excellence appears to us far preferable to that of men.   this clearness of view, this expertness in all emergencies, this sureness in details, which brings the whole so accurately out, although they never seem to think of it   You may well forgive me," added he, and turned to Wilhelm with a smile, "that I forsook Aurelia for Theresa   with the one I could expect a calm and cheerful life, with the other not a happy hour "

"I will confess," said Wilhelm, "that in coming hither, I had no small anger in my heart against you, that I proposed to censure with severity your conduct to Aurelia "

"It was really censurable," said Lothario   "I should not have exchanged my friendship for her with the sentiment of love, I should not, in place of the respect which she deserved,

have intruded an attachment she was neither calculated to
excite nor to maintain   Alas! she was not lovely when she
loved, the greatest misery that can befall a woman"

"Well, it is past!" said Wilhelm.   "We cannot always
shun the things we blame   in spite of us, our feelings and our
actions sometimes strangely swerve from their natural and
right direction, yet there are certain duties which we never
should lose sight of   Peace be to the ashes of our friend!
Without censuring ourselves or her, let us, with sympathising
hearts, strew flowers upon her grave   But at the grave in
which the hapless mother sleeps, let me ask why you acknowledge not the child, a son whom any father might rejoice in,
and whom you appear entirely to overlook?   With your pure
and tender nature, how can you altogether cast away the
instinct of a parent?   All this while, you have not spent one
syllable upon that precious creature, of whose attractions I
could say so much"

"Whom do you speak of?" asked Lothario   "I do not
understand you"

"Of whom but of your son, Aurelia's son, the lovely child,
to whose good fortune there is nothing wanting, but that a
tender father should acknowledge and receive him"

"You mistake, my friend," exclaimed Lothario   "Aurelia
never had a son, at least by me   I know of no child, or I
would with joy acknowledge it, and even in the present case,
I will gladly look upon the little creature as a relic of her,
and take charge of educating it   But did she ever give you
to believe that the boy was hers, was mine?"

"I cannot recollect that I ever heard a word from her
expressly on the subject   but we took it up so, and I never for
a moment doubted it"

"I can give you something like a clue to this perplexity,"
said Jarno   "An old woman, whom you must have noticed
often, gave Aurelia the child   she accepted it with passion,
hoping to alleviate her sorrows by its presence   and, in truth,
it gave her many a comfortable hour."

This discovery awoke anxieties in Wilhelm, he thought of his dear Mignon and his beautiful Felix with the liveliest distinctness He expressed his wish to remove them both from the state in which they were

"We shall soon arrange it," said Lothario "The little girl may be committed to Theresa, she cannot be in better hands As for the boy, I think you should yourself take charge of him what in us the women leave uncultivated, children cultivate, when we retain them near us "

"But first, I think," said Jarno, "you will once for all renounce the stage, as you have no talent for it "

Our friend was struck he had to curb himself, for Jarno's harsh sentence had not a little wounded his self-love "If you convince me of that," replied he, forcing a smile, "you will do me a service, though it is but a mournful service to rouse one from a pleasing dream."

"Without enlarging on the subject," answered Jarno, "I could merely wish you would go and fetch the children The rest will come in course "

"I am ready," answered Wilhelm "I am restless, and curious to see if I can get no farther knowledge of the boy I long to see the little girl, who has attached herself so strangely to me "

It was agreed that he should lose no time in setting out Next day, he had prepared himself, his horse was saddled he only waited for Lothario, to take leave of him At the dinner hour, they went as usual to table, not waiting for the master of the house He did not come till late, and then sat down by them

"I could bet," said Jarno, "that today you have again been making trial of your tenderness of heart, you have not been able to withstand the curiosity to see your quondam love "

"Guessed ! " replied Lothario

"Let us hear," said Jarno, "how it went I long to know "

"I confess," replied Lothario, "the affair lay nearer my

heart than it reasonably ought so I formed the resolution of
again riding out, and actually seeing the person, whose
renewed young image had affected me with such a pleasing
illusion I alighted at some distance from the house, and
sent the horses to a side, that the children, who were playing
at the door, might not be disturbed I entered the house,
by chance she met me just within the threshold, it was
herself, and I recognised her, notwithstanding the striking
change She had grown stouter, and seemed to be larger
her gracefulness was shaded by a look of staidness, her
vivacity had passed into a calm reflectiveness Her head,
which she once bore so airily and freely, drooped a little,
slight furrows had been traced upon her brow

"She cast down her eyes on seeing me, but no blush
announced any inward movement of the heart I held out
my hand to her, she gave me hers I inquired about her
husband, he was absent, about her children, she stept out
and called them, all came in and gathered round her
Nothing is more charming than to see a mother with a child
upon her arm, nothing is more reverend than a mother
among many children That I might say something, I asked
the name of the youngest She desired me to walk in, and
see her father I agreed, she introduced me to the room, ·
where everything was standing almost just as I had left it,
and what seemed stranger still, the fair cousin, her living
image, was sitting on the very seat behind the spinning-wheel,
where I had found my love so often in the self-same form
A little girl, the very figure of her mother, had come after
us, and thus I stood in the most curious scene, between the
future and the past, as in a grove of oranges, where, within
a little circle, flowers and fruits are living, in successive stages
of their growth, beside each other The cousin went away
to fetch us some refreshment, I gave the woman I had loved
so much my hand, and said to her 'I feel a true joy in
seeing you again' 'You are very good to say so,' answered
she 'but I also can assure you I feel the highest joy How

often have I wished to see you once more in my life ! I have
wished it in moments, which I regarded as my last' She
said this with a settled voice, without appearance of emotion,
with that natural air which of old delighted me so much
The cousin returned, the father with her and I leave you
to conceive with what feelings I remained, and with what I
came away "

CHAPTER VIII

In his journey to the town, our friend was thinking of the
lovely women whom he knew, or had heard of their curious
fortunes, which contained so little happiness, were present
to him with a sad distinctness   "Ah !" cried he, "poor
Mariana ! What shall I yet learn of thee ? And thou
noble A azon, glorious protecting spirit, to whom I owe so
much, whom I everywhere expect to meet, and nowhere see,
in what mournful circumstances may I find thee, shouldst
thou again appear before me ! "

On his arrival in the town, there was not one of his acquaintances at home   he hastened to the theatre, he supposed
they would be rehearsing   Here, however, all was still, the
house seemed empty, one little door alone was open   Passing
through it to the stage, he found Aurelia's ancient serving-
aid, employed in sewing linen for a new decoration   there
was barely light enough to let her work   Felix and Mignon
were sitting by her on the floor they had a book between
the   , and while Mignon read aloud, Felix was repeating all
the words, as if he too knew his letters, as if he too could read

The children started up and ran to him   he embraced them
with the tenderest feelings, and brought them closer to the
woman   "Art thou the person," said he to her, with an
earnest voice, "from whom Aurelia received this child ?"
She looked up from her work, and turned her face to him,
he saw her in full light, he started back in terror, it was old
Barbara

" Where is Mariana ? " cried he

" Far from here," replied the crone.

" And Felix—— ? "

" Is the son of that unhappy, and too true and tender-hearted girl !   May you never feel what you have made us suffer !   May the treasure which I now deliver you, make you as happy as he made us wretched ! "

She arose to go away   Wilhelm held her fast   " I mean not to escape you," said she , " let me fetch a paper that will make you glad and sorrowful "

She retired , and Wilhelm gazed upon the child with a painful joy   he durst not reckon him his own   " He is thine ! " cried Mignon , " he is thine ! " and pressed the child to Wilhelm's knee

Barbara came back, and handed him a letter   " Here are Mariana's last words," said she

" She is dead ! " cried he

" Dead," said the old woman   " I wish to spare you all reproaches "

Astonished and confounded, Wilhelm broke up the letter, but scarcely had he read the first words of it, when a bitter grief took hold of him , he let the letter fall , and sank upon a seat   Mignon hurried to him, trying to console him   In the mean time, Felix had picked up the letter , he teased his playmate till she yielded, till she knelt beside him, and read it over   Felix repeated the words, and Wilhelm was compelled to hear them twice   " If this sheet should ever reach thee, then lament thy ill-starred friend   Thy love has caused her death   The boy, whose birth I survive but a few days, is thine   I die faithful to thee, much as appearances ay be against me   with thee I lost everything that bound me to life   I die content, for they have assured me that the child is healthy and will live   Listen to old Barbara, forgive her , farewell, and forget me not "

What a painful, and yet to his comfort, half-enigmatic letter !   Its contents pierced through his heart, as the children, stuttering and stammering, pronounced and repeated them

"There you have it now !" said the crone, not waiting till he had recovered "Thank Heaven that having lost so true a love, you have still so fine a child remaining Your grief will be unequalled, when you learn how the poor good girl stood faithful to you to the end, how miserable she became, and what she sacrificed for your sake"

"Let me drain the cup of sorrow and of joy at once !" cried Wilhelm "Convince me, even persuade me that she was a good girl, that she deserved respect as well as love, then leave me to my grief for her irreparable loss"

"It is not yet time," said Barbara, "I have work to do, and I would not we were seen together Let it be a secret that Felix is your son I should have too much abuse to suffer from the company, for having formerly deceived them. Mignon will not betray us, she is good and close"

"I have known it long, and I said nothing," answered Mignon "How is it possible·" cried Barbara "Whence?" cried Wilhelm

"The spirit told it me"

"Where? Where ?"

"In the vault, when the old man drew his knife, it called to me 'Bring his father,' and I thought it must be thou"

"*Who* called to thee?"

"I know not, in my heart, in my head, I was terrified, I trembled, I prayed, then it called, and I understood it"

Wilhelm pressed her to his heart, recommended Felix to her, and retired He had not observed till then that she was grown much paler and thinner than when he left her Madam Melina was the first acquaintance he met she received hi in the friendliest manner "O, that you might find everything among us as you wished !" exclaimed she

"I doubt it," answered Wilhelm; "I do not expect it. Confess that they have taken all their measures to dispense with me'

" Why would you go away ? " replied his friend

" We cannot soon enough convince ourselves," said he, " how very simply we may be dispensed with in the world What important personages we conceive ourselves to be ! We think that it is we alone who animate the circle we move in , that, in our absence, life, nourishment and breath will make a general pause and, alas, the void which occurs is scarcely remarked, so soon is it filled up again , nay, it is often but the place, if not for something better, at least for something more agreeable "

" And the sorrows of our friends we are not to take into account ? "

" For our friends, too, it is well, when they soon recover their composure, when they say each to himself There where thou art, there where thou remainest, accomplish what thou canst, be busy, be courteous, and let the present scene delight thee "

On a narrower inquiry, he found what he had looked for, the opera had been set up, and was exclusively attracting the attention of the public His parts had in the mean while been distributed between Horatio and Laertes, and both of them were in the habit of eliciting from the spectators far more liberal applause than he had ever been enabled to obtain

Laertes entered, and Madam Melina cried " Look you here at this lucky fellow he is soon to be a capitalist, or Heaven knows what ! " Wilhelm, in embracing him, discovered that his coat was superfine the rest of his apparel was simple, but of the very best materials

" Solve me the riddle ! " cried our friend

" You are still in time to learn," replied Laertes, " that my running to and fro is now about to be repaid, that a partner in a large commercial house is turning to advantage my acquirements from books or observation, and allowing me a share with him I would give something, could I purchase b ck my confidence in women there is a pretty niece in the house , and I see well enough that, if I pleased, I might soon be a made man "

" You have not heard," said Frau Melina, " that a marriage has already taken place among ourselves ? Serlo is actually wedded to the fair Elmira , her father would not tolerate their secret correspondence "

They talked, in this manner, about many things that had occurred while he was absent   nor was it difficult for him to observe, that, according to the present temper and constitution of the company, his dismissal had already taken place

He impatiently expected Barbara, who had appointed him to wait for her far in the night   She was to come when all were sleeping, she required as many preparations as if she had been the youngest   aiden gliding in to her beloved   Meanwhile he read, a hundred times, the letter she had given him , read with unspeakable delight the word *faithful* in the hand of his darling , with horror the announcement of her death, whose approaches she appeared to view unmoved

Midnight was past, when something rustled at the half-open door, and Barbara came in with a little basket. " I am to tell you the story of our woes,' said she, " and I must believe that you will sit unmoved at the recital , that you are waiting for me but to satisfy your curiosity , that you will now, as you did formerly, retire within your cold selfishness, while our hearts are breaking   But look you here ! Thus, on that happy evening, did I bring you the bottle of champagne , thus did I place the three glasses on the table : and as you then began, with soft nursery tales, to cozen us and lull us asleep, so will I now with stern truths instruct you and keep you waking "

Wilhel   knew not what to say, when the old woman in fact let go the cork, and filled the three glasses to the brim

" Drink ! " cried she, having emptied at a draught her foaming glass   " Drink, ere the spirit of it pass ! This third glass shall froth away untasted to the memory of my unhappy

Mariana How red were her lips, when she then drank your health ' Ah, and now forevei pale and cold '"

"Sibyl ' Fuiy '" ciied Wilhelm, springing up and striking the table with his fist, " what evil spirit possesses thee and drives thee ? For what dost thou take me, that thou thinkest the si plest nariative of Mariana's death and sorrows will not harrow me enough, but usest these hellish arts to shaipen my toiment ? If thy unsatiable greediness is such, that thou must revel at the funeral table, drink and speak ' I have loathed thee fiom of old , and I cannot ieckon Mariana guiltless while I even look upon thee, hei companion "

"Softly, mein heir '" replied the crone , " you shall not ruffle me Your debts to us are deep and daik the iailing of a debtoi does not angei one But you aie iight the simplest nairative will punish you sufficiently Heai, then, the stiuggle and the victoiy of Maiiana striving to continue youis "

"Continue mine ? " ciied Wilhelm . " what fable dost thou mean to tell me ? "

"Interrupt me not," said she, " hear me, and then give what belief you list to me it is all one Did you not, the last night you were with us, find a letter in the room and take it with you ? "

"I found the letter *after* I had taken it with me it was lying in the neckerchief, which, in the waimth of my love, I had seized and cairied off "

"What did the sheet contain ? "

"The expectation of an angiy lover to be better tieated on the next, than he had been on the pieceding evening And that you kept youi word to him, I need not be told , for I saw him with my own eyes gliding from your house befoie daybreak "

"You may have seen him but what occurred within , how sadly Mariana passed that night, how fretfully I passed it, you are yet to leain I will be altogether candid , I will neither hide nor palliate the fact, that I persuaded Mariana to yield to the solicitations of a certain Norberg it was with repugnance that she followed my advice, nay, that she even heard it He was rich, he seemed attached, I hoped he would be constant Soon after, he was forced to go upon his journey, and Mariana became acquainted with you What had I then to abide' What to hinder, what to undergo' 'O!' cried she often, 'hadst thou spared my youth, my innocence but four short weeks, I might have found a worthy object of my love, I had then been worthy of him, and love might have given, with a quiet conscience, what now I have sold against my will' She entirely abandoned herself to her affection for you I need not ask if you were happy Over her understanding I had an unbounded power, for I knew the means of satisfying all her little inclinations but over her heart I had no control, for she never sanctioned what I did for her, what I counselled her to do, when her heart said nay. It was only to irresistible necessity that she would yield but ere long the necessity appeared to her extremely pressing In the first period of her youth, she had never known want by a complication of misfortunes her people lost their fortune, the poor girl had been used to have a number of conveniences, and upon her young spirit certain principles of honour had been stamped, which made her restless, without much helping her. She had not the smallest skill in worldly matters, she was innocent in the strictest meaning of the word She had no idea that one could buy without paying nothing frightened her more than being in debt, she always rather liked to give than take This, and this alone, was what made it possible, that she could be constrained to give herself away, in order to get rid of various little debts which weighed upon her "

"And couldst not thou," cried Wilhelm in an angry tone, "have saved her?"

"O yes!" replied the beldame, "with hunger and need, with sorrow and privation but for this I was not disposed"

"Abominable, base procuress' So thou hast sacrificed

the hapless creatuie? Offered her up to thy thioat, to thy insatiable maw?"

"It were better to compose yourself and cease your ieviling." said the dame. "If you will revile, go to your high noble houses. there you will meet with many a mother full of anxious cares to find out for some lovely, heavenly maiden the most odious of men, piovided he be the richest See the poor creatuie shivering and faltering before her fate, and nowhere finding consolation, till some moie experienced female lets her undeistand, that by marriage she acquires the right, in future, to dispose of hei heart and person as she pleases"

"Peace!" cried Wilhelm "dost thou think that one crime can be the excuse of another? To thy stoiy, without farther obseivations!"

"Do you listen then, without blaming! Maiiana became yours against my will In this adventure at least I have nothing to reproach myself with Norberg retuined, he made haste to visit Mariana she ieceived him coldly and angrily, would not even admit him to a kiss I employed all my ait in apologising for her conduct, gave hi to undeistand that her confessor had awakened her conscience, that so long as conscientious scruples lasted one was bound to respect the I at last so fai succeeded that he went away, I promising to do my utmost for him He was rich and iude, but there was a touch of goodness in him, and he loved Mariana without limit He promised to be patient, and I laboured with the greatest ardour not to try him too far With Maiiana I had a stubborn contest I peisuaded hei, nay, I may call it forced her, by the threat of leaving hei, to write to Norbeig and invite him for the night You came, and by chance picked up his answer in the neckerchief Your presence broke my game For scarcely were you gone, when she anew began her lamentation she swoie she would not be unfaithful to you, she was so passionate, so frantic, that I could not help sincerely pitying her In the end, I promised, that for this night also, I would pacify her lover, and send him off, under some pretence or other I entreated her to go to bed, but she did not seem to trust me, she kept on her clothes, and at last fell asleep, without undressing, agitated and exhausted with weeping as she was

"Norberg came representing in the blackest hues her conscientious agonies and her repentance, I endeavoured to retain him he wished to see her, and I went into the room to prepare her, he followed me, and both of us at once came forward to her bed She awoke, sprang wildly up, and tore herself from our arms. she conjured and begged, she entreated, threatened and declared she would not yield She was improvident enough to let fall some words about the true state of her affections, which poor Norberg had to understand in a spiritual sense. At length he left her, and she locked her door. I kept him long with me, and talked with him about her situation I told him that she was with child, that, poor girl, she should be humoured He was so delighted with his fatherhood, with his prospect of a boy, that he granted every-thing she wished, he promised rather to set out and travel for a time, than vex his dear, and injure her by these internal troubles With such intentions, at an early hour he glided out, and if you, mein herr, stood sentry by our house, there was nothing wanting to your happiness, but to have looked into the bosom of your rival, whom you thought so favoured and so fortunate, and whose appearance drove you to despair."

" Art thou speaking truth ? " said Wilhelm

" True," said the crone, " as I still hope to drive you to despair.

" Yes, certainly you would despair, if I could rightly paint to you the following morning. How cheerfully did she awake, how kindly did she call me in, how warmly thank me, how cordially press me to her bosom ! ' Now,' said she, stepping up to her mirror with a smile, ' can I again take pleasure in myself, and in my looks, since once more I am my own, am his, my one beloved friend's How sweet is it to conquer ' How I thank thee for taking charge of me, for having turned thy prudence and thy understanding, once, at least, to my advantage! Stand by me, and devise the means of making me entirely happy!"

"I assented, would not irritate her, I flattered her hopes, and she caressed me tenderly If she retired but a moment from the window, I was made to stand and watch, for you, of course, would pass, for she at least would see you Thus did we spend the restless day At night, at the accustomed hour, we looked for you with certainty I was already out waiting at the staircase, I grew weary, and came in to her again With surprise, I found her in her military dress she looked cheerful, and charming beyond what I had ever seen her 'Do I not deserve,' said she, 'to appear tonight in man's apparel? Have I not struggled bravely? My dearest shall see me as he saw me for the first time I will press him as tenderly and with greater freedom to my heart than then, for am not I his much more than I was then, when a noble resolution had not freed me? But,' added she, after pausing for a little, 'I have not yet entirely won him, I must still risk the uttermost, in order to be worthy, to be certain of possessing him, I must disclose the whole to him, discover to him all my state, then leave it to himself to keep or to reject me This scene I am preparing for my friend, preparing for myself and were his feelings capable of casting me away, I should then belong again entirely to myself, my punishment would bring me con- solation, I would suffer all that fate could lay upon me'

"With such purposes and hopes, mein herr, this lovely girl expected you you came not O! how shall I describe the state of watching and of hope? I see thee still before me, with what love, what heartfelt love, thou spokest of the man, whose cruelty thou hadst not yet experienced!"

"Good, dear Barbara!" cried Wilhelm, springing up, and seizing the old woman by the hand, "we have had enough of mummery and preparation! Thy indifferent, thy calm, con- tented tone betrays thee Give me back my Mariana! She is living, she is near at hand Not in vain didst thou choose

this late lonely hour to visit me   not in vain hast thou
prepared me by thy most delicious narrative   Where is she?
Where hast thou hidden her?   I believe all, I will promise to
believe all, so thou but show her to me, so thou give her to
my arms   The shadow of her I have seen already   let me
clasp her once more to my bosom.   I will kneel before her, I
will entreat forgiveness, I will congratulate her upon her
victory over herself and thee, I will bring my Felix to her.
Come! where hast thou concealed her?   Leave *her*, leave me
no longer in uncertainty!   Thy object is attained   Where
hast thou hidden her?   Let me light thee with this candle,
let me once more see her fair and kindly face!'"

He had pulled old Barbara from her chair   she stared at
him, tears started into her eyes, wild pangs of grief took hold
of her   "What luckless error," cried she, "leaves you still a
moment's hope?   Yes, I have hidden her, but beneath the
ground   neither the light of the sun, nor any social taper shall
again illuminate her kindly face   Take the boy Felix to her
grave, and say to him 'There lies thy mother, whom thy
father doomed unheard'   The heart of Mariana beats no
longer with impatience to behold you, not in a neighbouring
chamber is she waiting the conclusion of my narrative, or
fable, the dark chamber has received her, to which no bridegroom follows, from which none comes to meet a lover"

She cast herself upon the floor beside a chair, and wept
bitterly   Wilhelm now, for the first time, felt entirely convinced that Mariana was no more, his emotions it is easy to
conceive   The old woman rose   "I have nothing more to tell
you," cried she, and threw a packet on the table   "Here are
some writings that will put your cruelty to shame   peruse
these sheets with unwet eyes, if you can"   She glided softly
out   Our friend had not the heart to open the pocket-book
that night   he had himself presented it to Mariana, he knew
that she had carefully preserved in it every letter he had sent
her   Next morning he prevailed upon himself   he untied the
ribbon, little notes came forward written with pencil in his

own hand, and recalled to him every situation, from the first
day of their graceful acquaintance to the last of their stern
separation. In particular, it was not without acute anguish,
that he read a small series of billets, which had been addressed
to himself, and to which, as he saw from their tenor, Werner
had refused admittance.

"No one of my letters has yet penetrated to thee, my
entreaties, my prayers have not reached thee, was it thyself
that gave these cruel orders? Shall I never see thee more?
Yet again I attempt it I entreat thee, come, O come! I
ask not to retain thee, if I might but once more press thee to
my heart"

" When I used to sit beside thee, holding thy hands, looking
in thy eyes, and with the full heart of love and trust to call
thee, 'Dear, dear good Wilhelm!' it would please thee so,
that I had to repeat it over and over. I repeat it once again
'Dear, dear good Wilhelm! Be good as thou wert, come,
and leave me not to perish in my wretchedness'"

"Thou regardest me as guilty I am so, but not as thou
thinkest Come, let me have this single comfort to be altogether known to thee, let what will befall me afterwards"

"Not for my sake alone, for thy own too, I beg of thee to
come I feel the intolerable pains thou art suffering, whilst
thou fliest from me Come, that our separation may be less
cruel! Perhaps I was never worthy of thee till this moment,
when thou art repelling me to boundless woe"

"By all that is holy, by all that can touch a human heart,
I call upon thee! It involves the safety of a soul, it involves
a life, two lives, one of which must ever be dear to thee This,
too, thy suspicion will discredit yet I will speak it in the hour

of death   the child which I carry under my heart is thine
Since I began to love thee, no other man has even pressed my
hand   O that thy love, that thy uprightness, had been the
companions of my youth ' "

"Thou wilt not hear me ?   I must even be silent   But these
letters will not die , perhaps they will speak to thee, when the
shroud is covering my lips, and the voice of thy repentance
cannot reach my ear   Through my weary life, to the last
moment, this will be my only comfort   that though I cannot
call myself blameless, towards thee I am free from blame "

Wilhelm could proceed no farther   he resigned himself
entirely to his sorrow , which became still more afflicting,
when, Laertes entering, he was obliged to hide his feelings
Laertes showed a purse of ducats , and began to count and
reckon them, assuring Wilhelm that there could be nothing
finer in the world than for a man to feel himself on the way
to wealth , that nothing then could trouble or detain him
Wilhelm bethought him of his dream, and smiled , but at the
same time, he remembered with a shudder, that in his vision
Mariana had forsaken him, to follow his departed father, and
that both of them at last had moved about the garden, hovering in the air like spirits
Laertes forced him from his meditations , he brought him
to a coffee-house, where, immediately on Wilhelm's entrance,
several persons gathered round him   They were men who had
applauded his performance on the stage   they expressed their
joy at meeting him , lamenting that, as they had heard, he
meant to leave the theatre   They spoke so reasonably and
kindly of himself and his acting, of his talent and their hopes
from it, that Wilhelm, not without emotion, cried at last ·
"O how infinitely precious would such sympathy have been to
me some months ago '   How instructive, how encouraging '
Never had I turned my mind so totally from the concerns of
the stage, never had I gone so far as to despair of the public "

"So far as this," said an elderly man who now stept forward, "we should never go The public is large, true judgment, true feeling, are not quite so rare as one believes, only the artist ought not to demand an unconditional approval of his work Unconditional approval is always the least valuable, conditional you gentlemen are not content with In life, as in art, I know well, a person must take counsel with himself when he purposes to do or to produce anything but when it is produced or done, he must listen with attention to the voices of a number, and with a little practice, out of these many votes he will be able to collect a perfect judgment The few, who could themselves pronounce one, for the most part hold their peace"

"This they should not do," said Wilhelm "I have often heard people, who themselves kept silence in regard to works of merit, complaining and lamenting that silence was kept"

"Today, then, we will speak aloud," cried a young man "You must dine with us, and we will try to pay off a little of the debt we have owed to you, and sometimes also to our good Aurelia"

This invitation Wilhelm courteously declined he went to Frau Melina, whom he wished to speak with on the subject of the children, as he meant to take them from her

Old Barbara's secret was not too religiously observed by him He betrayed himself so soon as he again beheld the lovely Felix "O my child!" cried he, "My dear child!" He lifted him, and pressed him to his heart "Father! what hast thou brought for me?" cried the child Mignon looked at both, as if she meant to warn them not to blab

"What new phenomenon is this?" said Frau Melina They got the children sent away, and Wilhelm, thinking that he did not owe old Barbara the strictest secrecy, disclosed the whole affair to Frau Melina She viewed him with a smile "O! these credulous men!" exclaimed she "If anything is lying in their path, it is so easy to impose it on them, while in other cases they will neither look to the right nor left, and can value nothing, which they have not previously impressed with the stamp of an arbitrary passion!" She sighed, against her will If our friend had not been altogether blind, he must have noticed in her conduct an affection for him which had never been entirely subdued

He now spoke with her about the children, how he purposed to keep Felix with him, and to place Mignon in the country Madame Melina, though sorry at the thought of parting with them, said the plan was good, nay, absolutely necessary Felix was becoming wild with her, and Mignon seemed to need fresh air and other occupation, she was sickly, and was not yet recovering

"Let it not mislead you," added Frau Melina, "that I have lightly hinted doubts about the boy's being really yours The old woman, it is true, deserves but little confidence, yet a person who invents untruths for her advantage may likewise speak the truth when truths are profitable to her Aurelia she had hoodwinked to believe that Felix was Lothario's son and it is a property of us women that we cordially like the children of our lovers, though we do not know the mothers, or even hate them from the heart" Felix came jumping in, she pressed him to her with a tenderness which was not usual to her

Wilhelm hastened home, and sent for Barbara, who, however, would not undertake to meet him till the twilight He received her angrily "There is nothing in the world more shameful," said he, "than establishing oneself on lies and fables Already thou hast done much mischief with them, and now when thy word could decide the fortune of my life, now must I stand dubious, not venturing to call the child my own, though to possess him without scruple would form my highest happiness I cannot look upon thee, scandalous creature, without hatred and contempt"

"Your conduct, if I speak with candour," said the old woman, "appears to me intolerable Even if Felix were not yours, he is the fairest and the loveliest child in nature, one

might purchase him at any price, to have him always near one
Is he not worthy your acceptance? Do not I deserve for my
care, for the labour I have had with him, a little pension for
the small remainder of my life? O, you gentlemen who know
no want! It is well for you to talk of truth and honour but
how the miserable being whose smallest necessity is unprovided
for, who sees in her perplexities no friend, no help, no counsel,
how she is to press through the crowd of selfish men, and to
starve in silence, you are seldom at the trouble to consider.
Did you read Mariana's letters? They are the letters she
wrote to you at that unhappy season It was in vain that I
attempted to approach you to deliver you these sheets your
savage brother-in-law had so begirt you that craft and
cunning were of no avail, and at last, when he began to
threaten me and Mariana with imprisonment, I had then to
cease my efforts, and renounce all hope Does not everything
agree with what I told you? And does not Norberg's letter
put the story altogether out of doubt?"

"What letter?" asked he

"Did you not find it in the pocket-book?" said Barbara

"I have not yet read all of them"

"Give me the pocket-book on that paper everything
depends Norberg's luckless billet caused this sorrowful perplexity, another from his hand may loose the knots, so far as
aught may still depend upon unravelling them" She took a
letter from the book, Wilhelm recognised that odious writing,
he constrained himself and read

"Tell me, girl, how hast thou got such power over me? I
would not have believed that a goddess herself could make
a sighing lover of me Instead of hastening towards me with
open arms, thou shrankest back from me one might have
taken it for aversion Is it fair that I should spend the night
with old Barbara, sitting on a trunk, and but two doors
between me and my pretty Mariana? It is too bad, I tell
thee! I have promised to allow thee time to think, not
to press thee unrelentingly, I could run mad at every wasted

quartei of an hour   Have not I given thee gifts according to
my power ? Dost thou still doubt of my love ? What wilt thou
have ? Do but tell me   thou shalt want for nothing   Would
the Devil had the priest that put such stuff into thy head '
Why didst thou go to such a churl ? There aie plenty of them
that allow young people so ewhat   Enough ' I tell thee
things must altei   in two days I must have an answer , for
I am to leave the town , and if thou become not kind and
friendly to me, thou shalt never see me moie   "

In this style, the letter spun itself to great length , tuining,
to Wilhelm's painful satisfaction, still about the same point ,
and testifying foi the tiuth of the account which he had got
from Baibaia   A second lettei clearly proved, that Mariana
in the sequel also had maintained her puipose , and it was
not without heartfelt grief that out of these and other papers
Wilhelm learned the history of the unlucky gill to the veiy
hour of hei death

Baibaia had giadually tamed the rude Noiberg, by announcing to him Mariana's death, and leaving him in the
belief that Felix was his son   Once or twice he had sent
her money , which, howevei, she ietained for herself, having
talked Aurelia into taking charge of the child   But unhappily this secret source of riches did not long endure.
Norbeig by a life of riot had impaired his fortune , and by
repeated love-affaiis his heait was rendered callous to his
supposed first-born

Probable as all this seemed, beautifully as it all agreed,
Wilhelm did not venture to give way to joy   He still appeared
to dread a present coming fiom his evil Genius

"Your jealous fears," said Barbaia, who guessed his mood
of mind, "time alone can cure   Look upon the child as a
stranger one, take stricter heed of him on that account,
observe his gifts, his temper, his capacities , and if you do not,
by and by, discover in him the exact iesemblance of yourself,
your eyes must certainly be bad   Of this I can assure you,
were I a man, no one should foist a child on me   but it is a

happiness for women, that in these cases men are not so quick of sight "

These things over, Wilhelm and Barbara parted, he was to take Felix with him, she to carry Mignon to Theresa, and afterwards to live in any place she pleased, upon a small annuity which he engaged to settle on her

He sent for Mignon, to prepare her for the new arrangement   " Master !" said she, " keep me with thee   it will do me good and do me ill "

He told her that, as she was now grown up, there should be something farther done for her instruction   " I am sufficiently instructed," answered she, " to love and grieve "

He directed her attention to her health, and showed that she required continuous care, and the direction of a good physician   " Why care for me," said she, " when there are so many things to care for ? "

After he had laboured greatly to persuade her that he could not take her with him, that he would conduct her to a place where he might often see her, she appeared as if she had not heard a word of it.   " Thou wishest not to have me with thee ? " said she   " Perhaps it is better, send me to the old Harper, the poor man is lonely where he is "

Wilhelm tried to show her that the old man was in comfortable circumstances   " Every hour I long for him," replied the child

" I did not see," said Wilhelm, " that thou wert so fond of him when he was living with us "

" I was frightened for him, when he was awake, I could not bear his eyes, but when he was asleep, I liked so well to sit by him !   I used to chase the flies from him, I could not look at him enough   O ! he has stood by me in fearful moments, none knows how much I owe him   Had I known the road, I should have run away to him already "

Wilhelm set the circumstances in detail before her, he said, that she had always been a reasonable child, and that on this occasion also she might do as she desired.   " Reason is cruel,"

said she, " the heart is better , I will go as thou requirest,
only leave me Felix "

After much discussion, her opinion was not altered , and
Wilhelm at last resolved on giving Barbara both the children,
and sending them together to Theresa   This was the easier
for him, as he still feared to look upon the lovely Felix as his
son   He would take him on his arm, and carry him about
the child delighted to be held before the glass , Wilhelm also
liked, though unavowedly, to hold him there, and seek resem-
blances between their faces   If for a moment any striking
similarity appeared between them, he would press the boy in
his arms ; and then at once, affrighted by the thought that he
might be mistaken, he would set him down, and let him run
away   " O ! " cried he, " if I were to appropriate this priceless
treasure, and it were then to be snatched from me, I should be
the most unhappy man on earth ! "

The children had been sent away , and Wilhelm was about
to take a formal leave of the theatre, when he felt that in
reality he had already taken leave, and needed but to go
Mariana was no more , his two guardian spirits had departed,
and his thoughts hied after them   The fair boy hovered like
a beautiful uncertain vision in the eyes of his imagination   he
saw him, at Theresa's hand, running through the fields and
woods, forming his mind and person, in the free air, beside a
free and cheerful foster-mother   Theresa had become far
dearer to him since he figured her in company with Felix
Even while sitting in the theatre, he thought of her with
smiles , he was almost in her own case, the stage could now
produce no more illusion in him

Serlo and Melina were excessively polite to him, when they
observed that he was making no pretensions to his former
place   A portion of the public wished to see him act again
this he could not accede to , nor in the company did any one
desire it, saving Frau Melina

Of this friend he now took leave , he was moved at parting
with her , he exclaimed: " Why do we presume to promise

anything depending on an unknown future ? The most slight
engagement we have not power to keep , far less a purpose of
importance   I feel ashamed in recollecting what I promised
to you all, in that unhappy night, when we were lying
plundered, sick and wounded, crammed into a miserable tavern
How did misfortune elevate my courage , what a treasure did
I think I had found in my good wishes!   And of all this not a
jot has taken effect   I leave you as your debtor   and my
comfort is, that our people prized my promise at its actual
worth, and never more took notice of it "

"Be not unjust to yourself," said Frau Melina   "if no one
acknowledges what you have done for us, I at least will not
forget it   Our whole condition had been different, if you had
not been with us.   But it is with our purposes as with our
wishes   They seem no longer what they were, when they have
been accomplished, been fulfilled , and we think we have done,
have wished for nothing "

"You shall not, by your friendly statement," answered
Wilhelm, "put my conscience to peace   I shall always look
upon myself as in your debt "

"Nay, perhaps you are so," said Madam Melina , "but not
in the manner you suppose.   We reckon it a shame to fail in
the fulfilment of a promise we have uttered with the voice
O my friend, a worthy person by his very presence promises us
much!   The confidence which he elicits, the inclination he
inspires, the hopes which he awakens are unbounded   he is,
and he continues, in our debt, although he does not know it
Fare you well!   If our external circumstances have been
happily repaired by your direction, there is a void produced by
your departure, in my mind, which will not be so easily filled
up again "

Before leaving the city, Wilhelm wrote a copious sheet to
Werner   He had before exchanged some letters , but, not
being able to agree, they had at length ceased to write   Now,
however, Wilhelm had again approximated to his brother, he
was just about to do what Werner had so earnestly desired.

He could say 'I am abandoning the stage, I mean to join myself with men whose intercourse, in every sense, must lead me to a sure and suitable activity   He inquired about his property   and it now seemed strange to him, that he had never for so long a time disturbed himself about it   He knew not that it is the manner of all persons who attach importance to their inward cultivation, altogether to neglect their outward circumstances   This had been Wilhelm's case   he now for the first time seemed to notice, that to work effectively, he stood in need of outward means   He entered on his journey, this time, in a temper altogether different from that of last, the prospects he had in view were charming, he hoped to meet with something cheerful by the way

CHAPTER IX

On returning to Lothario's Castle, Wilhelm found that changes had occurred   Jarno met him with the tidings, that Lothario's uncle being dead, the Baron had himself set out to take possession of the heritage   "You come in time," said he, "to help the Abbé and me   Lothario has commissioned us to purchase some extensive properties of land in this quarter   he has long contemplated the bargain, and we have now got cash and credit just in season   The only point which made us hesitate was, that a distant trading house had also views upon the same estates, at length we have determined to make common cause with it, as otherwise we might outbid each other without need or reason   The trader seems to be a prudent man   At present we are making estimates and calculations   we must also settle economically how the lands are to be shared, so that each of us may have a fine estate."   The papers were submitted to our friend, the fields, meadows, houses, were inspected, and though Jarno and the Abbé seemed to understand the matter fully, Wilhelm could not help desiring that Theresa had been with them

In these labours several days were spent, and Wilhelm had scarcely time to tell his friends of his adventures and his dubious fatherhood   This incident, to him so interesting, they treated with indifference and levity

He had noticed, that they frequently in confidential conversation, while at table or in walks, would suddenly stop short, and give their words another application, thereby showing, at least, that they had on the anvil many things which were concealed from him   He bethought him of what Lydia had said, and he put the greater faith in it, as one entire division of the Castle had always been inaccessible to him   The way to certain galleries, particularly to the ancient tower, with which externally he was so well acquainted, he had often sought, and hitherto in vain

One evening Jarno said to him   " We can now consider you as ours, with such security, that it were unjust if we did not introduce you deeper into our mysteries   It is right that a man, when he first enters upon life, should think highly of himself, should determine to attain many eminent distinctions, should endeavour to make all things possible, but when his education has proceeded to a certain pitch, it is advantageous for him that he learn to lose himself among a mass of men, that he learn to live for the sake of others, and to forget himself in an activity prescribed by duty   It is then that he first becomes acquainted with himself, for it is conduct alone that compares us with others   You shall soon see what a curious little world is at your very hand, and how well you are known in it   Tomorrow morning before sunrise be dressed and ready "

Jarno came at the appointed hour   he led our friend through certain known and unknown chambers of the Castle, then through several galleries, till at last they reached a large old door, strongly framed with iron   Jarno knocked, the door went up a little, so as to admit one person   Jarno introduced our friend, and did not follow him   Wilhelm found himself in an obscure and narrow stand   all was dark

round him and when he tried to go a step forward, he found
himself hemmed in A voice not altogether strange to him
cried "Enter!" and he now discovered that the sides of the
place where he was were merely hung with tapestry, through
which a feeble light glimmered in to him "Enter!" cried
the voice again he raised the tapestry and entered

The hall, in which he now stood, appeared to have at one
time been a chapel, instead of the altar he observed a large
table raised some steps above the floor, and covered with a
green cloth hanging over it On the top of this, a drawn
curtain seemed as if it hid a picture, on the sides were spaces
beautifully worked, and covered-in with fine wire netting, like
the shelves of a library, only here, instead of books, a multitude of rolls had been inserted Nobody was in the hall, the
rising sun shone through the window, right on Wilhelm, and
kindly saluted him as he came in

"Be seated!" cried a voice, which seemed to issue from
the altar Wilhelm placed himself in a small arm-chair, which
stood against the tapestry where he had entered There was
no seat but this in the room, Wilhelm had to be content
with it, though the morning radiance dazzled him, the chair
stood fast, he could only keep his hand before his eyes

But now the curtain, which hung down above the altar,
went asunder with a gentle rustling, and showed, within a
picture-frame, a dark empty aperture A man stept forward
from it, in a commondress, saluted the astonished looker-on,
and said to him "Do you not recognise me? Among the
many things which you would like to know, do you feel no
curiosity to learn where your grandfather's collection of
pictures and statues are at present? Have you forgot the
painting which you once so much delighted in? Where,
think you, is the sick king's son now languishing?"
Wilhelm, without difficulty, recognised the stranger whom,
in that important night, he had conversed with at the inn
"Perhaps," continued his interrogator, "we should now be
less at variance in regard to Destiny and Character"

Wilhelm was about to answer, when the curtain quickly
flew together "Strange!" said Wilhelm to himself "Can
chance occurrences have a connexion? Is what we call
Destiny but Chance? Where *is* my grandfather's collection,
and why am I reminded of it in these solemn moments?"

He had not leisure to pursue his thoughts the curtain
once more parted, and a person stood before him, whom he
instantly perceived to be the country clergyman, that had
attended him and his companions on that pleasure sail of
theirs He had a resemblance to the Abbé, though he seemed
to be a different person With a cheerful countenance, in a
tone of dignity, he said "To guard from error, is not the
instructor's duty, but to lead the erring pupil, nay, to let
him quaff his error in deep satiating draughts, this is the
instructor's wisdom He who only tastes his error, will long
dwell with it, will take delight in it as in a singular felicity
while he who drains it to the dregs will, if he be not crazy,
find it out" The curtain closed again, and Wilhelm had a
little time to think "What error can he mean," said he
within himself, "but the error which has clung to me through
my whole life, that I sought for cultivation where it was not
to be found, that I fancied I could form a talent in me, while
without the smallest gift for it"

The curtain dashed asunder faster than before, an officer
advanced, and said in passing "Learn to know the men who
may be trusted!" The curtain closed, and Wilhelm did
not long consider, till he found this officer to be the one who
had embraced him in the Count's park, and had caused his
taking Jarno for a crimp How that stranger had come
hither, who he was, were riddles to our friend "If so many
men," cried he, "took interest in thee, knew thy way of life,
and how it should be carried on, why did they not conduct
thee with greater strictness, with greater seriousness? Why
did they favour thy silly sports, instead of drawing thee away
from them?"

"Dispute not with us!" cried a voice "Thou art saved,

thou art on the way to the goal None of thy follies wilt thou repent, none wilt thou wish to repeat, no luckier destiny can be allotted to a man " The curtain went asunder ; and in full armour stood the old King of Denmark in the space. " I am thy father's spirit," said the figure, " and I depart in comfort, since my wishes for thee are accomplished, in a higher sense than I myself contemplated Steep regions cannot be surmounted save by winding paths, on the plain, straight roads conduct from place to place Farewell, and think of me, when thou enjoyest what I have provided for thee "

Wilhelm was exceedingly amazed and struck he thought it was his father's voice, and yet in truth it was not the present and the past alike confounded and perplexed him

He had not meditated long, when the Abbé came to view, and placed himself behind the green table " Come hither ! " cried he to his marvelling friend He went, and mounted up the steps On the green cloth lay a little roll " Here is your indenture," said the Abbé " take it to heart, it is of weighty import " Wilhelm lifted, opened it, and read

INDENTURE

Art is long, life short, judgment difficult, opportunity transient To act is easy, to think is hard, to act according to our thought is troublesome Every beginning is cheerful , the threshold is the place of expectation The boy stands astonished, his impressions guide him , he learns sportfully, seriousness comes on him by surprise Imitation is born with us , what should be imitated is not easy to discover The excellent is rarely found, more rarely valued The height charms us, the steps to it do not with the summit in our eye, we love to walk along the plain It is but a part of art that can be taught, the artist needs it all Who knows it half, speaks much, and is always wrong , who knows it wholly, inclines to act, and speaks seldom or late The former have no secrets and no force the instruction they can give is like baked bread, savoury and satisfying for a single day, but flour cannot be sown and seed-corn ought not to be ground Words are good, but they are not the best   The best is not to be explained by words   The spirit in which we act is the highest matter   Action can be understood and again represented by the spirit alone   No one knows what he is doing, while he acts aright, but of what is wrong we are always conscious   Whoever works with symbols only, is a pedant, a hypocrite, or a bungler   There are many such, and they like to be together   Their babbling detains the scholar   their obstinate mediocrity vexes even the best   The instruction which the true artist gives us, opens the mind, for where words fail him, deeds speak   The true scholar learns from the known to unfold the unknown, and approaches more and more to being a master

"Enough !" cried the Abbé, " the rest in due time.   Now, look round you among these cases "

Wilhelm went, and read the titles of the rolls   With astonishment, he found *Lothario's Apprenticeship, Jarno's Apprenticeship*, and his own *Apprenticeship* placed there, with many others whose names he did not know

"May I hope to cast a look into these rolls ? "

"In this chamber there is now nothing hid from you "

"May I put a question ? "

"Without scruple, and you may expect a positive reply, if it concerns a matter which is nearest your heart, and ought to be so "

"Good then !   Ye marvellous sages, whose sight has pierced so many secrets, can you tell me whether Felix is in truth my son ? "

"Hail to you for this question !" cried the Abbé, clapping hands for joy   "Felix is your son !   By the holiest that lies hid among us, I swear to you, Felix is your son, nor, in our opinion, was the mother that is gone unworthy of you.

Receive the lovely child from our hands, turn round, and venture to be happy "

Wilhelm heard a noise behind him he turned round, and saw a child's face peeping archly through the tapestry at the end of the room, it was Felix The boy playfully hid himself, so soon as he was noticed "Come forward!" cried the Abbé, he came running, his father rushed towards him, took him in his arms, and pressed him to his heart "Yes! I feel it," cried he, "thou art mine! What a gift of Heaven have I to thank my friends for! Whence, or how, comest thou, my child, at this important moment?"

"Ask not," said the Abbé. "Hail to thee, young man! Thy Apprenticeship is done; Nature has pronounced thee free"

BOOK VIII

CHAPTER I

FELIX skipped into the garden, Wilhelm followed him with rapture a lovely morning was displaying everything with fresh charms, our friend enjoyed the most delightful moment Felix was new in the free and lordly world, nor did his father know much more than he about the objects, concerning which the little creature was repeatedly and unweariedly inquiring At last they joined the gardener, who had to tell them the names and uses of a multitude of plants Wilhelm looked on Nature as with unscaled eyes, the child's new-fangled curiosity first made him sensible how weak an interest he himself had taken in external things, how small his actual knowledge was Not till this day, the happiest of his life, did his own cultivation seem to have commenced he felt the necessity of learning, being called upon to teach

Jarno and the Abbé did not show themselves again till evening, when they brought a guest along with them Wilhelm viewed the stranger with amazement, he could scarce believe his eyes it was Werner, who, likewise, for a moment, hesitated in his recognition They embraced each other tenderly, neither of them could conceal that he thought the other greatly altered Werner declared that his friend was taller, stronger, straighter, that he had become more polished in his looks and carriage "Something of his old true-heartedness, I miss, however," added he "That too will soon appear again," said Wilhelm, "when we have recovered from our first astonishment"

The impression Werner made upon his friend was by no

means so favourable   The honest man seemed rather to have retrograded than advanced   He was much leaner than of old, his peaked face appeared to have grown sharper, his nose longer, brow and crown had lost their hair, the voice, clear, eager, shrill, the hollow breast and stooping shoulders, the sallow cheeks, announced indubitably that a melancholic drudge was there

Wilhelm was discreet enough to speak but sparingly of these great changes, while the other, on the contrary, gave free course to his friendly joy   "In truth," cried he, "if thou hast spent thy time badly, and, as I suppose, gained nothing, it must be owned thou art grown a piece of manhood such as cannot fail to turn to somewhat   Do not waste and squander me this too again, with such a figure thou shalt buy some rich and beautiful heiress"   "I see," said Wilhelm, smiling, "thou wilt not belie thy character   Scarcely hast thou found thy brother after long absence, when thou lookest on him as a piece of goods, a thing to speculate on, and make profit by"

Jarno and the Abbé did not seem at all astonished at this recognition, they allowed the two to expatiate on the past and present as they pleased   Werner walked round and round his friend, turned him to this side and to that, so as almost to embarrass him   "No!" cried he, "such a thing as this I never met with, and yet I know that I am not mistaken   Thy eyes are deeper, thy brow is broader, thy nose has grown finer, thy mouth more lovely   Do but look at him, how he stands, how it all suits and fits together!   Well, idling is the way to grow   But for me, poor devil," said he, looking at himself in the glass, "if I had not all this while been making store of money, it were over with me altogether"

Werner had got Wilhelm's last letter, the distant trading house, in common with which Lothario meant to purchase the estates, was theirs   On that business Werner had come hither, not dreaming that he should meet with Wilhelm on the way   The Baron's lawyer came, the papers were produced, Werner reckoned the conditions reasonable   "If you mean well," said he, 'as you seem to do, with this young man, you will of yourselves take care that our part be not abridged it shall be at my friend's option whether he will take the land, and lay out a portion of his fortune on it"   Jarno and the Abbé protested that they did not need this admonition Scarcely had the business been discussed in general terms, when Werner signified a longing for a game at ombre, to which, in consequence, Jarno and the Abbé set themselves along with him   He was now grown so accustomed to it, that he could not pass the evening without cards

The two friends, after supper, being left alone, began to talk, and question one another very keenly, touching everything they wished to have communicated   Wilhelm spoke in high terms of his situation, of his happiness in being received among such men   Werner shook his head and said   "Well, I see, we should believe nothing that we do not see with our eyes   More than one obliging friend assured me thou wert living with a wild young nobleman, wert supplying him with actresses, helping him to waste his money, that, by thy means, he had quarrelled with every one of his relations"   "For my own sake, and the sake of these worthy gentlemen, I should be vexed at this," said Wilhelm, "had not my theatrical experience made me tolerant to every sort of calumny   How can men judge rightly of our actions, which appear but singly or in fragments to them, of which they see the smallest portion, while good and bad takes place in secret, and for most part nothing comes to light but an indifferent show? Are not the actors and actresses in a play set up on boards before them, lamps are lit on every side, the whole transaction is comprised within three hours, yet scarcely one of them knows rightly what to make of it"

Our friend proceeded to inquire about his family, his young comrades, his native town   Werner told, with great haste, of changes that had taken place, of changes that were still in progress   "The women in our house," said he, "are satisfied and happy, we are never short of money One half of their time they spend in dressing, the other in showing themselves when dressed They are as domestic as a reasonable man could wish My boys are growing up to prudent youths I already, as in vision, see them sitting, writing, reckoning, running, trading, trucking each of them, as soon as possible, shall have a business of his own As to what concerns our fortune, thou wilt be contented with the state of it When we have got these lands in order, thou must come directly home with me, for it now appears as if thou too couldst mingle with some skill in worldly undertakings Thanks to thy new friends, who have set thee on the proper path I am certainly a fool I never knew till now how well I liked thee, now when I cannot gape and gaze at thee enough, so well and handsome thou lookest That is in truth another form than the portrait which was sent thy sister, which occasioned such disputes at home Both mother and daughter thought young master very handsome indeed, with his slack collar, half-open breast, large ruff, sleek pendent hair, round hat, short waistcoat, and wide pantaloons, while I, on the other hand, maintained that the costume was scarce two finger-breadths from that of Harlequin But now thou lookest like a man, only the queue is wanting, in which I beg of thee to bind thy hair, else some time or other, they will seize thee as a Jew, and demand toll and tribute of thee "

Felix in the mean time had come into the room, and as they did not mind him, he had laid himself upon the sofa, and was fallen asleep "What urchin is this?" said Werner Wilhelm at that moment had not the heart to tell the truth, nor did he wish to lay a still ambiguous narrative before a man, who was by nature anything but credulous

The whole party now proceeded to the lands, to view them, and conclude the bargain Wilhelm would not part with Felix from his side, for the boy's sake, he rejoiced exceedingly in the intended purchase The longing of the child for cherries and berries, the season for which was at hand, brought

to his mind the days of his own youth, and the manifold
duties of a father, to prepare, to procure, and to maintain
for his family a constant series of enjoyments With what
interest he viewed the nurseries and the buildings! How
zealously he contemplated repairing what had been neglected,
restoring what had fallen! He no longer looked upon the
world with the eyes of a bird of passage an edifice he did
not now consider as a grove that is hastily put together, and
that withers ere one leaves it Everything that he proposed
commencing was to be completed for his boy, everything that
he erected was to last for several generations In this sense,
his apprenticeship was ended. with the feeling of a father, he
had acquired all the virtues of a citizen He felt this, and
nothing could exceed his joy "O needless strictness of
morality," exclaimed he, "while Nature in her own kindly
manner trains us to all that we require to be! O strange
demands of civil society, which first perplexes and misleads us,
then asks of us more than Nature herself! Woe to every sort
of culture which destroys the most effectual means of all true
culture, and directs us to the end, instead of rendering us
happy on the way!"

Much as he had already seen in his life, it seemed as if the
observation of the child afforded him his first clear view of
human nature The theatre, the world had appeared before
him, only as a multitude of thrown dice, every one of which
upon its upper surface indicates a greater or a smaller value,
and which, when reckoned up together, make a sum But
here in the person of the boy, as we might say, a single die
was laid before him, on the many sides of which the worth
and worthlessness of man's nature were legibly engraved

The child's desire to have distinctions made in his ideas
grew stronger every day Having learned that things had
names, he wished to hear the name of everything supposing
that there could be nothing which his father did not know, he
often teased him with his questions, and caused him to inquire
concerning objects, which but for this he would have passed

without notice   Our innate tendency to pry into the origin and end of things was likewise soon developed in the boy When he asked whence came the wind, and whither went the flame, his father for the first time truly felt the limitation of his own powers, and wished to understand how far man may venture with his thoughts, and what things he may hope ever to give account of to himself or others   The anger of the child, when he saw injustice done to any living thing, was extremely grateful to the father, as the symptom of a generous heart Felix once struck fiercely at the cook for cutting up some pigeons   The fine impression this produced on Wilhelm was, indeed, ere long disturbed, when he found the boy unmercifully tearing sparrows in pieces, and beating frogs to death   This trait reminded him of many men, who appear so scrupulously just when without passion, and witnessing the proceedings of other men

The pleasant feeling, that the boy was producing so fine and wholesome an influence on his being, was in a short time troubled for a moment, when our friend observed that in truth the boy was educating him more than he the boy   The child's conduct he was not qualified to correct   its mind he could not guide in any path but a spontaneous one   The evil habits which Aurelia had so violently striven against, had all, as it seemed, on her death, assumed their ancient privileges   Felix still never shut the door behind him, he still would not eat from a plate, and no greater pleasure could befall him than when he happened to be overlooked, and could take his bit immediately from the dish, or let the full glass stand, and drink out of the bottle   He delighted also very much when he could set himself in a corner with a book, and say with a serious air   "I must study this scholar stuff!" though he neither knew his letters nor would learn them.

Thus, when Wilhelm thought how little he had done for Felix, how little he was capable of doing, there arose at times a restlessness within him, which appeared to counterbalance all his happiness   "Are we men, then," said he, "so selfishly formed that we cannot possibly take proper charge of any one without us? Am I not acting with the boy exactly as I did with Mignon? I drew the dear child towards me, her presence gave me pleasure, yet I cruelly neglected her What did I do for her education, which she longed for with such earnestness? Nothing! I left her to herself, and to all the accidents to which in a society of coarse people she could be exposed. And now for this boy, who seemed so interesting before he could be precious to thee, has thy heart ever bid thee do the smallest service to him? It is time that thou shouldst cease to waste thy own years and those of others awake, and think what thou shouldst do for thyself, and for this good being, whom love and nature have so firmly bound to thee"

This soliloquy was but an introduction to admit that he had already thought, and cared, and tried, and chosen he could delay no longer to confess it After sorrow, often and in vain repeated, for the loss of Mariana, he distinctly felt that he must seek a mother for the boy, and also that he could not find one equal to Theresa With this gifted lady he was thoroughly acquainted Such a spouse and helpmate seemed the only one to trust oneself to, in such circumstances Her generous affection for Lothario did not make him hesitate By a singular destiny, they two had been forever parted, Theresa looked upon herself as free, she had talked of marrying, with indifference indeed, but as of a matter understood

After long deliberation, he determined on communicating to her everything he knew about himself She was to be made acquainted with him, as he already was with her He accordingly began to take a survey of his history but it seemed to him so empty of events, and in general so little to his credit, that he more than once was on the point of giving up his purpose At last, however, he resolved on asking Jarno for the Roll of his Apprenticeship, which he had noticed lying in the Tower Jarno said it was the very time for that, and Wilhelm consequently got it

It is a feeling of awe and fear, which seizes on a man of
noble mind, when conscious that his character is just about to
be exhibited before him   Every transition is a crisis, and a
crisis presupposes sickness   With what reluctance do we look
into the glass after rising from a sick-bed!   The recovery we
feel   the effects of the past disease are all we see   Wilhelm
had, however, been sufficiently prepared , events had already
spoken loudly to him, and his friends had not spared him   If
he opened the roll of parchment with some hurry, he grew
calmer and calmer the farther he read   He found his life
delineated with large sharp strokes, neither unconnected
incidents, nor narrow sentiments perplexed his view , the most
bland and general reflections taught without shaming him
For the first time, his own figure was presented to him; not
indeed, as in a mirror, a second self, but as in a portrait,
another self: we do not, it is true, recognise ourselves in every
feature , but we are delighted that a thinking spirit has so
understood us, that such gifts have been employed in representing us, that an image of what we were exists, and may endure
when we ourselves are gone

Wilhelm next employed himself in setting forth the history
of his life, for the perusal of Theresa, all the circumstances of
it were recalled to memory by what he had been reading, he
almost felt ashamed that, to her great virtues, he had nothing
to oppose which indicated a judicious activity   He had been
minute in his written narrative, he was brief in the letter
which he sent along with it   He solicited her friendship her
love, if it were possible , he offered her his hand, and entreated
for a quick decision

After some internal contest whether it was proper to impart
this weighty business to his friends, to Jarno and the Abbé,
he determined not to do so   His resolution was so firm, the
business was of such importance, that he could not have submitted it to the decision of the wisest and best of men   He
was even cautious enough to carry his letter with his own hand
to the nearest post. From his parchment roll it appeared with

certainty enough that, in very many actions of his life, in which he had conceived himself to be proceeding freely and in secret, he had been observed, nay, guided, and perhaps the thought of this had given him an unpleasant feeling, and he wished at least in speaking to Theresa's heart, to speak purely from the heart, to owe his fate to her decision and determination only   Hence in this solemn point he scrupled not to give his overseers the slip

CHAPTER II

SCARCELY was the letter gone, when Lothario returned. Every one was gladdened at the prospect of so speedily concluding the important business which they had in hand Wilhelm waited with anxiety to see how all these many threads were to be loosed, or tied anew, and how his own future state was to be settled   Lothario gave a kindly salutation to them all   he was quite recovered and serene, he had the air of one who knows what he should do, and who finds no hindrance in the way of doing it.

His cordial greeting Wilhelm could scarcely repay   "This," he had to own within himself, "is the friend, the lover, bridegroom of Theresa, in his stead thou art presuming to intrude Dost thou think it possible for thee to banish, to obliterate an impression such as this?"   Had the letter not been sent away, perhaps he would not have ventured sending it at all. But happily the die was cast   it might be, Theresa had already taken up her resolution, and only distance shrouded with its veil a happy termination   The winning or the losing must soon be decided   By such considerations, he endeavoured to compose himself, and yet the movements of his heart were almost feverish   He could give but little attention to the weighty business, on which in some degree the fate of his whole property depended   In passionate moments, how trivial do we reckon all that is about us, all that belongs to us !

Happily for him, Lothario treated the affair with magnanimity, and Werner with an air of ease   The latter, in his violent desire of gain, experienced a lively pleasure in contemplating the fine estate which was to be his friend's Lothario, for his part, seemed to be revolving very different thoughts   "I cannot take such pleasure in the acquirement of property," said he, "as in the justness of it"

"And, in the name of Heaven," cried Werner, "is not this of ours acquired justly ?"

"Not altogether," said Lothario

" Are we not giving hard cash for it ?"

"Doubtless," replied Lothario , "and most probably you will consider what I am now hinting at as nothing but a whim. No property appears to me quite just, quite free of flaw, except it contribute to the state its due proportion "

"How !" said Werner   "You would rather that our lands, which we have purchased free from burden, had been taxable ?"

"Yes," replied Lothario, "in a suitable degree   It is only by this equality with every other kind of property, that our possession of it can be made secure   In these new times, when so many old ideas are tottering, what is the grand reason why the peasant reckons the possession of the noble less equitable than his own ?   Simply that the noble is not burdened, and lay a burden on him "

"But how would the interest of our capital agree with that ?" said Werner

"Perfectly well," returned the other   "if the state, for a regular and fair contribution, would relieve us from the feudal hocus-pocus , would allow us to proceed with our lands according to our pleasure   so that we were not compelled to retain such masses of them undivided, so that we might part them more equally among our children, whom we might thus introduce to vigorous and free activity , instead of leaving them the poor inheritance of these our limited and limiting privileges, to enjoy which we must ever be invoking the ghosts

of our forefathers How much happier were men and women
in our rank of life, if they might with unforbidden eyes look
round them, and elevate by their selection, here a worthy
maiden, there a worthy youth, regarding nothing farther than
their own ideas of happiness in marriage! The state would
have more, perhaps better citizens, and would not so often be
distressed for want of heads and hands "

"I can assure you honestly," said Werner, "I never in y
life thought about the state my taxes, tolls and tributes I
have paid because it was the custom "

"Still, however," said Lothario, "I hope to make a worthy
patriot of you As he alone is a good father, who at table
serves his children first, so is he alone a good citizen, who,
before all other outlays, discharges what he owes the state "

By such general reflections their special business was
accelerated rather than retarded It was nearly over, when
Lothario said to Wilhelm "I must send you to a place
where you are needed more than here My sister bids me beg
of you to go to her as soon as possible Poor Mignon seems
to be decaying more and more and it is thought your
presence might allay the malady Besides telling me in
person, my sister has despatched this note after me so that
you perceive she reckons it a pressing case " Lothario handed
him a billet Wilhelm, who had listened in extreme perplexity, at once discovered in these hasty pencil-strokes the
hand of the Countess, and knew not what to answer

"Take Felix with you," said Lothario "the little ones
will cheer each other You must be upon the road tomorrow
morning early, my sister's coach, in which my people travelled
hither, is still here I will give you horses half the way, the
rest you post A prosperous journey to you! Make many
compliments from me, when you arrive, tell my sister I shall
soon be back, and that she must prepare for guests Our
granduncle's friend, the Marchese Cipriani, is on his way to
visit us he hoped to find the old man still in life, they
meant to entertain each other with their common love of art,

and the recollection of their early intimacy The Marchese, much younger than my uncle, owed to him the greater part of his accomplishments We must exert all our endeavours to fill up in some measure the void which is awaiting him, and a larger party is the readiest means "

Lotharo went with the Abbé to his chamber, Jarno had ridden off before, Wilhelm hastened to his room There was none to whom he could unbosom his distress, none by whose assistance he could turn aside the project, which he viewed with so much fear The little servant came, requesting him to pack they were to put the luggage on tonight, meaning to set out by daybreak Wilhelm knew not what to do, at length he cried "Well, I shall leave this house at any rate, on the road I may consider what is to be done, at all events I will halt in the middle of my journey, I can send a message hither, I can write what I recoil from saying, then let come of it what will " In spite of this resolution, he spent a sleepless night a look on Felix resting so serenely was the only thing that gave him any solace "O! who knows,' cried he, "what trials are before me, who knows how sharply bygone errors will yet punish me, how often good and reasonable projects for the future shall miscarry! But this treasure, which I call my own, continue it to me, thou exorable or inexorable Fate ! Were it possible that this best part of myself were taken from me, that this heart could be torn from my heart, then farewell sense and understanding, farewell all care and foresight, vanish thou tendency to perseverance! All that distinguishes us from the beasts, pass away ! And if it is not lawful for a man to end his heavy days by the act of his own hand, may speedy madness banish consciousness, before Death, which destroys it forever, shall bring on his own long night "

He seized the boy in his arms, kissed him, clasped him and wetted him with plenteous tears

The child awoke his clear eye, his friendly look, touched his father to the inmost heart "What a scene awaits me,' cried he, " when I shall present thee to the beautiful unhappy

ountess, when she shall press thee to her bosom, which 'thy
ither has so deeply injured! Ought I not to fear that she
ill push thee from her with a cry, when the touch of thee
enews her real or fancied pain!" The coachman did not
eave him time for farther thought or hesitation, but forced
um into the carriage before day   Wilhelm wrapped his Felix
vell, the morning was cold but clear, the child, for the first
ime in his life, saw the sun rise   His astonishment at the first
iery glance of the luminary, at the growing power of the
light, his pleasure and his strange remarks rejoiced the father,
and afforded him a glimpse into the heart of the boy, before
which, as over a clear and silent sea, the sun was mounting and
hovering

In a little town the coachman halted, unyoked his horses,
and rode back   Wilhelm took possession of a room, and
asked himself seriously whether he would stay or proceed
Thus irresolute he ventured to take out the little note, which
hitherto he had never had the heart to look on   it contained
the following words   "Send thy young friend very soon,
Mignon for the last two days has been growing rather worse
Sad as the occasion is, I shall be happy to get acquainted with
him "

The concluding words Wilhelm, at the first glance, had not
seen   He was terrified on reading them, and instantly
determined not to go   "How?" cried he, "Lothario, knowing what occurred between us, has not told her who I am?
She is not, with a settled mind, expecting an acquaintance,
whom she would rather not see   she expects a stranger, and
I enter!   I see her shudder and start back, I see her blush!
No, it is impossible for me to encounter such a scene!"   Just
then his horses were led out and yoked   Wilhelm was
determined to take off his luggage and remain   He felt
extremely agitated   Hearing the maid running up-stairs to
tell him, as he thought, that all was ready, he began on the
spur of the instant to devise some pretext for continuing, his
eyes were fixed, without attention, on the letter which he still

held in his hand "In the name of Heaven!" cried he "what is this? It is not the hand of the Countess, it is the hand of the Amazon!"

The maid came in, requested him to walk down, and took Felix with her "Is it possible,' exclaimed he, "is it true? What shall I do? Remain, and wait, and certify myself? Or hasten, hasten and rush into an explanation? Thou art on the way to her, and thou canst loiter? This night thou mayest see her, and thou wilt voluntarily lock thyself in prison? It is her hand, yes, it is hers! This hand calls thee, her coach is yoked to lead thee to her! Now the riddle is explained Lothario has two sisters, my relation to the one he knows, how much I owe to the other is unknown to him Nor is she aware that the wounded stroller, who stands indebted to her for his health, if not his life, has been received with such unmerited attention in her brother's house"

Felix, who was swinging to and fro in the coach, cried up to him "Father! Come, O come! Look at the pretty clouds, the pretty colours!" "Yes, I come," cried Wilhelm. springing down-stairs, "and all the glories of the sky, which thou, good creature, so admirest, are as nothing to the moment which I look for"

Sitting in the coach, he recalled all the circumstances of the matter to his memory "So this is the Natalia, then, Theresa's friend! What a discovery, what hopes, what prospects! How strange that the fear of speaking about the one sister should have altogether concealed from me the existence of the other!" With what joy he looked on Felix! He anticipated for the child, as for himself, the best reception

Evening at last came on, the sun had set, the road was not the best, the postillion drove slowly, Felix had fallen asleep, and new cares and doubts arose in the bosom of our friend "What delusion, what fantasies are these that rule thee!" said he to himself "An uncertain similarity of handwriting has at once assured thee, and given thee matter for the strangest castles in the air " He again brought out the paper, in the departing light he again imagined that he recognised the hand of the Countess his eyes could no longer find in the parts what his heart had at once shown him in the whole. " These horses, then, are running with thee to a scene of terror ! Who knows but in a few hours they may have to bring thee back again ? And if thou shouldst meet with her alone ! But perhaps her husband will be there , perhaps the Baroness ? How altered will she be ! Shall I not fail, and sink to the earth, at sight of her ? "

Yet a faint hope that it might be his Amazon, would often gleam through these gloomy thoughts It was now night the carriage rolled into a courtyard, and halted , a servant with a link stept out of a stately portal, and came down the broad steps to the carriage-door " You have been long looked for, ' said he, opening it Wilhelm dismounted, took the sleeping Felix in his arms the first servant called to a second, who was standing in the door with a light " Show the gentleman up to the Baroness "

Quick as lightning, it went through Wilhelm's soul " What a happiness ! Be it by accident or of purpose, the Baroness is here ! I shall see her first , apparently the Countess has retired to rest Ye good spirits, grant that the moment of deepest perplexity may pass tolerably over ! "

He entered the house he found himself in the most earnest, and, as he almost felt, the holiest place that he had ever trod A pendent dazzling lustre threw its light upon a broad and softly rising flight of stairs, which lay before him, and which parted into two divisions at a turn above Marble statues and busts were standing upon pedestals and arranged in niches some of them seemed known to him The impressions of our childhood abide with us, even in their minutest traces He recognised a Muse, which had formerly belonged to his grandfather , not indeed by its form or worth, but by an arm which had been restored, and some new-inserted pieces of the robe He felt as if a fairy tale had turned out to be true   The child was heavy in his arms, he lingered on the stairs, and knelt down, as if to place him more conveniently His real want, however, was to get a moment's breathing-time He could scarcely raise himself again   The servant, who was carrying the light, offered to take Felix, but Wilhelm could not part with him   He had now mounted to an antechamber, in which, to his still greater astonishment, he observed the well-known picture of the sick king's son hanging on the wall He had scarcely time to cast a look on it, the servant hurried him along through two rooms into a cabinet   Here, behind a light-screen, which threw a shadow on her, sat a young lady reading   " O that it were she ! " said he within himself at this decisive moment   He set down the boy, who seemed to be awakening, he meant to approach the lady, but the child sank together drunk with sleep, the lady rose, and came to him   It was the Amazon !   Unable to restrain himself, he fell upon his knee, and cried   " It is she ! "   He seized her hand, and kissed it with unbounded rapture   The child was lying on the carpet between them, sleeping softly

Felix was carried to the sofa   Natalia sat down beside hi ; she directed Wilhelm to the chair which was standing nearest them   She proposed to order some refreshments, these our friend declined, he was altogether occupied convincing himself that it was she, closely examining her features, shaded by the screen, and accurately recognising them   She told him of Mignon's sickness, in general terms, that the poor child was gradually consuming under the influence of a few deep feelings, that, with her extreme excitability, and her endeavouring to hide it, her little heart often suffered violent and dangerous pains, that on any unexpected agitation of her mind, this primary organ of life would suddenly stop, and no trace of the vital movement could be felt in the good child's bosom   That when such an agonising cramp was past, the force of nature would again express itself in strong pulses, and now torment the child by its excess, as she had before suffered by its defect

Wilhelm recollected one spasmodic scene of that description, and Natalia referred him to the doctor, who would speak with him at large on the affair, and explain more circumstantially why he, the friend and benefactor of the child, had been at present sent for "One curious change," Natalia added, "you will find in her she now wears women's clothes, to which she had once such an aversion"

"How did you succeed in this?" said Wilhelm

"If it was indeed a thing to be desired," said she, "we owe it all to chance Hear how it happened Perhaps you are aware that I have constantly about me a number of little girls, whose opening minds I endeavour, as they grow in strength, to train to what is good and right From my mouth they learn nothing but what I myself regard as true yet I cannot and would not hinder them from gathering, among other people, many fragments of the common prejudices and errors which are current in the world If they inquire of me about them, I attempt, as far as possible, to join these alien and intrusive notions to some just one, and thus to render them, if not useful, at least harmless Some time ago, my girls had heard among the peasants' children many tales of angels, of Knecht Rupert and such shadowy characters, who, they understood, appeared at certain times in person, to give presents to good children, and to punish naughty ones They had an idea that these strange visitants were people in disguise in this I confirmed them, and without entering into explanations, I determined on the first opportunity, to let the see a spectacle of that sort It chanced that the birthday of two twin-sisters, whose behaviour had been always very good, was near, I promised that, on this occasion, the little present they had so well deserved should be delivered to them by an angel They were on the stretch of curiosity regarding this phenomenon I had chosen Mignon for the part, and accordingly. at the appointed day, I had her suitably equipt in a long light snow-white dress She was, of course, provided with a golden girdle round her waist, and a golden fillet on her hair I at first proposed to omit the wings, but the young ladies who were decking her, insisted on a pair of large golden pinions, in preparing which they meant to show their highest art Thus did the strange apparition, with a lily in the one hand, and a little basket in the other, glide in among the girls she surprised even me 'There comes the angel!' said I The children all shrank back, at last they cried 'It is Mignon!' yet they durst not venture to approach the wondrous figure

'Here are your gifts,' said she, putting down the basket They gathered around her, they viewed, they felt, they questioned her

'Art thou an angel?' asked one of them

'I wish I were,' said Mignon

'Why dost thou bear a lily?'

'So pure and so open should my heart be, then were I happy'

'What wings are these? Let us see them!'

'They represent far finer ones, which are not yet unfolded'

"And thus significantly did she answer all their other childlike, innocent inquiries The little party having satisfied their curiosity, and the impression of the show beginning to abate, we were for proceeding to undress the little angel This, however, she resisted she took her cithern, she seated herself here, on this high writing-table, and sang a little song with touching grace.

> Such let me seem till such I be,
>   Take not my snow-white dress away,
> Soon from this dusk of earth I flee
>   Up to the glittering lands of day.
>
> There first a little space I rest,
>   Then wake so glad, to scene so kind,
> In earthly robes no longer drest,
>   This band, this girdle left behind

> And those calm shining sons of morn
> They ask not who is maid or boy,
> No robes, no garments there are worn,
> Our body pure from sin's alloy

> Through little life not much I toil'd,
> Yet anguish long this heart has wrung,
> Untimely woe my blossom spoil'd,
> Make me again forever young!

"I immediately determined upon leaving her the dress," proceeded Natalia, "and procuring her some others of a similar kind These she now wears, and in them, I think, her form has quite a different expression"

As it was already late, Natalia let the stranger go he parted from her not without anxiety "Is she married or not?" asked he within himself He had been afraid, at every rustling, that the door would open, and her husband enter The serving-man, who showed him to his room, went off, before our friend had mustered resolution to inquire regarding this His unrest held him long awake, he kept comparing the figure of the Amazon with the figure of his new acquaintance The two would not combine the former he had, as it were, himself fashioned, the latter seemed as if it would almost new-fashion *him*.

CHAPTER III

NEXT morning, while all was yet quiet, he went about viewing the house It was the purest, finest, stateliest piece of architecture he had ever seen "True art," cried he, "is like good company it constrains us in the most delightful way to recognise the measure by which, and up to which, our inward nature has been shaped by culture" The impression which the busts and statues of his grandfather made upon him was exceedingly agreeable With a longing mind, he hastened to the picture of the sick king's son, and he still felt it to be charming and affecting The servant opened to him various

other chambers: he found a library, a museum, a cabinet
of philosophical instruments. In much of this he could not
help perceiving his extreme ignorance. Meanwhile Felix had
awakened, and come running after him. The thought of how
and when he might receive Theresa's letter gave him pain; he
dreaded seeing Mignon, and in some degree Natalia. How
unlike his present state was his state at the moment when he
sealed the letter to Theresa, and with a glad heart wholly
gave himself to that noble being!

Natalia sent for him to breakfast. He proceeded to a
room, where several tidy little girls, all apparently below ten
years, were occupied in furnishing a table, while another of
the same appearance brought in various sorts of beverage.

Wilhelm cast his eye upon a picture, hung above the sofa;
he could not but recognise in it the portrait of Natalia, little
as the execution satisfied him. Natalia entered, and the likeness seemed entirely to vanish. To his comfort, it was painted
with the cross of a religious order on its breast; and he now
saw another such upon Natalia's.

"I have just been looking at the portrait here," said he;
"and it seems surprising that a painter could have been at
once so true and so false. The picture resembles you in
general extremely well, and yet it neither has your features
nor your character."

"It is rather matter of surprise," replied Natalia, "that
the likeness is so good. It is not my picture; but the picture
of an aunt, whom I resembled even in childhood, though she
was then advanced in years. It was painted when her age
was just about what mine is: at the first glance every one
imagines it is meant for me. You should have been acquainted
with that excellent lady. I owe her much. A very weak
state of health, perhaps too much employment with her own
thoughts, and withal a moral and religious scrupulosity, prevented her from being to the world what, in other circumstances, she might have become. She was a light that shone
but on a few friends, and on me especially."

"Can it be possible," said Wilhelm, after thinking for a moment, while so many circumstances seemed to correspond so well, "can it be possible that the fair and noble Saint, whose meek Confessions I had liberty to study, was your aunt?"

"You read the manuscript?" inquired Natalia

"Yes," said Wilhelm, "with the greatest sympathy, and not without effect upon my life   What most impressed me in this paper was, if I may term it so, the purity of being, not only of the writer herself, but of all that lay round her, that self-dependence of nature, that impossibility of admitting anything into her soul which would not harmonise with its own noble lovely tone"

"You are more tolerant to this fine spirit," said Natalia, "nay. I will say more just, than many other men, to whom the narrative has been imparted   Every cultivated person knows how he has had to strive against a certain rudeness both in himself and others, how much his culture costs him, how apt he is, after all, in certain cases, to recollect himself alone, forgetting what he owes to others   How often has a worthy person to reproach himself for having failed to act with proper delicacy!   And when a fair nature too delicately, too conscientiously cultivates, nay, if you will, overcultivates itself, there seems to be no toleration, no indulgence for it in the world   Yet such persons are, without us, what the ideal of perfection is within us   models not for being imitated, but for being aimed at   We laugh at the cleanliness of the Dutch   but would our friend Theresa be what she is, if some such notion were not always present to her in her housekeeping?"

"I see before me then," cried Wilhelm, "in Theresa's friend, the same Natalia whom her amiable relative was so attached to, the Natalia, who from her youth was so affectionate, so sympathising and helpful!   It was only out of such a line that such a being could proceed   What a prospect opens before me, while I at once survey your ancestors, and all the circle you belong to!"

"Yes," replied Natalia, "in a certain sense, the story of my aunt would give you the faithfulest picture of us Her love to me, indeed, has made her praise the little girl too much in speaking of a child, we never speak of what is present, but of what we hope for "

Wilhelm, in the mean time, was rapidly reflecting that Lothario's parentage and early youth were now likewise known to him The fair Countess, too, appeared before him in her childhood, with the aunt's pearls about her neck he himself had been near those pearls, when her soft lovely lips bent down to meet his own These beautiful remembrances he sought to drive away by other thoughts He ran through the characters to whom that manuscript had introduced him " I am here then," cried he, " in your worthy uncle's house ! It is no house, it is a temple, and you are the priestess, nay, the Genius of it I shall recollect for life my impression yester-night, when I entered, and the old figures of my earliest days were again before me I thought of the compassionate marble statues in Mignon's song but these figures had not to lament about me , they looked upon me with a lofty earnestness, they brought my first years into immediate contact with the present moment That ancient treasure of our family, the joy of my grandfather, I find here placed among so many other noble works of art , and myself, whom nature made the darling of the good old man, my unworthy self I find here also, Heavens ! in what society, in what connexions ! "

The girls had by degrees gone out to mind their little occupations Natalia, left alone with Wilhelm, asked some farther explanation of his last remark The discovery, that a number of her finest paintings and statues had at one ti e been the property of Wilhelm's grandfather, did not fail to give a cheerful stimulus to their discourse As by that manuscript he had got acquainted with Natalia's house, so now he found himself too, as it were, in his inheritance At length he asked for Mignon His friend desired him to have patience till the Doctor, who had been called out into the neighbourhood, returned   It is easy to suppose that the Doctor was the same little active man, whom we already know, and who was spoken of in the Confessions of a Fair Saint

"Since I am now," said Wilhelm, "in the middle of your family circle, I presume the Abbé, whom that paper mentions, is the strange inexplicable person, whom, after the most singular series of events, I met with in your brother's house? Perhaps you can give some more accurate conception of him? '

"Of the Abbé there might much be said," replied Natalia "what I know best about him is the influence which he excited on our education   He was, for a time at least, convinced that education ought in every case to be adapted to the inclinations   his present views of it I know not   He maintained that with man the first and last consideration was activity, and that we could not act on anything, without the proper gifts for it, without an instinct impelling us to it 'You admit,' he used to say, 'that poets must be born such, you admit this with regard to all professors of the fine arts, because you must admit it, because those workings of human nature cannot very plausibly be aped   But if we consider well, we shall find that every capability, however slight, is born with us   that there is no vague general capability in men   It is our ambiguous dissipating education that makes men uncertain   it awakens wishes, when it should be animating tendencies, instead of forwarding our real capacities, it turns our efforts towards objects which are frequently discordant with the mind that aims at them   I augur better of a child, a youth who is wandering astray on a path of his own, than of many who are walking aright upon paths which are not theirs   If the former, either by themselves, or by the guidance of others, ever find the right path, that is to say, the path which suits their nature, they will never leave it, while the latter are in danger every moment of shaking off a foreign yoke, and abandoning themselves to unrestricted licence '"

"It is strange," said Wilhelm, "that this same extra-ordinary man should likewise have taken charge of me, should, as it seems, have, in his own fashion, if not led, at least confirmed me in my errors, for a time   How he will answer to the charge of having joined with others, as it were, to make game of me, I wait patiently to see "

"Of this whim, if it is one," said Natalia, "I have little reason to complain of all the family I answered best with it   Indeed I see not how Lothario could have got a finer breeding but for my sister, the Countess, some other treat-ment might have suited better, perhaps they should have studied to infuse more earnestness and strength into her nature   As to brother Friedrich, what is to become of him cannot be conjectured he will fall a sacrifice, I fear, to this experiment in pedagogy "

"You have another brother, then ? " cried Wilhelm

"Yes," replied Natalia , "and a light merry youth he is , and as they have not hindered him from roaming up and down the world, I know not what the wild dissipated boy will turn to   It is a great while since I saw him   The only thing which calms my fears is, that the Abbé, and the whole society about my brother, are receiving constant notice where he is and what he does "

Wilhelm was about to ask Natalia her opinion more pre-cisely on the Abbé's paradoxes, as well as to solicit informa-tion about that mysterious society , but the Physician entering changed their conversation   After the first compliments of welcome, he began to speak of Mignon

Natalia then took Felix by the hand, saying she would lead the child to Mignon, and prepare her for the entrance of her friend

The Doctor, now alone with Wilhelm, thus proceeded "I have wondrous things to tell you , such as you are not anti-cipating   Natalia has retired, that we might speak with greater liberty of certain matters, which, although I first learned them by her means, her presence would prevent us

fiom discussing freely   The stiange temper of the child
seems to consist almost exclusively of deep longing, the
desire of revisiting hei native land, and the desire for you,
my fiiend, aie, I might almost say, the only earthly things
about her   Both these feelings do but grasp towards an
immeasurable distance, both objects lie before her unattainable   The neighbourhood of Milan seems to be hei home
in very eaily childhood she was kidnapped fiom her paients
by a company of rope-dancers   A more distinct account we
cannot get from her, partly because she was then too young
to recollect the names of men and places, but especially
because she has made an oath to tell no living moital her
abode and paientage   Foi the strolling paity, who came up
with her when she had lost her way, and to whom she so
accurately desciibed hei dwelling, with such piercing entreaties
to conduct her home, but carried hei along with them the
faster, and at night in their quarters, when they thought
the child was sleeping, joked about their piecious captuie,
declaring she would nevei find the way home again   On this,
a hoiiid desperaticn fell upon the miseiable cieature, but at
last the Holy Virgin iose before her eyes, and promised that
she would assist hei   The child then swoie within herself a
sacred oath, that she would henceforth trust no human
creatuie, would disclose hei histoiy to no one, but live and
die in hope of immediate aid fiom Heaven   Even this,
which I am telling you, Natalia did not learn expiessly from
her, but gatheied it from detached expressions, songs and
childlike inadveitencies, betiaying what they meant to hide "

Wilhelm called to memory many a song and woid of this
dear child, which he could now explain   He earnestly
requested the Physician to keep fiom him none of the confessions or mysterious poetry of this peculiar being

"Prepare youiself," said the Physician, "foi a strange
confession, foi a story with which you, without remembering
it, have much to do, and which, as I greatly fear, has been
decisive for the death and life of this good creature "

"Let me hear," said Wilhelm, "my impatience is un-bounded"

"Do you recollect a secret nightly visit from a female," said the Doctor, "after your appearance in the character of Hamlet?"

"Yes, I recollect it well," cried Wilhelm, blushing, "but I did not look to be reminded of it at the present moment"

"Do you know who it was?"

"I do not! You frighten me! In the name of Heaven, not Mignon surely? Who was it? Tell me, pray"

"I know it not myself"

"Not Mignon, then?"

"No, certainly not Mignon but Mignon was intending at the time to glide in to you. and saw, with horror, from a corner where she lay concealed, a rival get before her"

"A rival!" cried our friend "Speak on, you more and more confound me"

"Be thankful," said the Doctor, "that you can arrive at the result so soon through means of me Natalia and I, with but a distant interest in the matter, had distress enough to undergo, before we could thus far discover the perplexed condition of the poor dear creature, whom we wished to help By some wanton speeches of Philina and the other girls, by a certain song which she had heard Philina sing, the child's attention had been roused, she longed to pass a night beside the man she loved, without conceiving anything to be implied in this beyond a happy and confiding rest A love for you, y friend, was already keen and powerful in her little heart, in your arms, the child had found repose from many a sorrow, she now desired this happiness in all its fulness At one time she proposed to ask you for it in a friendly manner, but a secret horror always held her back At last, that merry night and the excitement of abundant wine inspired her with the courage to attempt the adventure, and glide in to you on that occasion Accordingly she ran before, to hide herself in your apartment, which was standing open, but just when she had reached the top of the stairs, having heard a rustling, she concealed herself, and saw a female in a white dress slip into your chamber. You yourself arrived soon after, and she heard you push the large bolt

"Mignon's agony was now unutterable all the violent feelings of a passionate jealousy mingled themselves with the unacknowledged longing of obscure desire, and seized her half-developed nature with tremendous force Her heart, which hitherto had beaten violently with eagerness and expectation, now at once began to falter and stop, it pressed her bosom like a heap of lead, she could not draw her breath, she knew not what to do, she heard the sound of the old man's harp, hastened to the garret where he was, and passed the night at his feet in horrible convulsions"

The Physician paused a moment, then, as Wilhelm still kept silence, he proceeded "Natalia told me, nothing in her life had so alarmed and touched her as the state of Mignon while relating this indeed, our noble friend accused herself of cruelty in having, by her questions and management, drawn this confession from her, and renewed by recollection the violent sorrows of the poor little girl

"'The dear creature,' said Natalia, 'had scarcely come so far with her recital, or rather with her answers to my questions, when she sank all at once before me on the ground, and with her hand on her bosom piteously moaned that the pain of that excruciating night was come back She twisted herself like a worm upon the floor, and I had to summon all my composure, that I might remember and apply such means of remedy for mind and body as were known to me'"

"It is a painful predicament you put me in," cried Wilhelm, "by impressing me so vividly with the feeling of my manifold injustice towards this unhappy and beloved being, at the very moment when I am again to meet her If she is to see me, why do you deprive me of the courage to appear with freedom? And shall I confess it to you? Since her mind is so affected, I perceive not how my presence can be advantageous to her If you, as a Physician, are persuaded that this double longing has so undermined her being as to threaten death, why should I renew her sorrows by my presence, and perhaps accelerate her end ?"

"My friend," replied the Doctor, "where we cannot cure, it is our duty to alleviate, and how much the presence of a loved object tends to take from the imagination its destructive power, how it changes an impetuous longing to a peaceful looking, I could prove by the most convincing instances Everything in measure and with purpose ! For, in other cases, this same presence may rekindle an affection nigh extinguished But do you go and see the child, behave to her with kindness, and let us wait the consequence "

Natalia, at this moment coming back, bade Wilhelm follow her to Mignon "She appears to feel quite happy with the boy," observed Natalia, "and I hope she will receive our friend with mildness" Wilhelm followed, not without reluctance he was deeply moved by what he had been hearing; he feared a stormy scene of passion It was altogether the reverse that happened on his entrance

Mignon, dressed in long white women's-clothes, with her brown copious hair partly knotted, partly clustering out in locks, was sitting with the boy Felix on her lap, and pressing him against her heart She looked like a departed spirit, he like life itself it seemed as if Heaven and Earth were clasping one another She held out her hand to Wilhelm with a smile, and said "I thank thee for bringing back the child to me they had taken him away, I know not how, and since then I could not live So long as my heart needs anything on earth, thy Felix shall fill up the void "

The quietness, which Mignon had displayed on meeting with her friend, produced no little satisfaction in the party The Doctor signified that Wilhelm should go frequently and see her, that in body as in mind she should be kept as equable as possible He himself departed, promising to return soon

Wilhelm could now observe Natalia in her own circle   one would have desired nothing better than to live beside her Her presence had the purest influence on the girls, and young ladies of various ages, who resided with her in the house, or came to pay her visits from the neighbourhood

"The progress of your life," said Wilhelm once to her, "must always have been very even, your aunt's delineation of you in your childhood seems, if I mistake not, still to fit   It is easy to see, that you never were entangled in your path. You have never been compelled to retrograde "

"This I owe to my uncle and the Abbé," said Natalia, "who so well discriminated my prevailing turn of mind From my youth upwards, I can recollect no livelier feeling than that I was constantly observing people's wants, and had an irresistible desire to make them up   The child that had not learned to stand on its feet, the old man that could no longer stand on his, the longing of a rich family for children, the inability of a poor one to maintain their children, each silent wish for some particular species of employment, the impulse towards any talent, the natural gifts for many little necessary arts of life, were sure to strike me   my eye seemed formed by nature for detecting them   I saw such things, where no one had directed my attention, I seemed born for seeing them alone   The charms of inanimate nature, to which so many persons are exceedingly susceptible, had no effect upon me, the charms of art, if possible, had less   My most delightful occupation was and is, when a deficiency, a want appeared before me anywhere, to set about devising a supply, a remedy, a help for it

"If I saw a poor creature in rags, the superfluous clothes I had noticed hanging in the wardrobes of my friends immediately occurred to me, if I saw children wasting for want of care, I was sure to recollect some lady I had found oppressed with tedium amid riches and conveniences   if I saw too many persons crammed into a narrow space, I thought they should be lodged in the spacious chambers of palaces and

vacant houses This mode of viewing things was altogether
natural, without the least reflection , so that in my childhood
I often made the strangest work of it, and more than once
embarrassed people by my singular proposals Another of my
peculiarities was this, I did not learn till late, and after many
efforts, to consider money as a means of satisfying wants my
benefits were all distributed in kind, and my simplicity, I know,
was frequently the cause of laughter. None but the Abbé
seemed to understand me , he met me everywhere , he made
me acquainted with myself, with these wishes, these tendencies,
and taught me how to satisfy them suitably "

"Do you then," said Wilhelm, " in the education of your
little female world employ the method of these extraordinary
men ? Do you too leave every mind to form itself ? Do you
too leave your girls to search and wander, to pursue delusions,
happily to reach the goal, or miserably lose themselves in
error ? "

"No ! " replied Natalia " such treatment as that would
altogether contradict my notions To my mind, he who does
not help us at the needful moment, never helps , he who does
not counsel at the needful moment, never counsels I also
reckon it essential that we lay down and continually impress
on children certain laws, to operate as a kind of hold in life.
Nay, I could almost venture to assert that it is better to
be wrong by rule, than to be wrong with nothing but the
fitful caprices of our disposition to impel us hither and thither
and in my way of viewing men, there always seems to be a
void in their nature, which cannot be filled up, except by some
decisive and distinctly settled law "

"Your manner of proceeding, then," said Wilhelm, " is
entirely different from the manner of our friends ? "

"Yes," replied Natalia " and you may see the unexampled
tolerance of these men, from the fact, that they nowise disturb
me in my practice , but leave me on my own path, simply
because it is my own, and even assist me in everything that I
require of them "

A more minute description of Natalia's plans in managing her children we reserve for some other opportunity

Mignon often asked to be of their society, and this they granted her with greater readiness, as she appeared to be again accustoming herself to Wilhelm, to be opening her heart to him, and in general to have become more cheerful and contented with existence   In walking, being easily fatigued, she liked to hang upon his arm   " Mignon," she would say, " now climbs and bounds no more, yet she still longs to mount the summit of the hills, to skip from house to house, from tree to tree   How enviable are the birds, and then so prettily and socially they build their nests too ! "

Ere long it became habitual for her to invite her friend, more than once every day, into the garden   When Wilhelm was engaged or absent, Felix had to take his place, and if poor Mignon seemed at times quite loosened from the earth, there were other moments when she would again hold fast to father and son, and seem to dread a separation from them more than anything beside

Natalia wore a thoughtful look   " We meant," said she, " to open her tender little heart, by sending for you hither   I know not whether we did prudently "   She stopped, and seemed expecting Wilhelm to say something   To him also it occurred that by his marriage with Theresa, Mignon, in the present circumstances, would be fearfully offended   but in his uncertainty, he did not venture mentioning his project, he had no suspicion that Natalia knew of it

As little could he talk with freedom, when his noble friend began to speak about her sister, to praise her good qualities, and to lament her hapless situation   He felt exceedingly embarrassed when Natalia told him he would shortly see the Countess here   " Her husband," said she, " has now no object but replacing Zinzendorf in the Community, and by insight and activity supporting and extending that establishment   He is coming with his wife, to take a sort of leave, he then purposes visiting the various spots where the Community have settled They appear to treat him as he wishes and I should not wonder if, in order to be altogether like his predecessor, he ventured, with my sister, on a voyage to America, for being already well-nigh convinced that a little more would make a saint of him, the wish to superadd the dignity of martyrdom has probably enough often flitted through his mind "

CHAPTER IV

THEY had often spoken of Theresa, often mentioned her in passing, and Wilhelm almost every time was minded to confess that he had offered her his heart and hand A certain feeling, which he was not able to explain, restrained him; he paused and wavered, till at length Natalia, with the heavenly modest cheerful smile she often wore, said to him "It seems, then, I at last must break silence, and force myself into your confidence! Why, my friend, do you keep secret from me an affair of such importance to yourself, and so closely touching my concerns? You have made my friend the offer of your hand I do not mix uncalled in the transaction here are my credentials, here is the letter which she writes to you, which she sends you through my hands "

"A letter from Theresa!" cried he

"Yes, mein herr! Your destiny is settled, you are happy. Let me congratulate my friend and you on your good fortune "

Wilhelm spoke not, but gazed out before him Natalia looked at him, she saw that he was pale "Your joy is strong," continued she, "it takes the form of terror, it deprives you of the power to speak My participation is not the less cordial that I show it you in words I hope you will be grateful for I may say, my influence on the decision of your bride has not been small she asked me for advice, and as it happened, by a singular coincidence, that you were heie just then, I was enabled to destroy the few sciuples she still enteitained   Our messages went swiftly to and fro heie is her determination, here is the conclusion of the tieaty! And now you shall read hei other letters, you shall have a free clear look into the fair heait of your Theresa "

Wilhelm opened the letter, which she handed him unsealed. It contained these friendly woids

"I am youis, as I am and as you know me   I call you mine, as you are and as I know you   What in ourselves, what in oui connexion wedlock changes, we shall study to adjust, by ieason, cheerfulness and mutual goodwill   As it is no passion, but trust and inclination for each other that is leading us together, we iun less iisk than thousands of others   You will forgive me, will you not, if I still think often and kindly of my former fiiend, in return, I will piess your Felix to my heart, as if I weie his mothei   If you choose to shaie my little mansion stiaightway, we aie loid and master there, and in the meanwhile the puichase of your land might be concluded   I could wish that no new aniangements were made in it without me   I could wish at once to prove that I deserve the confidence which you repose in me   Adieu, dear, dear Fiiend!   Beloved Bridegroom, honouied Husband!   Theiesa clasps you to her bicast with hope and joy   My fiiend will tell you more, will tell you all "

Wilhelm, to whose mind this sheet recalled the image of Theresa with the liveliest distinctness, had now recovered his composure   While reading, thoughts had rapidly alteinated within his soul   With terror, he discoveied in his heart the most vivid traces of an inclination to Natalia   he blamed him-self, declaiing eveiy thought of that desciiption to be madness, he repiesented to himself Theiesa in her whole perfection, he again perused the letter, he grew cheeiful, or rather he so far regained his self-possession that he could appear cheeiful Natalia handed him the letters which had passed between Theresa and herself   out of Theresa's we propose extracting one or two passages

After delineating her bridegroom in her own peculiar way, Theresa thus proceeded

"Such is the notion I have formed of the man who now offers me his hand   What he thinks of himself thou shalt see by and by, in the papers he has sent me, where he altogether candidly draws his own portrait ; I feel persuaded that I shall be happy with him "

"As to rank, thou knowest my ideas on this point long ago Some people look on disagreement of external circumstances as a fearful thing, and cannot remedy it   I wish not to persuade any one, I wish to act according to my own persuasion.   I mean not to set others an example, nor do I act without example   It is interior disagreements only that frighten me a frame that does not fit what it is meant to hold , much pomp and little real enjoyment , wealth and avarice, nobility and rudeness, youth and pedantry, poverty and ceremonies,— these are the things which would annihilate me, however it may please the world to stamp and rate them "

"If I hope that we shall suit each other, the hope is chiefly founded upon this, that he resembles thee, my dear Natalia, thee, whom I so highly prize and reverence   Yes, he has thy noble searching and striving for the Better, whereby we of ourselves produce the Good which we suppose we find   How often have I blamed thee, not in silence, for treating this or that person, for acting in this or that case, otherwise than I should have done ! and yet in general the issue showed that thou wert right   'When we take people,' thou wouldst say, ' merely as they are, we make them worse , when we treat them as if they were what they should be, we improve them as far as they can be improved '   To see or to act thus, I know full well is not for   e   Skill, order, discipline, direction, that is my affair   I always recollect what Jarno said 'Theresa trains her pupils, Natalia forms the   Nay, once he went so far as to assert that of the three fair qualities, faith, love and

hope, I was entirely destitute 'Instead of faith,' said he,
'she has penetration, instead of love she has steadfastness,
instead of hope she has trust' Indeed I will confess that till
I knew thee, I knew nothing higher in the world than clearness and prudence it was thy presence only that persuaded,
animated, conquered me, to thy fair lofty soul I willingly
give place My friend too I honour on the same principle,
the description of his life is a perpetual seeking without finding, not empty seeking, but wondrous generous seeking, he
fancies others may give him what can proceed from himself
alone So, love, the clearness of my vision has not injured me,
on this occasion, more than others I know my husband
better than he knows himself, and I value him the more I
see him, yet I see not over him, all my skill will not enable
me to judge of what he can accomplish When I think of
him, his image always blends itself with thine I know not
how I have deserved to belong to two such persons But I will
deserve it, by endeavouring to do my duty, by fulfilling what
is looked for from me "

"If I recollect Lothario? Vividly and daily. In the company which in thought surrounds me, I cannot want him for a
moment O, what a pity for this noble character, related by
an error of his youth to me, that nature has related him to
thee! A being such as thou, in truth, were worthier of him
than I To thee I could, I would surrender him Let us be
to him all we can, till he find a proper wife, and then too let
us be, let us abide together "

"But what shall we say to our friends?" began Natalia —
"Your brother does not know of it?"—"Not a hint, your
people know as little we women have, on this occasion,
managed the affair ourselves Lydia had put some whims into
Theresa's head concerning Jarno and the Abbé There are
certain plans and secret combinations, with the general scheme
of which I am acquainted, and into which I never thought of

penetrating farther With regard to these, Theresa has, through Lydia, taken up some shadow of suspicion so in this decisive step she would not suffer any one but me to influence her With my brother it had been already settled, that they should merely announce their marriages to one another, not giving or asking counsel on the subject "

Natalia wrote a letter to her brother , she invited Wilhelm to subjoin a word or two, Theresa having so desired it They were just about to seal, when Jarno unexpectedly sent up his name His reception was of course as kind as possible he wore a sportful merry air , he could not long forbear to tell his errand " I am come," said he, " to give you very curious and very pleasing tidings they concern Theresa You have often blamed us, fair Natalia, for troubling our heads about so many things , but now you see how good it is to have one's spies in every place Guess, and let us see your skill for once ! "

The self-complacency with which he spoke these words, the roguish mien with which he looked at Wilhelm and Natalia, persuaded both of them that he had found their secret Natalia answered smiling " We are far more skilful than you think before we even heard your riddle, we had put the answer to it down in black and white "

With these words, she handed him the letter to Lotharo , satisfied at having met, in this way, the little triumph and surprise he had meant for them Jarno took the sheet with some astonishment ran it quickly over , started, let it drop from his hands, and stared at both his friends with an expression of amazement, nay, of fright, which on his countenance was rare He spoke no word

Wilhelm and Natalia were not a little struck , Jarno stept up and down the room " What shall I say ? " cried he " Or shall I say it at all ? But it must come out, the perplexity is not to be avoided So secret for secret, surprise against surprise ! Theresa is not the daughter of her reputed mother † The hinderance is removed I came to ask you to prepare her for a marriage with Lotharo "

Jarno saw the shock which he had given his friends, they cast their eyes upon the ground "The present case," said he, "is one of those which are worse to bear in company What each has to consider in it, he considers best in solitude I at least require an hour of leave" He hastened to the garden, Wilhelm followed him mechanically, yet without approaching near

At the end of an hour, they were again assembled Wilhelm opened the conversation "Formerly," said he, "while I was living without plan or object, in a state of carelessness, or I may say of levity, friendship, love, affection, trust came towards me with open arms, they pressed themselves upon me, but now when I am serious, destiny appears to take another course with me This resolution, of soliciting Theresa's hand, is probably the first that has proceeded altogether from myself I laid my plan considerately, my reason fully joined in it, by the consent of that noble maiden all my hopes were crowned But now the strangest fate puts back my outstretched hand, Theresa reaches hers to me, but from afar, as in a dream, I cannot grasp it, and the lovely image leaves me forever So fare thee well, thou lovely image ! and all ye images of richest happiness that gathered round it !'

He was silent for a moment, looking out before him Jarno was about to speak "Let me have another word," cried Wilhelm, "for the lot is drawing which is to decide the destiny of all my life At this moment I am aided and confirmed by the impression which Lothario's presence made upon me at the first glance, and which has ever since continued with me That man well merits every sort of friendship and affection, and without sacrifices friendship cannot be imagined For his sake, it was easy for me to delude a hapless girl, for his sake it shall be possible for me to give away the worthiest bride Return, relate the strange occurrence to him, and tell him what I am prepared for"

"In emergencies like this," said Jarno, "I hold that everything is done, if one do nothing rashly Let us take no step

till Lothario has agreed to it   I will go to him   wait
patiently for my return, or for his letter "

He rode away, and left his friends in great disquiet.   They
had time to reconsider these events, to think of them maturely.
It now first occurred to them, that they had taken Jarno's
statement simply by itself, and without inquiring into any
of the circumstances   Wilhelm was not altogether free from
doubts   but next day, their astonishment, nay, their bewilder-
ment, arose still higher, when a messenger arriving from
Theresa, brought the following letter to Natalia

" Strange as it may seem, after all the letters I have sent,
I am obliged to send another, begging that thou wouldst
despatch my bridegroom to me instantly   He shall be my
husband, what plans soever they may lay to rob me of him
Give him the enclosed letter, only not before witnesses,
whoever they may be ! "

The enclosed letter was as follows " What opinion will you
form of your Theresa, when you see her all at once insisting
passionately on a union which calm reason alone appeared to
have appointed ?   Let nothing hinder you from setting out,
the moment you have read this letter   Come, my dear, dear
friend, now three times dearer, since they are attempting to
deprive me of you "

" What is to be done ? " cried Wilhelm, after he had read
the letter

" In no case that I remember," said Natalia, after some
reflection, " have my heart and judgment been so dumb as in
the present one   what to do or to advise I know not "

" Can it be," cried Wilhelm vehemently, " that Lothario
does not know of it, or if he does, that he is but like us, the
sport of hidden plans ?   Has Jarno, when he saw our letter,
devised that fable on the spot ?   Would he have told us something different, if we had not been so precipitate ?   What can
they mean ?   What intentions can they have ?   What plan
can Theresa mean ?   Yes, it must be owned, Lothario is begirt
with secret influences and combinations. I myself have found

that they are active, that they take a certain charge of the
proceedings, of the destiny of several people, and contrive to
guide them   The ulterior objects of these mysteries I know
not, but their nearest purpose, that of snatching my Theresa
from me, I perceive but too distinctly   On the one hand, this
prospect of Lothario's happiness which they exhibit to me may
be but a hollow show, on the other hand, I see my dear, my
honoured bride inviting me to her affection   What shall I do?
What shall I forbear?"

"A little patience!" said Natalia, "a little time for
thought!   In these singular perplexities, I know but this, that
what can never be recalled should not be done in haste   To a
fable, to an artful plan we have steadfastness and prudence to
oppose   whether Jarno has been speaking true or false must
soon appear   If my brother has actually hopes of a connexion
with Theresa, it were hard to cut him off forever from that
prospect, at the moment when it seems so kindly inviting him
Let us wait at least till we discover whether he himself knows
anything of it, whether he believes and hopes"

These prudent counsels were confirmed by a letter from
Lothario   "I do not send Jarno," he wrote   "a line from
my hand is more to thee than the minutest narrative in the
mouth of a messenger.   I am certain, Theresa is not the
daughter of her reputed mother   and I cannot renounce hope
of being hers, till she too is persuaded, and can then decide
between my friend and me with calm consideration   Let him
not leave thee, I entreat it!   The happiness, the life of a
brother is at stake   I promise thee, this uncertainty shall not
be long"

"You see how the matter stands," said she to Wilhelm with
a friendly air, "give me your word of honour that you will
not leave the house!"

"I give it!" cried he, stretching out his hand, "I will not
leave this house against your will   I thank Heaven, and
my better Genius, that on this occasion I am led, and led by
you"

Natalia wrote Theresa an account of everything, declaring that she would not let her friend away   She sent Lothario's letter also

Theresa answered "I wonder not a little that Lothario is himself convinced   to his sister he would not feign to this extent   I am vexed, greatly vexed   It is better that I say no more   But I will come to thee, so soon as I have got poor Lydia settled   they are treating her cruelly   I fear we are all betrayed, and shall be so betrayed that we shall never reach the truth   If my friend were of my opinion, he would give thee the slip after all, and throw himself into the arms of his Theresa, whom none shall take away from him   But I, as I dread, shall lose him, and not regain Lothario   From the latter they are taking Lydia, by showing him afar off the prospect of obtaining me   I will say no more : the entanglement will grow still deeper   Whether, in the mean time, these beautiful relations to each other may not be so pushed aside, so undermined and broken down, that when the darkness passes off, the mischief shall no longer admit of remedy, time will show   If my friend do not tear himself away, in a few days I myself will come and seek him out beside thee, and hold him fast   Thou marvelest how this passion can have gained the mastery of thy Theresa   It is no passion, but conviction, it is a belief that since Lothario can never be mine, this new friend will make me happy   Tell him so in the name of the little boy that sat with him underneath the oak, and thanked him for his sympathy   Tell it him in the name of Theresa, who met his offers with a hearty openness   My first dream of living with Lothario has wandered far away from my soul, the drea of living with my other friend is yet wholly present to me. Do they hold me so light, as to think that it were easy to exchange the former with the latter ? "

"I depend on you," said Natalia to Wilhelm, handing hi the letter "you will not leave me   Consider that the comfort of my life is in your hands   My being is so intimately bound and interwoven with   y brother's, that he feels no sorrow which I do not feel, no joy which does not likewise gladden me Nay, I may truly say, through him alone I have experienced that the heart can be affected and exalted , that in the world there may be joy, love and an emotion which contents the soul beyond its utmost want "

She stopped , Wilhelm took her hand, and cried "O continue ! This is the time for a true mutual disclosure of our thoughts it never was more necessary for us to be well acquainted with each other "

" Yes, my friend ! " said she, smiling, with her quiet, soft, indescribable dignity , " perhaps it is not out of season, if I tell you that the whole of what so many books, of what the world holds up to us and names love, has always seemed to me a fable "

" You have never loved ? " cried Wilhelm.

" Never, or always ! " said Natalia

CHAPTER V

DURING this conversation, they kept walking up and down the garden, and Natalia gathered various flowers of singular forms, entirely unknown to Wilhelm, who began to ask their names, and occupy himself about them

" You know not," said Natalia, " for whom I have been plucking these ? I intend them for my uncle, whom we are to visit The sun is shining even now so bright on the Hall of the Past, I must lead you in, this moment , and I never go to it, without a few of the flowers which my uncle liked particularly, in my hand He was a peculiar man, susceptible of very strange impressions For certain plants and animals, for certain neighbourhoods and persons, nay, for certain sorts of minerals, he had an especial love, which he was rarely able to explain ' Had I not,' he would often say, ' from youth, withstood myself, and striven to form my judgment upon wide and

general principles, I had been the narrowest and most intolerable person living   For nothing can be more intolerable than
circumscribed peculiarity, in one from whom a pure and suitable
activity might be required'   And yet he was obliged to confess, that life and breath would almost leave him, if he did not
now and then indulge himself, not from time to time allow
hi self a brief and passionate enjoyment of what he could
not always praise and justify   'It is not my fault,' said he,
'if I have not brought my inclinations and my reason into
perfect harmony'   On such occasions he would joke with me,
and say   'Natalia may be looked upon as happy while she
lives   her nature asks nothing which the world does not wish
and use'"

So speaking, they arrived again at the house   Natalia led
him through a spacious passage, to a door, before which lay
two granite Sphinxes   The door itself was in the Egyptian
fashion, somewhat narrower above than below, and its brazen
leaves prepared one for a serious or even a gloomy feeling
Wilhelm was in consequence agreeably surprised, when his
expectation issued in a sentiment of pure cheerful serenity, as
he entered a hall, where art and life took away all recollection of death and the grave   In the walls all round, a series
of proportionable arches had been hollowed out, and large
sarcophaguses stood in them   among the pillars in the intervals
between them, smaller openings might be seen, adorned with
urns and similar vessels   The remaining spaces of the walls
and vaulted roof were regularly divided, and between bright
and variegated borders, within garlands and other ornaments,
a multitude of cheerful and significant figures had been painted,
upon grounds of different sizes   The body of the edifice was
covered with that fine yellow marble, which passes into
reddish, clear blue stripes of a chemical substance happily
imitating lapis-lazuli, while they satisfied the eye with contrast,
gave unity and combination to the whole   All this pomp and
decoration showed itself in the chastest architectural forms
and thus every one who entered felt as if exalted above him-

self, while the cooperating products of art, for the first time, taught him what man is and what he may become

Opposite the door, on a stately sarcophagus, lay a marble figure of a noble-looking man, reclined upon a pillow He held a roll before him, and seemed to look at it with still attention It was placed so that you could read with ease the words which stood there *Think of living*

Natalia took away a withered bunch of flowers, and laid the fresh one down before the figure of her uncle For it was her uncle whom the marble represented Wilhelm thought he recognised the features of the venerable gentleman, whom he had seen, when lying wounded in the green of the forest. "Here he and I passed many an hour," said Natalia, "while the hall was getting ready In his latter years, he had gathered several skilful artists round him, and his chief delight was to invent or superintend the drawings and cartoons for these pictures "

Wilhelm could not satisfy himself with looking at the objects which surrounded him "What a life," exclaimed he, "in this Hall of the Past ! One might with equal justice name it Hall of the Present and the Future Such all were, such all will be There is nothing transitory but the individual who looks at and enjoys it Here, this figure of the mother . pressing her infant to her bosom will survive many generations of happy mothers Centuries hence, perhaps some father will take pleasure in contemplating this bearded man, who has laid aside his seriousness, and is playing with his son Thus shamefaced will the bride sit for ages, and amid her silent wishes, need that she be comforted, that she be spoken to, thus impatient will the bridegroom listen on the threshold whether he may enter "

The figures Wilhelm was surveying with such rapture were of almost boundless number and variety From the first jocund impulse of the child, merely to employ its every limb in sport, up to the peaceful sequestered earnestness of the sage, you might, in fair and living order, see delineated how man possesses no capacity or tendency without employing and enjoying it   From the first soft conscious feeling, when the maiden lingers in pulling up her pitcher, and looks with satisfaction at her image in the clear fountain, to those high solemnities when kings and nations invoke the Gods at the altar to witness their alliances, all was depicted, all was forcible and full of meaning

It was a world, it was a heaven, that in this abode surrounded the spectator, and beside the thoughts which those polished forms suggested, beside the feelings they awoke, there still seemed something farther to be present, something by which the whole man felt himself laid hold of   Wilhelm too observed this, though unable to account for it   "What is this," exclaimed he, " which, independently of all signification, without any sympathy that human incidents and fortunes may inspire us with, acts on me so strongly and so gracefully ?   It speaks to me from the whole, it speaks from every part, though I have not fully understood the former, though I do not pecially apply the latter to myself !   What enchantment breathes from these surfaces, these lines, these heights and breadths, these masses and colours !   What is it that makes these figures so delightful, even when slightly viewed, and merely in the light of decorations ?   Yes, I feel it   one might tarry here, might rest, might view the whole, and be happy, and yet feel and think something altogether different from aught that stood before his eyes "

And certainly if we were able to describe how happily the whole was subdivided, how everything determined by its place, by combination or by contrast, by uniformity or by variety, appeared exactly as it should have done, producing an effect as perfect as distinct, we should transport the reader to a scene, from which he would not be in haste to stir

Four large marble candelabra rose in the corners of the hall, four smaller ones were in the midst of it, around a very beautifully worked sarcophagus, which, judging from its size, might once have held a young person of middle stature.

Natalia paused beside this monument ; she laid her hand

upon it as she said   "My worthy uncle had a great attachment to this fine antique   'It is not,' he would often say, 'the
first blossoms alone that drop, such you can keep above in
these little spaces, but fruits also, which, hanging on their
twigs, long give us the fairest hope, whilst a secret worm is
preparing their too early ripeness and their quick decay'   I
fear," continued she, "his words have been prophetic of that
dear little girl, who seems withdrawing gradually from our
cares, and bending to this peaceful dwelling"

As they were about to go, Natalia stopped and said
"There is something still which merits your attention
Observe these half-round openings aloft on both sides   Here
the choir can stand concealed while singing, these iron ornaments below the cornice serve for fastening-on the tapestry,
which, by order of my uncle, must be hung round at every
burial   Music, particularly song, was a pleasure he could not
live without   and it was one of his peculiarities that he wished
the singer not to be in view   'In this respect,' he would say
'they spoil us at the theatre, the music there is, as it were,
subservient to the eye, it accompanies movements, not
emotions   In oratorios and concerts, the form of the musician
constantly disturbs us   true music is intended for the ear
alone, a fine voice is the most universal thing that can be
figured, and while the narrow individual that uses it presents
himself before the eye, he cannot fail to trouble the effect
of that pure universality   The person whom I am to speak
with, I must see, because it is a solitary man, whose form and
character gives worth or worthlessness to what he says   but,
on the other hand, whoever sings to me must be invisible, his
form must not confuse me, or corrupt my judgment   Here, it
is but one human organ speaking to another, it is not spirit
speaking to spirit, not a thousandfold world to the eye, not a
heaven to the man'   On the same principles, in respect of
instrumental music, he required that the orchestra should as
much as possible be hid, because by the mechanical exertions,
by the mean and awkward gestures of the performers, our feel-

ing are so much dispersed and perplexed Accordingly he always used to shut his eyes while hearing music, thereby to concentrate his whole being on the single pure enjoyment of the ear."

They were about to leave the Hall, when they heard the children running hastily along the passage, and Felix crying "No, I! No, I!"

Mignon rushed in at the open door she was foremost, but out of breath, and could not speak a word Felix, still at some distance, shouted out · " Mamma Theresa is come!" The children had run a race, as it seemed, to bring the news Mignon was lying in Natalia's arms, her heart was beating fiercely

"Naughty child," said Natalia, " art not thou forbidden violent motions? See how thy heart is beating!"

"Let it break?" said Mignon with a deep sigh. "it has beat too long"

They had scarcely composed themselves from this surprise, this sort of consternation, when Theresa entered She flew to Natalia, clasped her and Mignon in her arms Then turning round to Wilhelm, she looked at him with her clear eyes, and said "Well, my friend, how is it with you? You have not let them cheat you?" He made a step towards her, she sprang to him, and hung upon his neck " O my Theresa!" cried he

"My friend, my love, my husband! Yes, forever thine!" cried she, amid the warmest kisses

Felix pulled her by the gown, and cried "Mamma Theresa, I am here too!" Natalia stood, and looked before her Mignon on a sudden clapped her left hand on her heart, and stretching out the right arm violently, fell with a shriek at Natalia's feet, as dead

The fright was great no motion of the heart or pulse was to be traced Wilhelm took her on his arm, and hastily carried her away, the body hung lax over his shoulders The presence of the Doctor was of small avail he and the young

Surgeon, whom we know already, strove in vain   The dear
little creature could not be recalled to life

Natalia beckoned to Theresa   the latter took her friend by
the hand and led him from the room   He was dumb, not
uttering a word, he durst not meet her eyes   He sat down
with her upon the sofa, where he had first found Natalia   He
thought with great rapidity along a series of fateful incidents,
or rather he did not think, but let his soul be worked on by
the thoughts which would not leave it   There are moments
in life, when past events, like winged shuttles, dart to and fro
before us, and by their incessant movements weave a web,
which we ourselves, in a greater or less degree, have spun and
put upon the loom   "My friend, my love!" said Theresa,
breaking silence, as she took him by the hand   "Let us stand
together firmly in this hour, as we perhaps shall often have
to do in similar hours   These are occurrences, which it takes
two united hearts to suffer   Think, my friend, feel that thou
art not alone, show that thou lovest thy Theresa by imparting
thy sorrows to her!"   She embraced him, and drew him softly
to her bosom   he clasped her in his arms and pressed her
strongly towards him   "The poor child," cried he, "used
in mournful moments to seek shelter and protection in my
unstable bosom   let the stability of thine assist me in this
heavy hour"   They held each other fast, he felt her heart
beat against his breast, but in his spirit all was desolate and
void, only the figures of Mignon and Natalia flitted like
shadows across the waste of his imagination

Natalia entered   "Give us thy blessing!" cried Theresa
"Let us, in this melancholy moment, be united before thee!"
Wilhelm had hid his face upon Theresa's neck   he was so
far relieved that he could weep   He did not hear Natalia
come, he did not see her, but at the sound of her voice his
tears redoubled.   "What God has joined I will not part,"
she answered, smiling, "but to unite you is not in my power,
nor am I gratified to see that sorrow and sympathy seem
altogether to have banished from your hearts the recollec-

tion of my brother " At these words, Wilhelm started from
Theresa's arms   " Whither are you going ? " cried the ladies
" Let me see the child," said he, " whom I have killed ! Misfortune when we look upon it with our eyes is smaller than
when our imagination sinks the evil down into the recesses
of the soul   Let us view the departed angel ! Her serene
countenance will say to us that it is well with her " As his
friends could not restrain the agitated youth, they followed
him, but the worthy Doctor with the Surgeon met them, and
prevented them from coming near the dead   " Keep away
from this mournful object," said he, " and allow me, so far as
I am able, to give some continuance to these remains   On this
dear and singular being I will now display the beautiful art
not only of embalming bodies, but of retaining in them a look
of life   As I foresaw her death, the preparations are already
made, with these helps I shall undoubtedly succeed   Give
me but a few days, and ask not to see the child again till I
have brought her to the Hall of the Past "

The young Surgeon had in his hands that well-known case
of instruments   " From whom can he have got it ? " Wilhelm
asked the Doctor   " I know it very well," replied Natalia
" he has it from his father, who dressed your wounds when we
found you in the forest "

" Then I have not been mistaken ! I recognised the band
at once ! " cried Wilhelm   " O get it for me ! It was this
that first gave me any hint of my unknown benefactress
What weal and woe will such a thing survive ! Beside how
many sorrows has this band already been, and its threads still
hold together ! How many men's last moments has it witnessed, and its colours are not yet faded ! It was near me
in one of the fairest hours of my existence, when I lay
wounded on the ground, and your helpful form appeared
before me, and the child whom we are now lamenting sat
with its bloody hair, busied with the tenderest care to save
my life ! "

sad occurrence, that Theresa could inquire about the child,
and the probable cause of its unexpected death for strangers
were announced, who, on making their appearance, proved
to be well-known strangers Lothario, Jarno, and the Abbé
entered Natalia met her brother among the rest, there was
a momentary silence Theresa, smiling on Lothario, said
"You scarcely expected to find me here, of course, it would
not have been advisable that we should visit one another at
the present time however, after such an absence, take my
cordial welcome"

Lothario took her hand, and answered "If we are to
suffer and renounce, it may as well take place in the presence
of the object whom we love and wish for I desire no influence on your determination, my confidence in your heart,
in your understanding and clear sense, is still so great, that
I willingly commit to your disposal my fate and that of my
friend"

The conversation turned immediately to general, nay, we
may say, to trivial topics The company soon separated
into single pairs, for walking Natalia was with her brother,
Theresa with the Abbé, our friend was left with Jarno in the
Castle

The appearance of the guests at the moment when a heavy
sorrow was oppressing Wilhelm, had, instead of dissipating
his attention, irritated him and made him worse he was
fretful and suspicious, and unable or uncareful to conceal it,
when Jarno questioned him about his sulky silence "What
is the use of saying more?" cried Wilhelm "Lothario with
his helpers is come and it were strange if those mysterious
watchmen of the tower, who are constantly so busy, did not
now exert their influence on us, to effect I know not what
strange purpose So far as I have known these saintly gentlemen, it seems to be in every case their laudable endeavour to
separate the united, and to unite the separated What sort
of web their weaving will produce, may probably to unholy
eyes be forever a riddle"

"You are cross and bitter," said the other, "that is as it should be. Would you get into a proper passion, it were still better."

"That too might come about," said Wilhelm. "I fear much some of you are in the mind to load my patience, natural and acquired, beyond what it will bear."

"In the mean time," said the other, "till we see what is to be the issue of the matter, I could like to tell you somewhat of the tower, which you appear to view with such mistrust."

"It stands with you," said Wilhelm, "whether you will risk your eloquence on an attention so distracted. My mind is so engaged at present, that I know not whether I can take a proper interest in these very dignified adventures."

"Your pleasing humour shall not hinder me," said Jarno, "from explaining this affair to you. You reckon me a clever fellow, I want to make you reckon me an honest one, and what is more, on this occasion I am bidden speak."—"I could wish," said Wilhelm, "that you did it of yourself, and with an honest purpose to inform me, but as I cannot hear without suspicion, wherefore should I hear at all?"—"If I have nothing better to do," said Jarno, "than tell you stories, you too have time to listen to me, and to this you may perhaps feel more inclined, when I assure you, that all you saw in that tower was but the relics of a youthful undertaking, in regard to which the greater part of the initiated were once in deep earnest, though all of them now view it with a smile."

"So, with these pompous signs and words, you do but mock?" cried Wilhelm. "With a solemn air, you lead us to a place inspiring reverence by its aspect, you make the strangest visions pass before us, you give us rolls full of glorious mystic apophthegms, of which in truth we understand but little, you disclose to us, that hitherto we have been pupils, you solemnly pronounce us free, and we are just as wise as we were."—"Have you not the parchment by you?" said the other. "It contains a deal of sense. those general seem obscure and empty to a man without experiences to recollect while reading them   But give me the Indenture as we call it, if it is at hand "—" Quite at hand," cried Wilhelm, "such an amulet well merits being worn upon one's breast " —" Well," said Jarno, smiling, " who knows whether the contents of it may not one day find place in your head and heart? "

He opened the Roll, and glanced over the first half of it. " This," said he, " regards the cultivation of our gifts for art and science , of which let others speak the second treats of life , here I am more at home "

He then began to read passages, speaking between-whiles, and connecting them with his remarks and narrative   " The taste of youth for secrecy, for ceremonies, for imposing words, is extraordinary , and frequently bespeaks a certain depth of character   In those years, we wish to feel our whole nature seized and moved, even though it be but vaguely and darkly The youth who happens to have lofty aspirations and fore-castings, thinks that secrets yield him much, that he must depend much on secrets, and effect much by means of them It was with such views that the Abbé favoured a certain Society of young men , partly according to his principle of aiding every tendency of nature, partly out of habit and inclination, for in former times he had himself been joined to an association, which appears to have accomplished many things in secret   For this business I was least of all adapted I was older than the rest , from youth I had thought clearly , I wished in all things nothing more than clearness, I felt no interest in men, but to know them as they were   With the same taste I gradually infected all the best of our associates, and this circumstance had almost given a false direction to our plan of culture   For we now began to look at nothing but the errors and the narrowness of others, and to think ourselves a set of highly-gifted personages   Here the Abbé came to our assistance he taught us, that we never should inspect the conduct of men, unless we at the same time took an interest in improving it, and that through action only could we ever be in a condition to inspect and watch ourselves He advised us, however, to retain the primary forms of the Society hence there was still a sort of law in our proceedings, the first mystic impressions might be traced in the constitution of the whole At length, as by a practical similitude, it took the form of a corporate trade, whose business was the arts Hence came the names of Apprentices, Assistants, and Masters We wished to see with our own eyes, and to form for ourselves a special record of our own experience in the world Hence those numerous confessions, which in part we ourselves wrote, in part made others write, and out of which the several *Apprenticeships* were afterwards compiled The formation of his character is not the chief concern with every man Many merely wish to find a sort of recipe for comfort, directions for acquiring riches, or whatever good they aim at All such, when they would not be instructed in their proper duties, we were wont to mystify, to treat with juggleries and every sort of hocus-pocus, and at length to shove aside We advanced none to the rank of Masters, but such as clearly felt and recognised the purpose they were born for, and had got enough of practice to proceed along their way with a certain cheerfulness and ease "

"In my case, then," cried Wilhelm, "your ceremony has been very premature, for since the day when you pronounced e free, what I can, will, or shall do, has been more unknown to me than ever "—"We are not to blame for this perplexity, perhaps good fortune will deliver us In the mean time listen "He in whom there is much to be developed will be later in acquiring true perceptions of himself and of the world There are few who at once have Thought and the capacity of Action Thought expands, but lames, Action animates, but narrows '"

"I beg of you," cried Wilhelm, "not to read me any more of that surprising stuff These phrases have sufficiently con-

Jarno, half rolling up the parchment, into which, however, he kept casting frequent glances "I myself have been of less service to the cause of our Society and of my fellow-men than any other member I am but a bad schoolmaster, I cannot bear to look on people making awkward trials, when I see a person wandering from his path, I feel constrained to call to him, although it were a night-walker going straight to break his neck On this point, I had a continual struggle with the Abbé, who maintains that error can never be cured except by erring About you, too, we often argued He had taken an especial liking to you, and it is saying something to have caught so much of his attention For me, you must admit, that every time we met, I told you just the naked truth "— "Certainly, you spared me very little," said the other, "and I think you still continue faithful to your principles "— "What is the use of sparing," answered Jarno, "when a young man of many good endowments is taking a quite false direction? "—"Pardon me," said Wilhelm, "you have rigorously enough denied me any talent for the stage, I confess to you, that though I have entirely renounced the art, I cannot think myself entirely incapable "—"And with me,' said Jarno, "it is well enough decided, that a person who can only play himself is no player Whoever cannot change himself, in temper and in form, into many forms, does not deserve the name Thus you, for example, acted Hamlet and some other characters extremely well, because in these, your form, your disposition and the temper of the moment suited For an amateur theatre, for any one who saw no other way before him, this would perhaps have answered well enough But," continued Jarno, looking on the roll, "'we should guard against a talent which we cannot hope to practise in perfection Improve it as we may, we shall always in the end, when the merit of the master has become apparent to us, painfully lament the loss of time and strength devoted to such botching '"

"Do not read!" cried Wilhelm "I entreat you earnestly;

speak on, tell, inform me ! So the Abbé aided me in Hamlet
he provided me a ghost ? "—" Yes, for he asserted that it was
the only way of curing you, if you were curable "—" And on
this account he left the veil, and bade me fly ? "—" Yes, he
hoped that having fairly acted Hamlet, your desire of acting
would be satiated He maintained that you would never go
upon the stage again I believed the contrary, and I was
right We argued on the subject, that very evening when
the play was over "—" You saw me act, then ? "—" I did
indeed "—" And who was it that played the Ghost ? "—" That
I cannot tell you, either the Abbé or his twin brother, but
I think the latter, for he is a little taller "—" You have
secrets from each other, then ? "—" Friends may and must *have*
secrets from each other, but they *are* not secrets to each
other "

" The very thought of that perplexity perplexes   e Let
me understand the man, to whom I owe so many thanks as
well as such reproaches "

" What gives him such a value in our estimation," answered
Jarno, " what in some degree secures him the dominion over
all of us, is the free sharp eye that nature has bestowed on
him for all the powers which dwell in man, and are susceptible
of cultivation, each according to its kind Most men, even
the most accomplished, are but limited each prizes certain
properties in others and himself, these alone he favours, these
alone will he have cultivated Directly the reverse is the-
procedure of our Abbé for every gift he has a feeling, every
gift he delights to recognise and forward But I must look
into my roll again ! ' It is all men that make up mankind,
all powers taken together that make up the world These
are frequently at variance and as they endeavour to destroy
each other, Nature holds them together, and again produces
them From the first animal tendency to handicraft attempts,
up to the highest practising of intellectual art, from the
inarticulate crowings of the happy infant, up to the polished

of boys up to the vast equipments by which countries are
conquered and retained, from the slightest kindliness and
the most transitory love, up to the fiercest passion and the
most earnest covenant, from the merest perception of sensible
presence up to the faintest presentiments and hopes of the
remotest spiritual future, all this and much more also lies in
man, and must be cultivated yet not in one, but in many
Every gift is valuable, and ought to be unfolded When one
encourages the beautiful alone, and another encourages the
useful alone, it takes them both to form a man The useful
encourages itself, for the multitude produce it, and no one
can dispense with it the beautiful must be encouraged, for
few can set it forth, and many need it "

"Hold! hold!" cried Wilhelm "I have read it all "—
"Yet a line or two!" said Jarno "Here is our worthy Abbé
to a hairsbreadth 'One power rules another, none can
cultivate another in each endow ent, and not elsewhere,
lies the force which must complete it, this many people do
not understand, who yet attempt to teach and influence'"—
"I too do not understand it," answered Wilhelm —" You will
often hear the Abbé preach on this text, and, therefore, 'Let
us merely keep a clear and steady eye on what is in ourselves,
on what endowments of our own we mean to cultivate, let us
be just to others, for we ourselves are only to be valued in so
far as we can value'"—" For Heaven's sake, no more of these
wise saws! I feel them to be but a sorry balsam for a wounded
heart Tell me rather, with your cruel settledness, what you
expect of me, how and in what manner you intend to sacrifice
me "—" For every such suspicion, I assure you, you will
afterwards beg our pardon It is your affair to try and
choose, it is ours to aid you A man is never happy till his
vague striving has itself marked out its proper limitation It
is not to me that you must look, but to the Abbé it is not of
yourself that you must think, but of what surrounds you.
Thus, for instance, learn to understand Lothario's superiority;
how his quick and comprehensive vision is inseparably united

with activity, how he constantly advances, how he expands
his influence, and carries every one along with him. Wherever
he may be, he bears a world about with him his presence
animates and kindles Observe our good Physician, on the
other hand ! His nature seems to be directly the reverse If
the former only works upon the general whole, and at a
distance, the latter turns his piercing eye upon the things that
are beside him, he rather furnishes the means for being active,
than himself displays or stimulates activity His conduct is
exactly like the conduct of a good domestic manager, he is
busied silently, while he provides for each in his peculiar sphere,
his knowledge is a constant gathering and expending, a taking
in and giving out on the small scale Perhaps Lothario in a
single day might overturn what the other had for years been
employed in building up but perhaps Lothario also might
impart to others, in a moment, strength sufficient to restore
a hundredfold what he had overturned ”—“ It is but a sad
employment,” answered Wilhelm, “ to contemplate the sublime advantages of others, at a moment when we are at
variance with ourselves Such contemplations suit the man
at ease, not him whom passion and uncertainty are agitating ”
—“ Peacefully and reasonably to contemplate is at no time
hurtful,” answered Jarno “ and while we use ourselves to
think of the advantages of others, our own mind comes in-
sensibly to imitate them, and every false activity, to which
our fancy was alluring us, is then willingly abandoned Free
your mind, if you can, from all suspicion and anxiety Here
comes the Abbé be courteous towards him, till you have
learned still farther what you owe him The rogue ! There
he goes between Natalia and Theresa, I could bet he is con-
triving something As in general he likes to act the part of
Destiny a little, so he does not fail to show a taste for making
matches, when he finds an opportunity ”

Wilhelm, whose angry and fretful humour all the placid
prudent words of Jarno had not bettered, thought his friend

like the present, he answered with a smile indeed, but a rather bitter one. "I thought the taste for making matches had been left to those that had a taste for one another"

CHAPTER VI

The company had met again, the conversation of our friends was necessarily interrupted Ere long a courier was announced, as wishing to deliver with his own hand a letter to Lothario The man was introduced he had a vigorous sufficient look, his livery was rich and handsome Wilhelm thought he knew him nor was he mistaken, for it was the man whom he had sent to seek Philina and the fancied Mariana, and who never came back Our friend was about to address him, when Lothario, who had read the letter, asked the courier with a serious, almost angry tone "What is your master's name?"

"Of all questions," said the other with a prudent air, "this is the one which I am least prepared to answer I hope the letter will communicate the necessary information verbally I have been charged with nothing"

"Be it as it will," replied Lothario with a smile, "since your master puts such trust in me as to indite a letter so exceedingly facetious, he shall be welcome to us"—"He will not keep you long waiting for him," said the courier with a bow, and withdrew

" Do but hear the distracted stupid message," said Lothario "'As of all guests, Good Humour is believed to be the most agreeable wherever he appears, and as I always keep that gentleman beside me by way of travelling companion, I feel persuaded that the visit I intend to pay your noble Lordship will not be taken ill, on the contrary, I hope the whole of your illustrious family will witness my arrival with complete satisfaction, and in due time also my departure; being always, et cetera, Count of Snailfoot'"

"'Tis a new family," said the Abbé

" A vicariat count, perhaps," said Jarno

" The secret is easy to unriddle," said Natalia " I wager it is none but brother Friedrich, who has threatened us with a visit ever since my uncle's death "

" Right! fair and skilful sister !" cried a voice from the nearest thicket, and immediately a pleasant, cheerful youth stept forward   Wilhelm could scarcely restrain a cry of wonder " How ?" exclaimed he " Does our fair-haired knave, too, meet me here ?"   Friedrich looked attentively, and recognising Wilhelm, cried   " In truth it would not have astonished me so much to have beheld the famous Pyramids, which still stand fast in Egypt, or the grave of King Mausolus, which, as I am told, does not exist, here placed before me in my uncle's garden, as to find you in it, my old friend, and frequent benefactor   Accept my best and heartiest service ! "

After he had kissed and complimented the whole circle, he again sprang towards Wilhelm, crying " Use him well, this hero, this leader of armies, and dramatical philosopher ! When we became acquainted first, I dressed his hair indifferently, I may say execrably, yet he afterwards saved me from a pretty load of blows   He is magnanimous as Scipio, munificent as Alexander, at times he is in love, yet he never hates his rivals   Far from heaping coals of fire on the heads of his enemies,—a piece of service, I am told, which we can do for any one,—he rather, when his friends have carried off his love, despatches good and trusty servants after them, that they ay not strike their feet against a stone "

In the same style, he ran along with a volubility which baffled all attempts to restrain it, and as no one could reply to him in that vein, he had the conversation mostly to himself " Do not wonder," cried he, " that I am so profoundly versed in sacred and profane writers you shall hear by and by how I attained my learning " They wished to know how matters stood with him, where he had been, but crowds of proverbs and old stories choked his explanation

Natalia whispered to Theresa "His gaiety afflicts me, I am sure at heart he is not merry"

As, except a few jokes which Jarno answered, Friedrich's merriment was met by no response from those about him, he was obliged at last to say "Well, there is nothing left for me, but among so many grave faces to be grave myself And as in such a solemn scene, the burden of my sins falls heavy on my soul, I must honestly resolve upon a general confession, for which, however, you, my worthy gentlemen and ladies, shall not be a jot the wiser This honourable friend already knows a little of my walk and conversation, he alone shall know the rest, and this the rather, as he alone has any cause to ask about it Are not you," continued he to Wilhelm, "curious about the how and where, the when and wherefore? And how it stands with the conjugation of the Greek verb φιλέω, φιλῶ, and the derivatives of that very amiable part of speech?"

He then took Wilhelm by the arm, and led him off, pressing him and skipping round him with the liveliest air of kindness

Scarcely had they entered Wilhelm's room, when Friedrich noticed, in the window, a powder-knife, with the inscription *Think of me* "You keep your valuables well laid up!" said he "This is the powder-knife Philina gave you, when I pulled your locks for you I hope, in looking at it, you have diligently thought of that fair damsel I assure you, she has not forgotten you, if I had not long ago obliterated every trace of jealousy from my heart, I could not look on you without envy"

"Talk no more of that creature," answered Wilhelm "I confess, it was a while before I could get rid of the impression, which her looks and manner made on me, but that was all"

"Fy! fy!" cried Friedrich "would any one deny his deary? You loved her as completely as a man could wish No day passed without your giving her some present, and when a German gives, you may be sure he loves. No alternative remained for me but whisking her away from you, and in this the little red officer at last succeeded"

"How! You were the officer whom we discovered with her, whom she travelled off with?"

"Yes," said Friedrich, "whom you took for Mariana We had sport enough at the mistake"

"What cruelty," cried Wilhel , "to leave me in such suspense!"

"And besides to take the courier, whom you sent to catch us, into pay!" said Friedrich "He is a very active fellow; we have kept him by us ever since And the girl herself I love as desperately as ever She has managed me in so e peculiar style I am almost in a mythologic case, every day I tremble at the thought of being metamorphosed"

"But tell me, pray," said Wilhelm, "where have you acquired this stock of erudition? It surprises me to hear the strange way you have assumed of speaking always with a reference to ancient histories and fables"

"It was by a pleasant plan," said Friedrich, "that I got my learning Philina lives with me at present we have got a lease of an old knightly castle from the farmer in whose ground it is and there we live, with the hobgoblins of the place, as merrily as possible In one of the rooms, we found a small but choice library, consisting of a folio *Bible*, *Gottfried's Chronicle*, two volumes of the *Theatrum Europæum*, an *Acerra Philologica*, *Gryphius' Writings*, and some other less important works As we now and then, when tired of romping, felt the time hang heavy on our hands, we proposed to read some books, and before we were aware, the time hung heavier than ever At last, Philina hit upon the royal plan of laying all the tomes, opened at once, upon a large table we sat down opposite to one another we read to one another; always in detached passages, first from this book, then from that Here was a proper pleasure! We felt now as if we were in good society, where it is reckoned unbecoming to dwell on any subject, or search it to the bottom; we thought

ourselves in witty gay society, where none will let his neighbour speak   We regularly treat ourselves with this diversion
every day, and the erudition we obtain from it is quite surprising   Already there is nothing new for us under the sun,
on everything we see or hear, our learning offers us a hint
This method of instruction we diversify in many ways   Frequently we read by an old spoiled sand-glass, which runs in
a minute or two   The moment it is down the silent party
turns it round like lightning, and commences reading from his
book, and no sooner is it down again, than the other cuts him
short, and starts the former topic   Thus we study in a truly
academic manner   only our hours are shorter, and our studies
are extremely varied "

"This rioting is quite conceivable," said Wilhelm, "when
a pair like you two are together   but how a pair so full of
frolic stay together, does not seem so easily conceivable "

"It is our good fortune," answered Friedrich, "and our
bad   Philina dare not let herself be seen, she cannot bear to
see herself, she is in the family way   Nothing ever was so
ludicrous and shapeless in the world   A little while before I
came away, she chanced to cast an eye upon the looking-glass
in passing   'Faugh!' cried she, and turned away her face
'the living picture of the Frau Melina! Shocking figure!
One looks entirely deplorable!'"

"I confess," said Wilhelm with a smile, "it must be rather
farcical to see a father and a mother such as you and she
together "

"'Tis a foolish business," answered Friedrich, "that I must,
at last, be raised to the paternal dignity   But she asserts, and
the time agrees   At first that cursed visit which she paid you
after Hamlet gave me qualms "

"What visit?"

"I suppose you have not quite slept off the memory of it
yet?   The pretty, flesh-and-blood spirit of that night, if you
do not know it, was Philina   The story was in truth a hard
dower for me, but if we cannot be content with such things,

we should not be in love Fatherhood at any rate depends
entirely upon conviction I am convinced, and so I am a
father There, you see, I can employ my logic in the proper
season too And if the brat do not laugh itself to death so
soon as it is born, it may prove, if not a useful, at least a
pleasant citizen of this world "

Whilst our friends were talking thus of mirthful subjects,
the rest of the party had begun a serious conversation
Scarcely were Friedrich and Wilhelm gone, when the Abbé
led his friends, as if by chance, into a garden-house, and
having got them seated, thus addressed them

" We have in general terms asserted that Fraulein Theresa
was not the daughter of her reputed mother it is fit that we
should now explain ourselves on this matter, in detail I shall
relate the story to you, which I undertake to prove and to
elucidate in every point

" Frau von * * * spent the first years of her wedlock in the
utmost concord with her husband , only they had this misfortune, that the children she brought him came into the world
dead , and on occasion of the third, the mother was declared
by the Physicians to be on the verge of death, and to be sure
of death if she should ever have another The parties were
obliged to take their resolution they would not break the
marriage , it was too suitable to both, in a civil point of view.
Frau von * * * sought in the culture of her mind, in a certain
habit of display, in the joys of vanity, a compensation for the
happiness of motherhood which was refused her She cheerfully indulged her husband, when she noticed in him an
attachment to a young lady, who had sole charge of their
domestic economy , a person of beautiful exterior, and very
solid character Frau von * * * herself, ere long, assisted in
procuring an arrangement by which the lady yielded to
the wishes of Theresa's father , continuing to discharge
her household duties, and testifying to the mistress of the
family, if possible, a more submissive zeal to serve her than
before

"After a while, she declared herself with child and both the father and his wife, on this occasion, though from very different causes, fell upon the same idea Herr von * * * wished to have the offspring of his mistress educated in the house as his lawful child, and Frau von * * *, angry that the indiscretion of her Doctor had allowed some whisper of her condition to go abroad, proposed by a supposititious child to counteract this, and likewise to retain, by such compliance, the superiority in her household, which otherwise she was like to lose However, she was more backward than her husband she observed his purpose, and contrived, without any formal question, to facilitate his explanation She made her own terms, obtaining almost everything that she required, and hence the will, in which so little care was taken of the child The old Doctor was dead they applied to a young, active and discreet successor, he was well rewarded, he looked forward to the credit of exposing and remedying the unskilfulness and premature decision of his deceased colleague The true mother, not unwillingly, consented, they managed the deception very well, Theresa came into the world, and was surrendered to a stepmother, while her mother fell a victim to the plot, having died by venturing out too early, and left the father inconsolable

"Frau von * * * had thus attained her object, in the eyes of the world she had a lovely child, which she paraded with excessive vanity, and she had also been delivered from a rival, whose fortune she envied, and whose influence, at least in prospect, she beheld with apprehension The infant she loaded with her tenderness, and by affecting, in trustful hours, a lively feeling for her husband's loss, she gained mastery of his heart, so that in a manner he surrendered all to her, laid his own happiness and that of his child in her hands, nor was it till a short while prior to his death, and in some degree by the exertions of his grown-up daughter, that he again assumed the rule in his own house This, fair Theresa, was in all probability the secret, which your father, in his last sickness, so

struggled to communicate, this is what I wish to lay circu-
stantially before you, at a moment when our young friend,
who by a strange concurrence has become your bridegroom,
happens to be absent   Here are the papers, which will prove
in the most rigorous manner everything that I have stated
You will also see from them how long I have been following
the trace of this discovery, though till now I could never
attain certainty respecting it   I did not risk imparting to
my friend the possibility of such a happiness, it would have
wounded him too deeply, had this hope a second time deceived
him   You will understand poor Lydia's suspicions   I readily
confess, I nowise favoured the attachment of our friend to her,
whenever I began to look for a connexion with Theresa "

To this recital no one replied   The ladies, some days
afterwards, returned the papers, not making any further
ention of them

There were other matters in abundance to engage the party
when they were together, and the scenery around was so
delightful, that our friends, singly or in company, on horseback, in carriages, or on foot, delighted to explore it   On
one of these excursions, Jarno took an opportunity of opening
the affair to Wilhelm   he delivered him the papers, not however seeming to require from him any resolution in regard to
them

"In the singular position I a   placed in," said our friend,
"I need only repeat to you what I said at first, in presence of
Natalia, and with the clear intention to fulfil it   Lothario
and his friends may require of me every sort of self-denial   I
here abandon in their favour all pretensions to Theresa, do
you procure me, in return, a formal discharge   There requires
no great reflection to decide.   For so e days, I have noticed
that Theresa has to make an effort in retaining any show of
the vivacity with which she welco ed me at first   Her affection is gone from me, or rather I have never had it "

"Such affairs are more conveniently explained," said Jarno,
"by a gradual process, in silence and expectation, than by

many words, which always cause a sort of fermentation and embarrassment "

" I rather think," said Wilhelm, " that precisely this affair admits of the most clear and calm decision on the spot   I have often been reproached with hesitation and uncertainty   why will you now, when I do not hesitate, commit against myself the fault you have often blamed in me ?   Do our neighbours take such trouble with our training, only to let us feel that they themselves are untrained ?   Yes, grant me soon the cheerful thought that I am out of a mistaken project, into which I entered with the purest feelings in the world "

Notwithstanding this request, some days elapsed without his hearing any more of the affair, or observing any further alteration in his friends   The conversation, on the contrary, was general and of indifferent matters

CHAPTER VII

JARNO and Wilhelm were sitting one day by Natalia   " You are thoughtful, Jarno," said the lady , " I have seen it in your looks for some time "

" I am so," answered Jarno   " a weighty business is before me, which we have for years been meditating, and must now begin to execute   You already know the outline of it   I may speak of it before our friend , for it will depend on himself, whether he too shall not share in it   You are going to get rid of me, before long   I mean to take a voyage to America "

" To America ?" said Wilhelm, smiling   " Such an adventure I did not anticipate from you , still less that you would have selected me for a companion "

" When you rightly understand our plan," said Jarno, " you will give it a more honourable name , and perhaps yourself be tempted to embark in it   Listen to me   It requires but a slight acquaintance with the business of the world to see that mighty changes are at hand, that property is almost nowhere quite secure "

" Of the business of the world I have no clear notion," interrupted Wilhelm, "and it is but of late that I ever thought about my property Perhaps I had done well to drive it out of my head still longer , the care of securing it, appears to give us hypochondria "

" Hear me out," said Jarno " Care beseems ripe age, that youth may live for a time free from care in the conduct of poor mortals, equilibrium cannot be restored except by contraries As matters go, it is anything but prudent to have property in only one place, to commit your money to a single spot , and it is difficult again to guide it well in many. We have therefore thought of something else From our old tower there is a society to issue, which must spread itself through every quarter of the world, and to which members from every quarter of the world shall be admissible We shall ensure a competent subsistence to each other, in the single case of a revolution happening, which might drive any part of us entirely from their possessions I am now proceeding to America, to profit by the good connexions which our friend established while he stayed there The Abbé means to go to Russia if you like to join us, you shall have the choice of continuing in Germany to help Lothario, or of accompanying me I conjecture you will choose the latter to take a distant journey is extremely serviceable to a young man "

Wilhelm thought a moment, and replied " The offer well deserves consideration , for ere long the word with me must be, The farther off the better You will let me know your plan, I hope, more perfectly It is perhaps my ignorance of life that makes me think so , but such a combination seems to me to be attended with insuperable difficulties "

" The most of which, till now, have been avoided," answered Jarno, " by the circumstance, that we have been but few in number, honourable, discreet, determined people, animated by a certain general feeling, out of which alone the feeling proper for societies can spring "—"And if you speak me fair," said Friedrich, who hitherto had only listened, "I too will go along with you " Jarno shook his head

"Well, what objections can you make?" cried Friedrich "In a new colony, young colonists will be required, these I bring with me merry colonists will also be required, of these I make you certain Besides, I recollect a certain damsel, who is out of place on this side of the water, the fair, soft-hearted Lydia What is the poor thing to do with her sorrow and mourning, unless she get an opportunity to throw it to the bottom of the sea, unless some brave fellow take her by the hand? You, my benefactor," said he, turning towards Wilhelm, "you have a taste for comforting forsaken persons what withholds you now? Each of us might take his girl under his arm, and trudge with Jarno "

This proposal struck Wilhelm offensively He answered with affected calmness "I know not whether she is unengaged, and as in general I seem to be unfortunate in courtship, I shall hardly think of making the attempt "

"Brother Friedrich," said Natalia, "though thy own conduct is so full of levity, it does not follow that such sentiments will answer others Our friend deserves a heart that shall belong to him alone, that shall not at his side be moved by foreign recollections It was only with a character as pure and reasonable as Theresa's, that such a venture could be risked "

"Risk!" cried Friedrich "In love it is all risk In the grove or at the altar, with a clasp of the arms or a golden ring, by the chirping of the cricket or the sound of trumpets and kettledrums, it is all but a risk, chance does it all "

"I have often noticed," said Natalia, "that our principles are just a supplement to our peculiar manner of existence We delight to clothe our errors in the garb of universal laws, to attribute them to irresistibly-appointed causes Do but think, by what a path thy dear will lead thee, now that she has drawn thee towards her, and holds thee fast there "

"She herself is on a very pretty path," said Friedrich, " on the path to saintship A by-path, it is true, and somewhat roundabout, but the pleasanter and surer for that Maria of Magdala travelled it, and who can say how many more? But on the whole, sister, when the point in hand is love, thou shouldst not mingle in it In my opinion, thou wilt never marry, till a bride is lacking somewhere, in that case, thou wilt give thyself, with thy habitual charity, to be the supplement of some peculiar manner of existence, not otherwise So let us strike a bargain with this soul-broker, and agree about our travelling company "

" You come too late with your proposals," answered Jarno, " Lydia is disposed of "

" And how ? " cried Friedrich

" I myself have offered her my hand," said Jarno

" Old gentleman," said Friedrich, " you have done a feat to which, if we regard it as a substantive, various adjectives might be appended, various predicates, if we regard it as a subject "

" I must honestly confess," replied Natalia, " it appears a dangerous experiment to make a helpmate of a woman, at the very moment when her love for another man is like to drive her to despair "

" I have ventured," answered Jarno, " under a certain stipulation, she is to be mine And, believe me, there is nothing in the world more precious than a heart susceptible of love and passion Whether it has loved, whether it still loves, are points which I regard not The love of which another is the object, charms me almost more than that which is directed to myself I see the strength, the force of a tender soul, and my self-love does not trouble the delightful vision "

" Have you talked with Lydia, then, of late ? " inquired Natalia

Jarno smiled and nodded Natalia shook her head, and said as he rose " I really know not what to make of you, but me you shall not mystify, I promise you "

She was about retiring, when the Abbé entered with a letter in his hand "Stay, if you please," said he to her. "I have a proposal here, respecting which your counsel will be welcome The Marchese, your late uncle's friend, whom for some time we have been expecting, will be here in a day or two He writes to me, that German is not so familiar to him as he had supposed, that he needs a person who possesses this and other languages to travel with him, that as he wishes to connect himself with scientific rather than political society, he cannot do without some such interpreter I can think of no one better suited for the post than our young friend here He knows the language, is acquainted with many things beside, and for himself, it cannot but be advantageous to travel over Germany in such society and such circumstances Till we have seen our native country, we have no scale to judge of other countries by What say you, my friend? What say you, Natalia?"

Nobody objected to the scheme Jarno seemed to think his Transatlantic project would not be a hindrance, as he did not mean to sail directly Natalia did not speak, and Friedrich uttered various saws about the uses of travel

This new project so provoked our friend, that he could hardly conceal his irritation He saw, in this proposal, a conceited plan for getting rid of him as soon as possible, and what was worse, they went so openly to work, and seemed so utterly regardless of his feelings The suspicions Lydia had excited in him, all that he himself had witnessed, rose again upon his mind, the simple manner in which everything had been explained by Jarno, now appeared to him another piece of artifice

He constrained himself, and answered "At all events, the offer will require mature deliberation"

"A quick decision may perhaps be necessary," said the Abbé

"For that I am not prepared," answered Wilhelm "We can wait till the Marchese comes, and then observe if we agree together One condition must, however, be conceded first of all that I take Felix with me "

"This is a condition," said the Abbé, " which will scarcely be conceded "

"And I do not see," cried Wilhelm, " why I should let any man prescribe conditions to me, or why, if I choose to view my native country, I must go in company with an Italian "

"Because a young man," said the Abbé, with a certain imposing earnestness, "is always called upon to form connexions "

Wilhelm, feeling that he could not long retain his self-command, as it was Natalia's presence only which in some degree assuaged his indignation, hastily made answer "Give me a little while to think I imagine it will not be very hard to settle whether I am called upon to form additional connexions, or ordered irresistibly, by heart and head, to free myself from such a multiplicity of bonds, which seem to threaten me with a perpetual, miserable thraldom "

Thus he spoke, with a deeply-agitated mind A glance at Natalia somewhat calmed him her form and dignity, in this impassioned moment, stamped themselves more deeply on his mind than ever

"Yes," said he, so soon as he was by himself, "confess it, thou lovest her, thou once more feelest what it means to love with thy whole soul Thus did I love Mariana, and deceive myself so dreadfully, I loved Philina, and could not help despising her Aurelia I respected, and could not love. Theresa I reverenced, and paternal tenderness assumed the form of an affection for her And now when all the feelings that can make a mortal happy meet within my heart, now am I compelled to fly! Ah ! why should these feelings and convictions be combined with an insuperable longing? Why, without the hope of its fulfilment, should they utterly subvert all other happiness? Shall the sun and the world, society or any other gift of fortune, ever henceforth yield me pleasure?

Shalt thou not for evei say Natalia is not here ! And yet, alas, Natalia will be always present to thee ! If thou closest thy eyes, she will appear to thee, if thou openest them, her form will flit befoie all outwaid things, like the image which a dazzling object leaves behind it in the eye   Did not the swiftly-passing figure of the Amazon dwell continually in thy imagination ? And yet thou hadst but seen her, thou didst not know her   Now, when thou knowest her, when thou hast been so long beside her, when she has shown such care about thee, now are her qualities impiessed as deeply upon thy soul, as her form was then upon thy fancy   It is painful to be always seeking, but fai more painful to have found, and to be forced to leave   What now shall I ask for farther in the world ?   What now shall I look for faither ?   Is there a countiy, a city that contains a treasuie such as this ?   And I must travel on, and ever find inferiority ?   Is life, then, like a race-course, where a man must rapidly return, when he has reached the utmost end ?   Does the good, the excellent stand before us like a firm unmoving goal, from which with fleet horses we are forced away, the instant we appeared to have attained it ?   Happier are they who strive for earthly wares ! They find what they are seeking in its proper climate, or they buy it in the faii

"Come, my own boy !" cried he to Felix, who now ran fiisking towards him "be thou, and remain thou, all to me ! Thou wert given me as a compensation for thy loved mother, thou wert to replace the second mother whom I meant for thee, and now thou hast a loss still greater to make good Occupy my heart, occupy my spirit with thy beauty, thy loveliness, thy capabilities, and thy desire to use them !'"

The boy was busied with a new plaything, his father tried to put it in a better state foi him, just as he succeeded, Felix had lost all pleasuie in it   "Thou art a true son of Adam !" ciied Wilhelm   "Come, my child ! Come, y brother ! let us wander, playing without object, through the world, as we best may "

His resolution to remove, to take the boy along with him, and recreate his mind by looking at the world, had now assumed a settled form He wrote to Werner for the necessary cash and letters of credit, sending Friedrich's courier on the message, with the strictest charges to return immediately. Much as the conduct of his other friends had grieved him, his relation to Natalia remained serene and clear as ever

He confided to her his intention she took it as a settled thing that he would go, and if this seeming carelessness in her chagrined him, her kindly manner and her presence made him calm She counselled him to visit various towns, that he might get acquainted with certain of her friends The courier returned, and brought the letter which our friend required, though Werner did not see content with this new whim "My hope that thou wert growing reasonable," so the letter ran, "is now again deferred Where are you all gadding? And where lingers the lady, who, thou saidst, was to assist us in arranging these affairs? Thy other friends also are absent they have thrown the whole concern upon the shoulders of the Lawyer and myself. Happy that he is as expert a jurist, as I am a financier, and that both of us are used to business Fare thee well! Thy aberrations shall be pardoned thee, since but for them, our situation here could not have been so favourable"

So far as outward matters were concerned, Wilhelm might now have entered on his journey, but there were still, for his heart, two hindrances that held him fast In the first place, they flatly refused to show him Mignon's body, till the funeral the Abbé meant to celebrate, and for this solemnity, the preparations were not ready. There had also been a curious letter from the country Clergyman, in consequence of which the Doctor had gone off It related to the Harper, of whose fate Wilhelm wanted to have farther information

In these circumstances, day or night he found no rest for mind or body When all were asleep, he wandered up and down the house The presence of the pictures and statues,

which he knew so well of old, alternately attracted and
repelled him   Nothing that surrounded him could he lay
hold of or let go, all things reminded him of all, the whole
ring of his existence lay before him, but it was broken into
fragments, and seemed as if it would never unite again   These
works of art, which his father had sold, appeared to him an
omen that he himself was destined never to obtain a lasting
calm possession of anything desirable in life, or always to be
robbed of it so soon as gained, by his own or other people's
blame   He waded so deep in these strange and dreary meditations, that often he almost thought himself a disembodied
spirit, and even when he felt and handled things without
him, he could scarcely keep himself from doubting whether he
was really there and alive

Nothing but the piercing grief, which often seized him, but
the tears he shed at being forced, by causes frivolous as they
were irresistible, to leave the good which he had found, and
found after having lost it,—restored him to the feeling of his
earthly life   It was in vain to call before his mind his happy
state in other respects   "All is nothing, then," exclaimed he,
"if the one blessing, which appears to us worth all the rest, is
wanting!"

The Abbé told the company that the Marchese was arrived
"You have determined, it appears," said he to Wilhelm, "to
set out upon your travels with your boy alone   Get acquainted
with this nobleman, however, he will be useful to you, if you
meet him by the way"   The Marchese entered   he was a
person not yet very far advanced in years, a fine, handsome,
pleasing Lombard figure   In his youth, while in the army
and afterwards in public business, he had known Lothario's
uncle, they had subsequently travelled through the greater
part of Italy together, and many of the works of art, which
the Marchese now again fell in with, had been purchased in his
presence, and under various happy circumstances, which he still
distinctly recollected

The Italians have in general a deeper feeling for the

high dignity of art than any other nation   In Italy, whoever
follows the employment, tries to pass at once for artist, master
and professor   by which pretensions, he acknowledges at least
that it is not sufficient merely to lay hold of some transmitted
excellency, or to acquire by practice some dexterity, but that
a an who aims at art, should have the power to think of
what he does, to lay down principles, and make apparent to
himself and others how and wherefore he proceeds in this way
or in that

The stranger was affected at again beholding these produc-
tions, when the owner of them was no more, and cheered to
see the spirit of his friend surviving in the gifted persons left
behind him   They discussed a series of works, they found
a lively satisfaction in the harmony of their ideas   The
Marchese and the Abbé were the speakers, Natalia felt herself
again transported to the presence of her uncle, and could enter
without difficulty into their opinions and criticisms, Wilhelm
could not understand them, except as he translated their
technology into dramatic language   Friedrich's facetious vein
was sometimes rather difficult to keep in check   Jarno was
seldom there

It being observed that excellent works of art were very rare
in latter times, it was remarked by the Marchese   " We can
hardly think or estimate how many circu stances must combine in favour of the artist   with the greatest genius, with the
ost decisive talent, the demands which he must make upon
himself are infinite, the diligence required in cultivating his
endowments is unspeakable   Now, if circumstances are not in
his favour, if he observed that the world is very easy to be
satisfied, requiring but a slight, pleasing, transitory show, it
were matter of surprise, if indolence and selfishness did not
keep him fixed at mediocrity, it were strange if he did not
rather think of bartering modish wares for gold and praises,
than of entering on the proper path, which could not fail in
some degree to lead him to a sort of painful martyrdom
Accordingly, the artists of our time are always offering and

never giving   They always aim at charming, and they never satisfy   everything is merely indicated, you can nowhere find foundation or completion   Those for whom they labour, it is true, are little better   If you wait a while in any gallery of pictures, and observe what works attract the many, what are praised and what neglected, you have little pleasure in the present, little hope in the future "

"Yes," replied the Abbé, "and thus it is that artists and their judges mutually form each other   The latter ask for nothing but a general vague enjoyment, a work of art is to delight them almost as a work of nature, they imagine that the organs for enjoying works of art may be cultivated altogether of themselves, like the tongue and the palate, they try a picture or a poem as they do an article of food   They do not understand how very different a species of culture it requires to raise one to the true enjoyment of art   The hardest part of it, in my opinion, is that sort of separation, which a man that aims at perfect culture must accomplish in himself   It is on this account that we observe so many people partially cultivated, and yet every one of them attempting to pronounce upon the general whole "

"Your last remark is not quite clear to me," said Jarno, who came in just then

"It would be difficult," replied the Abbé, "to explain it fully without a long detail   Thus much I may say   When any man pretends to mix in manifold activity or manifold enjoyment, he must also be enabled as it were to make his organs manifold and independent of each other   Whoever aims at doing or enjoying all and everything with his entire nature, whoever tries to link together all that is without him by such a species of enjoyment, will only lose his time in efforts that can never be successful   How difficult, though it seems so easy, is it to contemplate a noble disposition, a fine picture simply in and for itself, to watch the music for the music's sake, to admire the actor in the actor, to take pleasure in a building for its own peculiar harmony and dura-

bility ! Most men are wont to treat a work of art, though
fixed and done, as if it were a piece of soft clay   The hard
and polished marble is again to mould itself, the film-walled
edifice is to contract or to expand itself, according as their
inclinations, sentiments and whims may dictate, the picture
is to be instructive, the play to make us better, everything
is to do all   The reason is, that most men are themselves
unformed, they cannot give themselves and their being any
certain shape   and thus they strive to take from other things
their proper shape, that all they have to do with may be loose
and wavering like themselves   Everything is, in the long-run,
reduced by them to what they call effect, everything is relative,
say they, and so indeed it is, everything with them grows
relative, except absurdity and platitude, which truly are
absolute enough "

"I understand you," answered Jarno, " or rather I perceive
how what you have been saying follows from the principles
you hold so fast by   Yet with men, poor devils, we should
not go to quest so strictly   I know enow of them in truth,
who, beside the greatest works of art and nature, forthwith
recollect their own most paltry insufficiency, who take their
conscience and their morals with them to the opera, who
bethink them of their loves and hatreds in contemplating a
colonnade   The best and greatest that can be presented to
them from without, they must first, as far as possible, diminish
in their way of representing it, that they may in any measure
be enabled to combine it with their own sorry nature "

CHAPTER VIII

THE Abbé called them, in the evening, to attend the
obsequies of Mignon   The company proceeded to the Hall of
the Past, they found it magnificently ornamented and illuminated   The walls were hung with azure tapestry almost from
ceiling to floor, so that nothing but the friezes and socles,

above and below, were visible   On the four candelabra in the
corners, large wax-lights were burning, smaller lights were in
the four smaller candelabra placed by the sarcophagus in the
middle   Near this stood four Boys, dressed in azure with
silver, they had broad fans of ostrich feathers, which they
waved above a figure that was resting upon the sarcophagus
The company sat down   two invisible Choruses began in a soft
musical recitative to ask   " Whom bring ye us to the still
dwelling?"   The four Boys replied with lovely voices "'Tis
a tired playmate whom we bring you, let her rest in your still
dwelling, till the songs of her heavenly sisters once more
awaken her "

CHORUS

Firstling of youth in our circle, we welcome thee!   With
sadness welcome thee!   May no boy, no maiden follow!   Let
age only, willing and composed, approach the silent Hall, and
in the solemn company, repose this one dear child!

BOYS

Ah, reluctantly we brought her hither!   Ah, and she is to
remain here!   Let us too remain, let us weep, let us weep
upon her bier!

CHORUS

Yet look at the strong wings, look at the light clear robe!
How glitters the golden band upon her head!   Look at the
beautiful, the noble repose!

BOYS

Ah! the wings do not raise her, in the frolic game, her
robe flutters to and fro no more, when we bound her head
with roses, her looks on us were kind and friendly

CHORUS

Cast forward the eye of the spirit!   Awake in your souls

the imaginative power, which carries forth, what is fairest, what is highest, Life, away beyond the stars

BOYS

But ah ! we find her not here , in the garden she wanders not , the flowers of the meadow she plucks no longer   Let us weep, we are leaving her here !   Let us weep and remain with her !

CHORUS

Children, turn back into life !   Your tears let the fresh air dry, which plays upon the rushing water   Fly from Night ! Day and Pleasure and Continuance are the lot of the living

BOYS

Up !   Turn back into life !   Let the day give us labour and pleasure, till the evening brings us rest, and the nightly sleep refreshes us

CHORUS

Children !   Hasten into life !   In the pure garments of beauty, may Love meet you with heavenly looks and with the wreath of immortality !

The Boys had retired , the Abbé rose from his seat, and went behind the bier   "It is the appointment," said he, " of the Man who prepared this silent abode, that each new tenant of it shall be introduced with a solemnity   After him, the builder of this mansion, the founder of this establishment, we have next brought a young stranger hither   and thus already does this little space contain two altogether different victims of the rigorous, arbitrary, and inexorable Death-goddess   By appointed laws we enter into life , the days are numbered which make us ripe to see the light , but for the duration of our life there is no law   The weakest thread will spin itself to unexpected length , and the strongest is cut suddenly under by the scissors of the Fates, delighting, as it seems, in

contradictions   Of the child, whom we have here committed
to her final rest, we can say but little   It is still uncertain
whence she came , her parents we know not , the years of her
life we can only conjecture   Her deep and closely-shrouded
soul allowed us scaice to guess at its interior movements
there was nothing clear in her, nothing open but her affection
for the man, who had snatched her from the hands of a
barbaiian.   This impassioned tenderness, this vivid gratitude,
appeared to be the flame which consumed the oil of her life
the skill of the physician could not save that fair life, the most
anxious friendship could not lengthen it.   But if art could
not stay the departing spiiit, it has done its utmost to pieserve
the body, and withdraw it from decay   A balsamic substance
has been forced through all the veins, and now tinges, in place
of blood, these cheeks too early faded   Come neai, my friends,
and view this wonder of art and care ! "

He raised the veil   the child was lying in her angel's-dress,
as if asleep, in the most soft and graceful posture   They
appioached, and admired this show of life   Wilhelm alone
continued sitting in his place   he was not able to compose
himself   what he felt, he durst not think , and eveiy thought
seemed ready to destroy his feeling

For the sake of the Marchese, the speech had been pronounced in Fiench   That nobleman came forwaid with the
rest, and viewed the figure with attention   The Abbé thus
proceeded   "With a holy confidence, this kind heait, shut
up to men, was continually turned to its God   Humility,
nay, an inclination to abase heiself externally, seemed natuial
to her   She clave with zeal to the Catholic ieligion, in which
she had been born and educated   Often she expressed a still
wish to sleep on consecrated ground : and according to the
usage of the church, we have therefore consecrated this
marble coffin, and the little earth which is hidden in the
cushion that supports her head   With what ardour did she
in her last moments kiss the image of the Crucified, which
stood beautifully figured on her tender arm, with many

hundred points!" So saying, he stripped up her right
sleeve, and a crucifix, with marks and letters round it,
showed itself in blue upon the white skin

The Marchese looked at this with eagerness, stooping down
to view it more intensely "O God!" cried he, as he stood
upright, and raised his hands to Heaven "Poor child!
Unhappy niece! Do I meet thee here! What a painful
joy to find thee, whom we had long lost hope of, to find
this dear frame, which we had long believed the prey of
fishes in the ocean, here preserved, though lifeless! I assist
at thy funeral, splendid in its external circumstances, still
ore splendid from the noble persons who attend thee to thy
place of rest And to these," added he with a faltering
voice, "so soon as I can speak, I will express my thanks"

Tears hindered him from saying more By the pressure of
a spring, the Abbé sank the body into the cavity of the
marble Four Youths, dressed as the Boys had been, came
out from behind the tapestry, and lifting the heavy, beautifully ornamented lid upon the coffin, thus began their song

THE YOUTHS

Well is the treasure now laid up, the fair image of the
Past! Here sleeps it in the marble, undecaying, in your
hearts too it lives, it works Travel, travel, back into life!
Take along with you this holy Earnestness,—for Earnestness
alone makes life eternity

The invisible Chorus joined in with the last words but no
one heard the strengthening sentiment, all were too much
busied with themselves, and the emotions which these wonderful disclosures had excited. The Abbé and Natalia conducted
the Marchese out, Theresa and Lothario walked by Wilhelm
It was not till the music had altogether died away, that their
sorrows, thoughts, meditations, curiosity again fell on them
with all their force, and made them long to be transported
back into that exalting scene

CHAPTER IX

THE Marchese avoided speaking of the matter, but had long secret conversations with the Abbé   When the Company was met, he often asked for music, a request to which they willingly assented, as each was glad to be delivered from the charge of talking   Thus they lived for some time, till it was observed that he was making preparations for departure   One day he said to Wilhelm "I wish not to disturb the remains of this beloved child, let her rest in the place where she loved and suffered   but her friends must promise to visit me in her native country, in the scene where she was born and bred, they must see the pillars and statues, of which a dim idea remained with her   I will lead you to the bays, where she liked so well to roam and gather pebbles   You, at least, young friend, shall not escape the gratitude of a family that stands so deeply indebted to you   Tomorrow I set out on my journey   The Abbé is acquainted with the whole history of this matter   he will tell it you again   He could pardon me when grief interrupted my recital, as a third party he will be enabled to narrate the incidents with more connexion   If, as the Abbé had proposed, you like to follow me in travelling over Germany, you shall be heartily welcome   Leave not your boy behind   at every little inconvenience which he causes us, we will again remember your attentive care of my poor niece "

The same evening, our party was surprised by the arrival of the Countess   Wilhelm trembled in every joint as she entered   she herself, though forewarned, kept close by her sister, who speedily reached her a chair   How singularly simple was her attire, how altered was her form !   Wilhelm scarcely dared to look at her   she saluted him with a kindly air, a few general words addressed to him did not conceal her sentiments and feelings   The Marchese had retired betimes, and as the company were not disposed to part so early, the Abbé now produced a manuscript "The singular narrative which was intrusted to me," said he, "I forthwith put on paper The case where pen and ink should least of all be spared, is in recording the particular circumstances of remarkable events" They informed the Countess of the matter, and the Abbé read as follows, in the name of the Marchese

"Many men as I have seen, I still regard my father as a very extraordinary person His character was noble and upright, his ideas were enlarged, I may even say great, to hi self he was severe, in all his plans there was a rigid order, in all his operations an unbroken perseverance In one sense, therefore, it was easy to transact and live with him yet owing to the very qualities which made it so, he never could accommodate himself to life, for he required from the state, from his neighbours, from his children and his servants, the observance of all the laws which he had laid upon himself His most moderate demands became exorbitant by his rigour and he never could attain to enjoyment, for nothing ever was completed as he had forecast it At the moment when he was erecting a palace, laying out a garden, or acquiring a large estate in the highest cultivation, I have seen him inwardly convinced, with the sternest ire, that Fate had doomed him to do nothing but abstain and suffer In his exterior, he maintained the greatest dignity, if he jested, it was but displaying the preponderancy of his understanding Censure was intolerable to him, the only time I ever saw him quite transported with rage, was once when he heard that one of his establishments was spoken of as something ludicrous In the same spirit, he had settled the disposal of his children and his fortune My eldest brother was educated as a person that had large estates to look for I was to embrace the clerical profession, the youngest was to be a soldier I was of a lively temper, fiery, active, quick, apt for corporeal exercises the youngest rather seemed inclined to an enthusiastic quietism, devoted to the sciences, to music and poetry.

It was not till after the hardest struggle, the maturest
conviction of the impossibility of his project, that our father,
still reluctantly, agreed to let us change vocations, and
although he saw us both contented, he could never suit
himself to this arrangement, but declared that nothing good
would come of it   The older he grew, the more isolated did
he feel himself from all society   At last he came to live
almost entirely alone   One old friend, who had served in
the German armies, who had lost his wife in the campaign,
and brought a daughter of about ten years of age along with
him, remained his only visitor   This person bought a fine
little property beside us he used to come and see my father
on stated days of the week, and at stated hours, his little
daughter often came along with him   He was never heard
to contradict my father, who at length grew perfectly
habituated to him, and endured him as the only tolerable
company he had   After our father's death, we easily observed
that this old gentleman had not been visiting for naught, that
his compliances had been rewarded by an ample settlement
He enlarged his estates, his daughter might expect a handsome portion   The girl grew up, and was extremely beautiful my elder brother often joked with me about her, saying
I should go and court her

"Meanwhile brother Augustin, in the seclusion of his
cloister, had been spending his years in the strangest state
of mind   He abandoned himself wholly to the feeling of a
holy enthusiasm, to those half-spiritual, half-physical emotions, which, as they for a time exalted him to the third
heaven, ere long sank him down to an abyss of powerlessness
and vacant misery   While my father lived, no change could
be contemplated   what indeed could we have asked for or
proposed ? After the old man's death, our brother visited us
frequently his situation, which at first afflicted us, in time
became much more tolerable for his reason had at length
prevailed.   But the more confidently reason promised him
complete recovery and contentment on the pure part of

nature, the more vehemently did he require of us to free him from his vows   His thoughts, he let us know, were turned upon Sperata, our fair neighbour

" My elder brother had experienced too much suffering from the harshness of our father, to look on the condition of the youngest without sympathy   We spoke with the family confessor, a worthy old man, we signified to him the double purpose of our brother, and requested him to introduce and expedite the business   Contrary to custom, he delayed   and at last, when Augustin pressed us, and we recommended the affair more keenly to the clergyman, he had nothing left but to impart the strange secret to us

" Sperata was our sister, and that by both her parents   Our mother had declared herself with child at a time when both she and our father were advanced in years, a similar occurrence had shortly before been made the subject of some merriment in our neighbourhood, and our father, to avoid such ridicule, determined to conceal this late lawful fruit of love as carefully as people use to conceal its earlier accidental fruits   Our mother was delivered secretly, the child was carried to the country, and the old friend of the family, who, with the confessor, had alone been trusted with the secret, easily engaged to give her out for his daughter   The confessor had reserved the right of disclosing the secret in case of extremity   The supposed father was now dead, Sperata was living with an old lady, we were aware that a love of song and music had already led our brother to her, and on his again requiring us to undo his former bond, that he might engage himself by a new one, it was necessary that we should, as soon as possible, apprise him of the danger he stood in

" He viewed us with a wild contemptuous look   ' Spare your idle tales,' cried he, ' for children and credulous fools, from me, from my heart, they shall not tear Sperata, she is mine   Recall, I pray you, instantly, your frightful spectre, which would but harass me in vain   Sperata is not my sister, she is my wife !'   He described to us, in rapturous terms, how

this heavenly girl had drawn him out of his unnatural state of
separation from his fellow-creatures into true life, how their
spirits accorded like their voices, how he blessed his sufferings
and errors, since they had kept clear of women, till the moment
when he wholly and forever gave himself to this most amiable
being   We were shocked at the discovery, we deplored his
situation, but we knew not how to help ourselves, for he
declared with violence, that Sperata had a child by him within
her bosom   Our confessor did whatever duty could suggest to
him, but by this means he only made the evil worse   The
relations of nature and religion, moral rights and civil laws,
were vehemently attacked and spurned at by our brother
He considered nothing holy but his relation to Sperata,
nothing dignified but the names of father and wife   'These
alone,' cried he, ' are suitable to nature, all else is caprice and
opinion   Were there not noble nations which admitted marriage with a sister?   Name not your gods!   You never name
them but when you wish to befool us, to lead us from the
paths of nature, and, by scandalous constraint, to transform
the noblest inclinations into crimes   Unspeakable are the
perplexities, abominable the abuses, into which you force the
victims whom you bury alive

    " ' I may speak, for I have suffered like no other, from the
highest, sweetest feeling of enthusiasm, to the frightful deserts
of utter powerlessness, vacancy, annihilation and despair,
from the loftiest aspirations of preternatural existence, to the
most entire unbelief, unbelief in myself   All these horrid
grounds of the cup, so flattering at the brim, I have drained,
and my whole being was poisoned to its core   And now,
when kind Nature, by her greatest gift, by love, has healed
me, now, when in the arms of a heavenly creature, I again
feel that I am, that she is, that out of this living union a
third shall arise and smile in our faces, now ye open up the
flames of your Hell, of your Purgatory, which can only singe
a sick imagination, ye oppose them to the vivid, true, indestructible enjoyment of pure love!   Meet us under these

cypresses, which turn their solemn tops to heaven, visit us among those espaliers where the citrons and pomegranates bloom beside us, where the graceful myrtle stretches out its tender flowers to us, and then venture to disturb us with your dreary, paltry nets which men have spun!'

"Thus for a long time he persisted in a stubborn disbelief of our story, and when we assured him of its truth, when the confessor himself asseverated it, he did not let it drive him from his point. 'Ask not the echoes of your cloisters, not your mouldering parchments, not your narrow whims and ordinances! Ask Nature and your heart, she will teach you what you should recoil from, she will point out to you with the strictest finger, over what she has pronounced her everlasting curse. Look at the lilies do not husband and wife shoot forth on the same stalk? Does not the flower which bore them, hold them both? And is not the lily the type of innocence, is not their sisterly union fruitful? When Nature abhors, she speaks it aloud, the creature that shall not be is not produced, the creature that lives with a false life is soon destroyed. Unfruitfulness, painful existence, early destruction, these are her curses, the marks of her displeasure. It is only by immediate consequences that she punishes. Look around you, and what is prohibited, what is accursed, will force itself upon your notice. In the silence of the convent, in the tumult of the world, a thousand practices are consecrated and revered, while her curse rests on them. On stagnant idleness as on overstrained toil, on caprice and superfluity as on constraint and want, she looks down with mournful eyes. her call is to moderation, true are all her commandments, peaceful all her influences. The man who has suffered as I have done has a right to be free. Sperata is mine, death alone shall take her from me. How I shall retain her, how I may be happy, these are your cares! This instant I go to her, and part from her no more'

"He was for proceeding to the boat, and crossing over to her we restrained him, entreating that he would not take a

step, which might produce the most tremendous consequences.
He should recollect, we told him, that he was not living in the
free world of his own thoughts and ideas, but in a constitution of affairs, whose ordinances and relations had become inflexible as laws of nature The confessor made us promise not
to let him leave our sight, still less our house after this he
went away, engaging to return ere long What we had fore-
seen took place reason had made our brother strong, but his
heart was weak, the earlier impressions of religion rose on
him, and dreadful doubts along with them He passed two
fearful nights and days the confessor came again to his
assistance, but in vain! His enfranchised understanding
acquitted him his feelings, religion, all his usual ideas
declared him guilty

" One morning, we found his chamber empty on the table
lay a note, in which he signified that, as we kept him prisoner
by force, he felt himself entitled to provide for his freedom,
that he meant to go directly to Sperata, he expected to escape
with her, and was prepared for the most terrible extremities,
should any separation be attempted

" The news of course affrighted us exceedingly, but the
confessor bade us be at rest Our poor brother had been
narrowly enough observed the boatman, in place of taking
him across, proceeded with him to his cloister Fatigued with
watching for the space of four-and-twenty hours, he fell
asleep, as the skiff began to rock him in the moonshine, and
he did not awake, till he saw himself in the hands of his
spiritual brethren, he did not recover from his amazement,
till he heard the doors of the convent bolting behind him

" Sharply touched at the fate of our brother, we reproached
the confessor for his cruelty, but he soon silenced or convinced us by the surgeon's reason, that our pity was destructive
to the patient He let us know that he was not acting on
his own authority, but by order of the bishop and his chapter,
that by this proceeding, they intended to avoid all public
scandal, and to shroud the sad occurrence under the veil of a

secret course of discipline prescribed by the Church   Our
sister they would spare, she was not to be told that her lover
was her brother   The charge of her was given to a priest, to
whom she had before disclosed her situation   They contrived
to hide her pregnancy and her delivery   As a mother she felt
altogether happy in her little one   Like most of our women,
she could neither write, nor read writing   she gave the priest
many verbal messages to carry to her lover   The latter,
thinking that he owed this pious fraud to a suckling mother,
often brought pretended tidings from our brother, whom he
never saw, recommending her, in his name, to be at peace,
begging of her to be careful of herself and of her child, and
for the rest to trust in God

"Sperata was inclined by nature to religious feelings. Her
situation, her solitude increased this tendency, the clergyman
encouraged it, in order to prepare her by degrees for an
eternal separation   Scarcely was her child weaned, scarcely
did he think her body strong enough for suffering agony of
mind, when he began to paint her fault to her in most terrific
colours, to treat the crime of being connected with a priest as
a sort of sin against nature, as a sort of incest   For he had
taken up the strange thought of making her repentance equal
in intensity to what it would have been, had she known the
true circumstances of her error   He thereby produced so
much anxiety and sorrow in her mind, he so exalted the idea
of the Church and of its head before her, showed her the
awful consequences, for the weal of all men's souls, should
indulgence in a case like this be granted, and the guilty pair
rewarded by a lawful union, signifying too how wholesome it
was to expiate such sins in time, and thereby gain the crown
of immortality,—that at last, like a poor criminal, she willingly
held out her neck to the axe, and earnestly entreated that she
might forever be divided from our brother   Having gained so
much, the clergy left her the liberty (reserving to themselves a
certain distant oversight) to live at one time in a convent, at
another in her house, according as she afterwards thought good

"Her little girl meanwhile was glowing from her earliest years, she had displayed an extraordinary disposition   When still very young, she could run, and move with wonderful dexterity, she sang beautifully, and learned to play upon the cithern almost of herself   With words, however, she could not express herself, and the impediment seemed rather to proceed from her mode of thought, than from her organs of speech   The feelings of the poor mother to her, in the mean time, were of the most painful kind   the expostulations of the priest had so perplexed her mind, that though she was not quite deranged, her state was far from being sane   She daily thought her crime more terrible and punishable, the clergy-man's comparison of incest, frequently repeated, had impressed itself so deeply, that her horror was not less than if the actual circumstances had been known to her   The priest took no small credit for his ingenuity, with which he had contrived to tear asunder a luckless creature's heart   It was miserable to behold maternal love, ready to expand itself in joy at the existence of her child, contending with the horrid feeling, that this child should not be there   The two emotions strove together in her soul, love was often weaker than aversion

"The child had long ago been taken from her, and com-mitted to a worthy family residing on the sea-shore   In the greater freedom, which the little creature enjoyed here, she soon displayed her singular delight in climbing   To mount the highest peaks, to run along the edges of the ships, to imitate in all their strangest feats the rope-dancers, whom she often saw in the place, seemed a natural tendency in her

" To practise these things with the greater ease, she liked to change clothes with boys   and though her foster parents thought this highly blameable and unbecoming, we bade them indulge her as much as possible   Her wild walks and leapings often led her to a distance, she would lose her way, and be long from home, but she always came back   In general, as she returned, she used to set herself beneath the columns in the portal of a country house in the neighbourhood. her

people now had ceased to look for her, they waited for her
She would there lie resting on the steps, then run up and
down the large hall, looking at the statues, after which, if
nothing specially detained her, she used to hasten home

"But at last our confidence was balked, and our indulgence
punished The child went out, and did not come again her
little hat was found swimming on the water, near the spot
where a torrent rushes down into the sea It was conjectured
that, in clambering among the rocks, her foot had slipped, all
our searching could not find the body

" The thoughtless tattle of her house-mates soon communicated the occurrence to Sperata, she seemed calm and cheerful when she heard it, hinting not obscurely at her satisfaction
that God had pleased to take her poor child to himself, and
thus preserved it from suffering or causing some more dreadful
misery

" On this occasion, all the fables which are told about our
waters came to be the common talk The sea, it was said.
required every year an innocent child yet it would endure no
corpse, but sooner or later throw it to the shore, nay, the last
joint, though sunk to the lowest bottom, must again come
forth They told the story of a mother, inconsolable because
her child had perished in the sea, who prayed to God and his
saints to grant her at least the bones for burial The first
storm threw ashore the skull, the next the spine, and after all
was gathered, she wrapped the bones in a cloth, and took them
to the church but O ! miraculous to tell ! as she crossed the
threshold of the temple, the packet grew heavier and heavier,
and at last, when she laid it on the steps of the altar, the
child began to cry, and issued living from the cloth One
joint of the right-hand little finger was alone wanting this
too the mother anxiously sought and found, and in memory of
the event it was preserved among the other relics of the church

" On poor Sperata these recitals made a deep impression,
her imagination took a new flight, and favoured the emotion
of her heart. She supposed that now the child had expiated

by its death, both its own sins, and the sins of its parents
that the curse and penalty, which hitherto had overhung them
all, was at length wholly removed, that nothing more was
necessary, could she only find the child's bones, that she might
carry them to Rome, where upon the steps of the great altar
in St Peter's, her little girl, again covered with its fair fresh
skin, would stand up alive before the people With its own
eyes it would once more look on father and mother, and the
Pope, convinced that God and his saints commanded it, would,
amid the acclamations of the people, remit the parents their
sins, acquit them of their oaths, and join their hands in wedlock

"Her looks and her anxiety were henceforth constantly
directed to the sea and the beach When, at night in the
moonshine, the waves were tossing to and fro, she thought
every glittering sheet of foam was bringing out her child,
and some one about her had to run off, as if to take it up
when it should reach the shore

"By day she walked unweariedly along the places where the
pebbly beach shelved slowly to the water she gathered, in a
little basket, all the bones which she could find None durst
tell her that they were the bones of animals the larger ones
she buried, the little ones she took along with her In this
employment she incessantly persisted The clergyman, who,
by so unremittingly discharging what he thought his duty,
had reduced her to this condition, now stood up for her with
all his might By his influence, the people in the neighbourhood were made to look upon her not as a distracted person,
but as one entranced they stood in reverent attitudes as she
walked by, and the children ran to kiss her hand

"To the old woman, her attendant and faithful friend, the
secret of Sperata's guilt was at length imparted by the priest,
on her solemnly engaging to watch over the unhappy creature
with untiring care, through all her life And she kept this
engagement to the last, with admirable conscientiousness and
patience

"Meanwhile we had always had an eye upon our brother

Neither the physicians nor the clergy of his convent would allow us to be seen by him but, in order to convince us of his being well in some sort, we had leave to look at him as often as we liked, in the garden, the passages, or even through a window in the roof of his apartment

"After many terrible and singular changes, which I shall omit, he had passed into a strange state of mental rest and bodily unrest He never sat but when he took his harp and played upon it, and then he usually accompanied it with singing At other times, he kept continually in motion , and in all things he was grown extremely guidable and pliant, for all his passions seemed to have resolved themselves into the single fear of death You could persuade him to do anything, by threatening him with dangerous sickness or with death

"Besides this singularity of walking constantly about the cloister, a practice which he hinted it were better to exchange for wandering over hill and dale, he talked about an Apparition which perpetually tormented him He declared, that on awakening, at whatever hour of the night, he saw a beautiful boy standing at the foot of his bed, with a bare knife, and threatening to destroy him They shifted him to various other chambers of the convent , but he still asserted that the boy pursued him His wandering to and fro become more unrestful the people afterwards remembered too, that at this time they had often seen him standing at the window looking out upon the sea

"Our poor sister, on the other hand, seemed gradually wasting under the consuming influence of her single thought, of her narrow occupation It was at last proposed by the physician, that among the bones which she had gathered, the fragments of a child's skeleton should by degrees be introduced , and so the hapless mother's hopes kept up The experiment was dubious , but this at least seemed likely to be gained by it, that when all the parts were got together, she would cease her weary search, and might be entertained with hopes of going to Rome.

"It was accordingly resolved on her attendant changed, by imperceptible degrees, the small remains committed to her with the bones Speiata found An inconceivable delight arose in the poor sick woman's heart, when the parts began to fit each other, and the shape of those still wanting could be marked She had fastened every fragment in its proper place with threads and ribbons, filling up the vacant spaces with e broidery and silk, as is usually done with the relics of saints

"In this way nearly all the bones had been collected, none but a few of the extremities were wanting One morning, while she was asleep, the physician having come to ask for her, the old attendant, with a view to show him how his patient occupied herself, took away these dear remains from the little chest where they lay in poor Speiata's bedroom A few minutes afterwards, they heard her spring upon the floor, she lifted up the cloth and found the chest empty She threw herself upon her knees, they came and listened to her joyful ardent prayer 'Yes!' exclaimed she, 'it is true, it was no dream, it is real! Rejoice with me, my friends! I have seen my own beautiful good little girl again alive She arose and threw the veil from off her, her splendour enlightened all the room, her beauty was transfigured to celestial loveliness, she could not tread the ground, although she wished it Lightly was she borne aloft, she had not even time to stretch her hand to me *There!* cried she to me, and pointed to the road where I am soon to go Yes, I will follow her, soon follow her, my heart is light to think of it My sorrows are already vanished, the sight of my risen little one has given me a foretaste of the heavenly joys'

"From that time her soul was wholly occupied with prospects of the brightest kind she gave no farther heed to any earthly object, she took but little food, her spirit by degrees cast off the fetters of the body At last this imperceptible gradation reached its head unexpectedly her attendants found her pale and motionless, she opened not her eyes, she was what we call dead

"The report of her vision quickly spread abroad among the people, and the reverential feeling, which she had excited in her lifetime, soon changed, at her death, to the thought that she should be regarded as in bliss, nay, as in sanctity

"When we were bearing her to be interred, a crowd of persons pressed with boundless violence about the bier, they would touch her hand, they would touch her garment In this impassioned elevation, various sick persons ceased to feel the pains by which at other times they were tormented they looked upon themselves as healed, they declared it, they praised God and his new saint The clergy were obliged to lay the body in a neighbouring chapel, the people called for opportunity to offer their devotion The concourse was incredible, the mountaineers, at all times prone to lively and religious feelings, crowded forward from their valleys, the reverence, the wonder, the adoration daily spread and gathered strength The ordinances of the bishop, which were meant to limit, and in time abolish this new worship, could not be put in execution every show of opposition raised the people into tumults, every unbeliever they were ready to assail with personal violence 'Did not Saint Borromæus,' cried they, 'dwell among our forefathers? Did not his mother live to taste the joy of his canonisation? Was not that great figure on the rocks at Arona meant to represent to us, by a sensible symbol, his spiritual greatness? Do not the descendants of his kindred live among us to this hour? And has not God promised ever to renew his miracles among a people that believe?'

"As the body, after several days, exhibited no marks of putrefaction, but grew whiter, and as it were translucent, the general faith rose higher and higher Among the multitude were several cures, which even the sceptical observer was unable to account for, or ascribe entirely to fraud The whole country was in motion, those who did not go to see it, heard at least no other topic talked of

"The convent, where my brother lived, resounded, like the

land at large, with the noise of these wonders, and the people felt the less restraint in speaking of them in his presence, as in general he seemed to pay no heed to anything, and his connexion with the circumstance was known to none of them But on this occasion, it appeared, he had listened with attention He conducted his escape with such dexterity and cunning, that the manner of it still remains a mystery We learned afterwards, that he had crossed the water with a number of travellers, and charged the boatmen, who observed no other singularity about him, above all to have a care lest their vessel overset Late in the night, he reached the chapel, where his hapless loved one was resting from her woes Only a few devotees were kneeling in the corners of the place, her old friend was sitting at the head of the corpse, he walked up to her, saluted her, and asked how her mistress was 'You see it,' answered she with some embarrassment He looked at the corpse with a sidelong glance After some delay he took its hand Frightened by its coldness, he in the instant let it go he looked unrestfully around him, then turning to the old attendant 'I cannot stay with her at present,' said he, 'I have a long, long way to travel, but at the proper time I shall be back tell her so when she awakens'

"With this he went away It was a while before we got intelligence of these occurrences we searched, but all our efforts to discover him were vain How he worked his way across the mountains, none can say A long time after he was gone, we came upon a trace of him among the Grisons, but we were too late, it quickly vanished We supposed that he was gone to Germany, but his weak foot-prints had been speedily obliterated by the war"

CHAPTER X

THE Abbé ceased to read no one had listened without tears The Countess scarcely ever took her handkerchief from her eyes, at last she rose, and, with Natalia, left the room

The rest were silent, till the Abbé thus began, "The question now arises, whether we shall let the good Marchese leave us without telling him our secret For who can doubt a moment, that our Harper and his brother Augustin are one? Let us consider what is to be done, both for the sake of that unhappy man himself, and of his family. My advice is, not to hurry, but to wait till we have heard what news the Doctor, who is gone to see him, brings us back "

All were of the same opinion, and the Abbé thus proceeded "Another question, which perhaps may be disposed of sooner, still remains The Marchese is affected to the bottom of his heart, at the kindness which his poor niece experienced here, particularly from our young friend He ade me tell him, and repeat to him every circumstance connected with her, and he showed the liveliest gratitude on hearing it 'Her young benefactor,' he said, 'refused to travel with me, while he knew not the connexion that subsists between us I am not now a stranger, of whose manner of existence, of whose humours he might be uncertain I am his associate, his relation, and as his unwillingness to leave his boy behind was the impediment which kept him from accompanying me, let this child now become a fairer bond to join us still more closely Besides the services which I already owe him, let him be of service to me on my present journey let him then return along with me, my elder brother will receive him as he ought And let him not despise the heritage of his unhappy foster-child for by a secret stipulation of our father with his military friend, the fortune which he gave Sperata has returned to us and certainly we will not cheat our niece's benefactor of the recompense which he has merited so well '"

Theresa, taking Wilhelm by the hand, now said to him "We have here another beautiful example that disinterested well-doing yields the highest and best return Follow the call, which so strangely comes to you and while you lay a double load of gratitude on the Marchese, hasten to a fair land, which has already often drawn your heart and your imagination towards it "

"I leave myself entirely to the guidance of my friends and you," said Wilhelm "it is vain to think, in this world, of adhering to our individual will   What I purposed to hold fast, I must let go, and benefits which I have not deserved, descend upon me of their own accord "

With a gentle pressure of Theresa's hand, Wilhelm took his own away   "I give you full permission," said he to the Abbé, "to decide about me as you please   Since I shall not need to leave my Felix, I am ready to go anywhither, and to undertake whatever you think good "

Thus authorised, the Abbé forthwith sketched out his plan The Marchese, he proposed, should be allowed to depart, Wilhelm was to wait for tidings from the Doctor, he might then, when they had settled what was to be done, set off with Felix   Accordingly, under the pretence that Wilhelm's preparations for his journey would detain him, he advised the stranger to employ the mean while in examining the curiosities of the city, which he meant to visit   The Marchese did in consequence depart, and not without renewed and strong expressions of his gratitude, of which indeed the presents left by him, including jewels, precious stones, embroidered stuffs, afforded a sufficient proof

Wilhelm too was at length in readiness for travelling, and his friends began to be distressed that the Doctor sent them no news   They feared some mischief had befallen the poor old Harper, at the very moment when they were in hopes of radically improving his condition   They sent the courier off, but he was scarcely gone, when the Doctor in the evening entered with a stranger, whose form and aspect were expressive, earnest, striking, and whom no one knew   Both stood silent for a space, the stranger at length went up to Wilhelm, and holding out his hand said   "Do you not know your old friend, then?"   It was the Harper's voice, but of his form there seemed to remain no vestige   He was in the common garb of a traveller, cleanly and genteelly equipt, his beard had vanished, his hair was dressed with some attention to the mode, and what particularly made him quite irrecognisable was, that in his countenance the look of age was no longer visible Wilhelm embraced him with the liveliest joy, he w presented to the rest, and behaved himself with great propriety, not knowing that the party had a little while before become so well acquainted with him " You will have patience with a man," continued he with great composure, " who, grown up as he appears, is entering on the world, after long sorrows, inexperienced as a child   To this skilful gentleman I stand indebted for the privilege of again appearing in the company of my fellow-men "

They bade him welcome the Doctor motioned for a walk, to interrupt the conversation, and lead it to indifferent topics

In private, the Doctor gave the following explanation " It was by the strangest chance that we succeeded in the cure of this man   We had long treated him, morally and physically, as our best consideration dictated in some degree the plan was efficacious, but the fear of death continued powerful in him, and he would not lay aside his beard and cloak   For the rest, however, he appeared to take more interest in external things than formerly, and both his songs and his conceptions seemed to be approaching nearer life   A strange letter from the clergyman, as you already know, called me from you   I arrived   I found our patient altogether changed, he had voluntarily given up his beard, he had let his locks be cut into a customary form, he asked for common clothes, he seemed to have at once become another man   Though curious to penetrate the reason of this sudden alteration, we did not risk inquiring of himself at last we accidentally discovered it   A glass of laudanum was missing from the Parson's private laboratory we thought it right to institute a strict inquiry on the subject, every one endeavoured to ward off suspicion, and the sharpest quarrels arose among the inmates of the house   At last, this man appeared before us, and admitted

that he had the laudanum we asked if he had swallowed
any of it 'No!' said he 'but it is to this that I owe the
recovery of my reason It is at your choice to take the vial
from me, and to drive me back inevitably to my former state
The feeling that it was desirable to see the pains of life terminated by death, first put me on the way of cure, before long
the thought of terminating them by voluntary death arose in
me, and with this intention, I took the glass of poison The
possibility of casting off my load of griefs forever gave me
strength to bear them and thus have I, ever since this talis-
man came into my possession, pressed myself back into life, by
a contiguity with death Be not anxious lest I use the drug,
but resolve, as men acquainted with the human heart, by
granting me an independence of life, to make me properly and
wholesomely dependent on it' After mature consideration of
the matter, we determined not to meddle farther with him
and he now carries with him, in a firm little ground-glass vial,
this poison, of which he has so strangely made an antidote"

The Doctor was informed of all that had transpired since
his departure, towards Augustin, it was determined that they
should observe the deepest silence in regard to it The Abbé
undertook to keep beside him, and to lead him forward on the
healthful path he had entered

Meanwhile Wilhelm was to set about his journey over Germany with the Marchese If it should appear that Augustin
could be again excited to affection for his native country, the
circumstances were to be communicated to his friends, and
Wilhelm might conduct him thither

Wilhelm had at last made every preparation for his journey.
At first the Abbé thought it strange that Augustin rejoiced in
hearing of his friend and benefactor's purpose to depart, but
he soon discovered the foundation of this curious movement
Augustin could not subdue his fear of Felix, and he longed as
soon as possible to see the boy removed

By degrees so many people had assembled, that the Castle
and adjoining buildings could scarcely accommodate them all,

d the less, as such a mutitude of guests had not originally
en anticipated They breakfasted, they dined together,
ch endeavoured to persuade himself that they were living
a comfortable harmony, but each in secret longed in some
gree to be away Theresa frequently rode out attended by
)thalio, and oftener alone, she had already got acquainted
th all the landladies and landlords in the district, for she
ld it as a principle of her economy, in which perhaps she was
t far mistaken, that it is essential to be in good acceptance
th one's neighbours male and female, and to maintain with
em a constant interchange of civilities Of an intended
arriage with Lothario she appeared to have no thought
atalia and the Countess often talked with one another, the
bbé seemed to covet the society of Augustin, Jarno had
equent conversations with the Doctor, Friedrich held by
'ilhelm, Felix ran about, wherever he could meet with most
ausement It was thus too that in general they paired
emselves in walking, when the company broke up when it
is obliged to be together, recourse was quickly had to music,
unite them all by giving each back to himself
Unexpectedly the Count increased the party, intending to
move his lady, and, as it appeared, to take a solemn farewell
' his worldly friends Jarno hastened to the coach to meet
      the Count inquired what guests they had, to which the
her answered, in a fit of wild humour that would often seize
m "We have all the nobility in Nature, Marcheses, Mar-
uses, Milords and Barons we wanted nothing but a Count."
hey came upstairs Wilhelm was the first who met them
   the ante-chamber "Milord," said the Count to him in
rench, after looking at him for a moment, "I rejoice very
uch in the unexpected pleasure of renewing my acquaintance
ith your Lordship I am very much mistaken if I did not
e you at my Castle in the Prince's suite" "I had the
appiness of waiting on your Excellency at that time,"
iswered Wilhelm, "but you do me too much honour when
ou take me for an Englishman, and that of the first quality.

I am a German, and "   " A very brave young fellow," interrupted Jarno   The Count looked at Wilhelm with a smile,
and was about to make some reply, when the rest of the party
entered, and saluted him with many a friendly welcome
They excused themselves for being unable at the moment to
show him to a proper chamber, promising without delay to
make the necessary room for him

"Ay, ay! ' said he, smiling "we have left Chance, I see,
to act as our purveyor   Yet with prudence and arrangement,
how much is possible ! For the present, I entreat you not
to stir a slipper from its place, the disorder, I perceive,
would otherwise be great   Every one would be uncomfortably
lodged, and this no one shall be on my account, if possible,
not even for an hour   You can testify," said he to Jarno,
"and you too, Meister," turning to Wilhelm, "how many
people I commodiously stowed, that time, in my Castle   Let
me have the list of persons and servants, let me see how they
are lodged at present I will make a plan of dislocation, such
that, with the very smallest inconvenience, every one shall find
a suitable apartment, and there shall be room enough to hold
another guest if one should accidentally arrive "

Jarno volunteered to be the Count's assistant, procured him
all the necessary information, taking great delight, as usual, if
he could now and then contrive to lead him astray, and leave
him in awkward difficulties   The old gentleman at last,
however, gained a signal triumph   The arrangement was
completed, he caused the names to be written on their several
doors, himself attending, and it could not be denied that, by
a very few changes and substitutions, the object had been fully
gained   Jarno, among other things, had also managed that
the persons, who at present took an interest in each other,
should be lodged together

" Will you help me," said the Count to Jarno, after everything was settled, " to clear up my recollections of the young
man there, whom you call Meister, and who, you tell me, is a
German ?" Jarno was silent, for he knew very well that the

Count was one of those people who, in asking questions, merely wish to show their knowledge   The Count accordingly continued, without waiting for an answer   " You, I recollect, presented him to me, and warmly recommended him in the Prince's name   If his mother was a German woman, I'll be bound for it his father is an Englishman, and one of rank too who can calculate the English blood that has been flowing, these last thirty years, in German veins !   I do not wish to pump you   I know you have always family secrets of that kind, but in such cases it is in vain to think of cheating me "   He then proceeded to detail a great variety of things as having taken place with Wilhelm at the Castle, to the whole of which Jarno, as before, kept silence, though the Count was altogether in the wrong, confounding Wilhelm more than once with a young Englishman of the Prince's suite.   The truth was, the good old gentleman had in former years possessed a very excellent memory, and was still proud of being able to remember the minutest circumstances of his youth   but in regard to late occurrences, he used to settle in his mind as true, and utter with the greatest certainty, whatever fables and fantastic combinations in the growing weakness of his powers, imagination might present to him   For the rest, he was become extremely mild and courteous, his presence had a very favourable influence upon the company   He would call on them to read some useful book together, nay, he often gave them little games, which, without participating in them, he directed with the greatest care   If they wondered at his condescension, he would reply, that it became a man, who differed from the world in weighty matters, to conform to it the more anxiously in matters of indifference

In these games, our friend had, more than once, an angry and unquiet feeling to endure   Friedrich, with his usual levity, took frequent opportunity of giving hints that Wilhelm entertained a secret passion for Natalia   How could he have found it out ?   What entitled him to say so ?   And would not his friends think that, as they two were often together,

Wilhelm must have made a disclosure to him, so thoughtless and unlucky a disclosure?

One day, while they were merrier than common at some such joke, Augustin, dashing open the door, rushed in with a frightful look, his countenance was pale, his eyes were wild, he seemed about to speak, but his tongue refused its office The party were astounded, Lothario and Jarno, supposing that his madness had returned, sprang up and seized him With a choked and faltering voice, then loudly and violently, he spoke and cried "Not me! Haste! Help! Save the child! Felix is poisoned!"

They let him go, he hastened through the door   all followed him in consternation   They called the Doctor Augustin made for the Abbé's chamber, they found the child, who seemed amazed and frightened, when they called to him from a distance   "What hast thou been doing?"

"Dear papa!" cried Felix, "I did not drink from the bottle, I drank from the glass   I was very thirsty"

Augustin struck his hands together   "He is lost!" cried he, then pressed through the bystanders, and hastened away

They found a glass of almond-milk upon the table, with a bottle near it more than half empty   The Doctor came, was told what they had seen and heard   with horror he observed the well-known laudanum-vial lying empty on the table   He called for vinegar, he summoned all his art to his assistance

Natalia had the little patient taken to a room, she busied herself with painful care about him   The Abbe had run out to seek Augustin, and draw some explanation from him   The unhappy father had been out upon the same endeavour, but in vain   he returned, to find anxiety and fear on every face The Doctor, in the mean time, had been examining the almond-milk in the glass, he found it to contain a powerful mixture of opium   the child was lying on the sofa, seeming very sick, he begged his father "not to let them pour more stuff into him, not to let them plague him any more"   Lothario had sent his people, and had ridden off himself, endeavouring to find some trace of Augustin Natalia sat beside the child, he took refuge in her bosom, and entreated earnestly for her protection, earnestly for a little piece of sugar the vinegar, he said, was biting sour The Doctor granted his request, the child was in a frightful agitation, they were obliged to let him have a moment's rest The Doctor said that every means had been adopted, he would continue to do his utmost The Count came near, with an air of displeasure his look was earnest, even solemn he laid his hands upon the child, turned his eyes to Heaven, and remained some moments in that attitude. Wilhelm, who was lying inconsolable on a seat, sprang up, and casting a despairing look at Natalia, left the room Shortly afterwards the Count too left it

"I cannot understand," said the Doctor, having paused a little, "how it comes that there is not the smallest trace of danger visible about the child At a single gulp, he must have swallowed an immense dose of opium, yet I find no movement in his pulse but what may be ascribed to our remedies, and to the terror we have put him into "

In a few minutes Jarno entered, with intelligence that Augustin had been discovered in the upper story, lying in his blood, a razor had been found beside him, to all appearance he had cut his throat The Doctor hastened out he met the people carrying down the body The unhappy man was laid upon a bed, and accurately examined the cut had gone across the windpipe, copious loss of blood had been succeeded by a swoon, yet it was easy to observe that life, that hope was still there The Doctor put the body in a proper posture, joined the edges of the wound, and bandaged it The night passed sleepless and full of care to all Felix would not quit Natalia Wilhelm sat before her on a stool, he had the boy's feet upon his lap, the head and breast were lying upon hers Thus did they divide the pleasing burden and the painful anxiety, and continue, till the day broke, in their uncomfortable sad position Natalia had given her hand to Wilhelm, they did not speak a word, they looked at the

child and then at one another.   Lothario and Jarno were
sitting at the other end of the room, and carrying on a most
important conversation, which, did not the pressure of events
forbid us, we would gladly lay before our readers   The boy
slept softly, he awoke quite cheerful, early in the morning,
and demanded a piece of bread and butter

So soon as Augustin had in some degree recovered, they
endeavoured to obtain some explanation from him   They
learned with difficulty, and by slow degrees, that having, by
the Count's unlucky shifting, been appointed to the same
chamber with the Abbé, he had found the manuscript in
which his story was recorded   Struck with horror on perusing
it, he felt that it was now impossible for him to live, on
which he had recourse as usual to the laudanum   this he
poured into a glass of almond-milk, and raised it to his
mouth, but he shuddered when it reached his lips, he set it
down untasted, went out to walk once more across the
garden, and behold the face of nature, and on his return, he
found the child employed in filling up the glass out of which
it had been drinking

They entreated the unhappy creature to be calm, he seized
Wilhelm by the hand with a spasmodic grasp, and cried
"Ah! why did I not leave thee long ago?   I knew well that
I should kill the boy, and he me"   "The boy lives!" said
Wilhelm   The Doctor, who had listened with attention, now
inquired of Augustin if all the drink was poisoned   "No,"
replied he, "nothing but the glass"   "By the luckiest
chance, then," cried the Doctor, "the boy has drunk from the
bottle!   A benignant Genius has guided his hand, that he
did not catch at death, which stood so near and ready for
him"   "No! no!" cried Wilhelm with a groan, and clapping
both his hands upon his eyes   "How dreadful are the words!
Felix said expressly that he drank not from the bottle but the
glass   His health is but a show, he will die among our
hands"   Wilhelm hastened out, the Doctor went below,
and taking Felix up, with much caressing, asked   "Now

did not you, my pretty boy ?   You drank from the bottle,
not the glass ?"   The child began to cry   The Doctor
secretly informed Natalia how the matter stood   she also
strove in vain to get the truth from Felix. who but cried the
more, cried till he fell asleep

Wilhelm watched by him, the night went peacefully away
Next morning Augustin was found lying dead in bed, he had
cheated his attendants by a seeming rest, had silently
loosened the bandages, and bled to death   Natalia went to
walk with Felix, he was sportful as in his happiest days
"You are always good to me," said Felix, "you never scold,
you never beat me, I will tell you the truth, I did drink
from the bottle   Mamma Aurelia used to rap me over the
fingers every time I touched the bottle   father looked so
sour, I thought he would beat me "

With winged steps Natalia hastened to the Castle, Wilhelm
came, still overwhelmed with care, to meet her   "Happy
father !" cried she, lifting up the child, and throwing it into
his arms   "there is thy son again !   He drank from the
bottle   his naughtiness has saved him "

They told the Count the happy issue, but he listened with
a smiling, silent, modest air of knowingness, like one tolerating
the error of worthy men. Jarno, attentive to all, could not
explain this lofty self-complacency, till after many windings,
he at last discovered it to be his Lordship's firm belief that
the child had really taken poison, and that he himself, by
prayer and the laying-on of hands, had miraculously counter-
acted the effects of it   After such a feat, his Lordship now
determined on departing   Everything, as usual with him,
was made ready in a moment, the fair Countess, when about
to go, took Wilhelm's hand before parting with her sister's,
she then pressed both their hands between her own, turned
quickly round, and stept into the carriage

So many terrible and strange events, crowding one upon
the back of another, inducing an unusual mode of life, and
putting everything into disorder and perplexity, had brought

a sort of feverish movement into all departments of the
house. The hours of sleep and waking, of eating, drinking
and social conversation were inverted   Except Theresa, none
of them had kept in their accustomed course   The men
endeavoured, by increased potations, to recover their good
humour, and thus communicating to themselves an artificial
vivacity, they drove away that natural vivacity, which alone
imparts to us true cheerfulness and strength for action

Wilhelm, in particular, was moved and agitated by the
keenest feelings. Those unexpected, frightful incidents had
thrown him out of all condition to resist a passion which had
so forcibly seized his heart   Felix was restored to him, yet
still it seemed that he had nothing   Werner's letters, the
directions for his journey were in readiness, there was nothing
wanting but the resolution to remove   Everything conspired
to hasten him. He could not but conjecture that Lothario
and Theresa were awaiting his departure, that they might be
wedded   Jarno was unusually silent, you would have said
that he had lost a portion of his customary cheerfulness
Happily the Doctor helped our friend, in some degree, from
this embarrassment   he declared him sick, and set about
administering medicine to him

The company assembled always in the evening   Friedrich,
the wild madcap, who had often drunk more wine than suited
him, in general took possession of the talk, and by a thousand
frolicsome citations, fantasies and waggish allusions, often kept
the party laughing, often also threw them into awkward
difficulties, by the liberty he took to think aloud.

In the sickness of his friend he seemed to have little faith
Once when they were all together, "Pray, Doctor," cried he,
"how is it you call the malady our friend is labouring under?
Will none of the three thousand names, with which you
decorate your ignorance, apply to it? The disease at least is
not without examples   There is one such case," continued he
with an emphatic tone, "in the Egyptian or Babylonian
history"

The company looked at one another, and smiled

"What call you the king—?" cried he, and stopped short a moment "Well, if you will not help me, I must help myself" He threw open the folding-doors, and pointed to the large picture in the antechamber "What call you the goat-beard there, with the crown on, who is standing at the foot of the bed, making such a rueful face about his sick son? How call you the beauty, who enters, and in her modest roguish eyes at once brings poison and antidote? How call you the quack of a doctor, who at this moment catches a glimpse of the reality, and for the first time in his life takes occasion to prescribe a reasonable recipe, to give a drug which cures to the very heart, and is at once salutiferous and savoury?"

In this manner he continued babbling The company took it with as good a face as might be, hiding their embarrassment behind a forced laugh A slight blush overspread Natalia's cheeks, and betrayed the movements of her heart By good fortune, she was walking up and down with Jarno on coming to the door, with a cunning motion she slipped out, walked once or twice across the antechamber, and returned to her room

The company were silent Friedrich began to dance and sing.

> "O ye shall wonders see!
> What has been is not to be,
> What is said is not to say,
> Before the break of day
> Ye shall wonders see!"

Theresa had gone out to find Natalia, Friedrich pulled the Doctor forward to the picture, pronounced a ridiculous eulogium on medicine, and glided from the room

Lothario had been standing all the while in the recess of a window, he was looking, without motion, down into the garden Wilhelm was in the most dreadful state Left alone with his friends, he still kept silence for a time he ran with a hurried glance over all his history, and at last, with shuddering, surveyed his present situation, he started up and cried. "If

I am to blame for what is happening, for what you and I
are suffering, punish me   In addition to my other miseries,
deprive me of your friendship, and let me wander, without
comfort, forth into the wide world, in which I should have
mingled, and withdrawn myself from notice long ago   But if
you see in me the victim of a cruel entanglement of chance,
out of which I could not thread my way, then give me the
assurance of your love, of your friendship, on a journey which
I dare not now postpone   A time will come, when I may tell
you what has passed of late within me   Perhaps this is but
a punishment, which I am suffering, because I did not soon
enough disclose myself to you, because I hesitated to display
myself entirely as I was   you would have assisted me, you
would have helped me out in proper season   Again and
again have my eyes been opened to my conduct, but it was
ever too late, it was ever in vain!   How richly do I merit
Jarno's censure!   I imagined I had seized it, how firmly did
I purpose to employ it, to commence another life!   Could I,
ight I have done so?   It avails not for mortals to complain
of Fate or of themselves!   We are wretched, and appointed
for wretchedness, and what does it matter whether blame of
ours, higher influence or chance, virtue or vice, wisdom or folly
plunge us into ruin?   Farewell!   I will not stay another
moment in a house, where I have so fearfully violated the
rights of hospitality   Your brother's indiscretion is unpardonable, it aggravates my suffering to the highest pitch,
it drives me to despair "

"And what," replied Lothario, taking Wilhelm by the
hand, " what if your alliance with my sister were the secret
article on which depended my alliance with Theresa?   This
amends that noble maiden has appointed for you, she has
vowed that these two pairs should appear together at the altar.
'His reason has made choice of me,' said she, 'his heart
demands Natalia   my reason shall assist his heart'   We
agreed to keep our eyes upon Natalia and yourself, we told
the Abbé of our plan, who made us promise not to intermeddle

with this union, or attempt to forward it but to suffer everything to take its course   We have done so, Nature has
performed her part , our mad brother only shook the ripe
fruit from the branch   And now, since we have come together
so unusually, let us lead no common life , let us work together
in a noble manner, and for noble purposes !   It is inconceivable
how much a man of true culture can accomplish for himself
and others, if, without attempting to rule, he can be the
guardian over many , can induce them to do that in season,
which they are at any rate disposed enough to do , can guide
them to their objects, which in general they see with due distinctness, though they miss the road to them   Let us make a
league for this   it is no enthusiasm , but an idea which may
be fully executed, which indeed is often executed, only with
imperfect consciousness, by people of benevolence and worth
Natalia is a living instance of it   No other need attempt to
rival the plan of conduct which has been prescribed by nature
for that pure and noble soul "

He had more to say, but Friedrich with a shout came jumping in   ' What a garland have I earned ! " cried he   " how
will you reward me ?   Myrtle, laurel, ivy, leaves of oak, the
freshest you can find, come twist them   I have merits far
beyond them all   Natalia is thine ! I am the conjuror who
raised this treasure for thee "

" He raves," said Wilhelm , " I must go "

" Art thou empowered to speak ? " inquired Lothario, holding Wilhelm from retiring

" By my own authority," said Friedrich, " and the grace of
God   It was thus I was the wooer , thus I am the messenger
I listened at the door , she told the Abbé everything "

" Barefaced rogue ! who bade thee listen ? " said Lothario

" Who bade her bolt the door ? " cried Friedrich   " I heard
it all   she was in a wondrous pucker   In the night when
Felix seemed so ill, and was lying half upon her knees, and
thou wert sitting comfortless before her, sharing the beloved
load, she made a vow, that if the child died, she would confess

hei love to thee, and offer thee her hand   And now when the
child lives, why should she change her mind?   What we
promise under such conditions, we keep under any   Nothing
wanting but the paison ! He will come, and maivel what
strange news he biings "

The Abbé entered   "We know it all," ciied Friedrich
" be as brief as possible , it is mere formality you come for ,
they nevei send for you or me on any other score "

" He has listened," said the Baron —"Scandalous ! " exclaimed the Abbé

"Now, quick ! " said Friediich   "How stands it with the
ceiemonies? These we can reckon on our fingeis   You must
tiavcl , the Maichese's invitation answeis to a hairsbreadth
If we had you once bejond the Alps, it will all be right   the
people aie obliged to you for undei taking anything surprising ,
you piocuie them an amusement which they are not called to
pay foi   It is as if you gave a fiee ball , all ranks partake
in it "

" In such popular festivities," ieplied the Abbé, " you have
done the public much seivice in your time , but today, it
seems, you will not let me speak at all "

" If it is not just as I have told it," answered Fiiediich,
"let us have it better   Come iound, come round , we must
see them both together "

Lothaiio embiaced his fiiend, and led him to Natalia, who
with Theiesa came to meet them   All were silent

" No loiteiing ! " ciied Fiiedrich   " In two days you may
be ready for youi travels   Now, think you, fiiend," continued
he, addiessing Wilhelm, " when we first sciaped acquaintance,
and I asked you foi the pretty nosegay, who could have supposed you weie ever to ieceive a flower like this from me ? "

" Do not, at the moment of my highest happiness, remind
me of those times ! "

" Of which you need not be ashamed, any more than one
need be ashamed of his descent   The times were very good
times   only I cannot but laugh to look at thee, to my mind,

thou resemblest Saul the son of Kish, who went out to seek
his father's asses, and found a kingdom "

"I know not the worth of a kingdom," answered Wilhelm,
"but I know I have attained a happiness which I have not
deserved, and which I would not change with anything in life "

WILHELM MEISTER'S TRAVELS:

OR

THE RENUNCIANTS

A NOVEL

To travel now th' Apprentice does essay,
And every step is girt with doubt and danger
In truth he uses not to sing or play,
But is his path perplex'd, this toilsome ranger
Does turn an earnest eye, when mist's above him,
To his own heart, and to the hearts that love him

Scarce could tell you rightly
　Whether I'm the same or not,
If you task me very tightly
　Yes, this is my sense you've got,
Sense that vexes, then assuages,
　Now too light, and now too dark,
But in some few hundred pages
　May again come to the mark

Does Fortune try thee?   She had cause to do't,
She wish'd thee abstinent   obey, be mute!

———

What, shap'st thou here at the world! 'tis shapen long ago
The Maker shaped it, *he* thought it best even *so*
Thy lot is appointed, go follow its hest,
Thy course is begun, thou must walk, and not rest,
For sorrow and care cannot alter thy case,
And running, not raging, will win thee the race

———

Enwell tells us, a most royal man,
The deepest heart and highest head to scan
' In every place, at every time, thy surest chance
Lies in Decision, Justice, Tolerance '

———

My inheritance, how wide and fair !
Time is my estate, to Time I'm heir.

———

Now it is Day, be doing every one!
For the Night cometh, wherein work can none.

And so I, in Tale adjoining,
Lift old treasures into day,
If not gold or perfect coining,
They are metals anyway
Thou canst sort them, thou canst sunder,
Thou canst melt and make them one
Then take that with smiling wonder,
Stamp it like thyself, my son

WILHELM MEISTER'S TRAVELS

CHAPTER I

THE FLIGHT INTO EGYPT

WILHELM was sitting under the shadow of a huge crag, on a
shaggy impressive spot, where the steep mountain-path turned
abruptly round a corner down into the chasm   The sun was
still high, and brightening the tops of the pine-trees in the
clefts at his feet   He was looking at something in his note-
book, when Felix, who had been clambering about, came to
him with a stone in his hand   "What is the name of this
stone, father ? " said the boy

"I know not," answered Wilhelm

"Can this be gold that glitters in it so ? " said Felix

"No, no," replied Wilhelm , "and now I remember, people
call it mica, or cat-gold "

"Cat-gold ! " said the boy, smiling   "And why ? "

"I suppose because it is false, and cats are reckoned false
too "

"Well, I will note that," said the son, and put in the
stone beside the rest, with which he had already filled his
pockets

Scarcely was this over, when, adown the steep path, a
strange enough appearance came in sight   Two boys, beautiful
as day,—in coloured jackets, which you might have taken for
outer shirts,—came bounding down one after the other, and
Wilhelm had opportunity of viewing them more closely, as
they faltered, on observing him, and stopped for a moment
Round the elder boy's head waved rich fair locks, which you

looked at first, on observing him, and then his clear blue eyes
attracted your attention, which spread itself with delight over
his beautiful shape   The younger, more like a friend than
a brother, was decked with brown sleek hair, which hung
down over his shoulders, and the reflection of which appeared
to be imaged in his eyes

These strange, and in this wilderness quite unexpected
beings, Wilhelm had not time to view more narrowly, for he
heard a man's voice calling down round the corner of the crag,
in a serious but friendly tone

"Why do you stand still? Don't stop the way!"

Wilhelm looked upwards, and if the children had surprised
him, what he now saw filled him with astonishment   A stout,
firmset, not too tall young man, tucked up for walking, of
brown complexion and black hair, was stepping firmly and
carefully down the rock-way, and leading an ass behind hi ,
which first presented its glossy well-trimmed head, and then
the fair burden it bore   A soft lovely woman was seated on
a large and well-pannelled saddle in her arms, within a blue
mantle which hung over her, lay an infant, which she was
pressing to her breast, and looking at with indescribable
tenderness   The man did as the children had done, faltered
for a moment at sight of Wilhelm   The beast slackened its
step, but the descent was too precipitous, the travellers could
not halt, and Wilhelm with astonishment saw them vanish
behind the contiguous wall of rocks

Nothing was more natural than that this singular procession should cut short his meditations   He rose in no small
curiosity, and looked from his position towards the chasm,
to see whether they would not again make their appearance
somewhere below. He was just about descending to salute
these strange travellers when Felix came climbing up, and
said "Father, may I not go home with these boys to their
house? They want to take me with them   Thou must go
too, the man said to me   Come! They are waiting down
there!"

"I will speak with them," answered Wilhelm

He found them at a place where the path was more level, and he could not but gaze in wonder at the singular figures which had so strongly attracted his attention Not till now had it been in his power to note the peculiarities of the group The young stout man, he found, had a joiner's axe on his shoulder, and a long thin iron square The children bore in their hands large sedge-tufts, like palms, and if in this point they resembled angels, they likewise carried little baskets with shop-wares in them, thereby resembling the little daily posts, as they pass to and fro over the Mountains The mother also, he observed, on looking more leisurely, wore under her blue mantle a reddish mild-coloured lower garment, so that *The Flight into Egypt,* which our friend had so often seen painted, he now with amazement saw bodied forth before his eyes

The strangers exchanged salutations, and as Wilhelm, from surprise and attention, could not speak, the young man said "Our children have formed a friendship in these few moments Will you go with us, to see whether some kind relation will not spring up between the elder parties also? "

Wilhelm bethought himself an instant, and then answered "The aspect of your little family procession awakens trust and good-will, and to confess it frankly, curiosity no less, and a lively desire to be better acquainted with you For at the first glance, one might ask himself the question Whether you are real travellers, or only Spirits that take pleasure in enlivening these uninhabitable Mountains by pleasant visions ? "

"Then come home with us to our dwelling," said the other "Come with us!" cried the children, already drawing Felix along with them "Come with us!" said the woman, turning her soft kindliness from the suckling to the stranger

Without reflecting, Wilhelm answered "I am sorry that for the present moment I cannot follow you This night, at least, I must spend up at the Border-house My port-

manteau, my papers, all is lying up there, unpacked, intrusted
to no one   But that I may prove my wish and purpose to
satisfy your friendly invitation, take my Felix with you as a
pledge   Tomorrow I shall see you   How far is it?"

"We shall be home before sunset," said the carpenter
"and from the Border-house you are but a league and a half.
Your boy increases our household for this night, and tomorrow
we expect you"

The man and the animal set forth   Wilhelm smiled thoughtfully to see his Felix so soon received among the Angels   The
boy had already seized a sedge-tuft, and taken the basket from
the younger of his companions   The procession was again on
the point of vanishing behind a ledge of rock, when Wilhelm
recollected himself, and cried "But how shall I inquire you
out?"

"Ask for St Joseph!" sounded from the hollow, and the
whole vision had sunk behind the blue shady wall of cliffs   A
pious hymn, uplifted on a chorus of several voices, rose echoing
from the distance, and Wilhelm thought he could distinguish
the voice of his Felix among the rest

He ascended the path, and thus protracted the period of
sunset   The heavenly star, which he had more than once lost
sight of, illuminated him afresh as he mounted higher, and it
was still day when he reached his inn   Once more he delighted
himself with the vast mountain-prospect, then withdrew to
his chamber, where immediately he seized his pen, and passed
a part of the night in writing

Wilhelm to Natalia

Now at last I have reached the Summit, the summit of the
Mountains, which will place a stronger separation betwixt us
than all the tract I had passed over before   To my feeling,
one is still in the neighbourhood of those he loves, so long as
the streams run down from him towards them   Today I can
still fancy to myself that the twig, which I cast into the

forest-brook, may perhaps float down to her, may in a few days land at her garden, and thus our spirit sends its images more easily, our heart its sympathies, by the same downward course But over on the other side, I fear, there rises a wall of division against the imagination and the feelings Yet this perhaps is but a vain anxiety, for over on the other side, after all, it will not be otherwise than it is here What could part me from thee! From thee, whose own I am forever, though a strange destiny sunders me from thee, and unexpectedly shuts the heaven to which I stood so near I had time to compose myself, and yet no time could have sufficed to give me that composure, had I not gained it from thy mouth, from thy lips, in that decisive moment How could I have torn myself away, if the enduring thread had not been spun, which is to unite us for Time and Eternity? Yet I must not speak of all this Thy tender commands I will not break · on this mountain top. be it the last time that I name the word Separation before thee! My life is to become a restless wandering Strange duties of the wanderer have I to fulfil, and peculiar trials to undergo How I often smile within myself, when I read the terms which thou prescribedst to me, which I prescribed to myself Many of them have been kept, many broken, but even while breaking them, that sheet is of use to me, that testimonial of my last confession, of my last absolution it speaks to me as an authoritative conscience, and I again turn to the right path I watch myself, and my faults no longer rush like mountain-torrents, one over the other

Yet I will confess to thee, I many times wonder at those Teachers and Guides of men, who impose on their scholars nothing but external mechanical duties They make the task, for themselves and the world, a light one For this very part of my obligations, which at first seemed the heaviest, the strangest, I now observe with greatest ease, with greatest satisfaction

I am not to stay beyond three days under one roof I am

to quit no inn without removing at least one league from it
These regulations are in truth calculated to make my life a life
of Travel, and to prevent the smallest thought of settlement
from taking hold of me   Hitherto I have fulfilled this condition to the letter, not even using all the liberty it grants me
This is the first time that I have paused   here, for the first
ti e, I sleep three nights in the same bed   From this spot I
send thee much that I have heard, observed, laid up for thee
and early in the morning, I descend on the other side, in the
first place, to a strange family, I might almost say, a Holy
Family, of which, in my Journal, thou wilt find farther notice
For the present, farewell, and lay down this sheet with the
feeling that it has but one thing to say, but one thing which
it would say and repeat forever, yet will not say it, will not
repeat it now, till I have once more the happiness of lying at
thy feet, and weeping over thy hands for all that I renounce

Morning

My packing is done   The porter is girding the portmanteau
on his doisel   As yet the sun is not up, vapours are stream-
ing out of all the hollows, but the upper sky is clear   We step
down into the gloomy deeps, which also will soon brighten over
our heads   Let me send my last sigh home to thee !   Let my
last look towards thee be yet blinded with involuntary tears !
I am decided and determined   Thou shalt hear no more com-
plaints from me   thou shalt hear only what happens to the
wanderer   And yet now, when I am on the point of ending, a
thousand thoughts, wishes, hopes and purposes come crowding
through my soul   Happily the people force me away   The
porter calls me, and mine host has already in my presence
begun sorting the apartment, as if I were gone   thus feeling-
less, imprudent heirs do not hide, from the departing testator,
their preparations for assuming management

CHAPTER II

ST JOSEPH THE SECOND

ALREADY had the wanderer, following his porter on foot, left
the steep rocks behind and above him, already were they
traversing a softer mid range of hills, and hastening through
many a well-pruned wood, over many a friendly meadow,
forward and forward, till at last they found themselves on a
declivity, and looked down into a beautifully cultivated valley,
begirt on all sides with hills   A large monastic edifice, half
in ruins, half in repair, immediately attracted their attention.
"This is St Joseph," said the porter   "Pity for the fine
Church !   Do but look how fresh and firm it still holds up
its pillars through bush and tree, though it has lain many
hundred years in decay"

"The Cloister, on the contrary," said Wilhelm, "I observe,
is kept in good state"

"Yes," said the other, "there is a steward lives here,
he manages the husbandry, collects the dues and tithes, which
the people far and wide have to pay him "

So speaking, they had entered through the open gate into
a spacious court, surrounded with earnest-looking, well-kept
buildings, and announcing itself as the residence of some
peaceful community   Among the children playing in the
area, Wilhelm noticed Felix, the other two were the Angels
of last night   The friendly trio came running towards hi ,
with salutations and assurances that papa would soon be back
He, in the mean while, they said, must go into the hall, and
rest himself

How surprised was Wilhelm when the children led him into
this apartment which they named the hall   Passing directly
from the court, through a large door, our wanderer found
himself in a very cleanly undecayed Chapel, which, however, as
he saw well enough, had been fitted up for the domestic uses of

daily life   On the one side stood a table, a settle, some chairs
and benches, on the other side a neatly-carved dresser, with
variegated pottery, jugs and glasses   Some chests and trunks
were standing in suitable niches, and, simple as the whole
appeared, there was not wanting an air of comfort, and daily
household life looked forth from it with an aspect of invitation   The light fell in from high windows on the side   But
what most roused the attention of the wanderer, was a series
of coloured figures painted on the wall, stretching under the
windows, at a considerable height, round three quarters of the
Chapel, and hanging down to the wainscot, which covered
the remainder of the wall to the ground   The pictures represented the history of St Joseph   Here you might see him
first employed with his carpentry work, here he meets Mary,
and a lily is sprouting from the ground between them, while
Angels hover round observing them   Here his betrothing
takes place, next comes the salutation of the Angel   Here
he is sitting disconsolate among his neglected work, he has
laid-by the axe, and is thinking to put away his wife   But
now appears the Angel to him in a dream, and his situation
changes   With reverence he looks on the new-born Child in
the Stable at Bethlehem, and prays to it   Soon after this,
comes a wonderfully beautiful picture   You observe a
quantity of timber lying dressed, it is just to be put together,
and by chance two of the pieces form a cross   The Child has
fallen asleep on the cross, his mother sits by, and looks at
him with heartfelt love, and the foster-father pauses with his
labour, that he may not awaken him   Next follows the Flight
into Egypt   it called forth a smile from the gazing traveller,
for he saw here on the walls a repetition of the living figures
he had met last night.

He had not long pursued his contemplations, when the
landlord entered, whom he directly recognised as the leader
of the Holy Caravan   They saluted each other cordially
much conversation followed, yet Wilhelm's chief attention
continued fixed on the pictures   The host observed the feel-

ing of his guest, and began with a smile "No doubt you are wondering at the strange accordance of this building with its inhabitants, whom you got acquainted with last night Yet it is perhaps still more singular than you suppose the building has in truth formed the inhabitants.   For when the inanimate has life, it can also produce what has life "

"Yes, indeed !" answered Wilhelm, "I should be surprised if the spirit, which worked so powerfully in this mountain-solitude long centuries ago, and drew round it such a mighty body of edifices, possessions and rights, diffusing in return the blessings of manifold culture over the region, could not still, out of these ruins, manifest the force of its life on some living being But let us not linger on general reflections, make me acquainted with your history, let me know how it can possibly have happened, that without affectation and pre-sumption, the past again represents itself in you, and what .was, again is "

Just as Wilhelm was expecting responsive information from the lips of his host, a friendly voice in the court cried "Joseph !" The man obeyed it, and went out

"So he too is Joseph !" said Wilhelm to himself. "This is strange enough, and yet not so strange as that, in his life, he should personate his Saint " At the same time looking through the door, he saw the Virgin Mother of last night, speaking with her husband   They parted at last, the woman walked towards the opposite building "Mary," cried he after her, "a word more "

"So she too is Mary !" said Wilhelm inwardly "Little would make me feel as if I were transported eighteen hundred years into the past !" He thought of the solemn and secluded valley in which he was, of the wrecks and silence all round, and a strange antiquarian mood came over him   It was time for the landlord and children to come in   The latter called for Wilhelm to go and walk, as the landlord had still some business to do   And now came in view the ruins of the Church, with its many shafts and columns, with its high peaks and walls, which looked as if gathering strength in the influence of wind and weather, for strong trees from of old had taken root in the broad backs of the walls, and now in company with grass, flowers and moss in great quantities, exhibited bold hanging gardens vegetating in the air Soft sward-paths led you up the banks of a lively brook, and from a little elevation our wanderer could now overlook the edifice and its site with more interest, as its occupants had become still more singular in his eyes, and by their harmony with their abode had awakened his liveliest curiosity

The promenaders returned, and found in the religious hall a table standing covered At the upper end was an arm-chair, in which the mistress of the house took her seat Beside her she had placed a high wicker cradle, in which lay the little infant, the father sat next this on her left hand, Wilhelm on her right The three children occupied the lower space of the table An old serving-maid brought in a well-prepared meal Eating and drinking implements alike pointed to the past The children afforded matter for talk, while Wilhelm could not satisfy himself with looking at the form and the bearing of his saintly hostess.

Their repast over, the company separated The landlord took his guest to a shady spot in the Ruin, where, from an elevated station, the pleasant prospect down the valley lay entire before them, and farther off, the heights of the lower country, with their fruitful declivities and woody backs, were seen protruding one behind the other " It is fair," said the landlord, " that I satisfy your curiosity, and the rather, as I feel that you can view the strange with seriousness, when you find it resting on a serious ground This religious foundation, the remains of which are lying round us, was dedicated to the Holy Family, and in old times noted as a place of pilgrimage for many wonders done in it The Church was consecrated to the Mother and the Son It has lain for several centuries in ruins The Chapel, dedicated to the Holy Foster-father, still remains, as does likewise the serviceable part of the

Cloister The revenues have for many years belonged to a
temporal Prince, who keeps a steward here, this steward am
I, son of the last steward, who also succeeded his father in
the office

" St Joseph, though any regular worship of him has long
ceased here, had been so helpful to our family, that it is not
to be wondered at, if they felt particularly well inclined
towards him hence came it that they had me baptized by the
name of Joseph, and thereby, I may say, in some sense determined my whole future way of life I grew up and if I used
to help my father in managing the dues, I attached myself as
gladly, nay, still more gladly, to my mother, who cheerfully
distributed her bounty according to her fortune, and for her
kindness and good deeds was known and loved over all the
Mountains. Ere long she would send me out, now this way,
now that, now to fetch, now to carry, now direct, and I
very speedily began to be at home in this sort of pious
occupation

" In general, our Mountain life has something more humane
in it than the life of lowlanders The inhabitants here are
nearer, and, if you will, more remote also Our wants are
smaller, but more pressing Each man is placed more on his
own footing, he must learn to depend on his own hands, on
his own limbs The labourer, the post, the porter, all unite
in one person, each of us is more connected with the other,
meets him oftener, and lives with him in joint activity

" As I was still young, and my shoulders could not bear
heavy burdens, I fell upon a thought of furnishing a little ass
with panniers, which I might drive before me up and down
the steep footpaths In the Mountains the ass is no such
despicable animal as in the plain country, where the labourer
that ploughs with horses reckons himself better than he that
turns his furrow with oxen And I walked behind my beast
with the less hesitation, as I had before observed in the Chapel
that an animal of this same sort had been promoted to such
honour as to carry God and his Mother This Chapel was

not then, however, in the state you now see it in   It had been
treated as a carthouse, nay, almost as a stable   Firewood,
stakes, implements, barrels and ladders, everything that came
to hand, lay huddled together in it   Lucky that the pictures
were so high, and the wainscot could stand some hardships
But even in my childhood, I used many a time to clamber
over the wood, and delight myself with looking at the pictures,
which no one could properly explain to me   However, I
knew at least that the Saint whose life stood depicted on these
walls was my patron, and I rejoiced in him as much as if he
had been my uncle   I waxed in stature, and it being an
express condition, that whoever meant to aspire after this
post of Schaffner must practise some handicraft, our family,
desiring that I might inherit so good a benefice, determined
on putting me to learn some trade, and such a one, at the
same time, as might be useful here in our upland way of life

"My father was a cooper, and had been accustomed to
supply of himself whatever was required in that sort, from
which there arose no little profit, both to himself and the
country   But I could not prevail on myself to follow him in
this business   My inclination drew me irresistibly to the
joiner trade, the tools and materials of which I had seen,
from infancy upwards, so accurately and circumstantially
painted beside my Patron Saint   I signified my wish: nothing
could be objected to it, the less, as in our frequent buildings,
the carpenter is often wanted here, nay, if he have any sleight
in his trade and fondness for it, especially in forest districts,
the arts of the cabinet-maker, and even of the carver, lie close
beside his province   And what still farther confirmed me in
my higher purposes was a picture, which now, alas, is almost
effaced   If once you know what it is meant to represent, you
may still be able to decipher the figures, when I take you to
look at it   St Joseph had got no lower a commission than
to make a throne for King Herod   The royal seat was to be
erected between two given pillars   Joseph carefully measures
the breadth and height, and fashions a costly throne.   But

how astonished is he, how alarmed, on carrying his finished
work to the place   the throne is too high, and not broad
enough   King Herod, as we know, was a man that did not
understand jesting   the pious wright is in the greatest perplexity   The divine Child, accustomed to follow him everywhere, and in childlike humble sport to carry his tools after
him, observes his strait, and is immediately at hand with
advice and assistance   He requires of his Foster-father to
take hold of the throne by the one side, he himself grasps it
by the other, and both begin to pull.   Easily and pliantly, as
if it had been made of leather, the carved throne extends
in breadth, contracts proportionably in length, and fits itself
to the place with the nicest accuracy, to the great comfort
of the reassured Master, and the perfect satisfaction of the
King

"This throne was, in my youth, quite distinctly visible ,
and by the remains of the one side you will still be able to
discern, that there was no want of carving on it, which
indeed must have been easier for the painter, than it would
have been for the carpenter, had such a thing been required
of him

"That circumstance, however, raised no scruples in me ,
but I looked on the handicraft, to which I had devoted myself,
in so honourable a light, that I was all impatience to be
apprenticed to it , a longing which was the easier to fulfil, as
a master of the trade lived in our neighbourhood, who worked
for the whole district, and kept several apprentices and
journeymen about him   Thus I continued in the neighbourhood of my parents, and to a certain extent pursued my former
way of life also , seeing I employed my leisure hours and
holydays in doing those charitable messages which my mother
still intrusted to me

CHAPTER III

THE VISIT

"So passed several years," continued the narrator "I
very soon comprehended the principles of my trade, and my
frame, expanded by labour, was equal to the undertaking of
everything connected with the business   At the same time, I
kept managing my ancient service, which my good mother, or
rather the sick and destitute, required at my hands   I moved
with my beast through the Mountains, punctually distributed
my lading, and brought back from shopkeepers and merchants
what we needed here at home

"My master was contented with me, my parents also
Already I enjoyed the satisfaction, in my wanderings, of seeing
many a house which I had helped to raise, or had myself
decorated   For, in particular, that last notching of the bea -
ends, that carving of certain simple forms, that branding-in of
pretty figures, that red-painting of certain recesses, by which
a wooden house in the Mountains acquires so pleasant an
aspect, these arts were specially intrusted to me, as I always
made the best hand of such tasks, having Herod's Throne and
its ornaments constantly in my head

"Among the help-needing persons, whom my mother took
peculiar charge of, were particularly young wives near the
time of their confinement, as by degrees I could well enough
remark, though in such cases the commissions given me were
veiled in a certain mystery   My messages, on these occasions,
never reached directly to the party concerned   but everything
passed through the hands of a good old woman, who lived
down the dale, and was called Frau Elizabeth   My mother,
herself skilful in the art which saves life to so many at their
very entrance into life, constantly maintained a good understanding with Frau Elizabeth, and I often heard, in all
quarters, that many a one of our stout mountaineers stood

indebted for his existence to these two women   The secrecy
with which Elizabeth received me at all times, her pointed
replies to my enigmatical questions, which I myself did not
understand, awoke in me a singular reverence for her, and her
house, which was extremely clean, appeared to me to represent
a sort of sanctuary

"Meanwhile, by my acquirements and adroitness in my
craft, I had gained considerable influence in the family   As
my father, in the character of cooper, had taken charge of the
cellar and its contents, I now took charge of roof and room,
and repaired many a damaged part in the old building   In
particular, I contrived to make so e fallen barns and out-
houses once more serviceable for domestic use, and scarcely
was this done, when I set about cleaning and clearing out my
beloved Chapel   In a few days, it was put in order, almost as
you see it at present   and such pieces of the wainscot as were
damaged, or altogether wanting, I had endeavoured, as I went
along, to restore in the same fashion as the rest   These folding-
doors at the entrance too, you might think were old enough,
yet they are of my workmanship   I passed several years in
carving them at leisure hours, having first mortised the body
of them firmly together out of strong oaken planks   Whatever of the pictures had not been effaced or injured at that
ti e, has since continued unimpaired, and I assisted our
glazier in a new house he was erecting, under the condition of
his putting in coloured windows here

"If these figures and thoughts on the Saint's life had
hitherto occupied my imagination, the whole impressed itself
on me with much more liveliness, now that I could again regard
the place as a sanctuary, could linger in it, and muse at leisure
on what I saw or conjectured   There lay in me an irresistible
desire to follow in the footsteps of this Saint, and as a similar
history was not to be looked for in these times, I determined
on commencing my resemblance from the lowest point upwards, as indeed, by the use of my beast of burden, I had
already commenced it long ago. The small creature, which I

had hitherto employed, would no longer content me I chose
for myself a far more stately carrier, and got a large stout
saddle, which was equally adapted for riding and packing   A
pair of new baskets were also procured, and a net of many-
coloured knots, flakes and tufts, intermixed with jingling tags
of metal, decorated the neck of my long-eared beast, which
might now show itself beside its model on the wall   No one
thought of mocking me, when I passed over the Mountains
in this equipment people do not quarrel with Benevolence for
putting on a strange outside

"Meanwhile, war, or rather its consequences, had approached
our district, for dangerous bands of vagabond deserters had
more than once collected, and here and there practised much
violence and wanton mischief   By the good order of our Pro-
vincial Militia, by patrolling and prompt watchfulness, the
evil was very soon remedied but we too quickly relapsed into
our former carelessness, and, before we thought of it, new
disorders broke forth

"For a long time all had been quiet in our neighbourhood,
and I had travelled peacefully with my ass along the accustomed paths, till one day passing over a newly-sown glade of
the forest, I observed a female form sitting, or rather lying, at
the edge of the fence-ditch   She seemed to be asleep or in a
swoon   I endeavoured to recall her and as she opened her
eyes and sat upright, she cried with eagerness 'Where is he?
Did you see him?' I asked 'Whom?' She replied 'My
husband!' Considering her extremely youthful appearance, I
had not been expecting this reply yet I continued, so uch
the more kindly, to assist her, and assure her of my sympathy
I learned that the two travellers had left their carriage, the
road being so heavy, and struck into a footpath to make a
shorter cut   Hard by, they had been overtaken by armed
marauders, her husband had gone off fighting with the ,
she, not able to follow him far, had sunk on this spot, and lain
there she knew not how long   She pressingly begged of e
to leave her, and hasten after her husband   She rose to her

feet, and the fairest, loveliest form stood before me, yet I
could easily observe, that she was in a situation, in which she
might soon require the help of my mother and Frau Elizabeth
We disputed a while for I wished, before all, to bring her to
some place of safety, she wished, in the first place, to have
tidings of her husband   She would not leave the trace of him,
and all my arguments would, perhaps, have been unavailing,
had not a party of our Militia, which the tidings of fresh
misdeeds had again called out into service, chanced to pass
that way through the forest   These I informed of the matter,
with them the necessary arrangements were made, the place
of meeting appointed, and so the business settled for the time
With great expedition I hid my panniers in a neighbouring
cave, which had often served me before as a repository   I
adjusted my saddle for easy riding and not without a strange
emotion, lifted the fair burden on my willing beast, which
knowing of itself what path to choose, left me at liberty to
walk by her side

"You can figure to yourself, without my describing it at
large, in what a strange mood I was   What I had long been
seeking, I had now found   I felt as if I were dreaming, and
then again as if I were awakening from a dream   That
heavenly form, which I saw as it were hovering in the air, and
bending aside from the green branches, now seemed to me like
a dream which had risen in my soul through those figures in
the Chapel   Soon those figures themselves seemed to me to
have been only dreams, which were here issuing in a fair
reality   I asked her many things, she answered me softly
and kindly, as beseemed a dignified distress   She often desired
me, when we reached any open height, to stop, to look round,
to listen   She desired me with such grace, with such a deep
wistful look from under her long black eye-lashes, that I could
not but do whatever lay in my power, nay, at last I climbed
to the top of a high solitary branchless pine. Never had this
feat of my handicraft been more welcome to me, never had
I with greater joy brought down ribbons and silks from such

elevations at festivals and fairs   But for this ti e, alas, I
came back without booty , above, as below, I could hear or see
nothing   In the end, she herself called me down, and beckoned
to me earnestly with her hand , nay, at last, as in gliding
down, I quitted my hold a considerable way up, and dropt on
the ground, she gave a scream, and a sweet kindliness spread
over her face as she saw me before her unhurt

" Why should I tell you in detail of the hundred attentions,
with which I strove the whole way to be pleasing, to divert
her thoughts from her grief?   Indeed, how could I!   For it
is the very quality of true attention, that at the moment it
makes a nothing all   To my feeling, the flowers which I broke
for her, the distant scenes which I showed her, the hills, the
woods which I named to her, were so many precious treasures
which I was giving her to obtain for myself a place among her
interests, as one tries to do by presents

" Already she had gained me for my whole life, when we
reached our destination, at that good old woman's door, and I
saw a painful separation close at hand   Once more I ran over
all her for , and as my eyes came on her feet, I stooped as if
to adjust something in my girdle, and kissed the daintiest shoe
that I had ever seen, yet without her noticing me   I helped
her down, sprang up the steps, and called in at the door
'Frau Elizabeth, here is a visitor !'   The good old woman
came down   and I looked over her shoulders towards the
house, as the fair being mounted the steps, with graceful
sorrow, and inward painful self-consciousness, till she gratefully embraced my worthy old woman, and accompanied her
into the better chamber   They shut the door, and I was left
standing outside by my ass, like a man that has delivered a
loading of precious wares, and is again as poor a carrier
before

CHAPTER IV

THE LILY-STALK

"I was still lingering in my departure, for I knew not what to do if I were gone, when Frau Elizabeth came to the door, and desired me to send my mother down to her, and then to go about, and, if possible, get tidings of the husband 'Mary begs you very much to do this,' said she   'Can I not speak with her again myself?' replied I   'That will not do,' said Elizabeth, and we parted   In a short time I reached our dwelling, my mother was ready that same night to go over, and be helpful to the young stranger   I hastened down the country, thinking I should get the surest intelligence at the bailiff's   But the bailiff himself was still in uncertainty, and as I was known to him, he invited me to pass the night there   It seemed interminably long, and still I had the fair form before my eyes, as she sat gently swaying in the saddle, and looking down to me so sorrowful and friendly Every moment I hoped for news   To the worthy husband I honestly wished life and safety, and yet I liked so well to fancy her a widow ! The ranging troops by little and little collected, and after many variable rumours, the certainty at last came to light, that the carriage was saved, but the hapless traveller dead of his wounds in a neighbouring village   I learned also, that according to our first arrangement, some of the party had gone to communicate the melancholy tidings to Frau Elizabeth, consequently I had nothing more to do there Yet a boundless impatience, an immeasurable longing, drove me over wood and mountain once more to her threshold   It was dark, the door was shut, I saw light in the room, I saw shadows moving on the curtains, and thus I sat watching on a bench opposite the house ; still on the point of knocking, and still withheld by many considerations

"But why should I go-on describing to you what is in itself

of no interest?   In short, next morning too the house was
shut against me   They knew the heavy tidings, they needed
me no farther, they sent me to my father, to my work, they
would not answer my inquiries, they wanted to be rid of me

"For eight days this sort of treatment had continued,
when at last Frau Elizabeth called me in 'Step softly, my
friend,' said she, 'but enter without scruple'   She led me into
a trim apartment, where, in the corner, through the half-
opened curtains, I saw my fair one dressed, and sitting upright
in the bed   Frau Elizabeth went towards her as if to
announce me, lifted something from the bed, and brought it
me   wrapt in the whitest swathings, the prettiest boy! Frau
Elizabeth held it straight betwixt the mother and me; and
just then the Lily-stalk occurred to me, which in the picture
springs from the ground between Joseph and Mary, as witness
of their pure relation   From that moment, I was certain of
my cause, certain of my happiness   I could approach her with
freedom, speak with her, bear her heavenly eye, take the boy
on my arm, and imprint a warm kiss on his brow

"'How I thank you for your love to that orphan child!'
said the mother   Unthinkingly, and briskly, I cried 'It is
no orphan any longer, if you like!'

"Frau Elizabeth, more prudent than I, took the child from
my hands, and got me put away

"To this hour, when I chance to be wandering over our
mountains and forests, the remembrance of that time forms
my happiest entertainment   I can still recall the slightest
particulars, which, however, as is fit, I spare you at present
Weeks passed on, Mary was recovered, I could see her
oftener, my intercourse with her was a train of services and
attentions   Her family circumstances allowed her to choose
a residence according to her pleasure   She first stayed with
Frau Elizabeth, then she paid us a visit, to thank my mother
and me for so many and such friendly helps. She liked to live
with us, and I flattered myself that it was partly on my
account. What I wished to tell her, however, and durst not

utter, came to words in a singular and pretty wise, when I took
her into the Chapel, which I had then fitted up as a habitual
apartment   I showed her the pictures, and explained them
to her one after the other, and so doing, unfolded the duties
of a Foster-father in so vivid and cordial a manner, that the
tears came into her eyes, and I could not get to the end of my
picture-exhibition   I thought myself certain of her affection,
though I was not proud enough to wish so soon to efface the
memory of her husband   The law imposes on widows a year
of mourning, and, in truth, such an epoch, which includes in
it the change of all earthly things, is necessary for a feeling
heart, to alleviate the painful impressions of a great loss   We
see the flowers fade and the leaves fall, but we likewise see
fruits ripen, and new buds shoot forth   Life belongs to the
living, and he who lives must be prepared for vicissitudes

"I now spoke with my mother on the concern which lay so
near my heart   She thereupon disclosed to me how grievous
to Mary the death of her husband had been, and how she had
borne up and gathered courage again, solely from the thought
that she must live for her child   My inclination was not
unknown to the women, and already Mary had accustomed
herself to the idea of living with us   She stayed a while
longer in the neighbourhood ; then she came up to us, and we
lived for a time in the gentlest and happiest state of betrothment   At last we wedded   That feeling, which had first
drawn us together, did not fade away   The duties and joys
of the Father and the Foster-father were united. and so our
little family, as it increased, did certainly surpass its prototype
in number of persons, but the virtues of that pattern, in
respect to faithfulness and purity of sentiments, were sacredly
maintained and practised by us   And so also in friendly
habitude we keep up the external appearance which we, by
accident, arrived at, and which fits our internal state so well
for though all of us are good walkers, and stout bearers of
weight, the beast of burden still remains in our company, when
any business or visit takes us through these mountains and

valleys   As you met us last night, so does the whole country
know us, and we feel proud that our walk and conversation are
of such a sort as not to throw disgrace on the saintly name and
figure, whose imitators we profess to be "

Wilhelm to Natalia

I now conclude a pleasant half-marvellous history, which I
have just written down for thee, from the mouth of a very
worthy man   If I have not always given his very words, if
here and there, in describing his sentiments, I have expressed
my own, this, considering the relationship of mind I feel with
him, was natural enough   His reverence for his wife, does it
not resemble that which I entertain for thee ?   And is there
not, even in the first meeting of these lovers, something
similar to ours ?   But that he is fortunate enough to walk
beside his animal, as it bears the doubly-beautiful burden,
that he can enter at evenings with his family possession
through the old Cloister-gate, that he is inseparable from his
own loved ones, in all this I may well secretly envy him.
Yet I must not complain of my destiny, seeing I have
promised thee that I will suffer and be silent, as thou also hast
undertaken

Many a fair feature in the domestic union of these devout
and cheerful persons, I have been obliged to omit, for how
could it be depicted in writing ?   Two days have passed over
me agreeably, but the third warns me to be mindful of   y
farther wayfaring

With Felix I had a little quarrel today   He was almost for
compelling me to break through one wholesome regulation,
for which I stand engaged to thee   It has been an error, a
misfortune, in short an arrangement of Fate with me hitherto,
that before I am aware, my company increases, that I take a
new burden on my shoulders, which thenceforth I have to
bear and drag along with   e   So in my present wanderings -
no third party is to become a permanent associate with us,

We are, we will and must continue Two, and just now a new, and not very pleasing connexion seemed about to be established

To the children of the house with whom Felix has gaily passed these days in sporting, there had joined himself a little merry beggar-boy, who, submitting to be used or misused as the play required, had very soon got into favour with Felix By various hints and expressions, I now gathered that the latter had found himself a playmate for the next stage of our journey The boy is known in this quarter, and everywhere tolerated for his lively humour, and now and then obtains an alms Me, however, he did not please, and I desired our host to get him sent away This likewise took place, but Felix was angry at it, and we had a little flaw of discord

In the course of this affair, I discovered something which was pleasant to me In the corner of the Chapel, or hall, stood a box of stones, which Felix, who, since our wandering through the Mountains, has acquired an excessive fondness for minerals, eagerly drew forth and examined Many pretty eye-catching things were among them Our landlord said, the child might choose out what he liked these were the remains of a large collection which a friend had despatched thence a short while ago He called this person Montan, and thou wilt easily suppose how glad I was to hear this name, under which one of our best friends is travelling, one to whom we owe so much Having inquired into date and circumstances, I can now hope to meet him ere long on my pilgrimage.

CHAPTER V

The news that Montan was in the neighbourhood had made Wilhelm reflect He considered that it ought not to be left to chance alone whether he should meet with so estimable a friend, therefore he inquired of his landlord if they did not know towards what quarter this traveller had turned his

course   No one had any information on this point   and
Wilhelm had determined to pursue his pilgrimage on the
former plan, when Felix cried   "If Father were not so strange,
we might soon find Montan '

"What way?" said Wilhelm

Felix answered   "Little Fitz told us last night that he
could trace out the stranger gentleman, who had many fine
stones with him, and understood them well "

After some talking, Wilhelm at last resolved on making the
experiment, purposing, in the course of it, to keep so much
the sharper watch on the suspicious boy   Fitz was soon
found, and, hearing what was to be done, he soon produced
mallet and chisel, and a stout hammer, with a little bag, and
set forth, running merrily before the party, in his mining
accoutrements

The way went to a side, and up the Mountains   The
children skipped on together, from crag to crag, over stock
and stone, over brook and bourn, and without having any
path before him, Fitz pressed rapidly upwards, now looking to
the right hand, now to the left   As Wilhelm, and especially
the laden porter, could not follow so fast, the boys often ran
back and forward, singing and whistling   The aspect of some
new trees arrested the attention of Felix, who now for the
first time formed acquaintance with larches and fir-cones, and
curiously surveyed the strange gentian-shrubs   And thus, in
their toilsome wandering, there lacked not from time to time
a little entertainment   But all at once they were fronted by
a barricado of trees, which a storm had hurled together in a
confused mass   "This was not in my reckoning," said Fitz
"Wait here till I find my way again, only have a care of the
cave up there, no one goes into it, or near it, without getting
harm, or having tricks played on him "

The boy went off in an ascending direction   the porter, on
the other hand, grumbling at the excessive difficulty of the
way, set down his luggage, and searched sidewards and downwards for some beaten path

No sooner did Felix see himself alone with his father, than his curiosity awoke, and he glided softly towards the cave Wilhelm, who gave him leave, observed after some time that the child was no longer in sight He himself mounted to the cave, at the mouth of which he had last seen the boy, and, on entering, he found the place empty It was spacious, but could be taken in at a glance He searched for some other outlet, and found none The matter began to be serious He took the whistle, which he wore at his button-hole, an answer to his call came sounding out of the depth, so that he was uncertain whether he should take it for an echo, when, shortly afterwards, Felix peeped out of the ground, for the chink through which he looked was scarcely wide enough to let through his head

"What art thou about there?" cried his father

"Hush!" said Felix "art thou alone?"

"Quite alone," answered Wilhelm

"Then go quick," cried the boy, "and fetch me a couple of strong clubs"

Wilhelm went to the fallen timber, and with his hanger cut off a pair of thick staves, Felix took them, and vanished, having first called to his father "Let no one into the cave!"

After some time, Felix cried "Another pair of staves, and larger ones!" With these also his father provided him, and waited anxiously for the solution of his riddle At length the boy issued rapidly from the cleft, and brought a little box with him, not larger than an octavo volume, of rich, antique appearance, it seemed to be of gold, decorated with enamel "Put it up, father," said the boy, "and let none see it!" Wilhelm had not time to ask many questions, for they already heard the call of the returning porter, and scarcely had they joined him, when the little squire also began to shout and wave from above

On their approach, he cried out "Montan is not far off I bet we shall soon meet him"

"How canst thou know this," said Wilhelm, "in so wild

a forest, where no human being leaves any trace behind him ?"

"That is my knack," said Fitz, and, like a will-o'-wisp, he hopped off hither and thither, in a side direction, to lead his masters the stiangest road

Felix, in the mean while, highly satisfied in the treasure he had found, highly delighted at possessing a secret, kept close by his father, without, as formerly, skipping up and down beside his comrade   He nodded to Wilhelm with sparkling eyes, glancing towards his companion, and making significant faces, to indicate how much he was above Fitz now, in possessing a secret entirely wanting to the other.   He carried it so far at length, that Fitz, who often stopped and looked about, must very soon have noticed it   Wilhelm theiefore said to Felix "My son, whoevei wishes to keep a secret, must hide from us that he possesses one   Self-complaisance over the concealed destroys its concealment" Felix iestrained himself, but his formei gay free manner to his comrade he could not now attain

All at once little Fitz stood still   He beckoned the rest to him "Do you hear a beating?" said he   "It is the sound of a hammei striking on the rock "

"We hear it," answered they

"That is Montan," said he, "or some one who will tell us of him "

Following the sound, which was repeated from time to time, they reached an opening in the wood, and perceived a steep high naked rock, towering over all the rest, leaving even the lofty forest deep beneath it   On the top of it they descried a man · he was too far off to be iecognised   Immediately the boys set about ascending the precipitous path   Wilhelm followed with some difficulty, nay, danger for the person that climbs a rock foremost always proceeds with more safety, because he can look out for his conveniences, he who comes after sees only whither the other has arrived, but not how   The boys soon reached the top, and Wilhelm heard a shout of joy   "It is Jarno," cried Felix to his father   and Jarno immediately came forward to a rugged spot, stretched out his hand to his friend, and drew him up   They embraced, and welcomed each other into the free skyey air, with the rapture of old friends

But scarcely had they stept asunder, when a giddiness came over Wilhelm, not so much on his own account, as at seeing the boys hanging over the frightful abyss. Jarno observed it, and immediately bade all sit down   "Nothing is more natural," said he, " than that we should grow giddy at a great sight, which comes unexpectedly before us, to make us feel at once our littleness and our greatness   But there is not in the world any truer enjoyment, than at the moment when we are so made giddy for the first time "

"Are these, then, down there, the great Mountains we climbed over ?" inquired Felix   "How little they look ! And here," continued he, loosening a crumb of stone from the rock, "is the old cat-gold again   this is found everywhere, I suppose ? "

"It is found far and wide," answered Jarno, "and as thou art asking after such things, I may bid thee notice, that thou art now sitting on the oldest mountain, on the earliest rock of this world "

"Was the world not made at once, then ?" said Felix

"Hardly," answered Jarno, "good bread needs baking."

"Down there," said Felix, "is another sort of rock, and there again another, and still again another," cried he, pointing from the nearest mountains to the more remote, and so downward to the plain

It was a beautiful day, and Jarno let them survey the lordly prospect in detail   Here and there stood several other peaks, similar to the one our travellers were on   A secondary moderate range of mountains seemed as if struggling up, but did not by far attain that height   Farther off, the surface flattened still more, yet again some strangely-protruding forms rose to view   At last, in the remote distance, lakes were visible, and rivers, and a fruitful country spread itself out like a sea   And when the eye came back, it pierced into frightful depths, sounding with cataracts, and connected with each other in labyrinthic combination

Felix could not satisfy himself with questions, and Jarno was kind enough to answer all of them   in which, however, Wilhelm thought he noticed that the teacher did not always speak quite truly and sincerely.   So, after the unstaid boys had again clambered off, Wilhelm said to his friend   "Thou hast not spoken with the child, about these matters, as thou speakest to thyself"

"That indeed were a heavy requisition," answered Jarno "We do not always speak, even to ourselves, as we think, and it is not fit to tell others anything but what they can take up   A man understands nothing but what is commensurate with him   To fix a child's attention on what is present, to give him a description, a name, is the best thing we can do for him   He will soon enough begin to inquire after causes "

"One cannot blame this latter tendency," observed Wilhelm "The multiplicity of objects perplexes every one, and it is easier, instead of investigating them, to ask directly, Whence and Whither ?"

"And yet," said Jarno, "as children look at what is present only superficially, we cannot speak with them of Origin and Object otherwise than superficially also "

"Most men," answered Wilhelm, "continue all their days in this predicament, and never reach that glorious epoch, in which the Comprehensible appears to us common and insipid "

"It may well be called glorious," answered Jarno, "for it is a middle stage between despair and deification "

"Let us abide by the boy," said Wilhelm, "who is at present my first care   He has somehow got a fondness for minerals, since we began this journey   Canst thou not impart so much to me as would put it in my power to satisfy him, at least for a time ?"

"That will not do," said Jarno "In every new department, one must, in the first place, begin again as a child,
throw a passionate interest over the subject, take pleasure
in the shell, till one has the happiness to arrive at the
kernel "

"Tell me, then," said Wilhelm, "how hast thou attained
this knowledge? For it is not so very long, after all, since
we parted "

"My friend," said Jarno, "we were forced to resign ourselves, if not forever, at least for a long season The first
thing that occurs to a stout-hearted man, under such circumstances, is to begin a new life New objects will not suffice
him, these serve only for diversion of thought, he requires a
new whole, and plants himself in the middle of it "

"But why, then," interrupted Wilhelm, "choose this
strangest and loneliest of all pursuits? "

"Even because of its loneliness," cried Jarno "Men I
wished to avoid To them we can give no help, and they
hinder us from helping ourselves Are they happy, we must
let them persevere in their stolidities, are they unhappy, we
must save them without disturbing these stolidities, and no
one ever asks whether Thou art happy or unhappy."

"It is not quite so bad with the , surely," answered
Wilhelm, smiling

"I will not talk thee out of thy happiness," said Jarno
"Go on thy way, thou second Diogenes! Let not thy Lamp
in daylight go out! Down on that side lies a new world
before thee but I dare wager, things stand there as in the
old one. If thou canst not pimp, and pay debts, thou
availest nothing "

"Yet they seem to me more entertaining than thy dead
rocks," said Wilhelm

"Not they!" answered Jarno · "for my rocks are at least
incomprehensible."

CHAPTER VI

THE two friends had descended, not without care and labour, to reach the children, who were now lying in a shady spot down below   With almost greater eagerness than their picnic repast, the collected rock-specimens were unpacked by Montan and Felix   The latter had much to ask, the former much to nominate   Felix was delighted that his new teacher could give him names for all, and he speedily committed them to memory   At length he produced another specimen, and asked   "What do you call this, then?"

Montan viewed it with surprise, and said   "Where did you get it?"

Fitz answered promptly   "I found it myself, it is of this country"

"Not of this quarter," said Montan   Felix rejoiced to see his master somewhat puzzled   "Thou shalt have a ducat," said Montan, "if thou bring me to the spot where it lies"

"That is easy to earn," answered Fitz, "but not immediately"

" ᴛhen describe the place to me accurately, that I may not fail to find it   but the thing is impossible, for this is a cross-stone, which comes from Santiago in Compostella, and which some stranger has lost, if indeed thou hast not stolen it from him, for its curious look"

"Give your ducat into my master's hands," said Fitz, " and I will honestly confess where I got the stone   In the ruined church at St Joseph, there is likewise a ruined altar   Under the top-stones, which are all broken and heaped together, I discovered a layer of this rock, which has been the foundation of the other, and broke off from it as much as I could come at   If the upper stones were cleared away, one might find much more of it there"

"Take thy ducat," said Montan, "thou deservest it for

this discovery It is pretty enough Men naturally rejoice when inanimate nature produces any likeness of what they love and reverence Nature then appears to us in the form of a Sibyl, who has beforehand laid down a testimony of what had been determined from Eternity, and was not to be realised till late in Time On this rock, as on a sacred mysterious primeval basis, the priests had built their altar "

Wilhelm, who had listened for a while, and observed that many names, many designations, were repeatedly mentioned, again signified his former wish, that Montan would impart to him so much as was required for the primary instruction of the boy "Give that up," replied Montan "There is nothing more frightful than a teacher who knows only what his scholars are intended to know He who means to teach others, may indeed often suppress the best of what he knows, but he must not be half-instructed "

"But where are such perfect teachers to be had ?"

"These thou wilt find very easily," replied Montan

"Where, then ?" said Wilhelm, with some unbelief

"Where the thing thou art wishing to learn is in practice," said Montan "Our best instruction we obtain from complete conversance Dost thou not learn foreign languages best in the countries where they are at home ?—where only these and no other strike thy ear ?"

"And so it was among the Mountains," inquired Wilhelm, "that thy knowledge of Mountains was acquired ?"

"Of course "

"Without help from men ?"

"At least only from men who were miners There, where the Pygmies, allured by the metallic veins, bore through the rock, making the interior of the earth accessible, and in a thousand ways endeavouring to solve the hardest problems, there is the place where an inquiring thinker ought to take his stand He looks on action and effort, watches the progress of enterprises, and rejoices in the successful and the unsuccessful What is Useful forms but a part of the

Impoitant   Fully to possess, to command, and rule an object, we must first study it foi its own sake"

"Is there such a place in the neighbourhood?" said Wilhelm   "I should like to take Felix thither"

"The question I can answer in the affirmative," replied Montan, "the pioject not exactly assent to   At least, I must first tell thee, that thou hast the power of choosing among many other branches of activity, of knowledge, of art, for thy Felix, some of which might peihaps suit him better, than this sudden fancy which he has taken up at the moment, most probably from meie imitation"

"Explain thyself moie clearly," interrupted Wilhelm

"Thou must know, then," said Montan, "that we aie heie on the borders of a Piovince, which I might justly call a Pedagogic Utopia   In the conviction that only one thing can be carried on, taught and communicated with full advantages, several such points of active instruction have been, as it were, sown over a large tract of country   At each of these places thou wilt find a little world, but so complete within its limitation, that it may represent and model any other of these worlds, nay, the gieat busy world itself"

"I do not altogether comprehend what thou canst mean by this," interrupted Wilhelm

"Thou shalt soon comprehend it," said the other   "As down, not far from this, among the Mountains, thou wilt, in the first place, find collected round a mass of metalliferous iocks, whatever is of use for enabling man to appiopinate these treasures of Nature, and, at the same time, to acquiie general conceptions of moulding the ruggedness of inanimate things more dextrously to his own purposes, so, down in the lowest level, far out on the plain, where the soil spreads into large meadows and pastures, thou wilt find establishments foi anaging another important treasure which Nature has given to men"

"And this?" inquired Wilhelm

"Is the horse," replied the other   "In that last quarter,

thou art in the midst of everything which can instruct one on
the training, diet, growth, and likewise employment of this
noble animal   As in these hills all are busy digging, boring,
climbing, so there nothing is more anxiously attended to than
the young brood, springing, as it were, out of the ground;
and every one is occupied foddering, grazing, driving, leading,
curbing them, mounting their backs, and in all sorts of movements, natural and artificial, coursing with them over the
plain "

Felix, who had approached in the deepest attention, exclaimed, interrupting him   "O, thither will we !   That is the
prettiest, the best of all "

"It is far thither," answered Jarno, "and thou wilt find
something more agreeable and suitable, perhaps, by the way —
Any species of activity," continued he, "attracts the fondness
of a child , for everything looks easy that is practised to perfection.   All beginnings are hard, says the proverb   This, in
a certain sense, may be true , but we might say, with a more
universal application   All beginnings are easy , and it is the
last steps that are climbed most rarely and with greatest
difficulty "

Wilhelm, who had been reflecting in the mean while, now
said to Montan. "Is it actually so, as thou sayest, that these
people have separated the various sorts of activity, both in the
practice and teaching of them ?"

"They have done it," said Montan, "and with reason
Whatever any man has to effect must emanate from him like a
second self   and how could this be possible, were not his first
self entirely pervaded by it ?"

"Yet has not a general culture been reckoned very advantageous ?"

"It may really be so," replied the other   "everything in
its time   Now is the time of specialties   Happy he, who
understands this, and works for himself and others in that
spirit "

"In my spirit it cannot be," replied Wilhelm . " but tell

me, if I thought of sending Felix for a while into one of these
circles, which wouldst thou recommend to me?"

"It is all one," said Jarno "You cannot readily tell which
way a child's capacity particularly points For me, I should
still advise the merriest trade Take him to those horse-
subduers Beginning as a groom is in truth little easier than
beginning as an ore-beater, but the prospect is always gayer,
you can hope at least to get through the world riding"

It is easy to conceive, that Wilhelm had many other doubts
to state, and many farther explanations to require these
Jarno settled in his usual laconic way, but at last he broke
out as follows "In all things, to serve from the lowest station
upwards is necessary To restrict yourself to a trade is best
For the narrow mind, whatever he attempts is still a trade,
for the higher an art, and the highest, in doing one thing,
does all, or, to speak less paradoxically, in the one thing
which he does rightly, he sees the likeness of all that is done
rightly Take thy Felix," continued he, "through the Province, let the Directors see him, they will soon judge him,
and dispose of him to the best advantage The boy should be
placed among his equals, otherwise he seeks them for himself,
and then, in his associates, finds only flatterers or tyrants"

CHAPTER VII

THE third day being over, the friends, in conformity to
the engagement of our Renunciants, had to part, and Jarno
declared, he would now fly so far into the waste Mountains,
that no one should be able to discover him "There is nothing
more frightful," said he, "in a state like ours, than to meet
an old true friend, to whom we can communicate our thoughts
without reserve So long as one is by himself, one fancies
there is no end to the novelties and wonders he is studying,
but let the two talk a while together, right from the heart,
one sees how soon all this is exhausted Nothing is endless

but Inanity   Clever people soon explain themselves to one
another, and then they have done   But now I will dive into
the chasms of the rocks, and with them begin a mute un-
fathomable conversation "

" Have a care," said Wilhelm, smiling, " lest Fitz come
upon thy track   This time, at least, he succeeded in finding
thee "

" How didst thou manage that ? " said Montan   " After
all, it was only chance "

" Not in the least," answered Fitz   " I will tell you my
secret, for a fair consideration   You mineralogists, wherever
you go, keep striking to the right and left , from every stone,
from every rock, breaking off a piece, as if gold and silver
were hid in them   One has but to follow this trace , and
where any corner shows a fresh breakage, there some of you
have been   One notes and notes, forward and forward, and at
last comes upon the man "

Fitz was praised and rewarded   The friends parted ,
Montan alone, the little caravan in company   Wilhelm had
settled the place they should make for   The porter proposed
a road to it , but the children had taken a fancy for looking,
by the way, at the Giant's Castle, of which Fitz had talked so
much   Felix was curious about the large black pillars, the
great door, the cellar, the caves and vaults , and hoped he
might perhaps find something there, something of even greater
value than the box

How he came by this, he had, in the interim, informed his
father   Creeping through the cleft, it appeared, he had got
down into an open space pretty well lighted , and noticed, in
the corner of it, a large iron chest, the lid of which, though it
was not locked, he could not lift, but only raise a very little
To get into this, he had called to his father for the staves,
which he had employed partly as props under the lid, partly as
levers to heave it up , and so at length, forcing his way into
the chest, had found it wholly empty, except for the little box
which was lying in one of the nooks   This toy they had shown

Montan, who agreed with them in opinion, that it should be kept unopened, and no violence done to it, for it could not be unlocked except by a very complicated key

The porter declined going with the rest to the Giant's Castle, and proceeded down the smooth footpath by himself The others toiled after Fitz, through moss and tangle, and at length reached the natural Colonnade, which, towering over a huge mass of fragments, rose black and wondrous into the air. Yet, without uch regarding what he saw before his eyes, Felix instantly began inquiring for the other promised marvels, and as none of them was to be seen, Fitz could excuse himself no otherwise than by declaring that these things were never visible except on Sundays and particular festivals, and then only for a few hours   The boys remained convinced that the Pillared Palace was a work of men's hands   Wilhem saw well that it was a work of nature, but he could have wished for Montan to speak with on the subject

They now proceeded rapidly down hill, through a wood of high taper larches, which becoming more and more transparent, ere long exposed to view the fairest spot you can imagine, lying in the clearest sunshine

A large garden, see ingly appropriated to use, not ornament, lay richly furnished with fruit-trees, yet open before their eyes, for the ground, sloping on the whole, had been regularly cut into a number of divisions, now raised, now hollowed in manifold variety, and thus exhibited a complex waving surface   Several dwelling-houses stood scattered up and down, so that it seemed as if the space belonged to several proprietors   yet Fitz assured them, that one individual owned and directed the whole   Beyond the garden stretched a boundless landscape, beautifully cultivated and planted, in which lakes and rivers might be distinguished in the distance

Still descending, they had approached nearer and nearer, and were now expecting in a few moments to be in the garden, when Wilhelm all at once stopped short, and Fitz could not hide his roguish satisfaction, for a yawning chas   at the foot

of the mountain opened before them, and showed on the other
side a wall which had hitherto been concealed, steep enough
without, though within it was quite filled up with soil   A
deep trench, therefore, separated them from the garden, into
which they were directly looking   "We have still a good
circuit to make," said Fitz, " before we get the road that leads
in   However, I know an entrance on this side, which is much
shorter   The vaults where the hill-water in time of rain is let
through, in regular quantities, into the garden, open here
they are high and broad enough for one to walk along without
difficulty"   The instant Felix heard of vaults, he insisted on
taking this passage and no other   Wilhelm followed the
children, and the party descended the large steps of this
covered aqueduct, which was now lying quite dry   Down
below, they found themselves sometimes in light, sometimes in
darkness, according as the side openings admitted day, or the
walls and pillars excluded it   At last they reached a pretty
even space, and were slowly proceeding, when all at once a
shot went off beside them, and at the same time two secret
iron-grated doors started out, and enclosed them on both
sides   Not indeed the whole of them   Wilhelm and Felix
only were caught   For Fitz, the instant he heard the shot,
sprang back, and the closing grate caught nothing but his
wide sleeve   he himself nimbly throwing off his jacket, had
darted away without loss of a moment

   The two prisoners had scarcely time to recover from their
astonishment, till they heard voices which appeared to be
slowly approaching   In a little while, some armed men with
torches came forward to the grate, looking with eager eyes
what sort of capture they had made   At the same time, they
asked, if the prisoners would surrender peaceably?   "Surrender
is not the word here," said Wilhelm, " we are already in your
power   It is rather our part to ask, whether you will spare
us?   The only weapon we have, I give up to you"   And with
these words he handed his hanger through the grate   this
opened directly, and the two strangers were led forward by

the party, with great composure   Aftei a shoit while, they
found themselves in a singular place   it was a spacious cleanly
apartment, with many little windows at the veiy top of the walls,
and these, notwithstanding the thick iion giatings, admitted
light enough   Seats, sleeping-places, and whatever else is
expected in a middling inn, had been provided, and it seemed
as if any one placed here could want nothing but fieedom

Wilhelm, directly after entering, had sat down to considei
his situation   Felix, on the other hand, on iecoveiing from
his astonishment, bioke out into an inciedible fury   These
laige walls, these high windows, these strong doois, this
seclusion, this restiiction, were entiiely new to him.   He
looked iound and iound, he ian hithei and thithei., stamped
with his feet, wept, iattled the doors, struck against theui
with his fists, nay, was even on the point of running at them
with his head, had not Wilhelm seized him, and held him fast
between his knees   "Do but look at the thing calmly, my
son," began he   "for impatience and violence cannot help us
The mystery will clear up, and I must be widely mistaken, or
we are fallen into no wicked hands   Read these inscriptions.
'To the innocent, deliveiance and iepaiation, to the misled,
compassion, and to the guilty, avenging justice'   All this
bespeaks to us that these establishments aie woiks not of
ciuelty, but of necessity   Men have but too much cause to
secure themselves fiom men   Of ill-wisheis there are many,
of ill-doeis not few, and to live fitly, well-doing will not
always suffice"   Felix still sobbed, but he had pacified himself in some degree, moie by the caresses than the words of
his father   "Let this experience," continued Wilhelm, "which
thou gainest so eaily, and so innocently, iemain a lively
testimony to thy mind, in how complete and accomplished a
century thou livest   What a jouiney had human natuie to
travel, before it reached the point of being mild even to the
guilty, merciful to the injurious, humane to the inhuman!
Doubtless they weie men of godlike souls who fiist taught
this, who spent their lives in iendeiing the practice of it

possible, and recommending it to others Of the Beautiful
men are seldom capable, oftener of the Good and how highly
should we value those who endeavour, with great sacrifices, to
forward that Good among their fellows!"

Felix, in the course of this consolatory speech, had fallen
quietly asleep on his father's bosom, and scarcely had the
latter laid him down on one of the ready-made beds, when
the door opened, and a man of prepossessing appearance stept
in   After looking kindly at Wilhelm for some time, he began
to inquire about the circumstances, which had led him by the
private passage, and into this predicament   Wilhelm related
the affair as it stood, produced some papers, which served to
explain who he was, and referred to the porter, who, he said,
must soon arrive on the other side by the usual road   This
being so far explained, the official person invited his guest to
follow him   Felix could not be awakened, and his father
carried him asleep from the place which had incited him to
such violent passion

Wilhelm followed his conductor into a fair garden-apart-
ment, where refreshments were set down which he was invited
to partake of, while the other went to report the state of
matters to his superior   When Felix, on awakening, perceived
a little covered table, fruit, wine, biscuit, and at the same
time the cheerful aspect of a wide-open door, he knew not
what to make of it   He ran out, he ran back, he thought he
had been dreaming, and in a little while, with such dainty
fare and such pleasant sights, the preceding terror and all his
obstruction had vanished, like an oppressive vision in the
brightness of morning

The porter had arrived, the officer, with another man of
a still friendlier aspect, brought him in, and the business
now came to light, as follows   The owner of this property,
charitable in this higher sense, that he studied to awaken all
round him to activity and effort, had for several years been
accustomed, from his boundless young plantations, to give out
the small wood to diligent and careful cultivators, gratis, to

the negligent, for a certain price, and to such as wished to trade in it, likewise at a moderate valuation   But these two latter classes also had required their supplies gratis, as the meritorious were treated; and this being refused them, they had attempted stealing trees   Their attempt succeeded in many ways   This vexed the owner the more, as not only were the plantations plundered, but, by too early thinning, often ruined   It had been discovered that the thieves entered by this aqueduct, so the trap-gate had been erected in the place, with a spring gun, which, however, was only meant for a signal   The little boy had, under various pretexts, often made his appearance in the garden, and nothing was more natural, than that out of mischief and audacity he should lead the stranger by a road which he had formerly discovered for other purposes   The people could have wished to get hold of him   meanwhile his little jacket was brought in, and put by among other judicial seizures

Wilhelm was now made acquainted with the owner and his people, and by them received with the friendliest welcome Of this family we shall say nothing more here, as some farther light on them and their concerns is offered us by the subsequent history

CHAPTER VIII

Wilhelm to Natalia

MAN is of a companionable, conversing nature   his delight is great when he exercises faculties that have been given him, even though nothing farther came of it   How often in society do we hear the complaint, that one will not let the other speak   and in the same manner also we might say, that one would not let the other write, were not writing an employment commonly transacted in private and alone

How much people write one could scarcely ever conjecture

I speak not of what is printed, though that in itself is abundant enough, but of all that, in the shape of letters and memorials and narratives, anecdotes, descriptions of present circumstances in the life of individuals, sketches and larger essays, circulates in secret, of this you can form no idea till you have lived for some time in a community of cultivated families, as I am now doing.   In the sphere where I am moving at present, there is almost as much time employed in informing friends and relatives of what is transacted, as was employed in transacting it   This observation, which for several weeks has been constantly forced on me, I now make with the more pleasure, as the writing tendency of my new friends enables me at once and perfectly to get acquainted with their characters and circumstances   I am trusted, a sheaf of Letters is given to me, some quires of a Travelling Journal, the Confessions of some mind not yet in unity with itself, and thus everywhere, in a little while, I am at home I know the neighbouring circle, I know the persons whose acquaintance I am to obtain, I understand them better almost than they do themselves, seeing they are still implicated in their situation, while I hover lightly past them, ever with thy hand in mine, ever speaking with thee about all I see   Indeed it is the first condition I make, before accepting any confidence offered me, that I may impart it to thee   Here, accordingly. are some letters, which will introduce thee into the circle, in which, without breaking or evading my vow, I for the present revolve.

THE NUT-BROWN MAID

Lenardo to his Aunt

At last, dear Aunt, after three years, you receive my first letter, conformably to our engagement, which, in truth, was singular enough   I wished to see the world and mingle in it, and wished, during that period, to forget the home whence I had departed, whither I hoped to return   The whole impres-

sion of this home I purposed to retain, and the partial and
individual was not to confuse me at a distance   Meanwhile
the necessary tokens of life and welfare have, from time to
time, passed to and fro between us   I have regularly received
money, and little presents for my kindred have been delivered
you for distribution   By the wares I sent, you would see how
and where I was   By the wines, I doubt not my uncle has
tasted out my several places of abode, then the laces, nick-
nacks, steel-wares, would indicate to my fair cousins my progress through Brabant, by Paris, to London, and so, on their
writing-desks, work-boxes, tea-tables, I shall find many a
symbol wherewith to connect the history of my journeyings
You have accompanied me without hearing of me, and
perhaps may care little about knowing more   For me, on the
other hand, it is highly desirable to learn, through your kindness, how it stands with the circle into which I am once more
entering   I would, in truth, return from strange countries as
a stranger, who, that he may not be unpleasant, first informs
himself about the way and manner of the household, not
fancying that, for his fine eyes or hair, he shall be received
there quite in his own fashion   Write to me, therefore, of my
worthy uncle, of your fair nieces, of yourself, of our relations
near and distant, of servants also, old and new   In short, let
your practised pen, which for so long a time you have not
dipped into ink for your nephew, now again tint paper in his
favour.   Your letter of news shall forthwith be my credential,
with which I introduce myself so soon as I obtain it   On you,
therefore, it depends whether you will see me or not   We
alter far less than we imagine, and circumstances, too, continue much as they were   Not only what has altered, but
what has continued, what has by degrees waxed and waned, do
I now wish instantly to recognise at my return, and so once
more to see myself in a well-known mirror   Present my
heartiest salutations to all our people, and believe, that in
the singular manner of my absence and my return, there

participation and lively intercourse   A thousand compliments
to one and all !

Postscript —Neglect not also, my dear Aunt, to say a word
or two about our dependants , how it stands with our stewards
and farmers   What is become of Valerina, the daughter of
that farmer, whom my uncle, with justice certainly, but also,
as I thought, with some severity, ejected from his lands when
I went away ?   You see, I still remember many a particular,
I still know all   On the past you shall examine me, when you
have told me of the present

The Aunt to Julietta

At last, dear children, a letter from our three-years speech-
less traveller   What strange beings these strange men are !
He will have it that his wares and tokens were as good as
so many kind words, which friend may speak or write to friend
He actually fancies himself our creditor, requires from *us*, in
the first place, the performance of that service, which *he* so
unkindly refused   What is to be done ?   For me, I should
have met his wishes forthwith in a long letter, did not this
headache signify too clearly that the present sheet can scarcely
be filled   We all long to see him   Do you, my dears, undertake the business   Should I be recovered before you have
done, I will contribute my share   Choose the persons and
circumstances, as you like best to describe them   Divide the
task   You will do it all far better than I   The   essenger
will bring me back a note from you

Julietta to her Aunt

We have read and considered , and now send you by the
messenger our view of the matter, each in particular , having
first jointly signified that we are not so charitable as our dear
Aunt to her ever-perverse nephew   Now, when he has kept

hid, we forsooth are to spread ours on the table, and play an open against a secret game   This is not fair, and yet let it pass, for the craftiest is often caught, simply by his own over-anxious precautions   But as to the way and manner of transacting this commission, we are not agreed   To write of our familiars as we think of them, is for us at least a very strange problem   Commonly we do not think of them at all, except in this or that particular case, when they give us some peculiar satisfaction or vexation   At other times, each lets his neighbour go his way   You alone could manage it, dear Aunt, for you have both the penetration and the tolerance Hersilia, who you know is not difficult to kindle, has just, on the spur of the moment, given me a bird's-eye view of the whole family in all the graces of caricature   I wish it stood on paper, to entice a smile from yourself in your illness, but not that I would have it sent   My own project is, to lay before him our correspondence for these three years, then let him read, if he have the heart, or let him come and see with his eyes, if he have not   Your Letters to e, dear Aunt, are in the best order, and all at your service.   Hersilia dissents from this opinion, excuses herself with the disorder of her papers, and so forth, as she will tell you herself

Hersilia to her Aunt

I will and must be very brief, dear Aunt, for the messenger is clownishly impatient   I reckon it an excess of generosity, and not at all in season, to submit our correspondence to Lenardo   What has he to do with knowing all the good we have said of him, with knowing all the ill we have said of him, and finding out from the latter still more than from the former that we like him?   Hold him tight, I entreat you There is something so precise and presumptuous in this demand, in this conduct of his, just the fashion of your young gentlemen when they return from foreign parts   They can never look on those who have stayed at home as full-grown

persons, like themselves Make your headache an excuse He
will come, doubtless and if he do not come, we can wait a
little Perhaps his next idea may be to introduce himself in
some strange secret way, to become acquainted with us in
disguise, and who knows what more may be included in the
plan of so deep a gentleman? How pretty and curious this
would be! It could not fail to bring about all manner of
embroilments and developments, far grander than any that
could be produced by such a diplo atic entrance into his
family as he now purposes

The messenger! The messenger! Bring up your old
people better, or send young ones This man is neither to
be pacified with flattery nor wine A thousand farewells!

Postscript for Postscript —What does our cousin want, will
you tell me, with his postscript of Valerina? This question
of his has struck me doubly She is the only person whom
he mentions by name. The rest of us are nieces, aunts,
stewards, not persons, but titles Valerina, our Lawyer's
daughter! In truth, a pretty fair-haired girl, that may
have glanced in our gallant cousin's eyes before he went
away She is married well and happily, this to you is no
news, but to him it is, of course, as unknown as everything
that has occurred here Forget not to inform him, in a
postscript, that Valerina grew daily more and ore beautiful, and so at last made a very good match That she is the
wife of a rich proprietor That the lovely fair-haired maid
is married Make it perfectly distinct to hi But neither
is this all, dear Aunt How the man can so accurately
remember his flaxen-headed beauty, and yet confound her
with the daughter of that worthless farmer, with a wild
humble-bee of a brunette, whose name was Nachodina, and
who went away Heaven knows whither, this, I declare to you.
remains entirely incomprehensible, and puzzles me quite excessively For it seems as if our pretty cousin, who prides
himself on his good memory, could change names and persons
to a very strange degree Perhaps he feels this obscurely

himself, and would have the faded image refreshed by your delineation Hold him tight, I beg of you but try to learn, for our own behoof, how it does stand with these Valerinas and Nachodinas , and how many more Inas and Trinas have retained their place in his imagination, while the poor Ettas and Ilias have vanished The messenger! The cursed messenger !

The Aunt to her Nieces

(Dictated)

Why should we dissemble towards those we have to spend our life with ? Lenaido, with all his peculiarities, deserves confidence I send him both your letters from these he will get a view of you , and the rest of us, I hope, will ere long unconsciously find occasion to depict ourselves before him likewise Farewell ! My head is very painful

Hersilia to her Aunt

Why should we dissemble towards those we have to spend our life with ? Lenardo is a spoiled nephew It is horrible in you to send him our letters From these he will get no real view of us , and I wish with all my heart for opportunity to let him view me in some other light You give pain to others, while you are in pain yourself, and blind to boot Quick recovery to your head ! Your heart is irrecoverable.

The Aunt to Hersilia

Thy last note I should likewise have packed in for Lenaido, had I happened to continue by the purpose, which my irrecoverable heart, my sick head, and my love of ease, suggested to me Your letters are not gone I am just parting with the young man, who has been for some time living in our circle, who, by the strangest chance, has come to know us pretty well, and is withal of an intelligent and kindly nature Him I am despatching He undertakes the task with great

readiness   He will prepare our nephew, and send or bring
hi   Thus can your Aunt recollect herself in the course of
a rash enterprise, and bend into another path   Hersilia also
will take thought, and a friendly revocation will not long be
wanting from her hand.

Wilhelm having accurately and circumstantially fulfilled
this task, Lenardo answered with a smile   "Much as I am
obliged to you for what you tell me, I must still put another
question   Did not my Aunt, in conclusion, request you also
to inform me of another and seemingly an unimportant
matter ? "

Wilhelm thought a moment   "Yes," said he, then, "I
remember   She mentioned a lady, named Valerina   Of her
I was to tell you that she is happily wedded, and every way
well "

"You roll a stone from my heart," replied Lenardo.   "I
now gladly return home, since I need not fear that my recollection of this girl can reproach me there "

"It beseems not me to inquire what relation you have had
to her,' said Wilhelm   "only you may be at ease, if in any
way you feel concerned for her fortunes "

"It is the strangest relation in the world," returned
Lenardo   "nowise a love matter, as you might perhaps
conjecture   I may confide in you, and tell it, as indeed there
is next to nothing to be told   But what must you think,
when I assure you, that this faltering in my return, this fear
of revisiting our family, these strange preparatives, and
inquiries how things looked at home, had no other object
but to learn, by the way, how it stood with this young
woman ? "

"For you will believe," continued he, "I am very well
aware that we may leave people whom we know, without
finding them, even after a considerable time, much altered
and so I likewise expect very soon to be quite at home with
my relatives   This single being only made me pause   her

fortune, I knew, must have changed, and, thank Heaven, it has changed for the better"

"You excite my curiosity," said Wilhelm "There must be something singular in this"

"I at least think it so," replied Lenardo, and began his narrative as follows

"To accomplish, in my youth, the grand adventure of a tour through cultivated Europe, was a fixed purpose, which I had entertained from boyhood, but the execution of which was, as usually happens in these things, from time to time postponed   What was at hand attracted me, retained me, and the distant lost more and more of its charms, the more I read of it, or heard it talked of   However, at last, incited by my uncle, allured by friends who had gone forth into the world before me, I did form the resolution, and that more rapidly than any one had been expecting

"My uncle, who had to afford the main requisite for my enterprise, directly made this his chief concern   You know him, and the way he has, how he still rushes with his whole force on one single object, and everything else in the mean while must rest and be silent, by which means, indeed, he has effected much that seemed to lie beyond the influence of any private man   This journey came upon him, in so e degree, unawares, yet he very soon took his easures   Some buildings, which he had planned, nay, even begun, were abandoned, and as he never on any account meddles with his accumulated stock, he looked about him, as a prudent financier, for other ways and means   The most obvious plan was to call-in outstanding debts, especially remainders of rent   for this also was one of his habits, that he was indulgent to debtors, so long as he himself had, to a certain degree, no need of money   He gave his Steward the list, with orders to manage the business   Of individual cases we learned nothing   only I heard transiently, that the far er of one of our estates, with whom my uncle had long exercised patience, was at last actually to be ejected, his cautionary pledge, a scanty supplement to the produce of this prosecution, to be retained, and the land to be let to some other person   This man was of a religious turn, but not, like others of his sect among us, shrewd and active withal   for his piety and goodness he was loved by his neighbours, but at the same time censured for his weakness as the master of a house   After the death of his wife, a daughter, whom we usually named the Nut-brown Maid, though already giving promise of activity and resolution, was still too young for taking a decisive   anagement   in short, the man went back in his affairs, and my uncle's indulgence had not stayed the sinking of his fortune

" I had my journey in my head, and could not quarrel with the means for accomplishing it   All was ready, packing and sorting went forward, every moment was becoming full of business   One evening I was strolling through the park, for the last time, to take leave of my familiar trees and bushes, when all at once Valerina stept into my way   for such was the girl's name, the other was but a byname, occasioned by her brown complexion   She stept into   y way "

Lenardo paused for a moment, as if considering   " How is this, then?" said he   " Was her name really Valerina? Yes, surely," he continued, " but the byname was more co mon   In short, the brown   aid came into my path, and pressingly entreated me to speak a good word for her father, for herself, to my uncle   Knowing how the matter stood, and seeing clearly that it would be difficult, nay, impossible, to do her any service at this moment, I candidly told her so, and set before her the blameworthiness of her father in an unfavourable light

" She answered this with so much clearness, and at the same time with so much filial mitigation and love, that she quite gained me; and, had it been my own money, I should instantly have made her happy, by granting her request   But it was my uncle's income   these were his arrangements, his orders with such a temper as his, to attempt altering aught that had been done was hopeless From of old, I had looked on a promise as in the highest degree sacred Whoever asked anything of me embarrassed me I had so accustomed myself to refuse, that I did not even promise what I purposed to perform This habit came in good stead in the present instance Her arguments turned on individuality and affection, mine on duty and reason and I will not deny that at last they seemed too harsh even to myself Already we had more than once repeated our topics without convincing one another, when necessity made her more eloquent, the inevitable ruin which she saw before her pressed tears from her eyes Her collected manner she entirely lost, she spoke with vivacity, with emotion, and as I still kept up a show of coldness and composure, her whole soul turned itself outwards I wished to end the scene but all at once she was lying at my feet, had seized my hand, kissed it, and was looking up to me, so good, so gentle, with such supplicating loveliness, that in the haste of the moment I forgot myself Hurriedly I said, while raising her from her kneeling posture 'I will do what is possible, compose thyself, my child!' and so turned into a side-path 'Do what is impossible!' cried she after me I now knew not what I was saying, but answered 'I will,' and hesitated 'Do it!' cried she, at once enlivened, and with a heavenly expression of hope I waved a salutation to her, and hastened away

"To my uncle I did not mean to apply directly for I knew too well that with him it was vain to speak about the partial, when his purpose was the whole I inquired for the Steward, he had ridden off to a distance, visitors came in the evening, friends wishing to take leave of me They supped and played till far in the night They continued next day, and their presence effaced the image of my importunate petitioner The Steward returned, he was busier and more overloaded than ever All were asking for him he had no

him, but scarcely had I named that pious farmer, when he
eagerly repelled the proposal 'For Heaven's sake, not a word
of this to your uncle, if you would not have a quarrel with
him!' The day of y departure was fixed, I had letters to
write, guests to receive, visits in the neighbourhood to pay
My servants had been hitherto sufficient for my wants, but
were nowise adequate to forward the arrangements of a distant journey All lay on my own hands, and yet when
the Steward appointed me an hour in the night before my
departure, to settle our money concerns, I neglected not again
to solicit him for Valerina's father

"'Dear Baron,' said the unstable man, 'how can such a
thing ever come into your head? Today already I have had
a hard piece of work with your uncle, for the sum you need
is turning out to be far higher than we reckoned on This is
natural enough, but not the less perplexing To the old
gentleman it is especially unwelcome, when a business seems
concluded, and yet many odds and ends are found straggling
after it This is often the case, and I and the rest have to
take the brunt of it As to the rigour with which the outstanding debts were to be gathered in, he himself laid down
the law to me he is at one with himself on this point, and it
would be no easy task to move him to indulgence Do not try
it, I beg of you! It is quite in vain'

"I let him deter me from my attempt, but not entirely I
pressed hi , since the execution of the business depended on
himself, to act with mildness and mercy He promised everything, according to the fashion of such persons, for the sake of
momentary peace He got quit of me the bustle, the hurry
of business increased! I was in my carriage, and had turned
my back on all home concerns

"A keen impression is like any other wound, we do not
feel it in receiving it Not till afterwards does it begin to
smart and gangrene So was it with me in regard to this
occurrence in the park Whenever I was solitary, whenever I
was une ployed, that image of the entreating maiden, with

the whole accompaniment, with every tree and bush, the place
where she knelt, the side-path I took to get rid of her, the
whole scene rose like a fresh picture before my soul   It was
an indestructible impression, which, by other images and
interests, might indeed be shaded or overhung, but never
obliterated   Still, in every quiet hour, she came before me,
and the longer it lasted, the more painful did I feel the blame
which I had incurred against my principles, against my custom,
though not expressly, only while hesitating, and for the first
time caught in such a perplexity

   "I failed not in my earliest letters to inquire of our Steward
how the business had turned   He answered evasively   Then
he engaged to explain this point, then he wrote ambiguously,
at last he became silent altogether   Distance increased, more
objects came between me and my home, I was called to many
new observations, many new sympathies, the image faded
away, the maiden herself, almost to the name   The remembrance of her came more rarely before me, and, my whim of
keeping up my intercourse with home, not by letters, but by
tokens, tended gradually to make my previous situation, with
all its circumstances, nearly vanish from my mind   Now,
however, when I am again returning home, when I am purposing to repay my family with interest what I have so long
owed it, now at last this strange repentance, strange I myself
must call it, falls on me with its whole weight   The form of
the aiden brightens up with the forms of my relatives, and
I dread nothing more deeply than to learn that, in the misery
into which I drove her, she has sunk to ruin, for my negligence
appears in my own mind an abetting of her destruction, a
furtherance of her mournful destiny   A thousand times I
have told myself that this feeling was at bottom but a weakness, that my early adoption of the principle, never to
promise, had originated in my fear of repentance, not in any
noble sentiment   And now it seems as if Repentance, which
I had fled from, meant to avenge herself, by seizing this

the imagination which torments me, so agreeable withal, so lovely, that I like to linger over it. And when I think of the scene, that kiss which she imprinted on my hand, still seems to burn there "

Lenardo was silent, and Wilhelm answered quickly and gaily . "It appears, then, I could have done you no greater service than by that appendix to my narrative, as we often find in the postscript the most interesting part of the letter In truth, I know little of Valerina, for I heard of her only in passing but, for certain, she is the wife of a prosperous land-owner, and lives happily, as your aunt assured me, on taking leave "

" Good, and well," said Lenardo "now there is nothing to detain me   You have given me absolution, let us now to my friends, who have already waited for me too long " To this Wilhelm answered "Unhappily I cannot attend you , for a strange obligation lies on me to continue nowhere longer than three days, and not to revisit any place in less than a year Pardon me, if I am not at liberty to mention the cause of this singularity "

" I am very sorry," said Lenardo, " that we are to lose you so soon that I cannot, in my turn, do anything for you   But since you are already in the way of showing me kindness, you might make e very happy if you pleased to visit Valerina , to inform yourself accurately of her situation , and then to let me have, in writing or in speech (a place of meeting might easily be found), express intelligence for my complete com-posure "

This proposal was farther discussed , Valerina's place of residence had been named to Wilhel   He engaged to visit her , a place of meeting was appointed, to which the Baron should come, bringing Felix with him, who in the mean while, had remained with the ladies

Lenardo and Wilhelm had proceeded on their way for so e time, riding together through pleasant fields, with abundance of conversation, when at last they approached the highway, and found the Baron's coach in waiting, now ready to revisit with its owner the spot it had left three years before Here the friends were to part, and Wilhelm, with a few kindly words, took his leave, again promising the Baron speedy news of Valerina

"Now when I bethink me," said Lenardo, "that it were but a small circuit if I accompanied you, why should I not visit Valerina myself? Why not witness with my own eyes her happy situation? You were so friendly as engage to be my messenger, why should you not be my companion? For some companion I must have, some moral counsel, as we take legal counsel to assist us, when we think ourselves inadequate to the perplexities of a process "

Wilhelm's objections, that the friends at home would be anxiously expecting the long-absent traveller, that it would produce a strange impression if the carriage came alone, and other reasons of the like sort, had no weight with Lenardo, and Wilhelm was obliged at last to resolve on acting the companion to the Baron, a task on which, considering the consequences that might be apprehended, he entered with no great alacrity

Accordingly the servants were instructed what to say on their arrival, and the two friends now took the road for Valerina's house The neighbourhood appeared rich and fertile, the true seat of Agriculture Especially the grounds of Valerina's husband seemed to be managed with great skill and care Wilhelm had leisure to survey the landscape accurately, while Lenardo rode in silence beside him At last the latter said "Another in my place would perhaps try to meet Valerina undiscovered, for it is always a painful feeling to appear before those whom we have injured, but I had rather front this, and bear the reproach which I have to dread from her first look, than secure myself fro it by disguise and untruth Untruth may bring us into embarrassment quite as well as truth, and when we reckon up how often the former or the latter profits us, it really see s most prudent, once for all,

to devote ourselves to what is true   Let us go forward, therefore, with cheerful minds   I will give my name, and introduce
you as my friend and fellow-traveller "

They had now reached the house, and dismounted in the
court   A well-looking man, whom you might have taken for
a farmer, came out to them, and announced himself as master
of the family   Lenardo named himself, and the landlord
seemed highly delighted to see him, and obtain his acquaintance   " What will my wife say," cried he, " when she again
meets the nephew of her benefactor !   She never tires of
recounting and reckoning up what her father owes your
uncle "

What strange thoughts rushed in rapid disorder through
Lenardo's mind !   "Does this man, who looks so honest-
minded, hide his bitterness under a friendly countenance and
smooth words ?   Can he give his reproaches so courteous an
outside ?   For did not my uncle reduce that family to misery !
And can the man be ignorant of this ?   Or," so thought he
to himself, with quick hope, " has the business not been so
bad as thou supposest ?   For no decisive intelligence has ever
yet reached thee "   Such conjectures alternated this way and
that, while the landlord was ordering out his carriage to bring
home his wife, who, it appeared, was paying a visit in the
neighbourhood

" If in the mean while, till my wife return," said the latter,
" I might entertain you in my own way, and at the same time
carry on my duties, say you walk a few steps with me into the
fields, and look about you how I manage my husbandry, for,
no doubt, to you, as a great proprietor of land, there is nothing
of more near concernment than the noble science, the noble art
of Agriculture "

Lenardo made no objection, Wilhelm liked to gather infor-
ation   The landlord had his ground, which he possessed
and ruled without restriction, under the most perfect treatment, what he undertook was adapted to his purpose, what
he sowed and planted was always in the right place, and

he could so clearly explain his mode of procedure, and the reasons of it, and every one co prehended him, and thought it possible for himself to do the same a mistake one is apt to fall into, on looking at a master, in whose hand all moves as it should do

The strangers expiessed their satisfaction, and had nothing but praise and appioval to pronounce on everything they saw He received it gratefully and kindly, and at last added "Now, however, I must show you my weak side, a quality discernible in every one that yields himself exclusively to one pursuit" He led them to his court-yard, showed them his implements, his store of these, and besides this, a store of all 1 aginable sorts of farm-gear, with its appurtenances, kept by way of specimen "I am often blamed," said he, "for going too far in this matter, but I cannot quite blame myself Happy is he to whom his business itself becomes a puppet, who at length can play with it, and amuse himself with what his situation makes his duty"

The two friends were not behindhand with their questions and examinations Wilhelm, in particular, delighted in the general observations which this man appeared to have a turn for making, and failed not to answer them while the Baron, more immersed in his own thoughts, took silent pleasure in the happiness of Valerina, which, in this situation, he reckoned sure, yet felt underhand a certain faint shadow of dissatisfaction, of which he could give himself no account

The party had returned within doors, when the lady's cairiage drove up They hastened out to meet hei . but what was Lenardo's amazement, his fright, when she stept forth! This was not the person, this was no Nut-brown Maid, but directly the reverse, a fair slim form, in truth, but light-haired, and possessing all the charms which belong to that co plexion

This beauty, this grace affrighted Lenardo. His eyes had sought the brown maiden, now quite a different figure glanced before them These features, too, he recollected, her words,

her manner, soon banished all uncertainty it was the daughter
of the Lawyer, a man who stood in high favour with the
uncle, for which reason also the dowry had been so handsome, and the new pair so generously dealt with All this,
and much more, was gaily recounted by the young wife as an
introductory salutation, and with such a joy as the surprise of
an unexpected meeting naturally gives rise to The question,
whether they could recognise each other, was mutually put
and answered, the changes in look were talked of, which in
persons of that age are found notable enough Valerina was
at all times agreeable, but lovely in a high degree, when any
joyful feeling raised her above her usual level of indifference
The company grew talkative the conversation beca e so
lively, that Lenardo w enabled to co pose himself and hide
his confusion Wilhelm, to whom he had very soon given a
sign of this strange incident, did his best to help him, and
Valerina's little touch of vanity in thinking that the Baron,
even before visiting his own friends, had remembered her, ...u
come to see her, excluded any shadow of suspicion that another
purpose or a misconception could be concerned in the affair

The party kept together till a late hour, though the two
friends were longing for a confidential dialogue, which accordingly commenced, the moment they were left alone in their
allotted chambers

"It appears," said Lenardo, "I am not to get rid of this
secret pain A luckless confusion of names, I now observe,
redoubles it This fair-haired beauty I have often seen playing with the brunette, who could not be called a beauty, nay,
I myself have often run about with the over the fields and
gardens, though so uch older than they Neither of them
made the slightest impression on me, I have but retained the
name of the one, and applied it to the other And now her
who does not concern me, I find happy above measure in her
own way, while the other is cast forth, who knows whither,
into the wide world"

Next morning the friends were up al ost sooner than their

active entertainers   The happiness of seeing her guests had
also awakened Valerina early   She little fancied with what
feelings they came to breakfast   Wilhelm, seeing clearly that
without some tidings of the Nut-brown Maid, Lenardo must
continue in a painful state, led the conversation to old times,
to playmates, to scenes which he himself knew, and other such
recollections   so that Valerina soon quite naturally came to
speak of the Nut-brown Maid, and to mention her name

No sooner did Lenardo hear the name Nachodina, than he
perfectly remembered it   but with the name, the figure also,
of that supplicant returned to hi , with such violence, that
Valerina's farther narrative became quite agonising to him, as
with warm sympathy she proceeded to describe the distrain-
ment of the pious farmer, his submissive resignation and
departure, and how he went away leaning on his daughter,
who carried a little bundle in her hand   Lenardo was like to
sink under the earth   Unhappily, and happily, she went into
a certain circumstantiality in her details, which, while it tortured Lenardo's heart, enabled him with help of his associate
to put on some appearance of co posure

The travellers departed, amid warm sincere invitations on
the part of the married pair to return soon, and a faint hollow
assent on their own part   And as a person, who stands in any
favour with himself, takes everything in a favourable light,
so Valerina explained Lenardo's silence, his visible confusion
in taking leave, his hasty departure, entirely to her own
advantage, and could not, although the faithful and loving
wife of a worthy gentleman, help feeling some small satisfaction at this re-awakening or incipient inclination, as she
reckoned it, of her former landlord

After this strange incident, while the friends were proceeding on their way, Lenardo thus addressed Wilhelm   " For our
shipwreck with such fair hopes at the very entrance of the
haven, I can still console myself in some degree for the
moment, and go calmly to meet my people, when I think that
Heaven has brought me you.—you to whom, under your

peculiar mission, it is indifferent whither or how you direct
your path   Engage to find out Nachodina, and to give me
tidings of her   If she be happy, then am I content, if unhappy, then help her at my charges   Act without reserve,
spare, calculate nothing ! I shall return home, shall endeavour
to get intelligence, and send your Felix to you by some trusty
person   Place the boy, as your intention was, where many of
his equals are placed   it is almost indifferent under what
superintendence, but I am much mistaken, if, in the neighbourhood, in the place where I wish you to wait for your son
and his attendant, you do not find a man that can give you
the best counsel on this point. It is he to whom I owe the
training of my youth, whom I should have liked so much to
take along with me in my travels, whom at least I should
many a time have wished to meet in the course of them, had
he not already devoted himself to a quiet domestic life."

The friends had now reached the spot where they were
actually to part   While the horses were feeding, the Baron
wrote a letter, which Wilhelm took charge of, yet, for the
rest, could not help communicating his scruples to Lenardo

"In my present situation," said he, "I reckon it a desirable commission to deliver a generous man from distress of
mind, and, at the same time, to free a human creature from
misery, if she happen to be miserable   Such an object one
may look upon as a star, towards which one sails, not knowing
what awaits him, what he is to meet, by the way   Yet, with
all this, I must not be blind to the danger which, in every
case, still hovers over you   Were you not a man who regularly
avoid engagements, I should require a promise from you not
again to see this female, who has come to be so precious in
your eyes, but to content yourself, when I announce to you
that all is well with her, be it that I actually find her happy,
or am enabled to make her so.   But having neither power nor
wish to extort a promise from you, I conjure you by all you
reckon dear and sacred, for your own sake, for that of your
kindred, and of me your new-acquired friend, to allow yourself

no approximation to that lost maiden, under what pretext soever, not to require of me that I mention or describe the place where I find her, or the neighbourhood where I leave her, but to believe y word that she is well, and be enfranchised and at peace"

Lenardo gave a smile, and answered "Perform this service for me, and I shall be grateful What you are willing and able to do I commit to your own hands, and for myself, leave me to time, to common sense, and, if possible, to reason"

"Pardon me," answered Wilhelm "but whoever knows under what strange forms love glides into our hearts, cannot but be apprehensive, on foreseeing that a friend may come to entertain wishes, which, in his circumstances, his station, would of necessity produce unhappiness and perplexity"

"I hope," said Lenardo, "when I know the maiden happy, I have done with her"

The friends parted, each in his own direction.

CHAPTER IX

By a short and pleasant road Wilhel   had reached the town to which his letter was directed He found it gay and well built, but its new aspect showed too clearly that, not long before, it must have suffered by a conflagration The address of his letter led him into the last small uninjured portion of the place, to a house of ancient, earnest architecture, yet well kept, and of a tidy look Dim windows, strangely fashioned, indicated an exhilarating pomp of colours from within Nor, in fact, did the interior fail to correspond with the exterior In clean apartments, everywhere stood furniture which must have served several generations, intermixed with very little that was new The master of the house received our traveller kindly, in a little cha ber si ilarly fitted up. These clocks had already struck the hour of many a birth and

many a death, everything which met the eye reminded one
that the past might, as it were, be protracted into the present

The stranger delivered his letter, but the landlord, without
opening it, laid it aside, and endeavoured, in a cheerful conversation, immediately to get acquainted with his guest They
soon grew confidential, and as Wilhelm, contrary to his usual
habit, let his eye wander inquisitively over the room, the
good old man said to him. "My domestic equipment excites
your attention You here see how long a thing may last, and
one should make such observations now and then, by way of
counterbalance to so much in the world that rapidly changes
and passes away This same tea-kettle served my parents,
and was a witness of our evening family assemblages, this
copper fire-screen still guards me from the fire, which these
stout old tongs still help me to mend, and so it is with all
throughout I had it in my power to bestow my care and
industry on many other things, as I did not occupy myself with
changing these external necessaries, a task which consumes so
many people's time and resources An affectionate attention
to what we possess makes us rich, for thereby we accumulate
a treasure of remembrances connected with indifferent things
I knew a young man who got a common pin from his love,
while taking leave of her, daily fastened his breast-frill with
it, and brought back this guarded and not unemployed treasure from a long journeying of several years In us little men,
such little things are to be reckoned virtue"

"Many a one too," answered Wilhelm, "brings back, from
such long and far travellings, a sharp pricker in his heart,
which he would fain be quit of"

The old man seemed to know nothing of Lenardo's situation,
though in the   ean while he had opened the letter and read
it, for he returned to his former topics

"Tenacity of our possessions," continued he, "in many cases
gives us the greatest energy To this obstinacy in myself I
owe the saving of my house When the town was on fire,
some people wished to begin snatching and saving here too

I forbade this, bolted my doors and windows, and turned out with several neighbours, to oppose the flames Our efforts succeeded in preserving this summit of the town Next morning all was standing here as you now see it, and as it has stood for almost a hundred years "

" Yet you will confess," said Wilhelm, " that no an withstands the change which Time produces "

" That, in truth ! " said the other " but he who holds out longest has still done something

" Yes ! even beyond the limits of our being we are able to maintain and secure, we transmit discoveries, we hand down sentiments, as well as property and as the latter was my chief province, I have for a long time exercised the strictest foresight, invented the most peculiar precautions , yet not till lately have I succeeded in seeing my wish fulfilled

" Commonly the son disperses what the father has collected, collects something different, or in a different way Yet if we can wait for the grandson, for the new generation, we find the same tendencies, the same tastes, again making their appearance And so at last, by the care of our Pedagogic friends, I have found an active youth, who, if possible, pays more regard to old possession than even I, and has withal a vehement attachment to every sort of curiosities My decided confidence he gained by the violent exertions, with which he struggled to keep off the fire from our dwelling Doubly and trebly has he merited the treasure which I mean to leave him nay, it is already given into his hands , and ever since that time, our store is increasing in a wonderful way.

" Not all, however, that you see here is ours On the contrary, as in the hands of pawnbrokers you find many a foreign jewel, so with us I can show you precious articles, which people, under the most various circumstances, have deposited with us for the sake of better keeping "

Wilhelm recollected the beautiful Box, which, at any rate, he did not like to carry with him in his wanderings, and showed it to his landlord. The old man viewed it with atten-

tion, gave the date when it was probably made, and showed
some similar things. Wilhelm asked him if he thought it
should be opened. The old man thought not. "I believe,
indeed," said he, "it could be done, without special harm to
the casket, but as you found it in so singular a way, you must
try your luck on it. For if you are born lucky, and this little
box is of any consequence, the key will doubtless by and by be
found, and in the very place where you are least expecting it."

"There have been such occurrences," said Wilhelm.

"I have myself experienced such," replied the old man,
"and here you behold the strangest of them. Of this ivory
crucifix I have had, for thirty years, the body with the head
and feet, in one place. For its own nature, as well as for the
glorious art displayed in it, I kept the figure laid up in my
most private drawer. nearly ten years ago I got the cross
belonging to it, with the inscription, and was then induced to
have the arms supplied by the best carver of our day. Far,
indeed, was this expert artist from equalling his predecessor,
yet I let his work pass, more for devout purposes, than for any
admiration of its excellence.

"Now, conceive my delight! A little while ago the original
genuine arms were sent me, as you see them here united in
the loveliest harmony, and I, charmed at so happy a coincidence, cannot help recognising in this crucifix the fortunes of
the Christian religion, which, often enough dismembered and
scattered abroad, will ever in the end again gather itself together at the foot of the Cross."

Wilhelm admired the figure, and its strange combination.
"I will follow your counsel," added he, "let the casket
continue locked till the key of it be found, though it should
lie till the end of my life."

"One who lives long," said the old man, "sees much collected and much cast asunder."

The young partner in the house now chanced to enter, and
Wilhelm signified his purpose of intrusting the Box to their
keeping. A large book was thereupon produced, the deposit

inscribed in it, with many ceremonies and stipulations, a receipt granted, which applied in words to any bearer, but was only to be honoured on the giving of a certain token agreed upon with the owner

So passed their hours in instructive and entertaining conversation, till at last Felix, mounted on a gay pony, arrived in safety   A groom had accompanied him, and was now for some time to attend and serve Wilhelm   A letter from Lenardo, delivered at the same time, complained that he could find no vestige of the Nut-brown Maid, and Wilhelm was anew conjured to do his utmost in searching her out   Wilhelm imparted the matter to his landlord   The latter smiled, and said   "We must certainly make every exertion, for our friend's sake, perhaps I may succeed in learning something of her   As I keep these old primitive household goods, so likewise have I kept some old primitive friends   You tell   e that this maiden's father was distinguished by his piety   The pious have a more intimate connexion with each other than the wicked, though externally it may not always prosper so well   By this means I hope to obtain some traces of what you are sent to seek   But, as a preparative, do you now pursue the resolution of placing your Felix among his equals and turning him to some fixed department of activity   Hasten with him to the great Institution   I will point out the way you must follow in order to find the Chief, who resides now in one, now in another division of his Province   You shall have a letter, with my best advice and direction "

CHAPTER X

THE pilgrims, pursuing the way pointed out to the   , had, without difficulty, reached the limits of the Province, where they were to see so many singularities   At the very entrance, soft knolls, favourable to crops, in its higher hills, to sheep-husbandry, in its wide bottoms, to grazing   Harvest was near at hand, and all was in the richest luxuriance, yet what most surprised our travellers was, that they observed neither men nor women, but in all quarters boys and youths engaged in preparing for a happy harvest, nay, already making arrangements for a merry harvest-home   Our travellers saluted several of them, and inquired for the Chief, of whose abode, however, they could gain no intelligence   The address of their letter was *To the Chief, or the Three*   Of this also the boys could make nothing, however, they referred the strangers to an Overseer, who was just about mounting his horse to ride off   Our friends disclosed their object to this man   the frank liveliness of Felix seemed to please him, and so they all rode along together

Wilhelm had already noticed, that in the cut and colour of the young people's clothes a variety prevailed, which gave the whole tiny population a peculiar aspect, he was just about to question his attendant on this point, when a still stranger observation forced itself upon him, all the children, how employed soever, laid down their work, and turned with singular, yet diverse gestures, towards the party riding past them, or rather, as it was easy to infer, towards the Overseer, who was in it   The youngest laid their arms crosswise over their breasts, and looked cheerfully up to the sky, those of middle size held their hands on their backs, and looked smiling on the ground, the eldest stood with a frank and spirited air, their arms stretched down, they turned their heads to the right, and formed themselves into a line, whereas the others kept separate, each where he chanced to be

The riders having stopped and dismounted here, as several children, in their various modes, were standing forth to be inspected by the Overseer, Wilhelm asked the meaning of these gestures, but Felix struck in, and cried gaily   " What posture am I to take, then ?"

" Without doubt," said the Overseer, "as the first posture

The arms over the breast, the face earnest and cheerful towards the sky "

Felix obeyed, but soon cried "This is not much to my taste, I see nothing up there does it last long? But yes!" exclaimed he joyfully, "yonder are a pair of falcons flying from the west to the east, that is a good sign too?"

"As thou takest it, as thou behavest," said the other, "now mingle among them, as they mingle" He gave a signal, and the children left their postures, and again betook them to work, or sport, as before

"Are you at liberty," said Wilhelm then, "to explain this sight which surprises me? I easily perceive that these positions, these gestures, are salutations directed to you"

"Just so," replied the Overseer, "salutations which at once indicate in what degree of culture each of these boys is standing"

"But can you explain to me the meaning of this gradation?" inquired Wilhelm, "for that there is one is clear enough"

"This belongs to a higher quarter," said the other "so much, however, I may tell you, that these ceremonies are not mere grimaces, that, on the contrary, the import of them, not the highest, but still a directing, intelligible import, is communicated to the children, while, at the same time, each is enjoined to retain and consider for himself whatever explanation it has been thought meet to give him, they are not allowed to talk of these things, either to strangers or among themselves, and thus their instruction is modified in many ways Besides, secrecy itself has many advantages, for when you tell a man at once and straightforward the purpose of any object, he fancies there is nothing in it Certain secrets, even if known to every one, men find that they must still reverence by concealment and silence, for this works on modesty and good morals"

"I understand you," answered Wilhelm "why should not the principle which is so necessary in material things, be

applied to spiritual also ? But perhaps, in another point,
you can satisfy my curiosity   The great variety of shape and
colour in these children's clothes attracts my notice and yet
I do not see all sorts of colours, but a few in all their shades,
from the lightest to the deepest   At the same time, I observe
that by this no designation of degrees in age or merit can be
intended, for the oldest and the youngest boys may be alike
both in cut and colour, while those of similar gestures are
not similar in dress "

"On this matter also," said the other, "silence is prescribed
to me but I am much mistaken, or you will not leave us
without receiving all the information you desire "

Our party continued following the trace of the Chief, which
they believed themselves to be upon   But now the strangers
could not fail to notice, with new surprise, that the farther
they advanced into the district, a vocal melody more and more
frequently sounded towards them from the fields   Whatever
the boys might be engaged with, whatever labour they were
carrying on, they accompanied it with singing, and it seemed
as if the songs were specially adapted to their various sorts of
occupation, and in similar cases everywhere the same   If
there chanced to be several children in company, they sang
together in alternating parts   Towards evening, appeared
dancers likewise, whose steps were enlivened and directed by
choruses   Felix struck in with them, not altogether unsuc-
cessfully, from horseback, as he passed, and Wilhelm felt
gratified in this amusement, which gave new life to the scene

"Apparently," he said to his companion, "you devote
considerable care to this branch of instruction, the accomplishment, otherwise, could not be so widely diffused, and so
completely practised "

"We do," replied the other "on our plan, Song is the
first step in education, all the rest are connected with it, and
attained by means of it   The simplest enjoyment, as well as
the simplest instruction, we enliven and impress by Song;
nay, even what religious and moral principles we lay before

our children, are communicated in the way of Song   Other
advantages for the excitement of activity spontaneously arise
from this practice, for, in accustoming the children to write
the tones they are to utter, in musical characters, and as
occasion serves, again to seek these characters in the utterance
of their own voice, and besides this, to subjoin the text below
the notes, they are forced to practise hand, ear and eye at
once, whereby they acquire the art of penmanship sooner than
you would expect, and as all this in the long-run is to be
effected by copying precise measurements and accurately settled
numbers, they come to conceive the high value of Mensuration
and Arithmetic much sooner than in any other way   Among
all imaginable things, accordingly, we have selected music as
the element of our teaching, for level loads run out from
music towards every side "

Wilhelm endeavoured to obtain still farther information,
and expressed his surprise at hearing no instrumental music
"This is by no means neglected here," said the other, "but
practised in a peculiar district, one of the most pleasant valleys
among the Mountains, and there again we have arranged it
so that the different instruments shall be taught in separate
places   The discords of beginners, in particular, are banished
into certain solitudes, where they can drive no one to despair,
for you will confess that in well-regulated civil society there is
scarcely a more melancholy suffering to be undergone, than
what is forced on us by the neighbourhood of an incipient
player on the flute or violin

"Our learners, out of a laudable desire to be troubleso e
to no one, go forth of their own accord, for a longer or a
shorter time, into the wastes, and strive in their seclusion
to attain the merit which shall again admit them into the
inhabited world   Each of the , from time to time, is allowed
to venture an attempt for admission, and the trial seldom
fails of success, for bashfulness and modesty, in this, as in
all other parts of our system, we strongly endeavour to maintain and cherish. That your son has a good voice, I am

glad to observe all the rest is managed with so uch the
greater ease "

They had now reached a place where Felix was to stop, and
make trial of its arrange ents, till a formal reception should
be granted him   From a distance they had been saluted by
a jocund sound of music, it was a game in which the boys
were, for the present, amusing themselves in their hour of
play   A general chorus mounted up, each individual of a
wide circle striking in at his time, with a joyful, clear, firm
tone, as the sign was given him by the Overseer   The latter
more than once took the singers by surprise, when at a signal
he suspended the choral song, and called on any single boy,
touching him with his rod, to catch by himself the expiring
tone, and adapt to it a suitable song, fitted also to the spirit
of what had preceded   Most part showed great dexterity,
a few, who failed in this feat, willingly gave in their pledges,
without altogether being laughed at for their ill success   Felix
was child enough to mix among them instantly, and in his
new task he acquitted himself tolerably well   The First
Salutation was then enjoined on him   he directly laid his
hands on his breast, looked upwards, and truly with so roguish
a countenance, that it was easy to observe no secret meaning
had yet in his ind attached itself to this posture

The delightful spot, his kind reception, the merry playmates, all pleased the boy so well, that he felt no very deep
sorrow as his father moved away   the departure of the pony
was perhaps a heavier matter, but he yielded here also, on
learning that in this circle it could not possibly be kept, and
the Overseer promised him, in compensation, that he should
find another horse, as smart and well-broken, at a ti e when
he was not expecting it

As the Chief, it appeared, was not to be come at, the
Overseer turned to Wilhelm and said   "I must now leave
you, to pursue my occupations, but first I will bring you to
the Three, who preside over our sacred things   Your letter
is addressed to them likewise, and they together represent the

Chief" Wilhelm could have wished to gain some previous
knowledge of these sacred things, but his companion answered
"The Three will doubtless, in return for the confidence you
show in leaving us your son, disclose to you in their wisdom
and fairness what is most needful for you to learn   The
visible objects of reverence, which I named sacred things, are
collected in this separate circle, are mixed with nothing,
interfered with by nothing   at certain seasons of the year
only are our pupils admitted here, to be taught in their
various degrees of culture, by historical and sensible means,
and in these short intervals they carry off a deep enough
impression to suffice them for a time, during the performance
of their other duties"

Wilhelm had now reached the gate of a wooded vale,
surrounded with high walls   on a certain sign the little door
opened, and a man of earnest and imposing look received
our traveller   The latter found himself in a large beautifully
umbrageous space, decked with the richest foliage, shaded
with trees and bushes of all sorts, while stately walls and
magnificent buildings were discerned only in glimpses through
this thick natural boscage   A friendly reception from the
Three, who by and by appeared, at last turned into a general
conversation, the substance of which we now present in an
abbreviated shape

"Since you intrust your son to us," said they, "it is fair
that we admit you to a closer view of our procedure   Of what
is external you have seen much, that does not bear its meaning
on its front   What part of this do you chiefly wish to have
explained?"

"Dignified, yet singular gestures of salutation I have noticed,
the import of which I would gladly learn   with you, doubtless, the exterior has a reference to the interior, and inversely,
let me know what this reference is'

"Well-formed, healthy children," replied the Three, "bring
much into the world along with them   Nature has given to
each whatever he requires for time and duration, to unfold

this is our duty   often it unfolds itself better of its own
accord   One thing there is, however, which no child brings
into the world with him, and yet it is on this one thing that
all depends for making man in every point a man   If you
can discover it yourself, speak it out "   Wilhelm thought a
little while, then shook his head

The Three, after a suitable pause, exclaimed   *Reverence!*
Wilhelm seemed to hesitate   "Reverence!" cried they a
second time   "All want it, perhaps you yourself

"Three kinds of gestures you have seen, and we inculcate
a threefold Reverence, which, when commingled and formed
into one whole, attains its highest force and effect   The first
is Reverence for what is above us   That posture, the arms
crossed over the breast, the look turned joyfully towards
Heaven   that is what we have enjoined on young children,
requiring from them thereby a testimony that there is a God
above, who images and reveals himself in parents, teachers,
superiors   Then comes the second, Reverence for what is
under us   Those hands folded over the back, and, as it were,
tied together, that down-turned, smiling look, announce that
we are to regard the Earth with attention and cheerfulness
from the bounty of the Earth we are nourished   the Earth
affords unutterable joys, but disproportionate sorrows she
also brings us   Should one of our children do himself external hurt, blameably or blamelessly, should others hurt him
accidentally or purposely, should dead involuntary matter do
him hurt, then let him well consider it, for such dangers will
attend him all his days   But from this posture we delay not
to free our pupil, the instant we become convinced that the
instruction connected with it has produced sufficient influence
on him   Then, on the contrary, we bid him gather courage,
and turning to his comrades, range himself along with them
Now, at last, he stands forth, frank and bold, not selfishly
isolated, only in combination with his equals does he front the
world   Farther we have nothing to add "

"I see a glimpse of it!" said Wilhelm   "Are not the

mass of men so marred and stinted, because they take pleasure only in the element of evil-wishing and evil-speaking ?
Whoever gives himself to this, soon comes to be indifferent
towards God, contemptuous towards the world, spiteful towards his equals , and the true, genuine, indispensable sentiment of self-estimation corrupts into self-conceit and presumption   Allow me, however," continued he, "to state one
difficulty   You say that reverence is not natural to man
now, has not the reverence or fear of rude people for violent
convulsions of Nature, or other- inexplicable mysteriously-
foreboding occurrences, been heretofore regarded as the germ
out of which a higher feeling, a purer sentiment, was by
degrees to be developed ? "

"Nature is indeed adequate to fear," replied they , "but
to reverence not adequate   Men fear a known or unknown
powerful being   the strong seeks to conquer it, the weak to
avoid it , both endeavour to get quit of it, and feel themselves happy when for a short season they have put it aside,
and their nature has in some degree restored itself to freedom
and independence   The natural man repeats this operation
millions of times in the course of his life, from fear he
struggles to freedom , from freedom he is driven back to fear,
and so makes no advancement   To fear is easy, but grievous ,
to reverence is difficult, but satisfactory   Man does not
willingly submit himself to reverence , or rather he never
so submits himself   it is a higher sense, which must be
communicated to his nature , which only in some peculiarly
favoured individuals unfolds itself spontaneously, who on
this account too have of old been looked upon as saints
and gods   Here lies the worth, here lies the business of
all true Religions , whereof there are likewise only three,
according to the objects towards which they direct our
devotion "

The men paused , Wilhelm reflected for a time in silence ,
but feeling in himself no pretension to unfold the eaning of
these strange words, he requested the Sages to proceed with

their exposition   They immediately complied.   " No religion
that grounds itself on fear," said they, "is regarded among us
With the reverence, to which a man should give dominion
in his mind, he can, in paying honour, keep his own honour,
he is not disunited with himself, as in the former case   The
Religion which depends on reverence for what is above us, we
denominate the Ethnic, it is the religion of the nations, and
the first happy deliverance from a degrading fear   all Heathen
religions, as we call them, are of this sort, whatsoever names
they may bear   The Second Religion, which founds itself
on reverence for what is around us, we denominate the
Philosophical, for the philosopher stations himself in the
middle, and must draw down to him all that is higher, and
up to him all that is lower, and only in this medium condition
does he merit the title of Wise   Here, as he surveys with
clear sight his relation to his equals, and therefore to the
whole human race, his relation likewise to all other earthly
circumstances and arrangements necessary or accidental, he
alone, in a cosmic sense, lives in Truth   But now we have
to speak of the Third Religion, grounded on reverence for
what is beneath us. this we name the Christian, as in the
Christian religion such a temper is with most distinctness
manifested. it is a last step to which mankind were fitted
and destined to attain   But what a task was it, not only to
be patient with the Earth, and let it lie beneath us, we
appealing to a higher birthplace, but also to recognise
humility and poverty, mockery and despite, disgrace and
wretchedness, suffering and death, to recognise these things
as divine, nay, even on sin and crime to look not as hindrances, but to honour and love them as furtherances, of what
is holy   Of this, indeed, we find some traces in all ages. but
the trace is not the goal, and this being now attained, the
human species cannot retrograde, and we may say, that the
Christian religion having once appeared, cannot again vanish,
having once assumed its divine shape, can be subject to no
dissolution."

"To which of these religions do you specially adhere?" inquired Wilhelm

"To all the three," replied they "for in their union they produce what may properly be called the true religion   Out of those Three Reverences springs the highest reverence, reverence for oneself, and those again unfold themselves fro this , so that man attains the highest elevation of which he is capable, that of being justified in reckoning himself the best that God and Nature have produced   nay, of being able to continue on this lofty eminence, without being again by self-conceit and presumption drawn down from it into the vulgar level "

"Such a confession of faith, developed in this manner, does not repulse me," answered Wilhelm , " it agrees with much that one hears now and then in the course of life , only, you unite what others separate "

To this they replied   "Our confession has already been adopted, though unconsciously, by a great part of the world "

"How then, and where?" said Wilhelm

"In the Creed!" exclaimed they   "for the first Article is Ethnic, and belongs to all nations , the second, Christian, for those struggling with affliction and glorified in affliction , the third, in fine, teaches an inspired Communion of Saints, that is, of men in the highest degree good and wise   And should not therefore the Three Divine Persons, under the similitudes and names of which these threefold doctrines and commands are promulgated. justly be considered as in the highest sense One ? "

"I thank you," said Wilhelm, "for having pleased to lay all this before me in such clearness and combination, as before a grown-up person, to whom your three modes of feeling are not altogether foreign   And now, when I reflect that you communicate this high doctrine to your children, in the first place as a sensible sign, then with some symbolical accompaniment attached to it, and at last unfold to them its deepest meaning, I cannot but warmly approve of your method "

"Right," answered they "but now we must show you more, and so convince you the better that your son is in no bad hands This, however, may remain for the morrow, rest and refresh yourself, that you may attend us in the morning, as a man satisfied and unimpeded, into the interior of our Sanctuary "

CHAPTER XI

At the hand of the Eldest, our friend now proceeded through a stately portal, into a round, or rather octagonal hall, so richly decked with pictures, that it struck him with astonishment as he entered All this, he easily conceived, must have a significant import, though at the moment he saw not so clearly what it was While about to question his guide on this subject, the latter invited him to step forward into a gallery, open on the one side, and stretching round a spacious gay flowery garden The wall, however, not the flowers, attracted the eyes of the stranger, it was covered with paintings, and Wilhelm could not walk far without observing that the Sacred Books of the Israelites had furnished the materials for these figures

"It is here," said the Eldest, "that we teach our First Religion, the religion which, for the sake of brevity, I named the Ethnic The spirit of it is to be sought for in the history of the world, its outward form, in the events of that history Only in the return of similar destinies on whole nations, can it properly be apprehended "

"I observe," said Wilhelm, "you have done the Israelites the honour to select their history as the groundwork of this delineation, or rather, you have made it the leading object there "

"As you see," replied the Eldest, "for you will remark, that on the socles and friezes we have introduced another series of transactions and occurrences, not so much of a syn-

chromstic as of a sy phionistic kind, since, among all
nations, we discover records of a similar import, and grounded
on the same facts   Thus you perceive here, while in the
main field of the picture, Abraham receives a visit from his
gods in the for   of fair youths, Apollo, among the herdsmen
of Admetus, is painted above on the frieze   From which we
may learn, that the gods, when they appear to men, are
commonly unrecognised of them "

The friends walked on   Wilhelm, for the most part, met
with well-known objects, but they were here exhibited in a
livelier and more expressive manner than he had been used to
see them   On some few matters he requested explanation,
and at last could not help returning to his former question
Why the Israelitish history had been chosen in preference to
all others ?

The Eldest answered   "Among all Heathen religions, for
such also is the Israelitish, this has the most distinguished
advantages, of which I shall mention only a few   At the
Ethnic judgment-seat, at the judgment-seat of the God of
Nations, it is not asked Whether this is the best, the most
excellent nation, but whether it lasts, whether it has continued
The Israelitish people never was good for much, as its own
leaders, judges, rulers, prophets have a thousand times re-
proachfully declared, it possesses few virtues, and most of the
faults of other nations   but in cohesion, steadfastness, valour,
and when all this would not serve, in obstinate toughness, it has
no match   It is the most perseverant nation in the world   it
is, it was and will be, to glorify the name of Jehovah, through
all ages   We have set it up, therefore, as the pattern-figure,
as the main figure, to which the others only serve as a frame "

"It becomes not me to dispute with you," said Wilhelm,
"since you have instruction to impart   Open to me, therefore, the other advantages of this people, or rather of its
history, of its religion "

"One chief advantage," said the other, "is its excellent
collection of Sacred Books   These stand so happily combined

together, that even out of the most diverse elements, the feeling of a whole still rises before us   They are complete enough
to satisfy, fragmentary enough to excite, barbarous enough
to rouse, tender enough to appease   and for how many other
contradicting merits might not these Books, might not this
one Book, be praised '"

The series of main figures, as well as their relations to the
smaller which above and below accompanied them, gave the
guest so much to think of, that he scarcely heard the pertinent
remarks of his guide, who, by what he said, seemed desirous
rather to divert our friend's attention, than to fix it on the
paintings   Once, however, the old man said, on some occasion "Another advantage of the Israelitish religion, I must
here mention, it has not embodied its God in any form, and
so has left us at liberty to represent him in a worthy human
shape, and likewise, by way of contrast, to designate Idolatry
by forms of beasts and monsters "

Our friend had now, in his short wandering through this
hall, again brought the spirit of universal history before his
mind, in regard to the events, he had not failed to meet with
something new   So likewise, by the simultaneous presentment
of the pictures, by the reflections of his guide, many new views
had risen on him, and he could not but rejoice in thinking
that his Felix was, by so dignified a visible representation, to
seize and appropriate for his whole life those great, significant
and exemplary events, as if they had actually been present,
and transacted beside him   He came at length to regard the
exhibition altogether with the eyes of the child, and in this
point of view it perfectly contented him   Thus wandering on,
they had now reached the gloomy and perplexed periods of the
history, the destruction of the City and the Temple, the
murder, exile, slavery of whole masses of this stiff-necked
people   Its subsequent fortunes were delineated in a cunning
allegorical way, a real historical delineation of them would
have lain without the limits of true Art

At this point, the gallery abruptly terminated in a closed

door, and Wilhelm was surprised to see himself already at the
end   "In your historical series," said he, "I find a chasm
You have destroyed the Temple of Jerusalem, and dispersed
the people, yet you have not introduced the divine Man who
taught there shortly before, to whom, shortly before, they
would give no ear"

"To have done this, as you require it, would have been an
error   The life of that divine Man, whom you allude to,
stands in no connection with the general history of the world
in his time   It was a private life, his teaching was a teaching
for individuals   What has publicly befallen vast masses of
people, and the minor parts which compose them, belongs to
the general history of the world, to the general religion of the
world, the religion we have named the First   What inwardly
befalls individuals, belongs to the Second religion, the Philosophical   such a religion was it that Christ taught and
practised, so long as he went about on Earth   For this
reason, the external here closes, and I now open to you the
internal "

A door went back, and they entered a similar gallery,
where Wilhelm soon recognised a corresponding series of
pictures from the New Testament   They seemed as if by
another hand than the first   all was softer, forms, movements,
accompaniments, light and colouring   " Here," said the guide,
after they had looked over a few pictures, " you behold neither
actions nor events, but Miracles and Similitudes   There is
here a new world, a new exterior, different from the former,
and an interior, which was altogether wanting there   By
Miracles and Similitudes, a new world is opened up   Those
make the common extraordinary, these the extraordinary
common "

"You will have the goodness," said Wilhelm, "to explain
these few words more minutely, for, by my own light, I
cannot "

"They have a natural meaning," said the other, "though a
deep one   Examples will bring it out most easily and soonest.

There is nothing more common and customary than eating and drinking, but it is extraordinary to transform a drink into another of more noble sort, to multiply a portion of food that it suffice a multitude   Nothing is more common than sickness and corporeal diseases, but to remove, to mitigate these by spiritual or spiritual-like means, is extraordinary, and even in this lies the wonder of the Miracle, that the common and the extraordinary, the possible and the impossible, become one   With the Similitude again, with the Parable, the converse is the case   here it is the sense, the view, the idea, that forms the high, the unattainable, the extraordinary   When this embodies itself in a common, customary, comprehensible figure, so that it meets us as if alive, present, actual, so that we can seize it, appropriate, retain it, live with it as with our equal,—this is a second sort of miracle, and is justly placed beside the first sort, nay, perhaps preferred to it   Here a living doctrine is pronounced, a doctrine which can cause no argument   it is not an opinion about what is right and wrong, it is Right and Wrong themselves, and indisputably "

This part of the gallery was shorter, indeed it formed but the fourth part of the circuit enclosing the interior court   Yet if in the former part you merely walked along, you here liked to linger, you here walked to and fro   The objects were not so striking, not so varied   yet they invited you the more to penetrate their deep still meaning   Our two friends, accordingly, turned round at the end of the space, Wilhelm, at the same time, expressing some surprise that these delineations went no farther than the Supper, than the scene where the Master and his Disciples part   He inquired for the remaining portion of the history

" In all sorts of instruction," said the Eldest, " in all sorts of communication, we are fond of separating whatever it is possible to separate, for by this means alone can the notion of importance and peculiar significance arise in the young mind   Actual experience of itself mingles and mixes all

things together   here, accordingly, we have entirely disjoined
that sublime Man's life from its termination In life, he
appears as a true Philosopher—let not the expression stagger
you—as a wise man in the highest sense   He stands fir   to
his point, he goes on his way inflexibly , and while he exalts
the lower to hi self, while he makes the ignorant, the poor,
the sick, partakers of his wisdom, of his riches, of his strength,
he, on the other hand, in no wise conceals his divine origin ,
he dares to equal himself with God, nay, to declare that he
himself is God   In this manner is he wont, from youth
upwards, to astound his familiar friends , of these he gains a
part to his own cause, irritates the rest against him , and
shows to all men, who are aiming at a certain elevation in
doctrine and life, what they have to look for from the world
And thus, for the noble portion of mankind his walk and conversation are even more instructive and profitable than his
death   for to those trials every one is called, to this trial but
a few   Now, omitting all that results from this consideration,
do but look at the touching scene of the Last Supper   Here
the Wise Man, as it ever is, leaves those that are his own
utterly orphaned behind him , and while he is careful for the
Good, he feeds along with the   a traitor by who   he and
the Better are to be destroyed "

With these words the Eldest opened a door , and Wilhelm
faltered in surprise, as he found himself again in the first hall
at the entrance   They had, in the mean while, as he now saw,
passed round the whole circuit of the court   " I hoped," said
Wilhelm, " you were leading me to the conclusion, and you
take me back to the beginning "

" For the present," said the Eldest, " I can show you nothing
farther   ore we do not lay before our pupils, more we do not
explain to them, than what you have now gone through   All
that is external, worldly, universal, we communicate to each
from youth upwards , what is more particularly spiritual and
conversant with the heart, to those only who grow up with
so e thoughtfulness of temper , and the rest, which is opened

only once a-year, cannot be imparted save to those whom we are sending forth as finished   That last Religion which arises from the Reverence of what is beneath us , that veneration of the contradictory, the hated, the avoided, we give each of our pupils, in small portions by way of outfit, along with him into the world, merely that he may know where more is to be had, should such a want spring up within him   I invite you to return hither at the end of a year, to visit our general festival, and see how far your son is advanced   then shall you be admitted into the Sanctuary of Sorrow "

" Permit me one question," said Wilhelm   " as you have set up the life of this divine Man for a pattern and example, have you likewise selected his sufferings, his death, as a model of exalted patience ? "

" Undoubtedly we have," replied the Eldest   " Of this we make no secret   but we draw a veil over those sufferings, even because we reverence them so highly   We hold it a damnable audacity to bring forth that torturing Cross, and the Holy One who suffers on it, or to expose them to the light of the sun, which hid its face when a reckless world forced such a sight on it , to take these mysterious secrets, in which the divine depth of Sorrow lies hid, and play with them, fondle them, trick them out, and rest not till the   ost reverend of all solemnities appears vulgar and paltry.   Let so much, for the present, suffice to put your mind at peace respecting your son ; and to convince you, that on meeting him again, you will find him trained, more or less, in one department or another, but at least in a proper way, and, at all events, not wavering, perplexed and unstable "

Wilhelm still lingered, looking at the pictures in this entrance-hall, and wishing to get explanation of their meaning   " This too," said the Eldest, " we must still owe you for a twelvemonth   The instruction, which, in the interim, we give the children, no stranger is allowed to witness   then, however, come to us , and you will hear what our best speakers think it serviceable to make public on these matters "

Shortly after this conversation, a knocking was heard at the little gate. The Overseer of last night announced himself he had brought out Wilhelm's horse, and so our friend took leave of the Three, who, as he set out, consigned him to the Overseer with these words "This man is now numbered among the Trusted, and thou understandest what thou hast to tell him in answer to his questions, for doubtless, he still wishes to be informed on much that he has seen and heard while here purpose and circumstance are known to thee"

Wilhelm had, in fact, some questions on his mind; and these he ere long put into words As they rode along, they were saluted by the children, as on the preceding evening · but today, though rarely, he now and then observed a boy who did not pause in his work to salute the Overseer, but let him pass unheeded Wilhelm asked the cause of this, and what such an exception meant His companion answered. "It is full of meaning, for it is the highest punishment which we inflict on our pupils, they are declared unworthy to show reverence, and obliged to exhibit themselves as rude and uncultivated natures but they do their utmost to get free of this situation, and in general adapt themselves with great rapidity to any duty Should a young creature, on the other hand, obdurately make no attempt at return and amendment, he is then sent back to his parents, with a brief but pointed statement of his case Whoever cannot suit himself to the regulations, must leave the district where they are in force"

Another circumstance excited Wilhelm's curiosity today, as as it had done yesterday the variety of colour and shape apparent in the dress of the pupils Hereby no gradation could be indicated, for children who saluted differently, were sometimes clothed alike, and others agreeing in salutation, differed in apparel Wilhelm inquired the reason of this seeming contradiction   "It will be explained," said the other, "when I tell you, that by this means we endeavour to find out the children's several characters With all our general strictness and regularity, we allow in this point a certain latitude of choice   Within the limits of our own stores of cloth and garnitures, the pupils are permitted to select what colour they please   and so likewise, within moderate limits, in regard to shape and cut   Their procedure, in these matters, we accurately note, for by the colour we discover their turn of thinking, by the cut, their turn of acting   However, a decisive judgment in this is rendered difficult by one peculiar property of human nature, by the tendency to imitate, the inclination to unite with something.   It is very seldom that a pupil fancies any dress that has not been already there, for most part, they select something known, something which they see before their eyes   Yet this also we find worth observing, by such external circumstances, they declare themselves of one party or another, they unite with this or that, and thus some general features of their characters are indicated, we perceive whither each tends, what example he follows

" We have had cases where the dispositions of our children verged to generality ; where one fashion threatened to extend over all, and any deviation from it to dwindle into the state of exception   Such a turn of matters we endeavour softly to stop, we let our stores run out, this and that sort of stuff, this and that sort of decoration is no longer to be had   we introduce something new and attractive, by bright colours and short smart shape, we allure the lively, by grave shadings, by commodious many-folded make, the thoughtful, and thus, by degrees, restore the equilibrium

"For to uniform we are altogether disinclined, it conceals the character, and,   ore than any other species of distortion, withdraws the peculiarities of children from the eye of their superiors "

Amid this and other conversation, Wilhelm reached the border of the Province ; and this at the point, where, by the direction of his antiquarian friend, he was to leave it, to pursue his next special object

At parting, it was now settled with the Overseer, that after the space of a twelvemonth, Wilhelm should return, when the grand Triennial Festival was to be celebrated, on which occasion all the parents were invited, and finished pupils were sent forth into the tasks of chanceful life. Then too, so he was informed, he might visit at his pleasure all the other Districts, where, on peculiar principles, each branch of education was com unicated and reduced to practice in complete isolation, and with every furtherance

CHAPTER XII

Hersilia to Wilhelm

MY valued, and to speak it plainly, dear friend, you are wrong, and yet, as acting on your own conviction, not wrong either So the Nut-brown Maid is found, then, found, seen, spoken to, known and acknowledged ! And you tell us farther, that it is impossible to wish this strange person, in her own way, any happier condition, or, in her present one, to be of any real advantage to her

And now you make it a point of conscience not to tell us where that wondrous being lives This you may settle with your own conscience, but to us it is unconscionable You think to calm Lenardo by assuring him that she is well He had said, almost promised, that he would content hi self with this : but what will not the passionate promise for others and the selves ! Know then that the matter is not in the least concluded as it yet stands She is happy, you tell us, happy by her own activity and merit but the youth would like to learn the How, the When and the Where, and, what is worse than this, his sisters too would like to learn Half a year is gone since your departure, till the end of another half year we cannot hope to see you Could not you, like a shrewd and knowing man, contrive to play your eternal *Rouge-et-Noir* in

our neighbourhood ?   I have seen people that could make the
Knight skip over all the chess-board without ever lighting
twice on one spot   You should learn this feat, your friends
would not have to want you so long.

But to set my good-will to you in the clearest light, I now
tell you in confidence, that there are two most enchanting
creatures on the road, whence I say not, nor whither, described
they cannot be, and no eulogy will do the   justice   A younger
and an elder lady, between whom it always grieves one to
make choice, the former so lovely, that all must wish to be
loved by her, the latter so attractive, that you   ust wish to
live beside her, though she did not love you   I could like,
with all my heart, to see you he med in, for three days,
between these two Splendours, on the morning of the fourth,
your rigorous vow would stand you in excellent stead.

By way of foretaste, I send you a story, which in some degree
refers to them, what of it is true or fictitious, you can try to
learn from themselves

THE MAN OF FIFTY

The Major came riding into the court of the mansion, and
Hilaria, his niece, was already standing without to receive hi ,
at the bottom of the stairs which led up to the apart ents
carcely could he recognise her, for she had grown both in
stature and beauty   She flew to meet him, he pressed her to
his breast with the feeling of a father.

To the Baroness, his sister, he was likewise welcome, and as
Hilaria hastily retired to prepare breakfast, the Major said,
with a joyful air. " For this time I can come to the point at
once, and say that our business is finished   Our brother, the
Chief Marshal, has at last convinced himself that he can
neither manage farmers nor stewards   In his lifetime he
makes over the estates to us and our children   the annuity
he bargains for is high, indeed, but we can still pay it   we
gain something for the present, and for the future all   This
new arrangement is to be co pleted forthwith.   And as I

very soon expect my discharge, I can again look forward to an active life, which may secure decided advantages to us and ours   We shall calmly see our children growing up beside us, and it will depend on us, on them, to hasten their union "

"All this were well," said the Baroness, "had not I a secret to inform thee of, which I myself discovered first   Hilaria's heart is no longer free   on her side thy son has little or nothing to hope for "

"What sayest thou ?" cried the Major   "Is it possible ? While we have been taking all pains to settle economical concerns, does inclination play us such a trick ?   Tell me, love, quick tell me, who is it that has fettered Hilaria's heart ?   Or is it then so bad as this ?   Is it not, perhaps, some transient impression we may hope to efface again ? "

"Thou must think and guess a little first," replied the Baroness, and thereby heightened his impatience   It had mounted to the utmost pitch, when the entrance of Hilaria, with the servants bringing in breakfast, put a negative on any quick solution of the riddle

The Major himself thought he saw the fair girl with other eyes than a little while before   He almost felt as if jealous of the happy man, whose image had been able to imprint itself on a soul so lovely   The breakfast he could not relish, and he noticed not that all was ordered as he liked to have it, and as he had used to wish and require it

In this silence and stagnation, Hilaria herself almost lost her liveliness   The mother felt embarrassed, and led her daughter to the harpsichord   but Hilaria's sprightly and expressive playing scarcely extorted any approbation from the Major   He wished the breakfast and the lovely girl fairly out of the way, and the Baroness was at last obliged to resolve on breaking up, and proposed to her brother a walk in the garden

No sooner were they by themselves, than the Major pressingly repeated his question , to which, after a pause, his sister answered, smiling   "If thou wouldst find the happy man whom she loves, thou hast not far to go, he is quite at hand, she loves *thee* ! '"

The Major stopped in astonishment, then cried "It were a most unseasonable jest to trick me into such a thought, which, if true, would make me so embarrassed and unhappy For though I need time to recover from my amazement, I see at one glance how grievously our circumstances would be disturbed by so unlooked-for an incident The only thing that comforts me is my persuasion that attachments of this sort are apparent merely, that a self-deception lurks behind them, and that a good true soul will undoubtedly return from such mistakes, either by its own strength, or at least by a little help from judicious friends "

"I am not of that opinion," said the Baroness , "by all the symptoms, Hilaria's present feeling is a very serious one "

"A thing so unnatural I should not have expected from so natural a character," replied the Major

"So unnatural it is not, after all," said his sister "I myself recollect having, in my own youth, an attachment to a man still older than thou Thou art fifty , not so very great an age for a German, if perhaps other livelier nations do fail sooner "

"But how dost thou support thy conjecture ?" said the Major.

"It is no conjecture, it is certainty. The details thou shalt learn by and by."

Hilaria joined them , and the Major felt himself, against his will, a second time altered Her presence seemed to him still dearer and more precious than before, her manner more affectionate and tender, already he began to put some faith in his sister's statement The feeling was highly delightful, though he neither would permit nor confess this to his mind Hilaria was, in truth, peculiarly interesting, her manner blended in closest union a soft shyness as towards a lover, and a trustful frankness as towards an uncle, for she really, and with her whole soul, loved him The garden lay in all the

pomp of spring, and the Major, who saw so   any old trees
again putting on their vesture, might also believe in the
returning of his own spring   And who would not have been
tempted to it, at the side of this most lovely maiden ?

So passed the day with them, the various household epochs
were gone through in high cheerfulness   in the evening, after
supper, Hilaria returned to her harpsichoid, the Major listened
with other ears than in the morning, one melody winded into
another; one song produced a second, and scarcely could
midnight separate the little party

On retiring to his room, the Major found everything
arranged to suit his old habitual conveniences   some copperplates, even, which he liked to look at, had been shifted from
other apartments, and his eyes being at last opened, he
saw himself attended to and flattered in the most minute
particulars

A few hours' sleep sufficed on this occasion   his buoyant
spirits aroused him early   But now he soon found occasion to
observe, that a new order of things carries   any inconveniences
along with it   His old groom, who also discharged the func-
tions of lackey and valet, he had not once reproved during
many years, for all went its usual course in the most rigid
order, the horses were dressed, and the clothes brushed, at the
proper moment, but today the master had risen earlier, and
nothing suited as it used to do

Ere long a new circumstance combined with this to ruffle
him still farther   At other times all had been right, as his
servant had prepared it for him, now, however, on advancing
to the glass, he found himself not at all as he wished to be.
Some grey hairs he could not deny, and of wrinkles also there
appears to have been a trace or two   He wiped and powdered
more than usual, and was fain at last to let matters stand as
they could   Then, it seemed, there were still creases in his
coat, and still dust on his boots. The old   room knew not
what to make of this, and was am   ed to see so altered a
  aster before him.

In spite of all these hindrances, the Major got down to the garden in good time. Hilaria, whom he hoped to find there, he actually found She brought him a nosegay, and he had not the heart to kiss her as usual, and press her to his breast He felt himself in the   ost delightful embarrassment, and yielded to his feelings, without reflecting whither they might carry him

The Baroness soon joined the   , and directing her brother to a note which had just been brought her by a special messenger, she cried "Thou wilt not guess whom this announces to us!"

"Tell us at once, then," said the Major; and it now appeared that an old theatrical friend was travelling by a road not far off, and purposing to call for a moment. "I am anxious to see him again," said the Major "he is no chicken now, and I hear he still plays young parts"

"He must be ten years older than thou," replied the Baroness

"He must," said the Major, "from all that I remember"

They had not waited long, when a lively, handsome, courteous man stept forward to them. Yet the friends soon recognised each other, and recollections of all sorts enlivened the conversation They proceeded to questions, to answers, to narratives, they mutually made known their present situations, and in a short time felt as if they had never been separated

Secret history informs us that this person had, in former days, being then a very elegant and graceful youth, had the good or bad fortune to attract the favour of a lady of rank, that by this means he had come into perplexity and danger, out of which the Major, at the very moment when the saddest fate seemed impending, had happily delivered him From that hour he continued grateful, to the brother as well as to the sister, for it was she that, by timeful warning, had originated their precautions

For a while before dinner, the men were left alone Not without surprise, nay, in some measure, with amazement, had

the Majoi viewed as a whole, and in detail, the exterior condition of his old fiiend He seemed not in the smallest
alteied and it was not to be wondered at that he could still
appear on the stage as an actor of youthful paits "Thou
inspectest me moie strictly than is faii," said he at last to the
Major "I fear thou findest the difference between this and
bygone times but too great"

"Not at all," iepled the Major "on the contrary, it fills
me with astonishment to find thy look fiesher and younger
than mine, though I know thou wert a firmset man at the
time when I, with the boldness of a callow despeiado, stood
by thee in ceitain straits"

"It is thy own fault," replied the other, "it is the fault of
all like thee, and though you are not to be loudly censured
for it, you are still to be blamed You think only of the
needful, you wish to be, not to seem This is very well, so
long as one *is* anything But when, at last, Being comes to
iecommend itself by Seeming, and this Seeming is found to be
even more transient than the Being, then every one of you
discovers that he would not have done amiss, if, in his caie foi
what was inwaid, he had not entirely neglected what was
outward"

"Thou art right," replied the Major, and could scaicely
suppiess a sigh

"Peihaps not altogether right," said the aged youth, "for
though in my tiade it were unpardonable if one did not tiy to
parget-up the outward man as long as possible. you people
need to think of other things, which are moie important and
piofitable"

"Yet there aie occasions," said the Major, "when a man
feels fresh internally, and could wish, with all his heart, that
he were fresh exteinally too"

As the stranger could not have the slightest suspicion of
the Major's real state of mind, he took these words in a
soldieily sense, and copiously explained how much depended
on externals in the art military, and how the officer, who had

so much attention to bestow on dress, might apply a little also to skin and hair

" For example," continued he, " it is indubitable that your temples are already grey, that wrinkles are here and there gathering together, and that your crown threatens to grow bald   Now look at me, old fellow as I am !   See how I have held out !   And all this without witchcraft, and with far less pains and care than others take, day after day, in spoiling, or at least wearying themselves "

The Major found this accidental conversation too precious an affair to think of ending it soon, but he went to work softly, and with precaution towards even an old acquaintance. "This opportunity, alas, I have lost," cried he, "and it is past recalling now   I must even content myself as I am, and you will not think worse of me on that account "

" Lost it is not," said the other, " were not you grave gentlemen so stiff and stubborn, did you not directly call one vain, if he thinks about his person, and cast away from you the happiness of being in pleasant company, and pleasing there yourselves "

" If it is not magic," smiled the Major, " that you people use for keeping yourselves young, it is at all events a secret, or at least you have *arcana*, such as one often sees bepraised in newspapers, and from these you pick out the best "

" Joke or earnest," said the other, " thou hast spoken truth Among the many things that have been tried for giving some repair to the exterior, which often fails far sooner than the interior, there are, in fact, certain invaluable recipes, simple as well as compound, which, as imparted to me by brethren of the craft, purchased for ready money, or hit upon by chance, I have proved and found effectual   By these I now hold fast and persevere, yet without abandoning my farther researches So much I may tell thee, and without exaggeration   A dressing-box I carry with me beyond all price !   A box, whose influences I could like to try on thee, if we chanced any time to be a fortnight together "

The thought that such a thing was possible, and that this possibility was held out to him so accidentally at the very moment of need, enlivened the spirit of the Major to such a degree, that he actually appeared much fresher and brisker already   at table, excited by the hope of bringing head and face into harmony with his heart, and by eagerness to get acquainted with the methods of doing so, he was quite another man , he met Hilaria's graceful attentions with alacrity of soul, and even looked at her with a certain confidence, which in the morning he was far from feeling

If the dramatic stranger had contrived, by many recollections, stories and happy hits, to keep up the cheerful hu our once excited, he so much the more alarmed the Major, on signifying, when the cloth was removed, that he must now think of setting forth and continuing his journey   By every scheme in his power, the Major strove to facilitate his friend's stay, at least for the night , he pressingly engaged to have horses and relays in readiness next morning , in a word, the healing toilette was absolutely not to get out of the premises, till once he had obtained more light on its contents and use.

The Major saw very well that here no time must be lost, he accordingly endeavoured, soon after dinner, to take his old favourite aside, and speak with him in private   Not having the heart to proceed directly to the point, he steered towards it afar off, and, taking up the former conversation, signified That he, for his part, would willingly bestow more care on his exterior, were it not that people, the moment they observed a man making such an attempt, marked him down for vain ; and so deducted from him in regard to moral esteem, what they felt obliged to yield him in regard to sensible

"Do not vex me with such phrases !" said his friend "these are words to which society has got accustomed, without attaching any meaning to them , or if we take it up more strictly, by which it indicates its unfriendly and spiteful nature   If thou consider it rightly, what, after all, is this

sa e vanity they make so much ado about? Every man
should feel some pleasure in himself, and happy he who feels
it. But if he does feel it, how can he help letting others
notice it? How shall he hide, in the midst of life, that it
gives him joy to be alive? If good society, and I mean this
exclusively here, only blamed such indications when they
became too violent; when the joy of one man over his existence hindered others to have joy and to show it over theirs, it
were good and well, and from this excess the censure has, in
fact, originally sprung But what are we to make of that
strange, prim, abnegating rigour against a thing which cannot
be avoided? Why should not a display of feeling on the part
of others be considered innocent and tolerable, which, more
or less, we from time to time allow ourselves? For it is the
pleasure one has in himself, the desire to communicate this
consciousness of his to others, that makes a man agreeable,
the feeling of his own grace that makes him graceful Would
to Heaven all men were vain! that is, were vain with clear
perception, with moderation and in a proper sense, we should
then, in the cultivated world, have happy times of it Women,
it is told us, are vain from the very cradle, yet does it not
become them, do they not please us the more? How can a
youth form hi self, if he is not vain? An empty, hollow
nature, will, by this means, at least contrive to give itself an
outward show; and a proper man will soon train himself from
the outside inwards As to my own share, I have reason to
consider myself in this point a most happy man, for my
trade justifies e in being vain, and the vainer I am, the
more satisfaction I give I am praised when others are
blamed, and have still, in this very way, the happiness and
the right to gratify and charm the public at an age when
others are constrained to retire from the scene, or linger on it
only with disgrace "

The Major heard with no great joy the issue of these reflections The little word vanity, as he pronounced it, had been
meant to serve as a transition, for enabling him to introduce

with some piopriety the statement of his own wish   But now
he was afraid, if then dialogue proceeded thus, he should be
led still farther from his aim, so he hastened to the point
directly

"For my own part," said he, "I should by no means
disincline to enlist under thy flag, since thou still holdest it to
be in time, and thinkest I might yet in some degiee make up
for what is lost   Impart to me somewhat of thv tinctures,
pomades, and balsams, and I will make a trial of them"

"Imparting," said the other, "is a harder task than you
suppose   Here, for example, it were still to small purpose
that I poured thee out some liquors from my phials, and left
the half of the best ingredients in my toilette   the appliance
is the haidest   You cannot, on the instant, appiopriate what
is given you   how this and that suit togethei, under what
circumstances, in what sequence things are to be used, all this
requiies practice and study, nay, study and piactice themselves will scarcely profit, if one bring not to the business a
natural genius for it"

"Thou art now, it seems, for diawing back," said the Major
"Thou raisest difficulties when I would have thy truly somewhat fabulous assertions rendered certain   Thou hast no mind
to let me try thy words by the test of action"

"By such banteiings, my friend," replied the othei, "thou
wouldst not prevail on me to gratify thy wish, if it weie not
that I entertain such affection for thee, and indeed first made
the proposal myself   Besides, if we considei it, man has quite
a peculiar pleasure in making Pioselytes, in bringing what
he values in himself into view also without himself on others,
causing others to enjoy what he enjoys, finding in others his
own likeness, represented and reflected back to him   In sooth,
if this is selfishness, it is of the most laudable and lovable
sort, that selfishness which has made us men and keeps us so.
From this universal feeling, then, apart from my friendship to
thee, I shall be happy in having such a scholar in the great
youth-renewing art   But, as from a master it   ay be expected

that he shall produce no botcher by his training, I confess
myself a little at a loss how to set about it   I told thee
already that neither recipes nor instructions would avail , the
practice cannot be taught by universal rules   For thy sake,
and from the wish to propagate my doctrine, I am ready to
make any sacrifice   The greatest in my power for the present
moment I will now propose to thee   I shall leave my servant
here , a sort of waiting-man and conjuror, who, if he does
not understand preparing everything, if he has not yet been
initiated into all the mysteries, can apply my preparations
perfectly , and in the first stage of the attempt will be of
great use to thee, till once thou have worked thy way so
far into the art, that I may reveal to thee the higher secrets
also ”

"How !" cried the Major , "thou hast stages and degrees
in thy art of making young ? Thou hast secrets even for the
initiated ? "

"No doubt of it !" replied the other   "That were but
a sorry art which could be comprehended all at once , the
last point of which could be seen by one just entering its
precincts "

Without loss of time, the waiting-man was formally consigned to the Major, who engaged to treat him handsomely
The Baroness was called on for drawers, boxes, glasses, to
what purpose she knew not   the petition of the toilette store
went forward , the friends kept together in a gay and sprightly
mood till after nightfall   At moonrise, some time later, the
guest took his leave, promising ere long to return

The Major reached his chamber pretty much fatigued   He
had risen early, had not spared himself throughout the day,
and now hoped very soon to get to bed   But here instead of
one servant, he found two   The old groom, in his old way,
rapidly undressed him , but now the waiting-man stept forth
and signified, that for appliances of a renovating and cosmetic
nature, the peculiar season was night , that so their effects,
sisted by a peaceful sleep, might be stronger and safer   The

Major was obliged to content himself, and let his head be
anointed, his face painted, his eyebrows pencilled, and his lips
tipt with salve. Besides all this, there were various ceremonies
still required, nay, the very nightcap was not to be put on
immediately, not till a net, or even a fine leather cap, had
been drawn on next the head

The Major laid himself in bed with a sort of unpleasant
feeling, which, however, he had no time to investigate the
nature of, as he very soon fell asleep But if we might speak
with his spirit, we should say he felt himself a little mummy-
like, somewhat between a sick man and a man embalmed
Yet the sweet image of Hilaria, encircled with the gayest
hopes, soon led him into a refreshing sleep

In the morning, at the proper hour, the groom was ready
in his place All that pertained to his master's equipment lay
in wonted order on the chairs, and the Major was just on
the point of rising, when the new attendant entered, and
strongly protested against any such precipitation He must
rest, he must wait, if their enterprise was to prosper, if they
were to be rewarded for their pains and labour The Major
now learned that he had to rise by and by, to take a slight
breakfast, and then go into a bath, which was already prepared for him The regulations were inflexible, they required
a strict observance, and some hours passed away under these
occupations

The Major abridged the resting-time after his bath, and
thought to get his clothes about him, for he was by nature
expeditious, and at present he longed to see Hilaria but
in this point also his new servant thwarted him, and signified,
that in all cases he must drop the thought of being in a
hurry Whatever he did, it appeared, must be done leisurely
and pleasurably, but the time of dressing was especially
to be considered as a cheerful hour for conversation with
oneself

The valet's manner of proceeding completely agreed with
his words But, in return, the Major, when, on stepping

forward to the glass, he saw himself trimmed out in the neatest fashion, really thought that he was better dressed than formerly Without many words, the conjuror had changed the very uniform into a newer cut, having spent the night in working at it An apparently so quick rejuvenescence put the Major in his liveliest mood, so that he felt himself as if renovated both without and within, and hastened with impatient longing to his friends

He found his sister engaged in looking at the pedigree, which she had caused to be hung up, the conversation last night having turned on some collateral relations, unmarried persons, or resident in foreign countries, or entirely gone out of sight, from all of whom the Baroness and her brother had more or less hope of heritages for themselves or their families They conversed a while on these matters, without mentioning the circumstance that all their economical cares and exertions had hitherto been solely directed to their children By Hilaria's attachment the whole of this prospect had altered, yet neither the Major nor his sister could summon courage to mention it farther, at this moment

The Baroness left the room, the Major was standing alone before this laconic history of his family, Hilaria stept in to him, she leant herself on him in a kind child-like way, looked at the parchment, and asked him whom of all these he had known, and who of them were still left and living

The Major began his delineation with the oldest, of whom any dim recollection remained with him from childhood Then he proceeded farther, painted the characters of several fathers, the likeness or unlikeness of their children to them, remarked that the grandfather often reappeared in the grandson, spoke, by the way, of the influence of certain women, wedded out of stranger families, and sometimes changing the character of whole branches He eulogised the virtue of many an ancestor and relative, nor did he hide their failings Such as had brought shame on their lineage he passed in silence. At length he reached the lowest lines Here stood his brother, the Chief-Marshal, himself, and his sister, and beneath him his son, with Hilaria at his side

"These two look each other straight enough in the face," said the Major, not adding what he thought of the matter in his heart

After a pause Hilaria answered, in a meek small tone, and almost with a sigh " Yet those, surely, are not to blame who look upwards " At the same time she looked up to him with a pair of eyes, out of which her whole love was speaking

"Do I understand thee rightly?" said the Major, turning round to her

"I can say nothing," answered she, with a smile, "which you do not know already "

"Thou makest me the happiest man under the sun," cried he, and fell at her feet   "Wilt thou be mine?"

"For Heaven's sake rise! I am thine forever "

The Baroness entered   Though not surprised, she rather hesitated   "If it be wrong, sister," said the Major, "the blame is thine if it be right, we will thank thee forever "

The Baroness from youth upwards had so loved her brother, that she preferred him to all men, and perhaps Hilaria's attachment itself had, if not arisen from this sisterly partiality, at least been cherished by it   All three now united in one love, in one delight, and thus the happiest hours flew over them   Yet at last their eyes reopened to the world around them likewise, and this rarely stands in unison with such emotions.

They now again bethought them of the son   For him Hilaria had been destined, this he himself well knew   Directly after finishing the business with the Chief-Marshal, the Major had appointed his son to expect him in the garrison, that they might settle everything together, and conduct these purposes to a happy issue   But now, by an unexpected occurrence, the whole state of matters had been thrown out of joint, the circumstances which before plied into one another so kindly, now seemed to be assuming a hostile aspect, and it was not easy to foresee what turn the affair would take, what temper would seize the individuals concerned in it

Meanwhile the Major was obliged to resolve on visiting his son, to whom he had already announced himself Not without reluctance, not without singular forecastings, not without pain at even for a short time leaving Hilaria, he at last, after much lingering, took the road, and leaving groom and horses behind him, proceeded with his cosmetic valet, who had now become an indispensable appendage, towards the town where his son resided

Both saluted and embraced each other cordially, after so long a separation They had uch to communicate, yet they did not just commence with what lay nearest their hearts The son went into copious talk about his hopes of speedy advancement, in return for which, the father gave him precise accounts of what had been discussed and determined between the elder members of the family, both in regard to fortune in general, to the individual estates, and everything pertaining to the

The conversation was in some degree beginning to flag, when the son took heart, and said to his father, with a smile. "You treat me very tenderly, dear father, and I thank you for it You tell me of properties and fortune, and mention not the terms under which, at least in part, they are to be mine you keep back the name of Hilaria, you expect that I should bring it forth, that I should express my desire to be speedily united with that amiable maiden "

At these words the Major felt himself in great perplexity, but as, partly by nature, partly by old habit, it was his way to collect the purpose of the man he had to treat with before stating his own, he now said nothing, and looked at the son with an ambiguous smile "You will not guess, father, what I have to say," continued the Lieutenant, "I will speak it out briefly, and once for all I can depend on your affection, which, amid such manifold care for me, has doubtless an eye

to my true happiness as well as my fortune   Some time or
other it must be said , be it said then even now , Hilaria
cannot make me happy !   I think of Hilaria as of a lovely
relative, towards whom I would live all my days with the
friendliest feelings , but another has awakened my affection,
another has bound my heart   The attachment is irresistible ,
you will not make me miserable "

Not without effort did the Major conceal the cheerfulness
which was rising over his face , and in a tone of mild seriousness inquire of the son   Who the person was that had so
entirely subdued him ?—"You must see her yourself, father,"
said the other , " for she can as little be described as comprehended   I have but one fear,—that you yourself will
be led away by her, like every one that approaches her   By
Heaven, it will be so , and I shall see you the rival of your
son ! "

"But who is she, then ? " inquired the Major   "If it is
not in thy power to delineate her personal characteristics,
tell me at least of her outward circumstances , these at least
may be described "

"Well, then, father," replied the son   "and yet these
outward circumstances too would be different in a different
person, would act otherwise on another   She is a young
widow, heiress of an old rich man lately deceased , independent, and well meriting to be so , acquainted with many,
loved by just as many, courted by just as many , yet, if I
mistake not very greatly, in her heart wholly mine "

With joyful vivacity, as the father kept silence, and gave
no sign of disapproval, the son proceeded to describe the
conduct of the fair widow towards him , told of her all-
conquering grace, recounted one by one her tender expressions of favour , in which the father truly could see nothing
but the light friendliness of a universally-courted woman, who
among so many may indeed prefer some one, yet without on
that account entirely deciding for him   Under any other
circumstances he would doubtless have endeavoured to warn a

son, nay, even a friend, of the self-deception which might probably enough be at work here but in the present case he himself was so anxious for his son's being right, for the fair widow's really loving him, and as soon as possible deciding in his favour, that he either felt no scruple of this sort, or banished any such from his mind, perhaps even only concealed it

"Thou placest me in great perplexity," began the father, after some pause "The whole arrangement between the surviving members of our family depends on the understanding that thou wed Hilaria If she wed a stranger, the whole fair, careful combination of a fine fortune falls to the ground again, and thou thyself art not too well provided for There is certainly another way still, but one which sounds rather strange, and by which thou wouldst gain very little I, in my old days, might wed Hilaria, a plan which could hardly give thee any very high satisfaction "

"The highest in the world !" exclaimed the Lieutenant "for who can feel a true attachment, who can enjoy or anticipate the happiness of love, without wishing every friend, every one whom he values, the like supreme felicity ! You are not old, father, and how lovely is Hilaria ! Even the transient thought of offering her your hand bespeaks a youthful heart, an unimpaired spirit Let us take up this thought, this project, on the spot, and consider and investigate it thoroughly My own happiness would be complete, if I knew you happy I could then rejoice in good earnest, that the care you had bestowed on my destiny was repaid on your own by so fair and high a recompense I can now with confidence and frankness, and true openness of heart, conduct you to my fair one You will approve of my feelings, since you yourself feel you will not impede the happiness of your son, since you are advancing to your own happiness "

With these, and other importunate words, the Lieutenant repressed many a scruple which his father was for introducing, left him no time to calculate, but hurried off with him to the

fair widow whom they found in a commodious and splendid
house, with a select rather than numerous party, all engaged
in cheerful conversation She was one of those female souls
whom no man can escape With incredible address she contrived to make our Major the hero of this evening The rest
of the party seemed to be her family, the Major alone was
her guest His circumstances she already knew very well,
yet she had the skill to ask about them, as if she were wishing,
now at last, to get right information on the subject from himself, and so, likewise, every individual of the company was
made to show some interest in the stranger One must have
known his brother, a second his estates, a third something
else concerned with him, so that the Major, in the midst of
a lively conversation, still felt himself to be the centre Moreover, he was sitting next the fair one, her eyes were on him,
her smile was directed to him, in a word, he felt himself so
comfortable, that he almost forgot the cause which had
brought him She herself scarcely ever mentioned his son,
though the young man took a keen share in the conversation
it seemed as if in her eyes, he, like all the rest, was present
only on his father's account

The guests strolled up and down the rooms, and grouped
themselves into accidental knots The Lieutenant stept up
to his fair one, and asked "What say you to my father?"

With a smile she replied "Methinks you might well take
him as a pattern Do but look how neatly he is dressed!
If his manner and bearing are not better than his gentle
son's!" And thus she continued to cry up and praise the
father at the son's expense, awakening, by this means, a very
mixed feeling of contentment and jealousy in the young man's
heart

Ere long the Lieutenant came in contact with his father,
and recounted all this to him. It made the Major's manner
to his fair hostess so much the more friendly, and she, on her
side, began to treat him on a more lively and trustful footing
In short, we may say that, when the company broke up, the

Major, as well as the rest, already belonged to her, and to her circle

A heavy rain prevented the guests from returning home as they had come   Some coaches drove up, into which the walkers arranged themselves, only the Lieutenant, under the pietext that the carriage was already too crowded, let his father drive away, and stayed behind

The Major, on entering his apartment, felt actually confused and giddy in mind, uncertain of himself, as is the case with us, on passing rapidly from one state to the opposite   The land still seems in motion to a man who steps from shipboard, and the light still quivers in the eye of him who comes at once into darkness   So did the Major still feel himself encircled with the presence of that fair being   He wished still to see, to hear her, again to see, again to hear her, and after some consideration he forgave his son, nay, he thought him happy that he might pretend to the appropriation of such loveliness

From these feelings he was roused by the Lieutenant, who, with lively expressions of rapture, rushed into the room, embraced his father, and exclaimed   " I am the happiest man in the world ! "   After several more of such preliminary phrases, the two at last came to an explanation   The father remarked, that the fair lady in conversing with him had not mentioned the son, or hinted at him by a single syllable —" That is just her soft, silent, half-concealing, half-discovering way, by which you become certain of your wishes, and yet can never altogether get rid of doubt   So was she wont to treat me hitherto, but your presence, father, has done wonders   I confess it, I stayed behind, that I might see her one moment longer   I found her walking to and fro in her still shining rooms   for I know it is her custom, when the company is gone, no light must be extinguished   She walks alone up and down in her magic halls, when the spirits are dismissed which she had summoned thither   She accepted the pretext, under cover of which I came back   She spoke with kind grace,

though of indifferent matters   We walked to and fio through
the open doors, along the whole suite of chambers   We had
wandeied seveial times to the end, into the little cabinet,
which is lighted only by a dim lamp   If she was beautiful
while moving under the blaze of the lustres, she was infinitelȳ
more so when illuminated by the soft gleam of the lamp
We had again ieached the cabinet, and, in turning, we
paused for an instant   I know not what it was that foiced this
audacity on me, I know not how I could venture, in the midst
of the most ordinary conversation, all at once to seize her hand,
to kiss that soft hand, and to press it to my heait   It was not
diawn away   'Heavenly creature !' ciied I, 'conceal thyself
no longer from me   If in this fair heart dwells favoui foi
the happy man who stands befoie thee, disclose it, confess it '
The present is the best, the highest time   Banish me, or take
me to thy arms '"

   "I know not what all I said, what I looked and expressed
She withdiew not, she resisted not, she answered not   I ventured to clasp her in my arms, to ask hei if she would be mine
I kissed her with rapture, she pushed me away   'Well, yes,
then, yes !' or some such woids, said she, in a faint tone, as if
embariassed   I retired, and cried, 'I will send my fathei , he
shall speak for me '   'Not a word to him of this !' replied
she, following me some steps   'Go away, forget what has
happened '"

   What the Major thought, we shall not attempt to unfold
He said, however, to his son   "What is to be done now,
thinkest thou ?   To my mind, the affair is, by accident, so
well introduced, that we may now go to work a little more
formally, that perhaps it were well if I called there tomoriow,
and proposed in thy name "

   "For Heaven's sake, no, father !" cried the son   "it would
spoil the whole business   That look, that tone, must be disturbed and deranged by no foimality   It is enough, father,
that youi presence accelerates this union, without your uttering
a word on the subject   Yes, it is to you that I owe my

happiness !   The respect which my loved one enteitains for you has conquered every sciuple , and nevei would your son have found so good a moment, had not his fathei piepaied it for him ! "

These and such disclosures occupied them till far in the night   They mutually settled their plans   the Major, simply for foim's sake, was to make a parting call, and then set out to arrange his marriage with Hilaria , the son was to forward and acceleiate his, as he should find it possible

Hersilia's Postscript

Here I break off, paitly because I can write no more at piesent, but partly also to fix a thoin in your heart.   Now, answer the question for yourself   How strangely fiom all that you have read, must matters stand with these ladies at piesent !   Till now, they had no mutual relation to each other , they were stiangeis, though each seemed to have the prospect of a marriage which was to appioximate them   And now we find them in company, but by themselves, without male attendance, and wandeiing ovei the world   What can have passed, what can be to follow ?   You, my worthy sir, will doubtless get quit of the difficulty, by mournfully exclaiming to yourself   "These, also, are Renunciants ! " And here you are perfectly right   but Expectants too ? This I durst not discovei, even if I knew it

To show you the way how this amiable pair may be met with on your wandering, I adopt a singulai expedient   You heiewith receive a little clipping of a map ·   when you lay this in its place on the full map of the country, the magnetic needle painted here will point with its barb to the spot whither the Desirable are moving   This riddle is not so very hard to read   but I could wish that, from time to time, you would do the like for us, and send a little snip of chart over hither, we should then, in some measure, understand to what quartei our thoughts weie to be directed , and how glad should

we be, if the needle were at last attracted by ourselves   May
all good be given you, and all errors forgiven !

It is said of women, that they cannot send away a letter
without tacking postscripts to the end of it.   Whatever
inferences you   ay draw from the fact, I cannot deny that
this is my second postscript, and the place, after all, where
I am to tell you the flower of the whole matter   This arrow-
shaft, on the little patch of map, Hilaria herself was at the
pains to draw, and to decorate with such dainty plumage
the sharp point, however, was the fair Widow's work   Have
a care that it do not scratch, or perhaps pierce you   Our
bargain is, that whenever you meet, be this where it may, you
are forthwith to present the small shred of paper, and so be
the sooner and more heartily admitted into trust

A WORD FROM THE EDITOR

That a certain deficiency, perhaps discernible in the parts,
certainly discernible here and there in the whole, cannot henceforth be avoided, we ourselves take courage to forewarn the
reader, without fearing thereby to thwart his enjoyment   In
the present task, undertaken truly with forethought and good
heart, we still meet with all the inconveniences which have
delayed the publication of these little volumes for twenty
years   This period has altered nothing for the better   We
still find ourselves in more than one way impeded, at this or
that place, threatened with one obstruction or another   For
we have to solve the uncertain problem of selecting from
those most multifarious papers, what is worthiest and most
important, so that it be grateful to thinking and cultivated
minds, and refresh and forward them in many a province of
life   Now here are the Journals, more or less complete, lying
before us, sometimes communicable without scruple, sometimes, again, by reason of their unimportant, and likewise **of**
their too important contents, seemingly unfit for insertion

There aie not even wanting sections devoted to the actual world , on statistic, technical and other practical external subjects   To cut these off as incongruous, we do not deteimine without reluctance , as life and inclination, knowledge and passion, strangely combining together, go on here in the straitest union

Then we come on sketches written with cleai views and for glorious objects , but not so consequent and deep-searching, that we can fully approve of them, or suppose that, in this new and so far advanced time, they could be readable and influential

So likewise we fall in with little anecdotes, destitute of connexion, difficult to arrange under heads , some of them, when closely examined, not altogether unobjectionable   Here and there we discover more complete narratives, seveial of which, though already known to the world, nevertheless demand a place here, and at the same time requiie exposition and conclusion   Of poems, also, there is no want , and yet it is not always easy, not always possible, to decide where they should be intioduced, with best iegaid to the pieserving and assisting of theii true tone, which is but too easily disturbed and overturned   If we are not, therefore, as we have too often done in bygone years, again to stop in the middle of this business, nothing will remain for us but to impart what we possess, to give out what has been preserved. Some Chapters, accordingly, the completion of which might have been desirable, we now offei in theii first huiiied form , that so the readei may not only feel the existence of a want here, but also be informed what this want is, and complete in his own mind whatever, partly from the nature of the object, partly from the intervening circumstances, cannot be presented to him peifectly completed in itself, or furnished with all its requisite accompaniments.

CHAPTER XIII

THE proposed riddle raised some scruples in Wilhelm's mind, yet ere long he began to feel a still attraction in the matter, an impulse of longing to reach that appointed line, and follow its direction, as, indeed, we are wont to seize with eagerness any specific object, that excites our imagination, our active faculties, and to wish that we might accomplish it and partake of it

A child that, in asking alms of us, puts into our hand a card with five Lottery Numbers written on it, we do not lightly turn away unserved, and it depends on the moment, especially if it be shortly before the drawing, whether we shall not, with accidentally stimulated hope, quite against our usual custom, stake heavy shares upon these very numbers

The wanderer now tried on a large Map the little fragment which had been sent him, and stood surprised, amazed, affrighted, as he saw the needle pointing straight to Mignon's native place, to the houses where she had lived What his peculiar feelings were, we do not find declared, but whoever can bring back to memory the end of the *Apprenticeship*, will in his own heart and mind, without difficulty, call forth the like

The chief cause, however, why we meet with scantier records of this excursion than we could have wished, may probably be this that Wilhelm chanced to fall in with a young lively companion of his journey, by means of whom it became easy to retain for himself and his friends a vivid and strong remembrance of this pious pilgrimage, without any aid of writing Unexpectedly he finds himself beside a Painter, one of that class of persons whom we often see wandering about the world, and still oftener figuring in Romances and Dramas, but in this case, an individual who showed himself at once to be really a distinguished artist The two very soon got acquainted, mutually communicated their desires, projects, purposes And now it appears that this skilful artist, who delights in painting aquatic landscapes, and can decorate his pieces with rich, well-imagined, well-executed additions and accompaniments, has been passionately attracted by Mignon's form, destiny, and being He has often painted her already, and is now going forth to copy from nature the scenes where she passed her early years, amid these to represent the dear child, in happy and unhappy circumstances and moments, and thus to make her image, which lives in all tender hearts, present also to the sense of the eye

The friends soon reach the Lago Maggiore, Wilhelm endeavours, by degrees, to find out the places indicated Rural palaces, spacious monasteries, ferries and bays, capes and landings, are visited, nor are the dwellings of courageous and kind-hearted fishermen forgotten, or the cheerfully-built villages along the shore, or the gay mansions on the neighbouring heights All this the Artist can seize, to all of it communicate, by light and colouring, the feeling suitable for each scene, so that Wilhelm passes his days and his hours in heart-searching emotion

In several of the leaves stood Mignon represented on the foreground, as she had looked and lived, Wilhelm, striving by correct description, to assist the happy imagination of his friend, and reduce these general conceptions within the stricter limits of individuality.

And thus you might see the Boy-girl, set forth in various attitudes and manifold expression Beneath the lofty portal of the splendid Country-house, she is standing, thoughtfully contemplating the Marble Statues in the Hall Here she rocks herself, plashing to and fro among the waters, in the fastened boat, there she climbs the ast, and shows herself as a fearless sailor

But, distinguished beyond all the other pictures, was one which the Artist, on his journey hither, and prior to his meeting with Wilhelm, had combined and painted with all its characteristic features In the heart of the rude Mountains shines the graceful seeming-boy, encircled with toppling cliffs, besprayed with cataracts, in the middle of a motley horde Never, perhaps, was a grim, precipitous, primeval mountain-pass more beautifully or expressively relieved with living figures The particoloured, gipsy-looking group, at once rude and fantastic, strange and common, too loose to cause fear, too singular to awaken confidence Stout beasts of burden are bearing along, now over paths made of trees, now down by steps hewn in the rock, a tawdry chaotic heap of luggage, round which all the instruments of a deafening music hang dangling to and fro, to affright the ear from time to time with rude tones Amid all this, the lovely child, self-collected without defiance, indignant without resistance, led but not dragged Who would not have looked with pleasure at this singular and impressive picture ? Given in strong characters, frowned the stern obstruction of these rock masses, riven asunder by gloomy chasms, towered up together, threatening to hinder all outgate, had not a bold bridge betokened the possibility of again coming into union with the rest of the world Nor had the Artist, with his quick feeling of fictitious truth, forgot to indicate the entrance of a Cave, which you might equally regard as the natural laboratory of huge crystals, or as the abode of a fabulously frightful brood of Dragons

Not without a holy fear did our friends visit the Marchese's palace The old man was still absent on his travels , but in this circle also, the two wanderers, knowing well how to apply and conduct themselves both towards spiritual and temporal authorities, were kindly received and entertained

The absence of the owner also was to Wilhelm very pleasant , for although he could have wished to see the worthy gentleman, and would have heartily saluted him, he felt afraid of the Marchese's thankful generosity, and of any forced recompense of that true loving conduct, for which he had already obtained the fairest reward.

And thus our friends went floating in gay boats from shore to shore, cruising the Lake in every direction   It was the fairest season of the year , and they missed neither sunrise nor sunset, nor any of the thousand shadings which the heavenly light first bounteously dispenses over its own firmament, and from thence over lake and land; not appearing itself in its perfect glory, till imaged back from the waters

A luxuriant vegetable world, planted by Nature, watched over and forwarded by Art, on every side surrounded them The first chestnut forests they had already greeted with welcome, and now they could not restrain a mournful smile, as, lying under the shade of cypresses, they saw the laurel mounting up , the pomegranates reddening , orange and lemon trees unfolding themselves in blossoms, and fruit at the same time glowing forth from the leafy gloom

Through means of his vivid associate, Wilhelm had another enjoyment prepared for him   Our old friend had not been favoured by Nature with the eye of a painter   Susceptible of visual beauty only in the human form, he now felt that, by the presence of a companion, alike disposed, but trained to quite different enjoyments and activities, the surrounding world also was opened to his sight

By viewing, under conversational direction, the changing glories of the region, and still more by concentrated imitation, his eyes were opened, and his mind freed from all its once obstinate doubts   Hitherto all copies of Italian scenery had seemed to him suspicious , the sky, he thought, was too blue , the violet tone of those charming distances was lovely but untrue, and the abundant fresh green too bright and gay   but now he united in his inmost perceptions with his new friend , and learned, susceptible as he was, to look at the Earth with that friend's eyes , and while Nature unfolded the open secret of her beauty, he could not but feel an irresistible attraction towards Art, as towards her most fit expositor

But his pictorial friend quite unexpectedly anticipated his wishes in another point   The Artist had already many times

started some gay song, and thus, in hours of rest, delightfully
enlivened and accompanied their movement, when out in long
voyages over the water   But now it happened, that in one of
the palaces they were visiting, he found a curious peculiar
stringed instrument, a lute of small size, strong, well-toned,
convenient, and portable   he soon contrived to tune it, and
then handled the strings so pleasantly, and so well entertained
those about him, that, like a new Orpheus, he subdued by soft
harmonies the usually rigorous and dry castellain, and kindly
constrained him to lend the instrument for a time, under the
condition that before departing, the singer should faithfully
return it, and in the interim, should come back some Sunday
or holyday, and again gratify them by his music

Quite another spirit now enlivened lake and shore, boat
and skiff strove which should be nearest our friends, even
freight and market barges lingered in their neighbourhood,
rows of people on the beach followed their course, when
landing, they were encircled by a gay-minded throng, when
departing, each blessed them, with a heart contented, yet full
of longing

And now, at last, to any third party who had watched our
friend, it must have been apparent enough that their mission
was, in fact, accomplished   all scenes and localities referring
to Mignon had been not only sketched, but partly brought
into light, shade and colour, partly, in warm, midday hours,
finished with the utmost fidelity   In effecting this, they had
shifted from place to place in a peculiar way, as Wilhelm's
vow frequently impeded them   this, however, they had now
and then contrived to evade, by explaining it as valid only
on land, and on water not applicable

Indeed Wilhelm himself now felt that their special purpose
was attained, yet he could not deny that the wish to see
Hilaria and the fair Widow must also be satisfied, if he wished
to leave this country with a free mind   His friend, to whom
he had imparted their story, was no less curious, and already
prided himself in the thought that in one of his paintings

there was a vacant space, which, as an artist, he might decorate with the forms of these gentle persons

Accordingly, they now cruised to and fro, watching the points where strangers are wont first to enter this paradise Their hope of meeting friends here had already been made known to the boatmen, and the search had not lasted long, when there came in sight a splendid barge, which they instantly made chase of, and forbore not passionately to grapple with, on reaching it The dames, in some degree alarmed at this movement, soon recovered their composure as Wilhelm produced his little piece of chart, and the two, without hesitation, recognised the arrow which themselves had drawn on it The friends were then kindly invited to come on board the ladies' barge, which they did without an instant's delay.

And now let us figure to ourselves these four, as they sit together in the daintiest apartment, the most blissful world lying round them, looking in each other's faces, fanned by soft airs, rocked on glittering waves Imagine the female pair, as we lately saw them described, the male, as they have together for weeks been leading a wayfaring life, and after a little reflection, we behold them all in the most delightful, but also the most dangerous situation.

For the three who have before, willingly or unwillingly, ranked themselves in the number of Renunciants, we have not the worst to fear, the fourth, however, may probably enough too soon see himself admitted into that order, like the others

After crossing the Lake several times, and pointing out the most interesting spots both on the shore and the islands, our two wanderers conducted their fair friends to the place they were to pass the night in, where a dextrous guide, selected for this voyage, had taken care to provide all possible conveniences Wilhelm's vow was now a harsh but suitable master of the ceremonies for he and his companion had already passed three days in this very station, and exhausted

all that was remarkable in the environs   The Artist, not
restrained by any vow, begged permission to attend the dames
on shore; this, however, they declined   and so the party
separated at some distance from the harbour

Scarcely had the singer stept into his skiff, which hastily
drew back from the beach, when he seized his lute, and gracefully began raising that strangely plaintive song, which the
Venetian gondoliers send forth in clear melody from land to
sea and from sea to land   Expert enough in this feat, which,
in the present instance, proceeded with peculiar tenderness
and expression, he strengthened his voice in proportion to the
increasing distance, so that on the shore you would have
thought you heard him still singing in the same place   He
at last laid his lute aside, trusting to his voice alone, and had
the satisfaction to observe that the dames, instead of retiring
into their house, were pleased to linger on the shore   He felt
so inspired that he could not cease, not even when night and
remoteness had withdrawn everything from view, till at last
his calmer friend reminded him that, if darkness did favour his
tones, the skiff had already long passed the limits within which
these could take effect

According to promise, the two parties again met next day
on the open Lake   Flying along, they formed acquaintance
with the lovely series of prospects, now standing forth in
separate distinction, then gathering into rows, and seen behind
each other, and at last fading away, as the higher eclipsed the
lower, all which, repeating itself in the waters, affords in such
excursions the most varied entertainment   Nor, in the course
of these sights, did the copies of them, from our Artist's port-
folio, fail to awaken thoughts and anticipations of what, in
the present hour, was not imparted.   For all such matters the
still Hilaria seemed to have a free and fair feeling

But towards noon, singularity again came into play   the
ladies landed alone, the men cruised before the harbour. And
now the singer endeavoured to accommodate his music to a
shorter distance, where not only the general, soft and quickly-

warbling tone of desire, but likewise a certain gay, graceful importunity, might be expected to tell   And here, now and then, some one or other of the songs, for which we stand indebted to our friends in the *Apprenticeship*, would come hovering over his strings, over his lips, but out of well-meant regard to the feelings of his hearers, as well as to his own, he restrained himself in this particular, and roved at large in foreign images and emotions, whereby his performance gained in effect, and reached the ear with so   uch the   ore insinuating blandishment   The two friends, blockading the harbour in this way, would not have recollected the trivial concern of eating and drinking, had not the more provident fair ones sent them over a supply of dainty bits, to which an accompanying draught of wine had the best possible relish

Every separation, every stipulation that comes in the way of our gathering passions, sharpens instead of stifling the   , and in this case, as in others, it may be presumed that the short absence had awakened equal longing in both parties. At all events, the dames, in their gay dazzling gondola, were very soon to be seen coming back

This word gondola, however, let us not take up in the melancholy Venetian   eaning   here it signifies a cheerful, commodious, social bark, which, had our little company been twice as large, would still have been spacious enough for them

Some days were spent in this peculiar way, between meeting and parting, between separation and social union, but amid the enjoyment of the most delightful intercourse, departure and bereavement still hovered before the agitated soul   In presence of the new friends, the old came back into the mind, were these new ones absent, each could not but admit that already they had taken deep root in his re e brance   None but a composed and tried spirit, like our fair Widow, could in such mo ents have maintained herself in complete equilibriu

Hilaria's heart had been too deeply wounded to admit of

any new entire impression but as the grace of a fair scene
encircles us of itself with soothing influences , so when the
mildness of tender-hearted friends conspires with it, there
comes over sense and soul a peculiar mood of softness, that
recalls to us, as in dreaming visions, the past and the absent,
and withdraws the present, as if it were but a show, into
spiritual remoteness   Thus, alternately rocked this way and
that, attracted and repelled, approximated and removed, they
wavered and wended for several days

Without more narrowly investigating these circumstances,
the shrewd, experienced guide imagined he observed some
alteration in the calm demeanour of his heroines , and when,
at last, the whimsical part of their predicament became known
to him, he contrived here also to devise the most grateful
expedient   For as our two shipmen were again conducting
the ladies to their usual place of dinner, they were met by
another gay bark , which, falling alongside of theirs, exhibited
a well-covered table, with all the cheerful invitations of a festive
repast   the friends could now wait in company the lapse of
several hours, and only night decided the customary separation.

Happily the Artist and Wilhelm had in their former
voyagings neglected, out of a certain natural caprice, to visit
the most highly ornamented of all the islands, and had even
yet never thought of showing to their fair friends the many
artificial and somewhat dilapidated curiosities of the place,
before these glorious scenes of creation were entirely gone
through   At last, however, new light rose on their minds
They took counsel with the guide   he contrived forthwith
to expedite their voyage, and all looked on it as the most
blissful they had yet undertaken   They could now hope and
expect, after so many interrupted joys, to spend three whole
heavenly days, assembled together in a sequestered abode

And here we cannot but bestow on this guide our high
commendation , he belonged to that nimble, active, dextrous
class, who, in attendance on successive parties, often travel
the same roads ; perfectly acquainted with the conveniences

and inconveniences on all of them, they understand how to
use the one and evade the other, and, without leaving their
own profit out of sight, still to conduct their patrons more
cheaply and pleasantly through the country, than without such
aid would have been possible

At this time, also, a sufficient female train belonging to our
dames, for the first time stept forth in decided activity, and
the fair Widow could now make it one of her conditions that
the friends were to remain with her as guests, and content
themselves with what she called her moderate entertainment
In this point too all prospered for the cunning functionary
had, on this occasion as on others, contrived to make so good
a use of the letters and introductions which his heroines had
brought with them, that, the owner of the place they were
now about to visit being absent, both castle and garden,
kitchen included, were thrown open for the service of the
strangers, nay, some prospect was held out even of the cellar
All things cooperated so harmoniously, that our wanderers,
fro the very first moment, felt themselves as if at home, as if
born lords of this paradise

The whole luggage of the party was now carried to the
island, an arrangement producing much convenience to all;
though the chief advantage aimed at was, that the portfolios
of our Artist, now, for the first time, all collected together,
might afford him means to exhibit, in continuous sequence, to
his fair hostesses the route he had followed This task was
undertaken by all parties with delight. Not that they proceeded in the common style of amateur and artist, mutually
eulogising here was a gifted man, rewarded by the most
sincere and judicious praise But that we fall not into the
suspicion of attempting, with general phrases, to palm on
credulous readers what we could not openly show them, let us
here insert the judgment of a critic, who some years afterwards viewed with studious admiration both the pieces here
in question, and the others of a like or similar sort, by the
same hand :

"He succeeds in representing the cheerful repose of lake
prospects, where houses in friendly approximation, imaging
themselves in the clear wave, seem as if bathing in its depths,
shores encircled with green hills, behind which rise forest
mountains, and icy peaks of glaciers   The tone of colouring
in such scenes is gay, mirthfully clear, the distances, as if
overflowed with softening vapour, which from watered hollows
and river valleys mounts up greyer and mistier, and indicates
their windings   No less is the Master's art to be praised in
views from valleys lying nearer the high Alpine ranges,
where declivities slope down, luxuriantly overgrown, and fresh
streams roll hastily along by the foot of rocks

"With exquisite skill, in the deep shady trees of the foreground, he gives the distinctive character of the several species,
satisfying us in the form of the whole, as in the structure of
the branches, and the details of the leaves   no less so, in the
fresh green with its manifold shadings, where soft airs appear
as if fanning us with benignant breath, and the lights as if
thereby put in motion

"In the middle-ground, his lively green tone grows fainter
by degrees, and at last, on the more distant mountain-tops,
passing into weak violet, weds itself with the blue of the sky
But our Artist is above all happy in his paintings of his
Alpine regions, in seizing the simple greatness and stillness of
their character, the wide pastures on the slopes, clothed with
the freshest green, where dark solitary firs stand forth from
the grassy carpet, and from high cliffs foaming brooks rush
down   Whether he relieve his pasturages with grazing cattle,
or the narrow winding rocky path with mules and laden pack-
horses, he paints all with equal truth and richness, still
introduced in the proper place, and not in too great copious-
ness, they decorate and enliven these scenes, without interrupting, without lessening their peaceful solitude   The
execution testifies a master's hand, easy, with a few sure
strokes, and yet complete   In his later pieces, he employed
glittering English permanent-colours on paper. these pictures,

accordingly, are of preeminently blooming tone , cheerful, yet, at the same time, strong and sated

" His views of deep mountain chasms, where round and round nothing fronts us but dead rock , where, in the abyss, overspanned by its bold arch, the wild stream rages, are indeed of less attraction than the former   yet their truth excites us , we admire the great effect of the whole, produced at so little cost, by a few expressive strokes, and masses of local colours

" With no less accuracy of character can he represent the regions of the topmost Alpine ranges, where neither tree nor shrub any more appears , but only, amid the rocky teeth and snow summits, a few sunny spots clothe themselves with a soft sward   Beautiful, and balmy, and inviting as he colours these spots, he has here wisely forborne to introduce grazing herds , for these regions give food only to the chamois, and a perilous employment to the Wild-hay-men "

" We shall not deviate from our purpose of bringing the condition of these waste scenes as close as possible to the conception of our readers, if to this word, Wild-hay-man, or *Wildheuer*, we subjoin a short explanation   It is a name given to the poorer inhabitants of the upland Alpine ranges, who occupy themselves in making hay from such grassy spots as are inaccessible to cattle.   For this purpose, they climb, with cramps on their feet, the steepest and most dangerous cliffs, or from high crags let themselves down by ropes, when this is necessary   and so reach these grassy patches   The grass once cut and dried to hay, they throw it down from the heights into the deeper valleys , where being collected together, it is sold to cattle-owners, with whom, on account of its superior quality, it finds a ready market "

These paintings, which must have gratified and attracted any eye, were viewed by Hilaria, in particular, with great

attention, and from her observations it became clear, that in
this department she herself was no stranger   To the Artist,
least of all, did this continue secret, nor could approval from
any one have been more precious to him, than from this most
graceful of all persons   Her companion, therefore, kept
silence no longer, but blamed Hilaria for not coming forward
with her own accomplishment, but lingering in this case as she
always did, now where the question was not, of being praised
or blamed, but of being instructed   A fairer opportunity, she
said, might not easily occur.

And now it came to light, when she was thus forced to
exhibit her portfolios, what a talent was lying hid behind this
still and most lovely nature   the capacity had been derived
from birth, and diligently cultivated by practice   She possessed a true eye, a delicate hand, such as women, accustomed
to use it in their dressing and decorating operations, find
available in higher art   You might, doubtless, observe un-
sureness in the strokes, and, in consequence, a too undecided
character in the objects   but you could not help admiring the
most faithful execution, though the whole was not seized in
its happiest effect, nor grouped and adjusted with the skill of
an artist   She is afraid, you would say, of profaning her
object, if she keep not completely true to it, hence she becomes precise and stiff, and loses herself in details

But now, by the great free talent, by the bold hand of the
Artist, she feels rising, awakening within her, whatever genuine
feeling and taste had till now slumbered in her mind, she
perceives that she has but to take heart, and earnestly and
punctually to follow some fundamental maxims, which the
Artist, with penetrating judgment and friendly importunity,
is repeating and impressing on her   That sureness of stroke
comes of its own accord, she by degrees dwells less on the
parts than on the whole   and thus the fairest capability rises
on a sudden to fulfilment, as a rose-bud, which in the evening
we passed-by unobservant, breaks forth in the morning at
sunrise before our face   and the living quivering movement of

this lordly blossom, struggling out to the light, seems almost visible before our eyes

Nor did this intellectual culture remain without moral effects for on a pure spirit it produces a magic impression to be conscious of that heartfelt thankfulness, natural towards any one to whom it stands indebted for decisive instruction In this case it was the first glad emotion which had risen in Hilaria's soul for many a week. To see this lordly world lying round her day after day, and now at once to feel the instantly acquired, more perfect gift of representing it ! What delight, in figures and tints, to be approaching nearer the Unspeakable ! She felt herself surprised as with a new youth, and could not refuse a peculiar kindliness to the man who had procured for her such happiness

Thus did the two sit together, you could scarcely have determined whether he was leader in communicating secret advantages in art, or she in seizing them and turning them to practice The happiest rivalry, such as too seldom rises between scholar and master, here took place Many a time you might observe the friend preparing with some decisive stroke to influence her drawing, which she, on the other hand, would gently decline, hastening to do the wished, the necessary, of her own accord, and always to her master's astonishment

The fair Widow, in the mean while, walked along the terraces with Wilhelm, under cypresses and pines, now under vine, now under orange groves, and at last could not but fulfil the faintly indicated wish of her new friend, and disclose to him the strange entanglement by which the two fair pilgrims, cut off from their former ties, and straitly united to one another, had been sent forth to wander over the world

Wilhelm, who wanted not the gift of accurately noting what he saw, took down her narrative sometime afterwards in writing this, as he compiled it and transmitted it by Hersilia to Natalia, we purpose by and by communicating to our readers

The last evening was now come, and a rising, most clear,

full moon concealed the transition from day to night The
party had assembled and seated themselves on one of the
highest terraces, to see distinct and unimpeded, and glitterin
in the sheen of east and west, the peaceful Lake, hidden partly
in its length, but visible over all its breadth

Whatever in such circumstances might be talked of, it was
natural once more to repeat the hundred times repeated, to
mention the beauties of this sky, of this water, of this land,
under the influences of a strong sun and milder moon, nay,
exclusively and lyrically to recognise and describe them

But what none of them uttered, what each durst scarcely
avow to himself, was the deep mournful feeling which, stronger
or weaker, but with equal truth and tenderness, was beating
in every bosom   The presentiment of parting diffused itself
over present union, a gradual stagnation was becoming almost
painful

Then at last the Singer roused himself, summoned up his
resolution; with strong tones, preluding on his instrument,
heedless of the former well-meant reserve   Mignon's figure,
with the first soft song of the gentle child, were hovering before him   Passionately hurried over the limits, with longing
touch awakening the sweetly-sounding strings, he began to
raise

> Know'st thou the land where lemon-trees do bloom,
> And oranges like gold — — — — —

Hilaria rose in deepest agitation, and hurried away, veiling
her face, our fair Widow, with a motion of refusal, waved her
hand towards the Singer, while she caught Wilhelm's arm with
the other. The perplexed and half-unconscious youth followed
Hilaria, Wilhelm, by his more considerate guide, was led after
them   And now when they stood all four under the high
moonshine, the general emotion was no longer to be concealed
The women threw themselves into each other's arms, the men
embraced each other, and Luna was witness of the noblest,
chastest tears   Some recollection slowly returned, they forced
themselves asunder, silent, under strange feelings and wishes,

from which hope was already cut off   And now our Artist, whom his friend dragged with him, felt himself heie under the void heaven, in the solemn lovely hour of night, initiated in the first stage of Renunciation, which those friends had already passed through, though they now saw themselves again in danger of being sharply tried

Not till late had the young men gone to rest; awakening in the eaily orning, they took heart, thought themselves now strong enough for a faiewell to this paradise, devised many plans for still, without violation of duty, at least lingering in the pleasant neighbourhood.

While purposing to introduce their projects to this effect, they were cut short by intelligence that, with the earliest break of day, the ladies had departed   A lettei from the hand of our Queen of Hearts gave them   ore precise information. You might have doubted whether sense rather than goodness, love rather than friendship, acknowledgment of merit rather than soft bashful favour, was expressed in it   But alas, in the conclusion stood the hard request, that our two wanderers weie neithei to follow their heroines, nor anywhere to seek them, nay, if they chanced to see each other, they were faithfully to avoid meeting

And now the paradise, as if by the touch of an enchanter's rod, was changed for our friends into an utter desert   and certainly they would have smiled at themselves, had they per- ceived at this moment how unjust and unthankful they were on a sudden become to so fair and remaikable a scene   No self-seeking hypochondriac could so sharply and spitefully have rated and censuied the decay of the buildings, the neglected condition of the walls, the weathered aspect of the towers, the grassy obstruction of the walks, the peiishing of the trees, the mossiness and mouldering of the artificial grottoes, and what- ever else of that sort was to be observed, as our two travellers now did   By degiees, however, they settled themselves as circumstances would admit   the Artist carefully packed up his work   they both set sail, Wilhelm accompanying him to the

upper quarter of the Lake, where by previous agreement, the
former set forth on his way to Natalia, to introduce her by his
fair landscape papers, into scenes which perhaps she might not
soon have an opportunity of viewing with her eyes   He was
at the same time commissioned to inform her confessionally
of the late incident, which had reduced him to a state such
that he might be received with hearty kindness by the Con-
federates in the vow of Renunciation, and with soft friendly
treatment, in the midst of them, be comforted, if he could not
be healed.

CHAPTER XIV

IN this division of our work, the exculpatory Word from
the Editor might have been more requisite than even in the
foregoing Chapter   for there, though we had not the paintings
of the master and his fair scholar, on which all depended, to
exhibit before our readers, and could neither make the perfection of the finished artist, nor the commencing stintedness
nor rapid development of the art-loving beauty visible to their
eyes   yet still the description might not be altogether ineffi-
cient, and many genial and thought-exalting matters re ained
to be imparted   But here, where the business in hand is a
great object, which one could have wished to see treated in
the most precise manner, there is, unhappily, too little noted
down, and we cannot hope that a complete view will be
attained from our communications
  Again, it is to be observed, that in the Novel, as in
Universal History, we have to struggle with uncertain com-
putations of time, and cannot always decisively fix what has
happened sooner, and what later   We shall hold, therefore,
by the surest points.

  That a year must have passed since Wilhel   left the Pedagogic Province, is rendered certain, by the circumstance, that
we now meet him at the Festival to which he had been invited

but as our wandeiing Renunciants sometimes unexpectedly
dive down and vanish fiom our sight, and then again emeige
into view at a place where they were not looked for, it cannot
be determined with certainty what tiack they have followed in
the inteiim.

Now, however, the Tiaveller advances from the side of the
plain country into the Pedagogic Province   he comes over
fields and pasturages, skiits, on the dry lea, many a little
fieshet, sees bushy rather than woody hills, a free prospect
on all sides, over a surface but little undulated   On such
tracks, he did not long doubt that he was in the horse-
producing region, and accordingly he failed not here and
there to observe greater or smaller herds of mares and foals
But all at once the hoiizon daikens with a fierce cloud of
dust, which rapidly swelling neaier and neaier, covers all the
breadth of the space, yet at last, rent asundei by a sharp side
wind, is foiced to disclose its interior tumult

At full gallop rushes foiwaid a vast multitude of these
noble animals, guided and held togethei by mounted keepers.
The monstrous huilyburly whirls past the wandeier, a fair
boy among the keepers looks at him with suiprise, pulls in,
leaps down, and embraces his father

Now commences a questioning and answering, the boy
relates that an agiicultural life had not agreed with him,
the harvest-home he had indeed found delightful, but the
subsequent ariangements, the ploughing and digging, by no
means so   This the Supeiiors iemark, and obseive at the
same time that he likes to employ himself with animals, they
direct him to the useful and necessary domestic breeds, try
him as a sequestered herdsman and keeper, and at last
piomote him to the moie lively equestrian occupation, where
accordingly he now, himself a young foal, has to watch over
foals, and to forward their good nourishment and training,
undei the oversight of skilful comiades

Fathei and son, following the heid, by various lone-lying
spacious faimyards, reached the town or hamlet, near which

the great annual Market was held   Here rages an incredible confusion, in which it is hard to determine whether merchants or wares raise more dust   From all countries purchasers assemble here to procure animals of noble blood and careful training, all the languages of the Earth, you would fancy, meet your ear   Amid all this hubbub, too, rises the lively sound of powerful wind-instruments   everything bespeaks motion, vigour and life

The Wanderer meets his Overseer of last year, who presents him to the others   he is even introduced to one of the Three, and by him, though only in passing, paternally and expressively saluted

Wilhelm, here again observing an example of exclusive culture and life-leading, expresses a desire to know in what else the pupils are practised, by way of counterpoise, that so in this wild, and, to a certain degree, savage occupation of feeding animals, the youth may not himself roughen into an animal   And, in answer, he is gratified to learn, that precisely with this violent and rugged-looking occupation the softest in the world is united,—the learning and practising of languages.

"To this," it was said, "we have been induced by the circumstance, that there are youths from all quarters of the world assembled here   now to prevent them from uniting, as usually happens when abroad, into national knots, and forming exclusive parties, we endeavour by a free communication of speech to approximate them

"Indeed, a general acquaintance with languages is here in some degree rendered necessary, since, in our yearly market festivals, every foreigner wishes to converse in his own tones and idiom, and, in the course of cheapening and purchasing, to proceed with all possible convenience   That no Babylonish confusion of tongues, however, no corruption of speech, may arise from this practice, we employ a different language month by month, throughout the year   according to the maxim, that in learning anything, its first principles alone should be taught by constraint

"We look upon our scholars," said the Overseer, "as so many swimmers, who, in the element which threatened to swallow them, feel with astonishment that they are lighter, that it bears and carries them forward and so it is with everything that man undertakes

"However, if any one of our young men show a special inclination for this or the other language, we neglect not, in the midst of this tumultuous-looking life, which nevertheless offers very many quiet, idly solitary, nay, tedious hours, to provide for his true and substantial instruction Our riding grammarians, among whom there are even some pedagogues, you would be surprised to discover among these bearded and beardless Centaurs Your Felix has turned himself to Italian, and in the monotonous solitude of his herdsman life, you shall hear him send forth many a dainty song with proper feeling and taste Practical activity and expertness are far more compatible with sufficient intellectual culture than is generally supposed "

Each of these districts was celebrating its peculiar festival, so the guest was now conducted to the Instrumental Music department This tract, skirted by the level country, began from its very border to exhibit kind and beautifully-changing valleys, little trim woods, soft brooks, by the side of which, among the sward, here and there, a mossy crag modestly stood forth Scattered, bush-encircled dwellings you might see on the hillsides, in soft hollows, the houses clustered nearer together Those gracefully separated cottages lay so far apart, that neither tones nor mistones could be heard from one to the other

They now approached a wide space, begirt with buildings and shady trees, where crowded, man on man, all seemed on the stretch of expectation and attention Just as the stranger entered, there was sent forth from all the instruments a grand symphony, the full rich power and tenderness of which he could not but admire Opposite the spacious main orchestra was a smaller one, which failed not to attract his notice here

stood various youngei and elder scholars, each held his instrument in readiness without playing, these were they who as
yet could not, or durst not, join in with the whole It was
interesting to observe how they stood as it were on the stait,
and our fiiend was informed that such a festival seldom
passed over, without some one oi othei of them suddenly
developing his talent

As among the instrumental music, singing was now introduced, no doubt could remain that this also was favoured
To the question, What other sort of culture was here blended
in kind union with the chief employment, oui wanderer
learned in reply, that it was Poetry, and of the lyrical kind
In this matter, it appeared, their main concern was, that both
arts should be developed each for itself and from itself, but
then also in contrast and combination with each other   The
scholars were first instructed in each according to its own
limitations, then taught how the two ieciprocally limit, and
again reciprocally free each other

To poetical rhythm the musical artist opposes measure of
tone and movement of tone   But here the mastery of Music
over Poesy soon shows itself, foi if the latter, as is fit and
necessary, keep hei quantities never so steadily in view, still
for the musician few syllables are decidedly short or long, at
his pleasure he can overset the most conscientious procedure
of the rhythmer, nay, change prose itself into song, from
which, in truth, the richest possibilities present themselves,
and the poet would soon feel himself annihilated, if he could
not, on his own side, by lyrical tenderness and boldness,
inspire the musician with ieverence, and, now in the softest
sequence, now by the most abrupt tiansitions, awaken new
feelings in the mind

The singers to be met with here are mostly poets themselves   Dancing also is taught in its fundamental principles,
that so all these accomplishments may iegulaily spread the -
selves into eveiy district

The guest, on being led across the next boundary, at once

perceived an altogether different mode of building   The houses were no longer scattered into separation, no longer in the shape of cottages   they stood regularly united, beautiful in their exterior, spacious, convenient and elegant within, you here saw an unconfined, well-built, stately town, corresponding to the scene it stood in   Here the Plastic Arts, and the trades akin to them, have their home, and a peculiar silence reigns over these spaces

The plastic artist, it is true, must still figure himself as standing in relation to all that lives and moves among men, but his occupation is solitary, and yet, by the strangest contradiction, there is perhaps no other that so decidedly requires a living accompaniment and society   Now here, in that circle, is each in silence forming shapes that are forever to engage the eyes of men, a holyday stillness reigns over the whole scene, and did you not here and there catch the picking of stone-hewers, and the measured stroke of carpenters, who are now busily employed in finishing a lordly edifice, the air were unmoved by any sound

Our wanderer was struck, moreover, by the earnestness, the singular rigour with which beginners, as well as more advanced pupils, were treated, it seemed as if no one by his own power and judgment accomplished anything, but as if a secret spirit, striving towards one single great aim, pervaded and vivified the all   Nowhere did you observe a scheme or sketch, every stroke was drawn with forethought   As the wanderer inquired of his guide the reason of this peculiar procedure, he was told   That Imagination was in itself a vague, unstable power, which the whole merit of the plastic artist consisted in more and more determining, fixing, nay, at last exalting to visible presence.

The necessity for sure principles in other arts was mentioned   "Would the musician," it was said, "permit his scholar to dash wildly over the strings, nay, to invent bars and intervals for himself at his own good pleasure?   Here it is palpable that nothing can be left to the caprice of the learner: the

element he is to work in is irrevocably given , the implement
he is to wield is put into his hands , nay, the very way and
manner of his using it, I mean the changing of the fingers, he
finds prescribed to him , so ordered that the one part of his
hand shall give place to the other, and each prepare the proper
path for its follower   by such determinate cooperation only
can the impossible at last become possible

"But what chiefly vindicates the practice of strict requisi-
tions, of decided laws, is that genius, that native talent, is
precisely the readiest to seize them, and yield them willing
obedience   It is only the half-gifted that would wish to put
his own contracted singularity in the place of the unconditional
whole, and justify his false attempts under cover of an uncon-
strainable originality and independence   To this we grant no
currency   we guard our scholars from all such misconceptions,
whereby a large portion of life, nay, often the whole of life, is
apt to be perplexed and disjointed

"With genius we love most to be concerned   for this is
animated just by that good spirit of quickly recognising what
is profitable for it   Genius understands that Art is called Art
because it is *not* Nature   Genius bends itself to respect even
towards what may be named conventional   for what is this
but agreeing, as the most distinguished men have agreed, to
regard the unalterable, the indispensable as the best ?   And
does not such submission always turn to good account ?

"Here too, as in all our departments, to the great assistance
of the teachers, our three Reverences and their signs, with
some changes suitable to the nature of the main employment,
have been introduced and inculcated "

The wanderer, in his farther survey, was surprised to observe
that the Town seemed still extending , street unfolding itself
from street, and so offering the most varied prospects   The
exterior of the edifices corresponded to their destination , they
were dignified and stately, not so much magnificent as beautiful   To the nobler and more earnest buildings in the centre
of the Town, the more cheerful were harmoniously appended ,

till farther out, gay decorated suburbs, in graceful style, stretched forth into the country, and at last separated into garden-houses

The stranger could not fail to remark, that the dwellings of the musicians in the preceding district were by no means to be compared, in beauty or size, with the present, which painters, sculptors and architects inhabited He was told that this arose from the nature of the thing The musician, ever shrouded in himself, must cultivate his inmost being, that so he may turn it outwards The sense of the eye he may not flatter The eye easily corrupts the judgment of the ear, and allures the spirit from the inward to the outward Inversely, again, the plastic artist has to live in the external world, and to manifest his inward being, as it were, unconsciously, in and upon what is outward Plastic artists should dwell like kings and gods how else are they to build and decorate for kings and gods ? They must at last so raise themselves above the common, that the whole mass of a people may feel itself ennobled in and by their works

Our friend then begged an explanation of another paradox Why at this time, so festive, so enlivening, so tumultuously excited, in the other regions, the greatest stillness prevailed here, and all labours were continued ?

"A plastic artist," it was answered, "needs no festival. When he has accomplished something excellent, it stands, as it has long done before his own eye, now at last before the eye of the world in his task he needed no repetition, no new effort, no fresh success, whereas the musician constantly afflicts himself with all this, and to him, therefore, the most splendid festival, in the most numerous assemblage, should not be refused "

"Yet at such a season," replied Wilhelm, "something like an exhibition might be desirable, in which it would be pleasant to inspect and judge the triennial progress of your best pupils "

"In other places," it was answered, "an exhibition may be

necessary , with us it is not   Our whole being and nature is
exhibition   Look round you at these buildings of every sort
all erected by our pupils , and this not without plans a hundred
ti es talked of and meditated , for the builder must not
grope and experiment , what is to continue standing, must
stand rightly, and satisfy, if not forever, yet at least for a long
space of time   If we cannot help *committing* errors, we   ust
build none

" With sculptors we proceed more laxly, most so of all with
painters ; to both we give liberty to try this and that, each in
his own way   It stands in their power to select in the interior
or exterior compartments of edifices in public places, some
space which they may incline to decorate   They give forth
their ideas, and if these are in some degree to be approved of,
the completion of them is permitted, and this in two ways
either with liberty, sooner or later, to remove the work, should
it come to displease the artist , or, with the condition that
what is once set up shall remain unalterable in its place
Most part choose the first of these offers, retaining in their
own hands this power of removal ; and in the performance,
they constantly avail themselves of the best advice   The
second case occurs seldomer, and we then observe that the
artist trusts less to himself, holds long conferences with companions and critics, and by this means produces works really
esti able, and deserving to endure "

After all this, our Traveller neglected not to ask   What
other species of instruction was combined with the main one
here ? and received for answer, that it was Poetry, and of the
Epic sort

This to our friend must have seemed a little singular, when
he heard farther that the pupils were not allowed to read or
hear any finished poems by ancient or modern poets   "We
merely impart to them," it was said, "a series of myths, tradi-
tions and legends, in the most laconic form   And now, from
the pictorial or poetic execution of these subjects, we at once
discover the peculiar productive gift of the genius devoted to

the one or the other ait   Both poet and painter thus labour
at the same fountain, and each endeavours to diaw off the
water to his own side, to his own advantage, and attain his
own required objects with it, in which he succeeds much
better than if he attempted again to fashion something that
has been fashioned already "

The Traveller himself had an opportunity of seeing how
this was accomplished   several painteis were busy in a room;
a gay young friend was relating with great minuteness a very
simple stoiy, so that he employed almost as   any words as
the others did pencil-stiokes, to complete the same exhibition
and round it fully off.

He was told, that in woiking togethei the friends were wont
to carry on much pleasant conversation, and that in this way
several improvisatoii had unfolded their gifts, and succeeded
in exciting great enthusiasm for this twofold mode of representation

Our friend now reverted his inquiries to the subject of
plastic art   " You have no exhibition," said he, " and therefoie I suppose give no piize either ? "

"No," said the other, "we do not, but here, close by, we
can show you something which we ieckon more useful "

They entered a large hall, beautifully lighted fiom above,
a wide circle of busy artists fiist attiacted the eye, and from
the midst of these rose a colossal group of figures, elevated in
the centre of the place   Male and female foims of gigantic
power, in violent postures, reminded one of that lordly fight
between Heroic youths and Amazons, wherein hate and enmity
at last issue in mutually regretful alliance   This strikingly
intertwisted piece of ait presented an equally favourable
aspect from every point of its circuit   In a wide ring round
it were many artists sitting and standing, each occupied in his
own way, the painter at his easel, the drawer at his sketch-
board, some were modelling it in full, others in bas-ielief,
there were even architects engaged in planning the pedestal,
on which a similar group, when wrought in maible, was to be

erected   Each individual was proceeding by his own method
in this task   painters and drawers were bringing out the group
to a plain surface, careful, however, not to destroy its figures,
but to retain as much of it as possible   In the same manner
were works in bas-relief going forward   One man only had
repeated the whole group in a miniature scale, and in certain
movements and arrangements of limbs he really seemed to
have surpassed his model

And now it came out that this man was the maker of the
model, who, before working it in marble, had here submitted
his performance not to a critical, but to a practical trial, and
by accurately observing whatever any of his fellow-artists in
his special department and way of thought might notice,
retain or alter in the group, was purposing, in subsequent
consideration, to turn all this to his own profit, so that,
when at length the grand work stood finished in marble,
though undertaken, planned and executed by one, it might
seem to belong to all

The greatest silence reigned throughout this apartment
also, but the Superior raised his voice, and cried   " Is there
any of you, then, who in presence of this stationary work can,
with gifted words, so awaken our imagination, that all we here
see concreted shall again become fluid, without losing its character, and so convince us, that what our artist has here laid
hold of, was indeed the worthiest ? "

Called forth on all sides by name, a fair youth laid down his
work, and as he stept forward, began a quiet speech, seemingly
intended merely to describe the present group of figures, but
ere long he cast himself into the region of poetry, plunged
into the middle of the action, and ruled this element like a
master, by degrees, his representation so swelled and mounted
by lordly words and gestures, that the rigid group seemed
actually to move about its axis, and the number of its figures
to be doubled and trebled   Wilhelm stood enraptured, and
at last exclaimed   " Can we now forbear passing over into
song itself, into rhythmic melody ? "

"This I should wish to hinder," said the Overseer, "for if our excellent sculptor will be candid, he will confess to us that our poet scarcely pleases him, and this because their arts lie in the most opposite regions on the other hand, I durst bet, that here and there a painter has not failed to appropriate some living touches from the speech A soft kindly song, however, I could wish our friend to hear there is one, for instance, which you sing to an air so lovely and earnest, it turns on Art in general, and I myself never listen to it without pleasure"

After a pause, in which they beckoned to each other, and settled their arrangements by signs, the following heart and spirit stirring song resounded in stately melody from all sides

> While inventing and effecting,
>   Artist, by thyself continue long
> The result art thou expecting,
>   Haste and see it in the throng
> Here in others look, discover
>   What thy own life's course has been,
> And thy deeds of years past over
>   In thy fellow man be seen
>
> The devising, the uniting,
>   What and how the forms shall be,
> One thing will the other lighten,
>   And at last comes joy to thee !
> Wise and true what thou impartest,
>   Fairly shaped, and softly done
> Thus of old the cunning artist
>   Artist-like his glory won
>
> As all Nature's thousand changes
>   But one changeless God proclaim,
> So in Art's wide kingdoms ranges
>   One sole meaning still the same
> This is Truth, eternal Reason,
>   Which from Beauty takes its dress,
> And serene through time and season
>   Stands for aye in loveliness

While the oiator, the singei,
　　Poui their hearts in rhyme and piose,
'Neath the painter's busy fingei
　　Shall bloom foith Life's cheerful rose ,
Girt with sisters , in the middle,
　　And with Autumn's fruitage blent ,
That of life's mysterious riddle
　　Some short glimpses may be hent

Thousandfold, and graceful, show thou
　　Form fiom foims evolving fair ,
And of man's bright image know thou
　　That a God once tarried there ·
And whate'er your tasks or prizes,
　　Stand as biethren one and all,
While, like song, sweet incense iises
　　Fiom the altar at your call

All this Wilhelm could not but let pass, though it must
have seemed paradoxical enough , and had he not seen it with
his eyes, might even have appeaied impossible   But now,
when it was explained and pointed out to him, openly and
freely, and in fair sequence, he scarcely needed to put any
farther question on the subject   Howevei, he at last addressed
his conductor as follows " I see here a most prudent provision
made for much that is desirable in life   but tell me farther,
which of your regions exhibits a similai attention to Dramatic
Poetry, and where could I instiuct myself in that matter ?   I
have looked round over all youi edifices, and observed none
that seemed destined for such an object "

" In reply to this question, we must not hide from you,
that, in our whole Province, theie is no such edifice to be seen
The drama presupposes the existence of an idle multitude,
perhaps even of a populace , and no such class finds harbour
with us , for birds of that feather, when they do not in spleen
forsake us of their own accord, we soon take caie to conduct
over the marches   Doubt not, however, that in our Institution, so universal in its character, this point was carefully
meditated   but no region could be found for the purpose

everywhere some important scruple came in the way   Indeed, who among our pupils could readily determine, with pretended mirth, or hypocritical sorrow, to excite in the rest a feeling untrue in itself, and alien to the moment, for the sake of calling forth an always dubious satisfaction?   Such juggleries we reckoned in all cases dangerous, and could not reconcile with our earnest objects "

"It is said, however," answered Wilhelm, " that this far-stretching art promotes all the rest, of whatever sort "

"Nowise," answered the other , " it employs the rest, but spoils them   I do not blame a player for uniting himself with a painter   but the painter, in such society, is lost   Without any conscience, the player will lay hold of whatever art or life presents hi , and use it for its fugitive objects, indeed with no small profit   the painter, again, who could wish in return to extract advantage from the theatre, will constantly find himself a loser by it , and so also in the like case will the musician   The combined Arts appear to me like a family of sisters, of whom the greater part were inclined to good economy, but one was light-headed, and desirous to appropriate and squander the whole goods and chattels of the household   The Theatre is this wasteful sister   it has an ambiguous origin, which in no case, whether as art or trade or amusement, it can wholly conceal "

Wilhelm cast his eyes on the ground with a deep sigh , for all that he had enjoyed or suffered on the Stage rose at once before his mind , and he blessed the good men who were wise enough to spare their pupils such pain, and, out of principle and conviction, to banish such errors from their sphere.

His attendant, however, did not leave him long in these meditations, but continued   " As it is our highest and holiest principle, that no talent, no capacity be misdirected, we cannot hide from ourselves, that among so large a number, here and there a mimical gift will sometimes decidedly come to light , exhibiting itself in an irresistible desire to ape the characters, for s, movements, speech of others   This we certainly do not

encourage, but we observe our pupil strictly, and if he continue faithful to his nature, then we have already established
an intercourse with the great theatres of all nations, and so
thither we send any youth of tried capability, that, as the
duck on the pond, so he on the boards, may be forthwith
conducted, full speed, to the future quack-quacking, and
gibble-gabbling of his life "

Wilhelm heard this with patience, but only with half-
conviction, perhaps with some spleen   for so strangely is man
tempered, that he may be persuaded of the worthlessness of
any darling object, may turn away from it, nay, even execrate
it, but yet will not see it treated in this way by others, and
perhaps the Spirit of Contradiction which dwells in all men,
never rouses itself more vehemently and stoutly than in such
cases

And the Editor of these sheets may himself confess, that he
lets not this strange passage through his hands without some
touch of anger   Has not he too, in many senses, expended
more life and faculty than was right on the Theatre?   And
would these men convince him that this has been an unpardonable error, a fruitless toil?

But we have no time for appending, in splenetic mood,
such remembrances and after-feelings to the narrative   for
our friend now finds himself agreeably surprised, as one of the
Three, and this a particularly prepossessing one, again comes
before his eyes   Kind, open meekness, announcing the purest
peace of soul, came in its refreshing effluences along with him
Trustfully the Wanderer could approach, and feel his trust
returned

Here he now learned that the Chief was at present in the
Sanctuary, instructing, teaching, blessing, while the Three
had separated to visit all the Regions, and everywhere, after
most thorough information obtained, and conferences with the
subordinate Overseers, to forward what was in progress, to
found what was newly planned, and thereby faithfully discharge
their high duty.

This same excellent peison now gave him a more com-
piehensive view of theii internal situation and external connexions, explained to him the mutual influences of one Region
on another, and also by what steps, after a longer oi a shorter
date, a pupil could be transferred from the one to the other.
All this haimonised completely with what he already knew
At the same time, he was much gratified by the desciiption
given of his son, and their faither plan of education met with
his entire approval

He was now, by the Assistants and Oveiseer, invited to a
Miners' Festival, which was forthwith to be celebrated The
ascent of the Mountains was difficult, and Wilhelm fancied he
observed that his guide walked even slowei towards evening,
as if the darkness had not been likely to obstruct their path
still moie   But when deep night came round them, this
enigma was solved our Wanderer observed little flames come
glimmeiing and wavering forth from many dells and chasms,
gradually stretch themselves into lines, and roll over the
summits of the mountains   Much kindliei than when
a volcano opens, and its belching ioai thieatens whole
countries with destruction, did this fair light appeai , and
yet, by degrees, it glowed with new brightness, giew
stronger, broadei, more continuous, glitteied like a stream
of stars, soft and lovely indeed, yet spreading boldly ovei
all the scene

After the attendant had a little while enjoyed the surpiise
of his guest, for they could cleaily enough observe each other,
their faces and forms as well as their path being illuminated
by the light from the distance,—he began "You see here, in
truth, a curious spectacle these lights which, day and night,
the whole year ovei, gleam and work under giound, foiwarding
the acquisition of concealed and scaicely attainable treasures,
these now mount and well foith from theii abysses, and gladden
the upper night Scaicely could one anywhere enjoy so brave
a review as here, where this most useful occupation, which in
its subterranean concealment is dispersed and hidden fiom the

eye, rises before us in its full co pleteness, and bespeaks a great secret combination "

Amid such speeches and thoughts, they had reached the spot where these fire-brooks poured themselves into a sea of flame, surrounding a well-lighted insular space The Wanderer placed himself in the dazzling circle, within which, glittering lights by thousands formed an imposing contrast with the miners, ranked round it like a dark wall Forthwith arose the gayest music, accompanied by becoming songs Hollow masses of rock came forward on machinery, and opened a resplendent interior to the eye of the delighted spectator. Mimetic exhibitions, and whatever else at such a moment can gratify the multitude, combined with all this at once to excite and to satisfy a cheerful attention

But with what astonishment was Wilhelm filled, when, on being introduced to the Superiors, he observed Friend Jarno, in solemn stately robes, among the number ! "Not in vain," cried Jaino, "have I changed my former name with the more expressive title of Montan thou findest e here initiated in mountain and cave, and now, if questioned, I could disclose and explain to thee much that a year ago was still a riddle to myself "

At this point our manuscripts forsake us of the conversation of these friends there is nothing specified , as little can we discover the connexion of what follows next, an incident of which in the same bundle, in the same paper, we find brief notice That a meeting had taken place between our Wanderer and Lothario and the Abbé Unhappily, in this, as in so many other leaves, the date has been neglected

Some passages, introduced rather in the way of exclamation than of narrative, point to the high meaning of Renunciation, by which alone the first real entrance into life is conceivable Then we come upon a Map, marked with several Arrows pointing towards one another, and along with this we find, in a certain sequence, several days of the month written down, so that we might fancy ourselves again walking in the real world, and moderately certain as to the next part of our friend's route, were it not that here also various

arks and ciphers, appended in different ways, awoke so e fear that a secret eaning at the bottom of it would forever lie hid from us

But what drives us out of all historical composure, is the strange circumstance, that immediately on all this there comes in the most improbable narration ; of a sort like those tales, whereby you long keep the hearer's curiosity on the stretch with a series of wonders, and at last explain That you were talking of a dream However, we shall communicate without change what lies before us

" If hitherto we had continued in the metalliferous part of the ountains, which externally is soft and by no eans of a wild aspect, I was now conducted through precipitous and scarcely passable rocks and chasms at last I gained the topmost summit, a cliff, the peak of which afforded room only for a single person, who, if he looked down from it into the horrid depth, ight see furious mountain-torrents foaming through black abysses In the present case, I looked down without giddiness or terror, for I was light of heart but now my attention fixed itself on some huge crags rising opposite me, precipitous like my own, yet offering on their summits a larger space of level Though parted by a monstrous chasm, the jutting masses came so near together that I could distinctly enough, with the naked eye, observe several persons assembled on the summit They were for most part ladies, one of whom coming forward to the very verge, awakened in me double and treble anxiety, as I became completely convinced that it was Natalia herself The danger of such an unexpected interview increased every moment, but it grew boundless, when a perspective came before my eyes, and brought me over to her, and her over to me. There is

something magical at all times in perspectives   Were we
not accustomed fiom youth to look through them, we should
shudder and tremble every time we put them to oui eyes
It is we who are looking, and it is not we, a being it is
whose organs are raised to a higher pitch, whose limitations
are done away, who has become entitled to stretch foith into
infinitude

"When, for example, we observe far-distant persons, by
means of such an instrument, and see them in unsuspicious
thoughtlessness following their business as if they were solitaiy
and unwatched, we could almost feel afiaid lest they might
discover us, and indignantly upbiaid us for our tieacherous
curiosity

"And so likewise did I, hemmed in by a stiange feeling,
waver between proximity and distance, and fiom instant to
instant alteinate between the two

"Those otheis in their turn had observed us, as a signal
with a white handkerchief put beyond a doubt   Foi a moment
I delayed in my answer to it, finding myself thus close beside
the being whom I adored   This is hei pure benign foim,
these are hei taper arms, which once so helpfully appeared
before me, after unblessed sorrows and perplexities, and at last
too, though but foi moments, sympathisingly embraced me

"I saw distinctly enough that she too had a perspective,
and was looking over to me, and I failed not, by such tokens
as stood at my command, to express the profession of a true
and heartfelt attachment

"And as experience teaches that remote objects, which we
have once clearly recognised thiough a perspective, afterwards
appear even to the naked eye as if standing shaped in distinct
neainess, be it that more accurate knowledge sharpens the
sense, or that imagination supplies what is wanting, so now
did I see this beloved being as accurately and distinctly as if
I could have touched her, though her company continued
still iriecognisable   And as I was tiampling round my narrow
station, struggling towards her the more, the abyss was like

to swallow me, had not a helpful hand laid hold of mine,
and snatched me at once fiom my danger and my fairest
happiness "

CHAPTER XV

HERE at last we again step on fiimer ground, the localities
of which we can settle with some piobability, though still
here and there on oui way there occur a few uncertainties,
which it is not in oui power altogether to clear up

As Wilhelm, in ordei to reach any point of the line marked
out by the first Arrow, had to proceed obliquely through the
country, he found himself necessitated to perform the journey
on foot, leaving his luggage to be carried after him   For this
walk of his, however, he was iichly iewarded, meeting at every
step, quite unexpectedly, with loveliest tracts of scenery   They
were of that sort, which the last slope of a mountain region
forms in its meeting with the plain country, bushy hills, their
soft declivities employed in domestic use, all level spaces
green, nowhere aught steep, unfruitful or unploughed to be
noticed   Ere long he reached the main valley, into which the
side-waters flowed, and this too was caiefully cultivated,
graceful when you looked over it, with taper tices marking
the bends of the iiver, and of the brooks which poured into
it   On looking at his map, his indicator, he observed with
surprise that the line drawn for him cut directly through
this valley, so that, in the fiist place, he was at least on the
right road

An old castle, in good iepaii, and seemingly built at different periods, stood foith on a bushy hill, at the foot of
which a gay hamlet stretched along, with its large inn rising
prominent among the othei houses   Hithei he proceeded,
and was received by the landlord kindly enough, yet with an
excuse that he could not be admitted, unless by the peimission
of a party who had hired the whole establishment foi a time,
on which account he, the landloid, was undei the necessity of

sending all his guests to the older inn, which lay farther up
the hamlet   After a short conference, the man seemed to
bethink himself, and said   " Indeed there is no one of them
at home even now, but this is Saturday, and the Bailiff will
not fail to be here soon   he comes every week to settle the
accounts of the last, and make arrangements for the next
Truly, there is a fair order reigns among these men, and a
pleasure in having to do with them, though they are strict
enough   for if they yield one no great profit, it is sure and
constant " He then desired his new guest to amuse himself in
the large upper hall, and await what farther might occur

Here Wilhelm, on entering, found a large clean apartment,
except for benches and tables, altogether empty   So much the
more was he surprised to see a large tablet inserted above one
of the doors, with these words marked on it in golden letters,
Ubi homines sunt modi sunt, which in modern tongue may
signify, that where men combine in society, the way and
manner in which they like to be and to continue together is
directly established   This motto made our Wanderer think
he took it as a good omen, finding here, expressed and confirmed, a principle which he had often, in the course of life,
perceived for himself to be furthersome and reasonable   He
had not waited long, when the Bailiff made his appearance,
who being forewarned by the landlord, after a short conversation, and no very special scrutiny, admitted Wilhelm on the
following terms   To continue three days, to participate
quietly in whatever should occur, and happen what might, to
ask no questions about the reason, and at taking leave, to
ask none about the score   All this our Traveller was obliged
to comply with, the deputy not being allowed to yield in a
single point

The Bailiff was about retiring, when a sound of vocal music
rolled up the stairs   two pretty young men entered singing,
and these the Bailiff, by a simple sign, gave to understand
that their guest was accepted   Without interrupting their
son, they kindly saluted the stranger, and continued their

duet with the finest grace, showing clearly enough that they were well trained, and complete masters of their art   As Wilhelm testified the most attentive interest, they paused and inquired   If in his own pedestrian wanderings no song ever occurred to him, which he went along singing by himself?   "A good voice," answered Wilhelm, "Nature has in truth denied me   yet I often feel as if a secret Genius were whispering some rhythmic words in my ear, so that, in walking, I move to musical measure fancying, at the same time, that I hear low tones, accompanying some song, which, in one way or another, has pleasantly risen before me"

"If you recollect such a song, write it down for us," said they "we shall see if we have skill to accompany your singing Demon"   He took a leaf from his note-book, and handed them the following lines

> From the mountains to the champaign,
>   By the glens and hills along,
> Comes a rustling and a tramping,
>   Comes a motion as of song
> And this undetermined roving
>   Brings delight, and brings good heed,
> And thy striving, be't with Loving,
>   And thy living, be't in Deed !

After brief study, there arose at once a gay marching melody, which, in its repetition and restriction still stepping forward, hurried on the hearer with it he was in doubt whether this was his own tune, his former theme, or one now for the first time so fitted to the words, that no other movement was conceivable   The singers had for some time pleasantly proceeded in this manner, when two stout young fellows ca e in, whom, by their accoutrements, you directly recognised as masons, two others, who followed them, being as evidently carpenters   These four, softly laying down their tools, listened to the music, and soon struck in with sure and decided voices, so that to the mind it seemed as if a real wayfaring company were stepping along over hill and valley,

and Wilhelm thought he had never heard anything so graceful, so enlivening to heart and mind   This enjoyment, however, was to be increased yet farther, and raised to the highest
pitch, by the entrance of a gigantic figure, mounting the stairs
with a hard firm tread, which, with all his efforts, he could
scarcely moderate   A heavy-laden dorsel he directly placed
in the corner, himself he seated on a bench, which beginning
to creak under his weight, the others laughed, yet without
going wrong in their music   Wilhelm, however, was exceedingly surprised, when, with a huge bass voice, this Son of Anak
joined in also   The hall quivered, and it was to be observed
that in his part he altered the burden, and sang it thus

> Life's no resting, but a moving,
> Let thy life be Deed on Deed !

Farther, you could very soon perceive that he was drawing
down the time to a slower step, and forcing the rest to follow
him   Of this, when at last they were satisfied and had concluded, they accused him, declaring he had tried to set them
wrong

"Not at all !" cried he   "it is you who tried to set me
wrong, to put me out of my own step, which must be measured
and sure, if I am to walk with my loading up hill and down
dale, and yet, in the end, arrive at my appointed hour, to
satisfy your wants "

One after the other, these persons now passed into an
adjoining room to the Bailiff, and Wilhelm easily observed
that they were occupied in settling accounts, a point, however, as to which he was not allowed at present to inquire
farther.   Two fair lively boys in the mean while entered, and
began covering a table in all speed, moderately furnishing it
with meat and wine, and the Bailiff, coming out, invited them
all to sit down along with him   The boys waited, yet forgot
not their own concern, but enjoyed their share in a standing
posture   Wilhelm recollected witnessing similar scenes during
his abode among the players, yet the present company seemed

to be of a much more serious cast, constituted not out of
sport, for show, but with a view to important concerns of life

The conversation of the craftsmen with the Bailiff added
strength to this conviction   These four active young people,
it appeared, were busy in the neighbourhood, where a violent
conflagration had destroyed the fairest village in the country,
nor did Wilhelm fail to learn that the worthy Bailiff was
employed in getting timber and other building materials, all
which looked the more enigmatical, as none of these persons
seemed to be resident here, but in all other points announced
themselves as transitory strangers   By way of conclusion to
the meal, St Christopher, such was the name they gave the
giant, brought out, for good-night, a dainty glass of wine,
which had before been set aside   a gay choral song kept the
party still some time together, after they were out of sight,
and then Wilhelm was at last conducted to a chamber of the
loveliest aspect and situation   The full moon, enlightening a
rich plain, was already up, and in the bosom of our Wanderer
it awoke remembrances of similar scenes   The spirits of all
dear friends hovered past him, especially the image of Lenardo
rose in him so vividly, that he might have fancied the man
himself was standing before his eyes   All this had prepared
him with its kind influences for nightly rest, when, on a
sudden, there arose a tone of so strange a nature, that it
almost frightened him   It sounded as from a distance, and
yet seemed to be in the house itself, for the building quivered
many times, and the floors reverberated when the sound rose
to its highest pitch   Wilhelm, though his ear was usually
delicate in discriminating tones, could make nothing of this
he compared it to the droning roar of a huge organ-pipe,
which, for sheer compass, produces no determinate note.
Whether this nocturnal terror passed away towards morning,
or Wilhelm by degrees became accustomed to the sound, and
no longer heeded it, is difficult to discover   at any rate, he fell
asleep, and was in due time pleasantly awakened by the rising
sun

Scarcely had one of the boys who were in waiting brought him breakfast, when a figure entered, who he had already noticed last night at supper, without clearly ascertaining his quality   A well-formed, broad-shouldered, yet nimble man, who now, by the implements which he spread out, announced himself as Barber, and forthwith piepared for performing his much-desired office on Wilhelm   For the rest, he was quite silent and with a light hand he went through his task, without once having opened his lips   Wilhelm therefore began, and said " Of your art you are completely master, and I know not that I have ever had a softer razor on my cheeks, at the same time, however, you appear to be a strict observer of the laws of the Society "

Roguishly smiling, laying his finger on his lips, the taciturn shaver glided through the door   " By my sooth," cried Wilhelm after him, " I think you must be old Redcloak, if not himself, at least a descendant of his it is lucky for you that you ask no counter service of me, your turn would have been but sorrily done "

No sooner had this curious personage retired, than the well-known Bailiff came in, inviting our friend to dinner for this day, in words which sounded pretty strange the BOND, so said the speaker expressly, gave the stranger welcome, requested his company at dinner, and took pleasure in the hope of being more closely connected with him   Inquiries were then made as to the guest's health, and how he was contented with his entertainment, to all which he could only answer in terms of satisfaction   He would, in truth, have liked much to ask of this man, as previously of the silent Barber, some information touching the horrid sound which throughout the night had, if not tormented, at least discomposed him, but, mindful of his engagement, he forbore all questions, hoping that, without importunity, from the good-will of the Society, or in some other accidental way, he might be informed according to his wishes

Our friend now, when left alone, began to reflect on the

strange person who had sent him this invitation, and knew not well what to make of the matter To designate one or more superiors by a neuter noun, seemed to him a somewhat precarious mode of speech For the rest, there was such a stillness all round, that he could not recollect of ever having passed a stiller Sunday. He went out of doors, and, hearing a sound of bells, walked towards the village Mass was just over, and among the villagers and country-people crowding out of church, he observed three acquaintances of last night, a ason, a carpenter, and a boy. Farther on, he met among the Protestant worshippers the other corresponding three How the rest managed their devotion was unknown to him but so much he thought himself entitled to conclude, that in this Society a full religious toleration was practised.

About mid-day, at the castle-gate, he was met by the Bailiff, who then conducted him through various halls into a large ante-chamber, and there desired him to take a seat Many persons passed through into an adjoining hall Those already known were to be seen among them, St Christopher himself went by all saluted the Bailiff and the stranger But what struck our friend most in this affair was, that the whole party seemed to consist of artisans, all dressed in the usual fashion, though extremely neat and clean a few among the number you might at most perhaps have reckoned of the clerk species

No more guests now making their appearance, the Bailiff led our friend through the stately door into a spacious hall Here a table of immense length had been covered, past the lower end of which he was conducted, towards the head, where he saw three persons standing in a cross direction But what was his astonishment when he approached, and Lenardo, scarcely yet recognised, fell upon his neck From this surprise he had not recovered, when another person, with no less warmth and vivacity, likewise embraced him, announcing himself as our strange Friedrich, Natalia's brother The rapture of these friends diffused itself over all present an

exclamation of joy and blessing sounded along the whole table
But in a moment, the company being seated, all again became
silent, and the repast, served up with a certain solemnity, was
enjoyed in like manner

Towards the conclusion of the ceremony, Lenardo gave a
sign two singers rose, and Wilhelm was exceedingly surprised to hear in this place his yesternight's song, which we,
for the sake of what follows, shall beg permission to insert
once more

> From the mountains to the champaign,
>   By the glens and hills along,
> Comes a rustling and a tramping,
>   Comes a motion as of song
> And this undetermined roving
>   Brings delight, and brings good heed,
> And thy striving, be 't with Loving,
>   And thy living, be 't in Deed!

Scarcely had this duet, accompanied by a chorus of agreeable
number, approached its conclusion, when two other singers, on
the opposite side, started up impetuously, and, with earnest
vehemence, inverted rather than continued the song, to
Wilhelm's astonishment, proceeding thus

> For the tie is snapt asunder,
>   Trust and loving hope are fled,
> Can I tell, in fear and wonder,
>   With what dangers round bestead,
> I, cut off from friend and brother,
>   Like the widow in her woe,
> With the one and not the other,
>   Now my weary way must go!

The chorus, taking up the strophe, grew more and more
numerous, more and more vociferous, and yet the voice of St
Christopher, from the bottom of the table, could still be distinctly recognised among them   The lamentation, in the end,
rose almost to be frightful a spirit of disquietment, combining with the skilful execution of the singers, introduced

something unnatural into the whole, so that it pained our friend, and almost made him shudder   In truth, they all seemed perfectly of one mind , and as if lamenting their own fate on the eve of a separation   The strange repetitions, the frequent resuscitation of a fatiguing song, at length became dangerous in the eyes of the Bond itself   Lenardo rose, and all instantly sat down, abruptly breaking off their hymn   The other, with friendly words, thus began

"Indeed I cannot blame you for continually recalling to your minds the destiny which stands before us all, that so, at any hour, you may be ready for it   If aged and lifeweary men have called to their neighbours   Think of dying ' we younger and lifeloving men may well keep encouraging and reminding one another with the cheerful words   Think of wandering ' Yet, withal, of a thing which we either voluntarily undertake, or believe ourselves constrained to, it were well to speak with cheerfulness and moderation   You yourselves know best what, in our situation, is fixed, and what is moveable   let us enjoy the former too, in sprightly and gay tones , and to its success be this parting cup now drunk ' "   He emptied his glass, and sat down   the four singers instantly rose, and in flowing connected tones thus began

> Keep not standing fix'd and rooted,
>   Briskly venture, briskly roam
> Head and hand, where'er thou foot it,
>   And stout heart, are still at home
> In each land the sun does visit
>   We are gay, whate'er betide
> To give room for wand'ring is it
>   That the world was made so wide

As the chorus struck in with its repetition of these lines, Lenardo rose, with him all the rest   His nod set the whole company into singing movement , those at the lower end marched out, St Christopher at their head, in pairs through the hall , and the uplifted wanderers' song grew clearer and freer, the farther they proceeded , producing at last a particularly good effect, when, from the terraces of the castle-garden, you looked down over the broad valley, in whose fulness and beauty you might well have liked to lose yourself   While the multitude were dispersing this way and that, according to their pleasure, Wilhelm was made acquainted with the third Superior   This was the Amtmann, by whose kind influence many favours had been done the Society, in particular, the Castle of his patron the Count, situated among several families of rank, had been given up to their use, so long as they might think fit to tarry here

Towards evening, while the friends were in a far-seeing grove, there came a portly figure over the threshold, whom Wilhelm at once recognised as the Barber of this morning To a low mute bow of the man, Lenardo answered " You now come, as always, at the right season, and will not delay to entertain us with your talent   I may be allowed," continued he, turning towards Wilhelm, " to give you some knowledge of our Society, the Bond of which I may flatter myself that I am No one enters our circle unless he have some talents to show, which may contribute to the use or enjoyment of society in general   This man is an excellent surgeon, of his skill as a beard-artist you yourself can testify   for these reasons he is no less welcome than necessary to us   Now, as his employment usually brings with it a great and often burdensome garrulity, he has engaged, for the sake of his own culture, to comply with a certain condition, as, indeed, every one that means to live with us must agree to constrain himself in some particular point, if the greater freedom be left him in all other points Accordingly our Barber has renounced the use of his tongue, in so far as aught common or casual is to be expressed by it but by this means, another gift of speech has been unfolded in him, which acts by forethought, cunningly and pleasurably ; I mean the gift of narration

" His life is rich in wonderful experiences, which he used to split in pieces, babbling of them at wrong times, but which he now, constrained by silence, repeats and arranges in his

quiet thought.   This also his powers of imagination now forwards, lending life and movement to past occurrences   With
no common art and skill, he can relate to us genuine Antique
Tales, or modern stories of the same fabulous cast ; thereby
at the right hour affording us a most pleasant entertainment,
when I loose his tongue for him, which I now do, giving him,
at the same time, this praise, that in the considerable period
during which I have known him, he has never once been guilty
of a repetition.   I cannot but hope that, in the present case,
for love and respect to our dear guest, he will especially
distinguish himself."

A sprightly cheerfulness spread over Redcloak's face, and
without delay he began speaking as follows

CHAPTER XVI

THE NEW MELUSINA

"RESPECTED gentlemen !   Being aware that preliminary
speeches and introductions are not much to your taste, I shall
without farther talk assure you, that in the present instance, I
hope to fulfil your commission moderately well   From me has
many a true history gone forth already, to the high and universal satisfaction of hearers   but, today I may assert that I
have one to tell, which far surpasses the former, and which,
though it happened to me several years ago, still disquiets me
in recollecting it, nay, still gives hope of some farther
development

"By way of introduction, let me confess, that I have not
always so arranged my scheme of life as to be certain of the
next period in it, or even of the next day   In my youth, I was
no first-rate economist, and often found myself in manifold
perplexity   At one time I undertook a journey, thinking to
derive good profit in the course of it   but the scale I went
upon was too liberal, and after having commenced my
travel with Extra-post, and then prosecuted it for a time in

the Diligence, I at last found myself obliged to front the end
of it on foot

"Like a gay young blade, it had been from of old my
custom on entering any inn, to look round for the landlady,
or even the cook, and wheedle myself into favour with her,
whereby, for most part, my shot was somewhat reduced

"One night at dusk, as I was entering the Post-house of a
little town, and purposing to set about my customary operations, there came a fair double-seated coach with four horses
rattling up to the door behind me   I turned round, and
observed in it a young lady, without maid, without servants
I hastened to open the carriage for her, and to ask if I could
help her in anything   On stepping out, a fair form displayed
itself, and her lovely countenance, if you looked at it narrowly,
was adorned with a slight shade of sorrow   I again asked
if there was aught I could do for her   'O yes!' said she, 'if
you will lift that little Box carefully, which you will find
standing on the seat, and bring it in   but I beg very much of
you to carry it with all steadiness, and not to move or shake it
in the least'   I took out the Box with great care, she shut
the coach door, we walked up-stairs together, and she told
the servants that she was to stay here for the night

"We were now alone in the chamber   she desired me to
put the Box on the table, which was standing at the wall, and
as, by several of her movements, I observed that she wished to
be alone, I took my leave, reverently but warmly kissing her
hand

"'Order supper for us two,' said she then   and you may
well conceive with what pleasure I executed the commission,
scarcely deigning, in my pride of heart, to cast even a side-
look on landlady and menials   With impatience I expected
the moment that was to lead me back to her   Supper was
served, we took our seats opposite each other, I refreshed
my heart, for the first time during a considerable while, with
a good meal, and no less with so desirable a sight beside me,

nay, it seemed as if she were growing fairer and fairer every
moment

"Her conversation was pleasant, yet she carefully waived
whatever had reference to affection and love   The cloth was
removed   I still lingered, I tried all sorts of manœuvres to get
near her, but in vain, she kept me at my distance, by a certain dignity which I could not withstand, nay, against my
will, I had to part from her at a rather early hour

"After a night passed in waking or unrestfully dreaming, I
rose early, inquired whether she had ordered horses, and
learning that she had not, I walked into the garden, saw her
standing dressed at the window, and hastened up to her
Here, as she looked so fair, and fairer than ever, love, roguery
and audacity all at once started into motion within me   I
rushed towards her, and clasped her in my arms   'Angelic,
irresistible being,' cried I, 'pardon! but it is impossible— !'
With incredible dexterity she whisked herself out of my arms,
and I had not even time to imprint a kiss on her cheek
'Forbear such outbreakings of a sudden foolish passion,' said
she, 'if you would not scare away a happiness which lies close
beside you, but which cannot be laid hold of till after some
trials'

"'Ask of me what thou pleasest, angelic spirit!' cried I
'but do not drive me to despair'   She answered with a smile
'If you mean to devote yourself to my service, hear the terms
I am come hither to visit a lady of my friends, and with her I
purpose to continue for a time   in the mean while, I could
wish that my carriage and this Box were taken forward   Will
you engage with it?   You have nothing to do, but carefully
to lift the Box into the carriage and out, to sit down beside
it, and punctually take charge that it receive no harm   When
you enter an inn, it is put upon a table, in a chamber by
itself, in which you must neither sit nor sleep   You lock the
chamber-door with this key, which will open and shut any
lock, and has the peculiar property, that no lock shut by it
can be opened in the interim'

" I looked at her, I felt strangely enough at heart I promised to do all, if I might hope to see her soon, and if she
would seal this hope to me with a kiss She did so , and from
that moment, I had become entirely her bondman   I was
now to order horses, she said   We settled the way I was to
take , the places where I was to wait, and expect her   She at
last pressed a purse of gold into my hand, and I pressed my
lips on the fair hand that gave it me   She seemed moved at
parting , and for me, I no longer knew what I was doing or
was to do

" On my return from giving my orders, I found the room-
door locked.   I directly tried my master-key, and it performed its duty perfectly   The door flew up   I found the
chamber empty , only the Box standing on the table where I
had laid it

" The carriage drove up   I carried the Box carefully down
with me, and placed it by my side   The hostess asked
' Where is the lady, then ?'   A child answered ' She is gone
into the town '   I nodded to the people and rolled off in
triumph from the door, which I had last night entered with
dusty gaiters   That in my hours of leisure I diligently
meditated on this adventure, counted my money, laid many
schemes, and still now and then kept glancing at the Box,
you will readily imagine   I posted right forward , passed
several stages without alighting , and rested not till I had
reached a considerable town, where my fair one had appointed
me to wait   Her commands had been pointedly obeyed
the Box always carried to a separate room, and two wax
candles lighted beside it, for such also had been her order   I
would then lock the chamber , establish myself in my own,
and take such comfort as the place afforded

" For a while I was able to employ myself with thinking of
her   but by degrees the time began to hang heavy on my
hands   I was not used to live without companions   these
I soon found, at tables-d'hôte, in coffee-houses and public
places, altogether to my wish   In such a mode of living my

money began to melt away, and one night, it vanished entirely from my purse, in a fit of passionate gaming, which I had not had the prudence to abandon   Void of money, with the appearance of a rich man, expecting a heavy bill of charges, uncertain whether and when my fair one would again make her appearance, I felt myself in the deepest embarrassment   Doubly did I now long for her, and believe that, without her and her gold, it was quite impossible for me to live

"After supper, which I had relished very little, being forced for this time to consume it in solitude, I took to walking violently up and down my room   I spoke aloud to myself, cursed my folly with horrid execrations, threw myself on the floor, tore my hair, and indeed behaved in the most outrageous fashion   Suddenly, in the adjoining chamber where the Box was, I heard a slight movement, and then a soft knocking at the well-bolted door, which entered from my apartment   I gather myself, grope for my aster-key, but the folding-doors fly open of themselves, and in the splendour of those burning wax-lights enters my Beauty   I cast myself at her feet, kiss her robe, her hands, she raises me, I venture not to clasp her, scarcely to look at her, but candidly and repentantly confess to her my fault   'It is pardonable,' said she, 'only it postpones your happiness and   me   You must now   ake another tour into the world before we can meet again   Here is more money,' continued she, 'sufficient if you husband it with any kind of reason.   But as wine and play have brought you into this perplexity, be on your guard in future against wine and women, and let me hope for a glad meeting when the time comes'

"She retired over the threshold, the folding-doors flew together   I knocked, I entreated, but nothing farther stirred   Next morning, while presenting his bill, the waiter smiled, and said 'So we have found out at last, then, why you lock your door in so artful and incomprehensible a way, that no master-key can open it   We supposed you must

have much money and precious ware laid up by you   but
now we have seen your treasure walking down-stairs, and in
good truth it seemed worthy of being well kept '

"To this I answered nothing, but paid my reckoning, and
mounted with my Box into the carriage   I again rolled forth
into the world, with the firmest resolution to be heedful in
future of the warning given me by my fair and mysterious
friend   Scarcely, however, had I once more reached a large
town, when forthwith I got acquainted with certain interesting
ladies, from whom I absolutely could not tear myself away.
They seemed inclined to make me pay dear for their favour:
for while they still kept me at a certain distance, they led me
into one expense after the other, and I, being anxious only
to promote their satisfaction, once more ceased to think of
my purse, but paid and spent straightforward, as occasion
needed   But how great was my astonishment and joy, when,
after some weeks, I observed that the fulness of my store was
not in the least diminished, that my purse was still as round
and crammed as ever ! Wishing to obtain more strict knowledge of this pretty quality, I set myself down to count, I
accurately marked the sum, and again proceeded in my
joyous life as before   We had no want of excursions by land,
and excursions by water, of dancing, singing, and other
recreations   But now it required small attention to observe
that the purse was actually diminishing, as if by my cursed
counting I had robbed it of the property of being uncountable.
However, this gay mode of existence had been once entered
on, I could not draw back, and yet my ready money soon
verged to a close   I execrated my situation, upbraided my
fair friend, for having so led me into temptation, took it as
an offence that she did not again show herself to me, renounced, in my spleen, all duties towards her, and resolved
to break open the Box, and see if peradventure any help
might be found there   I was just about proceeding with my
purpose but I put it off till night, that I might go through
the business with full composure, and, in the mean time, I

hastened off to a banquet, for which this was the appointed hour Here again we got into a high key, the wine and trumpet-sounding had flushed me not a little, when by the most villainous luck it chanced, that during the dessert, a former friend of my dearest fair one, returning from a journey, entered unexpectedly, placed himself beside her, and, without much ceremony, set about asserting his old privileges Hence very soon arose ill-humour, quarrelling and battle we plucked out our spits, and I was carried home half dead of several wounds

"The surgeon had bandaged me and gone away it was far in the night, my sick-nurse had fallen asleep, the door of the side-room opened; my fair mysterious friend came in, and sat down by me on the bed She asked how I was I answered not, for I was faint and sullen She continued speaking with much sympathy she rubbed my temples with a certain balsam, whereby I felt myself rapidly and decidedly strengthened, so strengthened that I could now get angry and upbraid her In a violent speech I threw all the blame of my misfortune on her, on the passion she had inspired me with, on her appearing and vanishing, and the tedium, the longing which in such a case I could not but feel I waxed more and more vehement, as if a fever had been coming on, and I swore to her at last, that if she would not be mine, would not now abide with me and wed me, I had no wish to live any longer, to all which I required a peremptory answer As she lingered and held back with her explanation, I got altogether beside myself, and tore off my double and triple bandages, in the firmest resolution to bleed to death But what was my amazement, when I found all my wounds healed, my skin smooth and entire, and this fair friend in my arms!

"Henceforth we were the happiest pair in the world We both begged pardon of each other, without either of us rightly knowing why She now promised to travel on along with me and soon we were sitting side by side in the carriage, the little Box lying opposite us on the other seat

Of this I had never spoken to her, nor did I now think of speaking, though it lay there before our eyes, and both of us, by tacit agreement, took charge of it, as circumstances might require, I, however, still carrying it to and from the carriage, and busying myself, as formerly, with the locking of the doors

"So long as aught remained in my purse, I had continued to pay. but when my cash went done, I signified the fact to her 'That is easily helped,' said she, pointing to a couple of little pouches fixed at the top, to the sides of the carriage These I had often observed before, but never turned to use She put her hand into the one, and pulled out some gold pieces, as from the other some coins of silver, thereby showing me the possibility of meeting any scale of expenditure which we might choose to adopt And thus we journeyed on from town to town, from land to land, contented with each other and with the world and I fancied not that she would again leave me, the less so, that for some time she had evidently been as loving wives wish to be, a circumstance by which our happiness and mutual affection was increased still farther But one morning, alas, she could not be found and as my actual residence, without her company, became displeasing, I again took the road with my Box, tried the virtue of the two pouches, and found it still unimpaired

"My journey proceeded without accident But if I had hitherto paid little heed to the mysteries of my adventure, expecting a natural solution of the whole, there now occurred something which threw me into astonishment, into anxiety, nay, into fear. Being wont, in my impatience for change of place, to hurry forward day and night, it was often my hap to be travelling in the dark and when the lamps, by any chance, went out, to be left in utter obscurity Once in the dead of such a night, I had fallen asleep, and on awakening I observed the glimmer of a light on the covering of my carriage I examined this more strictly, and found that it was issuing from the Box, in which there seemed to be a chink, as if it had been chapped by the warm and dry weather of summer, which was now come on My thoughts of jewels again came into my head, I supposed there must be so e carbuncle lying in the Box, and this point I forthwith set about investigating I postured myself as well as might be, so that my eye was in immediate contact with the chink But how great was my surprise, when a fair apartment, well lighted, and furnished with much taste and even costliness, met my inspection, just as if I had been looking down through the opening of a dome into a royal saloon! A fire was burning in the grate, and before it stood an arm-chair I held my breath and continued to observe And now there entered from the other side of the apartment a lady with a book in her hand, whom I at once recognised for my wife, though her figure was contracted into the extreme of diminution She sat down in the chair by the fire to read, she trimmed the coals with the most dainty pair of tongs, and in the course of her movements, I could clearly perceive that this fairest little creature was also in the family way But now I was obliged to shift my constrained posture a little, and the next moment, when I bent down to look in again, and convince myself that it was no dream, the light had vanished, and my eye rested on empty darkness

"How amazed, nay, terrified I was, you may easily conceive I started a thousand thoughts on this discovery, and in truth could think nothing In the midst of this, I fell asleep; and on awakening, I fancied that it must have been a mere dream, yet I felt myself in some degree estranged fro my fair one, and though I watched over the Box but so uch the more carefully, I knew not whether the event of her reappearance in human size was a thing which I should wish or dread

"After some time she did in fact re-appear one evening, in a white robe, she came gliding in, and as it was just then growing dusky in my roo , she seemed to e taller than when

I had seen her last and I remembered having heard that all
beings of the mermaid and gnome species increased in stature
very perceptibly at the fall of night   She flew, as usual, to
my arms , but I could not with light gladness press her to my
obstructed breast

" 'My dearest,' said she, ' I now feel by thy reception of me,
what, alas, I already knew too well   Thou hast seen me in
the interim   thou art acquainted with the state in which, at
certain times, I find myself, thy happiness and mine is interrupted, nay, it stands on the brink of being annihilated
altogether   I must leave thee, and I know not whether I
shall ever see thee again ' Her presence, the grace with
which she spoke, directly banished from my memory almost
every trace of that vision, which indeed had already hovered
before me as little more than a dream   I addressed her with
kind vivacity, convinced her of my passion, assured her that
I was innocent, that my discovery was accidental , in short, I
so managed it that she appeared composed, and endeavoured
to compose me

" ' Try thyself strictly,' said she, ' whether this discovery has
not hurt thy love, whether thou canst forget that I live in two
forms beside thee, whether the diminution of my being will not
also contract thy affection '

" I looked at her   she was fairer than ever , and I thought
within myself Is it so great a misfortune, after all, to have a
wife who from time to time becomes a dwarf, so that one can
carry her about with him in a casket ? Were it not much
worse if she became a giantess, and put her husband in the
box ? My gaiety of heart had returned   I would not for the
whole world have let her go   ' Best heart,' said I, ' let us be
and continue ever as we have been   Could either of us wish
to be better ? Enjoy thy conveniency , and I promise thee to
guard the Box with so much the more faithfulness   Why
should the prettiest sight I have ever seen in my life make a
bad impression on me ? How happy would lovers be, could

it was but a pictuie, a little sleight-of-hand deception   Thou
art trying and teasing me   but thou shalt see how I will
stand it '

" 'The matter is moie seiious than thou thinkest,' said the
fair one   'however, I am truly glad to see thee take it so
lightly, for much good may still be awaiting us both   I
will tiust in thee, and for my own part do my utmost .
only piomise me that thou wilt never mention this discovery
by way of iepioach   Anothei prayer likewise I must eainestly
make to thee   Be moie than ever on thy guard against wine
and anger '

" I piomised what she requiied, I could have gone on
promising to all lengths   but she herself tuined aside the
conversation, and thencefoith all proceeded in its former
routine   We had no inducement to alter our place of residence   the town was laige, the society various, and the fine
season gave iise to many an excuision and gaiden festival

" In all such amusements the piesence of my wife was welcome, nay, eageily desiied, by women as well as men   A kind
insinuating manner, joined with a certain dignity of beaiing,
secuied to her on all hands praise and estimation   Besides,
she could play beautifully on the lute, accompanying it with
hei voice, and no social night could be peifect, unless ciowned
by the graces of this talent

" I will be free to confess that I have never got much good
of music, on the contraiy, it has always rather had a disagreeable effect on me   My faii one soon noticed this, and
accordingly, when by ourselves, she nevei tiied to entertain
me by such means   in return, howevei, she appeaied to in-
demnify herself while in society, wheie indeed she always found
a ciowd of admireis

" And now, why should I deny it, our late dialogue, in spite
of my best intentions, had by no means sufficed to abolish the
mattei within me   on the contrary, my temper of mind had
by degiees got into the strangest tune, almost without my

hidden grudge broke loose, and by its consequences produced to   yself the greatest damage

"When I look back on it now, I in fact loved my beauty far less, after that unlucky discovery   I was also growing jealous of her, a whim that had never struck   e before   This night at table, I found myself placed very much to my mind beside my two neighbours, a couple of ladies, who, for some time, had appeaied to me very char ing   A id jesting and soft small talk, I was not sparing of my wine. while, on the other side, a pair of musical dilettanti had got hold of my wife, and at last contrived to lead the company into singing separately, and by way of chorus   This put me into ill-humour   The two amateuis appeared to me impertinent; the singing vexed me, and when, as   y turn came, they even requested a solo-strophe from   e, I grew truly indig-nant, I emptied my glass, and set it down again with no soft movement

"The grace of my two fair neighbours soon pacified me, indeed, but there is an evil natuie in wrath, when once it is set a-going   It went on fermenting within me, though all things were of a kind to induce joy and complaisance   On the contrary, I waxed more splenetic than ever when a lute was produced, and my faii one began fingering it and singing, to the admiration of all the rest   Unhappily, a general silence was requested   So then, I was not even to talk any more, and these tones were going through   e like a toothache Was it any wonder that, at last, the smallest spark should blow-up the mine?

"The songstress had just ended a song amid the loudest applauses, when she looked over to me, and this truly with the most loving face in the world   Unluckily, its lovingness could not penetrate so far   She peiceived that I had just gulped down a cup of wine, and was pouring out a fresh one   With her right fore-finger she beckoned to   e in kind threatening   'Considei that it is wine!' said she, not louder than for myself to hear it —'Water is foi meimaids!' ciied

I.—'My ladies,' said she to my neighbours, 'crown the cup with all your gracefulness, that it be not too often emptied.' —'You will not let yourself be tutored?' whispered one of them in my ear —'What ails the Dwarf?' cried I, with a more violent gesture, in which I overset the glass —'Ah, what you have spilt!' cried the paragon of women, at the same ti e, twanging her strings, as if to lead back the attention of the company from this disturbance to herself Her attempt succeeded, the more completely as she rose to her feet, seemingly that she might play with greater convenience, and in this attitude continued preluding.

"At sight of the red wine running over the table-cloth, I returned to yself I perceived the great fault I had been guilty of, and it cut me through the very heart Never till now had music spoken to me the first verse she sang was a friendly good-night to the company, here as they were, as they might still feel themselves together With the next verse they became as if scattered asunder, each felt himself solitary, separated, no one could fancy that he was present any longer But what shall I say of the last verse? It was directed to e alone, the voice of injured Love bidding farewell to Moroseness and Caprice

"In silence I conducted her home, foreboding no good. rcely, however, had we reached our chamber, when she began to show herself exceedingly kind and graceful, nay, even roguish, she made me the happiest of all men

"Next morning, in high spirits and full of love, I said to her 'Thou hast so often sung, when asked in company, as, for example, thy touching farewell song last night Come now, for my sake, and sing me a dainty gay welcome to this morning hour, that we may feel as if we were meeting for the first time'

"'That I may not do, my friend,' said she seriously 'The song of last night referred to our parting, which must now forthwith take place for I can only tell thee, the violation of thy promise and oath will have the worst consequences for us both, thou hast scoffed away a great felicity, and I too must renounce my dearest wishes'

" As I now pressed and entreated her to explain herself more clearly, she answered 'That, alas, I can well do, for, at all events, my continuance with thee is over   Hear, then, what I would rather have concealed to the latest times   The form, under which thou sawest me in the Box, is my natural and proper form   for I am of the race of King Eckwald, the dread Sovereign of the Dwarfs, concerning whom authentic History has recorded so much.   Our people are still as of old laborious and busy, and therefore easy to govern   Thou must not fancy that the Dwarfs are behindhand in their manufacturing skill   Swords which followed the foe, when you cast them after him, invisible and mysteriously binding chains, impenetrable shields, and suchlike ware, in old times, formed their staple produce   But now they chiefly employ themselves with articles of convenience and ornament, in which truly they surpass all people of the Earth   I may well say, it would astonish thee to walk through our workshops and warehouses   All this would be right and good, were it not that with the whole nation in general, but more particularly with the royal family, there is one peculiar circumstance connected'

" She paused for a moment, and I again begged farther light on these wonderful secrets, which accordingly she forthwith proceeded to grant

" 'It is well known,' said she, 'that God, so soon as he had created the world, and the ground was dry, and the mountains were standing bright and glorious, that God, I say, thereupon, in the very first place, created the Dwarfs, to the end that there might be reasonable beings also, who, in their passages and chasms, might contemplate and adore his wonders in the inward parts of the Earth   It is farther well known, that this little race by degrees became uplifted in heart, and attempted to acquire the dominion of the Earth, for which reason God then created the Dragons, in order to drive back the Dwarfs

into their mountains   Now, as the Dragons themselves were
wont to nestle in the large caverns and clefts, and dwell there,
and many of them, too, were in the habit of spitting fire, and
working much other mischief, the poor little Dwarfs were by
this means thrown into exceeding straits and distress, so that
not knowing what in the world to do, they humbly and fer-
vently turned to God, and called to him in prayer, that he
would vouchsafe to abolish this unclean Dragon generation
But though it consisted not with his wisdom to destroy his
own creatures, yet the heavy sufferings of the poor Dwarfs
so moved his compassion, that anon he created the Giants,
ordaining them to fight these Dragons, and if not root them
out, at least lessen their numbers

"'Now, no sooner had the Giants got moderately well
through with the Dragons, than their hearts also began to
wax wanton , and, in their presumption, they practised much
tyranny, especially on the good little Dwarfs, who then once
more in their need turned to the Lord , and he, by the power
of his hand, created the Knights, who were to make war on
the Giants and Dragons, and to live in concord with the
Dwarfs   Hereby was the work of creation completed on this
side   and it is plain, that henceforth Giants and Dragons, as
well as Knights and Dwarfs, have always maintained themselves
in being   From this, my friend, it will be clear to thee, that
we are of the oldest race on the Earth , a circumstance which
does us honour, but, at the same time, brings great disadvan-
tage along with it

"'For as there is nothing in the world that can endure forever, but all that has once been great, must become little and
fade, it is our lot also, that ever since the creation of the
world we have been waning and growing smaller , especially
the royal family, on whom, by reason of their pure blood, this
destiny presses with the heaviest force   To remedy this
evil, our wise teachers have many years ago devised the
expedient of sending forth a Princess of the royal house from
time to ti e into the world, to wed some honourable Knight,

that so the Dwarf progeny may be refected, and saved from
entire decay'

"Though my fair one related these things with an air of
the utmost sincerity, I looked at her hesitatingly, for it
seemed as if she meant to palm some fable on me   As to her
own dainty lineage, I had not the smallest doubt   but that
she should have laid hold of me in place of a Knight, occasioned some mistrust, seeing I knew   yself too well to suppose
that my ancestors had come into the world by an immediate
act of creation

"I concealed my wonder and scepticism, and asked her
kindly 'But tell me, my dear child, how hast thou attained
this large and stately shape? For I know few women that in
richness of form can compare with thee '—'Thou shalt hear,'
replied she 'It is a settled maxim in the Council of the
Dwarf Kings, that this extraordinary step be forborne as long
  it possibly can, which, indeed, I cannot but say is quite
natural and proper   Perhaps they might have lingered still
longer, had not my brother, born after me, come into the
world so exceedingly small, that the nurses actually lost him
out of his swaddling-clothes, and no   creature yet knows
whither he is gone   On this occurrence, unexampled in the
annals of Dwarfdom, the Sages were assembled , and without
more ado, the resolution was taken, and I sent out in quest of
a husband '

" 'The resolution!' exclaimed I 'that is all extremely
well   One can resolve, one can take his resolution   but to
give a Dwarf this heavenly shape, how did your Sages manage
that?'

" 'It had been provided for already,' said she, 'by our
ancestors   In the royal treasury lay a monstrous gold ring
I speak of it as it then appeared to me, when I saw it in   y
childhood   for it was this same ring, which I have here on my
finger   We now went to work as follows

" 'I was informed of all that awaited me, and instructed
what I had to do and to forbear   A splendid palace, after the

pattern of my father's favourite summer-residence, was then got ready a main edifice, wings, and whatever else you could think of It stood at the entrance of a large rock-cleft, which it decorated in the handsomest style On the appointed day, our court moved thither, y parents also and myself The army paraded, and four-and-twenty priests, not without difficulty, carried on a costly litter the ysterious ring It was placed on the threshold of the building, just within the spot where you entered Many ceremonies were observed, and after a pathetic farewell, I proceeded to my task I stept forward to the ring, laid my finger on it, and that instant began perceptibly to wax in stature In a few oments I had reached my present size; and then I put the ring on my finger But now, in the twinkling of an eye, the doors, windows, gates flapped-to; the wings drew up into the body of the edifice, instead of a palace, stood a little Box beside me, which I forthwith lifted and carried off with me, not without a pleasant feeling in being so tall and strong, still, indeed, a dwarf to trees and mountains, to streams and tracts of land, yet a giant to grass and herbs, and above all to ants, from whom we Dwarfs, not being always on the best terms with them, often suffer considerable annoyance

"'How it fared with me on my pilgri age, I might tell thee at great length Suffice it to say I tried many, but no one save thou seemed worthy of being honoured to renovate and perpetuate the line of the glorious Eckwald'

"In the course of these narrations, my head had now and then kept wagging, without myself having absolutely shaken it I put several questions, to which I received no very satisfactory answers, on the contrary, I learned, to y great affliction, that after what had happened, she must needs return to her parents She had hopes still, she said, of getting back to me but for the present, it was indispensably necessary to present herself at court, as otherwise, both for her and me, there was nothing but utter ruin The purses would soon cease to pay, and who knew what all the consequences would be?

"On hearing that our money would run short, I inquired no farther into consequences I shrugged my shoulders, I was silent, and she seemed to understand me

"We now packed up, and got into our carriage, the Box standing opposite us; in which, however, I could still see no symptoms of a palace   In this way we proceeded several stages   Post-money and drink-money were readily and richly paid from the pouches to the right and left, till at last we reached a mountainous district, and no sooner had we alighted here, than my fair one walked forward, directing me to follow her with the Box   She led me by rather steep paths to a narrow plot of green ground, through which a clear brook now gushed in little falls, now ran in quiet windings   She pointed to a little knoll, bade me set the Box down there, then said 'Farewell'   Thou wilt easily find the way back, remember me, I hope to see thee again'

"At this moment, I felt as if I could not leave her   She was just now in one of her fine days, or if you will, her fine hours   Alone with so fair a being, on the greensward, among grass and flowers, girt in by rocks, waters murmuring round you, what heart could have remained insensible'   I came forward to seize her hand, to clasp her in my arms   but she motioned me back, threatening me, though still kindly enough, with great danger, if I did not instantly withdraw

"'Is there no possibility, then,' exclaimed I, 'of my staying with thee, of thy keeping me beside thee?'   These words I uttered with such rueful tones and gestures, that she seemed touched by them, and after some thought confessed to me that a continuance of our union was not entirely impossible   Who happier than I'   My importunity, which increased every moment, compelled her at last to come out with her scheme, and inform me that if I too could resolve on becoming as little as I had once seen her, I might still remain with her, be admitted to her house, her kingdom, her family   The proposal was not altogether to my mind, yet at this moment I positively could not tear myself away, so, having already for a good while been accustomed to the marvellous, and being at all times prone to bold enterprises, I closed with her offer, and said she might do with me as she pleased

"I was thereupon directed to hold out the little finger of my right hand. she placed her own against it, then with her left hand, she quite softly pulled the ring from her finger, and let it run along mine   That instant, I felt a violent twinge on my finger   the ring shrunk together, and tortured me horribly   I gave a loud cry, and caught round me for my fair one, but she had disappeared   What state of mind I was in during this moment, I find no words to express, so I have nothing more to say, but that I very soon, in my miniature size, found myself beside my fair one in a wood of grass-stalks   The joy of meeting after this short yet most strange separation, or, if you will, of this reunion without separation, exceeds all conception   I fell on her neck, she replied to my caresses, and the little pair was as happy as the large one

"With some difficulty, we now mounted a hill   I say difficulty, because the sward had become for us an almost impenetrable forest   Yet at length we reached a bare space, and how surprised was I at perceiving there a large bolted mass, which, ere long, I could not but recognise for the Box, in the same state as when I had set it down

"'Go up to it, my friend,' said she, 'and do but knock with the ring   thou shalt see wonders'   I went up accordingly, and no sooner had I rapped, than I did, in fact, witness the greatest wonder   Two wings came jutting out, and at the same time there fell, like scales and chips, various pieces this way and that, while doors, windows, colonnades, and all that belongs to a complete palace at once came into view.

"If ever you have seen one of Rontchen's desks, how, at one pull, a multitude of springs and latches get in motion, and writing-board and writing-materials, letter and money compartments, all at once, or in quick succession, start forward, you will partly conceive how this palace unfolded itself, into which my sweet attendant now introduced me   In the large

saloon, I directly recognised the fireplace which I had for erly
seen from above, and the chair in which she had then been
sitting.   And on looking up, I actually fancied I could still
see something of the chink in the dome, through which I had
peeped in   I spare you the description of the rest   in a word,
all was spacious, splendid, and tasteful   Scarcely had I
recovered from my astonishment, when I heard afar off a
sound of military music   My better half sprang up, and with
rapture announced to me the approach of His Majesty her
Father.   We stept out to the threshold, and here beheld a
magnificent procession moving towards us, from a considerable
cleft in the rock   Soldiers, servants, officers of state and
glittering courtiers, followed in order.   At last you observed
a golden throng, and in the midst of it the King himself   So
soon as the whole procession had drawn up before the palace,
the King, with his nearest retinue, stept forward   His loving
daughter hastened out to him, pulling me along with her
We threw ourselves at his feet, he raised me very graciously,
and on coming to stand before hi , I perceived, that in this
little world I was still the   ost considerable figure.   We proceeded together to the palace, where His Majesty, in presence
of his whole court, was pleased to welco e me with a well-
studied oration, in which he expressed his surprise at finding
us here   acknowledged me as his son-in-law, and appointed
the nuptial ceremony to take place on the morrow

"A cold sweat went over me as I heard him speak of
marriage, for I dreaded this even more than music, which
otherwise appeared to me the   ost hateful thing on Earth
Your music-makers, I used to say, enjoy at least the conceit of
being in unison with each other, and working in concord, for
when they have tweaked and tuned long enough, grating our
ears with all manner of screeches, they believe in their hearts
that the matter is now adjusted, and one instrument accurately
suited to the other   The band-master hi self is in this happy
delusion, and so they set forth joyfully, though still tearing
our nerves to pieces   In the   arriage-state, even this is not

the case   for although it is but a duet, and you   ight think
two voices, or even two instruments, might in some degree be
attuned to each other, yet this happens very seldom , for while
the man gives out one tone, the wife directly takes a higher
one, and the man again a higher, and so it rises from the
chamber to the choral pitch, and farther and farther, till at
last wind-instruments themselves cannot reach it   And now,
as harmonical music itself is an offence to   e, it will not be
surprising that disharmonical should be a thing which I cannot
endure.

   " Of the festivities in which the day was spent, I shall and
can say nothing , for I paid small heed to any of the . The
sumptuous victuals, the generous wine, the loyal amusements,
I could not relish   I kept thinking and considering what I
was to do   Here, however, there was but little to be considered   I determined, once for all, to take myself away, and
hide somewhere   Accoidingly, I succeeded in reaching the
chink of a stone, where I intrenched and concealed myself as
well as might be   My first caie after this was to get the
unhappy ring off   y finger, an enteiprise, however, which
would by no means piosper, for, on the contrary, I felt that
eveiy pull I gave, the   etal grew straiter and cramped   e
with violent pains, which again abated so soon as I desisted
from my purpose.

   " Eaily in the morning I awoke (for my little person had
slept, and very soundly), and was just stepping out to look
faither about me, when I felt a kind of rain coming on.
Through the grass, flowers and leaves, there fell as it were
something like sand and grit in large quantities : but what was
   y horror when the whole of it became alive, and an innu er-
able host of Ants rushed down on me ! No sooner did they
observe me, than they made an attack on all sides , and
though I defended myself stoutly and gallantly enough, they
at last so hem ed   e in, so nipped and pinched me, that I
was glad to hear them calling to surrender   I surrendered
instantly and wholly, whereupon an Ant of iespectable stature

approached me with courtesy, nay, with reverence, and even recommended itself to my good graces   I learned that the Ants
had now become allies of my father-in-law, and by him been
called out in the present emergency, and commissioned to fetch
me back   Here, then, was little I in the hands of creatures
still less   I had nothing for it but looking forward to the
marriage, nay, I must now thank Heaven, if my father-in-law
were not wroth, if my fair one had not taken the sullens

"Let me skip over the whole train of ceremonies, in a
word, we were wedded   Gaily and joyously as matters went,
there were nevertheless solitary hours, in which you were led
astray into reflection, and now there happened to me something which had never happened before   what, and how, you
shall learn

"Everything about me was completely adapted to my
present form and wants, the bottles and glasses were in a fit
ratio to a little toper, nay, if you will, better measure, in
proportion, than with us   In my tiny palate, the dainty
titbits tasted excellently, a kiss from the little mouth of my
spouse was still the most charming thing in nature, and I
will not deny that novelty made all these circumstances highly
agreeable   Unhappily, however, I had not forgotten my
former situation   I felt within me a scale of bygone greatness, and it rendered me restless and cheerless   Now, for the
first time, did I understand what the philosophers might mean
by their Ideal, which they say so plagues the mind of man   I
had an Ideal of myself, and often in dreams I appeared as a
giant   In short, my wife, my ring, my dwarf figure, and so
many other bonds and restrictions, made me utterly unhappy,
so that I began to think seriously about obtaining my
deliverance

"Being persuaded that the whole magic lay in the ring, I
resolved on filing this asunder   From the court-jeweller,
accordingly, I borrowed some files   By good luck, I was
left-handed, as indeed, throughout my whole life, I had never
done aught in the right-handed way   I stood tightly to the

work it was not small, for the golden hoop, so thin as it appeared, had grown proportionably thicker in contracting from its former length   All vacant hours I privately applied to this task   and at last, the metal being nearly through, I was provident enough to step out of doors   This was a wise measure, for all at once the golden hoop started sharply from my finger, and my flame shot aloft with such violence, that I actually fancied I should dash against the sky, and, at all events, I must have bolted through the dome of our palace, nay, perhaps, in my new awkwardness, have destroyed this summer-residence altogether

"Here, then, was I standing again, in truth, so much the larger, but also, as it seemed to me, so much the more foolish and helpless   On recovering from my stupefaction, I observed the royal strong-box lying near me, which I found to be moderately heavy, as I lifted it, and carried it down the footpath to the next stage, where I directly ordered horses, and set forth   By the road, I soon made trial of the two side-pouches   Instead of money, which appeared to be run out, I found a little key   it belonged to the strong-box, in which I got some moderate compensation   So long as this held out, I made use of the carriage   by and by I sold it, and proceeded by the Diligence   The strong-box too I at length cast from me, having no hope of its ever filling again   And thus in the end, though after a considerable circuit, I again returned to the kitchen-hearth, to the landlady and the cook, where you were first introduced to me."

CHAPTER XVII

LENARDO was overwhelmed with business, his writing-office in the greatest activity, clerks and secretaries finding no moment's rest, while Wilhelm and Friedrich, strolling over field and meadow, were entertaining each other with the most pleasant conversation

And here, first of all, as necessarily happens between friends meeting after some separation, the question was started How far they had altered in the interim ? Friedrich would have it that Wilhelm was exactly the same as before to Wilhel again it seemed that his young friend, though no whit abated in mirth and discursiveness, was somewhat more staid in his manner   " It were pity," interrupted Friedrich, " if the father of three children, the husband of an exemplary matron, had not likewise gained a little in dignity of bearing "

Now, also, it came to light, that all the persons whom we got acquainted with in the *Apprenticeship* were still living and well , nay, better than before , being now in full and decisive activity , each, in his own way, associated with many fellow-labourers, and striving towards the noblest aim   Of this, however, it is not for the present permitted us to impart any more precise information , as, in a little book like ours, reserve and secrecy may be no unseemly qualities

But whatever, in the course of this confidential conversation, transpired respecting the Society in which we now are, as their more intimate relations, maxims and objects, by little and little, came to view, it is our duty and opportunity to disclose in this place

" The whim of Emigration," such was the substance of Friedrich's talk on this matter, " the whim of Emigration may, in straitened and painful circumstances, very naturally lay hold of men , if particular cases chance to be favoured by a happy issue, this whim will, in the general mind, rise to the rank of passion , as we have seen, as we still see, and withal cannot deny that we, in our time, have been befooled by such a delusion ourselves

" Emigration takes place in the treacherous hope of an improvement in our circumstances , and it is too often counter-balanced by a subsequent emigration , since, go where you ay, you still find yourself in a conditional world, and if not constrained to a new emigration, are yet inclined in secret to cherish such a desire

" We have therefoie bound ouiselves to ienounce all Emigration, and to devote ouiselves to Migration Heie one does not turn his back on his native countiy forever, but hopes, even after the gieatest circuit, to ariive theie again, richer, wiser, cleverer, bettei, and whatever else such a way of life can make him Now, in society all things aie easier, more ceitain in theii accomplishment, than to an individual, in which sense, my friend, consider what thou shalt obseive heie, for whatever thou mayest see, all and eveiy part of it is meant to forwaid a great movable connexion among active and sufficient men of all classes

" But as where men are, manneis are too, I may explain thus much of our constitution by way of pieliminary When two of our numbei anywhere by accident meet, they conduct themselves towards each othei according to theii iank and fashion, accoiding to custom of handiciaft oi ait, or by some other such mode adapted to their mutual ielations Three meeting together are considered as a Unity, which governs itself but if a fouith join them, they instantly elect the BOND, one chief and thiee subjects This Bond, however many more combine with them, can still only be a single newly-elected person, foi, in the great as in the small scale, co-regents are found to be mutually obstructive

" Thou mayest observe that Lenaido unites, in this way, more than a hundred active and able men, unites, employs, calls home, sends forth, as tomoriow, an impoitant day with us, thou wilt perceive and undeistand Thou wilt then see the Bond dissolved, the multitude divided into smallei societies, and the Bond multiplied, all the rest will at the same ti e become cleai to thee

" But, for the piesent, I invite thee to a shoit bout of reading Heie, under the shadow of these whispering tiees, by the side of this still-flowing water, let us peiuse a story, this little paper, which Lenaido, from the rich tieasures of his Collection, has intiusted to me, that so both of us may see thoroughly what a difference there is between a mad pilgiimage, such as many lead in the world, and a well-meditated, happily-commenced undertaking like ours, of which I shall at this time say no more in praise "

The quaint, fitful and most dainty story of *The Foolish Pilgrimess*, with which our two friends now occupied their morning, we feel ourselves constrained, not unreluctantly, by certain grave calculations, to reserve for some future and better season

CHAPTER XVIII

LENARDO having freed himself from business for an hour, took dinner with his friends, and at table he began to explain to them his family circumstances   His eldest sister was married   A rich brother-in-law, to the great satisfaction of the Uncle, had undertaken the management of all the estates, with him Valerina's husband was stoutly cooperating, they were labouring on the great scale, strengthening their enterprises by connexion with distant countries and places

Here likewise our oldest friends once more make their appearance   Lothario, Werner, the Abbé, are on their side proceeding in the highest diligence, while Jarno occupies himself with mining   A general Insurance has been instituted, we discern a vast property in Land, and on this depends the existence of a large Wandering Society, the individual members of which, under the condition of the greatest possible usefulness, are recommended to all the world, are forwarded in every undertaking, and secured against all mischances, while they again, as scattered colonists, may be supposed to react on their mother country with favourable influences

Throughout all this, we observe Lenardo recognised as the wandering Bond, in smaller and greater combinations, he, for most part, is elected   on him is placed the most unrestricted confidence.

So far had the disclosure, partly from Lenardo, partly from

Friedrich, proceeded without let, when both of them on a sudden became silent, each seeming to have scruples about communicating more   After a short pause, Wilhelm addressed them, and cried   " What new secret again suddenly over-shadows the friendliest explanation ?   Will you again leave me in the lurch ? "

"Not at all ! " exclaimed Friedrich   " Do but hear me ! He has found the Nut-brown Maid , and for her sake   "

" Not for her sake," interrupted Lenardo

" And just for her sake ! " persisted Friedrich   " Do not deceive yourself for her sake you are changing yourself into a lawful vagabond, as some others of us, not, in truth, for the most praiseworthy purposes, have in times past changed ourselves into lawless vagrants "

" Let us go along calmly," said Lenardo   " our friend here must be made acquainted with the state of our affairs , but, in the first place, let him have a little touch of discipline for him-self   You had found the Nut-brown Maid , but to me you refused the knowledge of her abode   For this I will not blame you but what good did it do ? To discover this secret, I was passionately incited , and, notwithstanding your sagacious caution, I at length came upon the right trace   You have seen the good Maiden yourself , her circumstances you have accurately investigated , and yet you did not judge them rightly   It is only the Loving who feels and discovers what the Beloved wishes and wants , he can read it in her from her deepest heart   Let this at present suffice   for explanation we have no time left today   Tomorrow I have the hottest press of business to front   next day we part   But for your infor-mation, composure and participating interest, accept this copy of a week from my Journal   it is the best legacy which I can leave you   By reading it, you will not indeed become wiser than you are and than I am   but let this for the present suffice   The nearest future, or a more remote one, will arrange and direct   that is to say, in this case, as in so many others, we know not what is to become of us "

By way of dessert, Lenardo received a packet, at the opening of which, he, with some tokens of surprise, handed a letter to Wilhelm " What secrets, what speedy concerns can sister Hersilia have with our friend ? 'To be delivered instantly, and opened privately, without the presence of any one, friend or stranger !' let us give him all possible convenience, Friedrich , let us withdraw !" Wilhelm hastily broke open the sheet, and read

Hersilia to Wilhelm

Wherever this letter may reach you, my noble friend, to a certainty it will find you in some nook, where you are striving in vain to hide from yourself By making you acquainted with my two fair dames, I have done you a sorry service.

But wherever you may be lurking, and doubtless it will search you out, my promise is, that if, after reading this letter, you do not forthwith leap from your seat, and, like a pious pilgrim, appear in my presence without delay, I must declare you to be the manliest of all men that is to say, the one most completely void of the finest property belonging to our sex , I mean Curiosity, which at this moment is afflicting me in its sharpest concentration

In one word, then, your Casket has now got its key , this, however, none but you and I are to know How it came into my hands, let me now tell you

Some days ago, our Man of Law gets despatches from a distant Tribunal , wherein he was asked if, at such and such a time, there had not been a boy prowling about our neighbourhood, who had played all manner of tricks, and at length, in a rash enterprise, lost his jacket

By the way this brat was described, no doubt remained with us but he was Fitz, the gay comrade whom Felix talked so much of, and so often wished back to play with hi .

Now, for the present, those Authorities request that said article of dress may be sent to them, if it is still in existence , as the boy, at last involved in judicial examinations, refers to

it   Of this demand our Lawyer chances to make mention ; he
shows us the little frock before sending it off

Some good or evil spirit whispers me to grope the breast-
pocket   a little angular prickly Something comes into my
hand , I, so timorous, ticklish and startlish as I usually am,
clench my hand, clench it, hold my peace, and the jerkin is
sent away.   Directly, of all feelings, the strangest seizes me
At the first stolen glance, I saw, I guessed that it was the key
of your little Box   And now came wondrous scruples of conscience, and all sorts of moral doubts   To discover, to give
back my windfall, was impossible , what have those long-
wigged judges to do with it, when it may be so useful to my
friend!   And then, again, all manner of questions about Right
and Duty begin lifting up their voices , but I would not let
them outvote me

From this you perceive into what a situation my friendship
for you has reduced me   a choice faculty develops itself, all on
a sudden, for your sake , what an occurrence!   May it not be
something more than Friendship that so holds the balance of
my conscience?   Between guilt and curiosity I am wonderfully
discomposed , I have a hundred whims and stories about what
may follow: Law and Judgment will not be trifled with
Hersilia, the careless, and as occasion served, capricious Hersilia, entangled in a criminal process, for this is the scope and
tendency of it!   And what can I do, but think of the friend
for whose sake I suffer all this?   I thought of you before, yet
with pauses   but now I think of you incessantly , now when
my heart throbs, and I think of the Eighth Commandment, I
must turn to you, as to the Saint, who has caused this sin, and
will also procure me an absolution   thus the opening of the
Casket is the only thing that can compose me   My curiosity
is growing stronger and doubly strong   come and bring the
Casket with you!   To what judgment-seat it properly belongs
we will make out between us   till then let it remain between
us , no one must know of it, be who he will

But now, in conclusion, look here, my friend!   And tell

me, what say you to this picture of the riddle? Does it not
remind you of Arrows with barbs? God help us! But the
Box must first stand unopened between you and me, and then
when opened, tell us farther what we have to do I wish there
were nothing whatever in it, and who knows what all I wish,
and what all I could tell but do you look at this, and hasten
so much the faster to get upon the road.

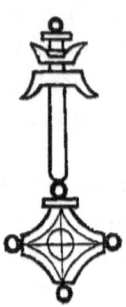

Friedrich returned more gay and lively than he had gone.
"Good news!" cried he "good luck! Lenardo has received
some pretty letters, to facilitate the parting credit more than
sufficient, and thou too shalt have thy share in it Fortune
herself surely knows not what she is about, for once in her
time she has done wise worthy fellows a favour "
Hereupon he handed to his friend some clipped fragments
of maps, with directions where they were to be produced, and
changed for hard cash or bills, as he might choose Wilhelm
was obliged to accept them, though he kept assuring his companion, that for the present he had no need of such things
"Then others will need them!" cried Friedrich "constrain
not thy good feelings, and wherever thou art, appear as a
benefactor But now come along, let us have a look at this
manuscript it is long till night, one tires of talking and
listening, so I have begged some writing for our entertainment.
Every leaf in Lenardo's Archives is penned in the spirit of the
whole in giving me this he said 'Well, take it and read it,

our friend will acquire more confidence in our Society and
Bond, the more good members he becomes acquainted with.'"
The two then retired to a cheerful spot, and Friedrich read,
enlivening with much natural energy and mirth what he found
set down for him

WHO CAN THE TRAITOR BE?

"No! no!" exclaimed he, violently and hastily rushing into
the chamber allotted him, and setting down his candle · "No!
it is impossible! But whither shall I turn? For the first
time, I think otherwise than he, for the first time, I feel, I
wish otherwise O father! couldst thou but be present
invisibly, couldst thou but look through and through me,
thou wouldst see that I am still the same, still thy true,
obedient, affectionate son Yet to say No! To contradict
my father's dearest, long-cherished wish! How shall I disclose
it? How shall I express it? No, I cannot marry Julia!
While I speak of it, I shudder And how shall I appear
before him, tell him this, him the good, kind father? He
looks at me with astonishment, without speaking the
prudent, clear-sighted, gifted man can find no words Woe
is me! Ah, I know well to whom I would confide this pain,
this perplexity, who it is I would choose for my advocate!
Before all others, thou, Lucinda! And I would first tell thee
how I love thee, how I give myself to thee, and pressingly
entreat thee to speak for me, and if thou canst love me
again, if thou wilt be mine, to speak for us both"

To explain this short pithy monologue will require some
details

Professor N of N had an only boy of singular beauty,
whom, till the child's eighth year, he had left entirely in
charge of his wife This excellent woman had directed the
hours and days of her son, in living, learning, and all good
behaviour She died, and the father instantly felt, that to
prosecute this parental tutelage was impossible In their
lifetime, all had been harmony between the parents, they

had laboured for a common aim, had determined in concert what was next to be done, and the mother had not wanted skill to execute wisely, by herself, what the two had planned together   Double and treble was now the widower's anxiety, seeing, as he could not but daily see, that for the sons of professors, even in universities, it was only by a sort of miracle that a happy education could be expected

In this strait he applied to his friend the Oberamtmann of R, with whom he had already been treating of plans for a closer alliance between their families   The Oberamtmann gave him counsel and assistance, so the son was established in one of those Institutions, which still flourish in Germany, and where charge is taken of the whole man, and body, soul and spirit are trained with all attention

The son was thus provided for, the father, however, felt himself very lonely   robbed of his wife, shut out from the cheerful presence of the boy, whom he had seen, without effort of his, growing up in such desirable culture   But here again the friendship of the Oberamtmann served him in good stead, the distance of their abodes vanished before his affection, his desire for movement, for diversion of thought. In this hospitable home the widowed Man of Letters found, in a family-circle motherless like his own, two beautiful little daughters growing up in diverse loveliness, a state of things which more and more confirmed the fathers in their purpose, in their hope, of one day seeing their families united in the most joyful bonds

They lived under the sway of a mild good Prince   the meritorious Oberamtmann was certain of his post during life, and in the appointment of a successor his recommendation was likely to go far   And now, according to the wise family arrangement, sanctioned also by the Minister, Lucidor was to train himself for the important office of his future father-in-law   This in consequence he did from step to step   Nothing was neglected in communicating to him all sorts of knowledge, in developing in him all sorts of activity, which the State in

any case requires practice in rigorous judicial law, and also
in the laxer sort, where prudence and address find their proper
field, foresight for daily ways and means, not excluding
higher and more comprehensive views, yet all tending towards
practical life, and so as with effect and certainty to be
employed in its concerns

With such purposes had Lucidor spent his school-years
by his father and his patron, he was now warned to make
ready for the university In all departments he already
showed the fairest talents, and to Nature he was farther
indebted for the singular happiness of inclining, out of love
for his father, out of respect for his friend, to turn his capabilities, first from obedience, then from conviction, on that
very object to which he was directed He was placed in a
foreign university, and here, both by his own account in his
letters, and by the testimony of his teachers and overseers,
he continued walking in the path that led towards his
appointed goal It was only objected to him, that in certain
cases he had been too impetuously brave The father shook
his head at this, the Oberamtmann nodded. Who would
not have been proud of such a son?

Meanwhile, the two daughters, Julia and Lucinda, were
waxing in stature and graces Julia, the younger, waggish,
lovely, unstable, highly entertaining, the other difficult to
portray, for in her sincerity and purity she represented all
that we prize most in woman Visits were paid and repaid,
and, in the Professor's house, Julia found the most inex-
haustible amusement

Geography, which he failed not to enliven by Topography,
belonged to his province, and no sooner did Julia cast her
eyes on any of the volumes, of which a whole series from
Homann's Warehouse were standing there, than the cities
all and sundry had to be mustered, judged, preferred or
rejected all havens especially obtained her favour, other
towns, to acquire even a slight approval from her, must stand
forth well supplied with steeples, domes and minarets.

Julia's father often left her for weeks to the care of his tried friend She was actually advancing in knowledge of her science, and already the inhabited world, in its main features, in its chief points and places, stood before her with some accuracy and distinctness   The garbs of foreign nations attracted her peculiar attention, and often when her foster-father asked her in jest If among the many young handsome men who were passing to and fro before her window, there was not some one or other whom she liked? she would answer "Yes, indeed, if he do but look odd enough"   And as our young students are seldom behindhand in this particular, she had often occasion to take notice of individuals among them they brought to her mind the costume of foreign nations, however, she declared in the end, that if she was to bestow her undivided attention on any one, he must be at least a Greek, equipped in the complete fashion of his country, on which account, also, she longed to be at some Leipzig Fair, where, as she understood, such persons were to be seen walking the streets

After his dry and often irksome labours, our Teacher had now no happier moments than those he spent in mirthfully instructing her, triumphing withal, in secret, that a being so attractive, ever entertaining, ever entertained, was in the end to be his own daughter   For the rest, the two fathers had mutually agreed, that no hint of their purpose should be communicated to the girls, from Lucidor, also, it was kept secret

Thus had years passed away, as indeed they very lightly pass, Lucidor presented himself completed, having stood all trials to the joy even of the superior overseers, who wished nothing more heartily than being able, with a good conscience, to fulfil the hopes of old, worthy, favoured and deserving servants

And so the business had at length by quiet regular steps come so far, that Lucidor, after having demeaned himself in subordinate stations to universal satisfaction, was now to be placed in a very advantageous post, suitable to his wishes and merits, and lying just midway between the University and the Oberamtmannship

The father now spoke with his son about Julia, of whom he had hitherto only hinted, as about his bride and wife, without any doubt or condition, congratulating him on the happiness of having appropriated such a jewel to himself   The Professor saw in fancy his daughter-in-law again from time to time in his house, occupied with charts, plans and views of cities   the son recalled to mind the gay and most lovely creature, who, in times of childhood, had, by her rogueries as by her kindliness, always delighted him   Lucidor was now to ride over to the Oberamtmann's to take a closer view of the full-grown fair one, and, for a few weeks, to surrender himself to the habitudes and familiarity of her household   If the young people, as was to be hoped, should speedily agree, the Professor was forthwith to appear, that so a solemn betrothment might forever secure the anticipated happiness

Lucidor arrives, is received with the friendliest welcome, a chamber is allotted him, he arranges himself there, and appears   And now he finds, besides the members of the family already known to us, a grown-up son, misbred certainly, yet shrewd and good-natured, so that if you liked to take him as the jesting Counsellor of the party, he fitted not ill with the rest   There belonged, moreover, to the house, a very old, but healthy and gayhearted man, quiet, wise, discreet, completing his life, as it were, and here and there requiring a little help.   Directly after Lucidor, too, there had arrived another stranger, no longer young, of an impressive aspect, dignified, thoroughly well-bred, and, by his acquaintance with the most distant quarters of the world, extremely entertaining   He was called Antoni

Julia received her announced bridegroom in fit order, yet with an excess rather than a defect of frankness   Lucinda, on the other hand, did the honours of the house, as her sister did

those of herself   So passed the day, peculiarly agreeable to
all, only to Lucidor not he, at all times silent, had been
forced, that he might avoid sinking dumb entirely, to employ
himself in asking questions, and in this attitude no one
appears to advantage

Throughout he had been absent-minded, for at the first
glance he had felt, not aversion or repugnance, yet estrange-
ment, towards Julia Lucinda, on the contrary, attracted him,
so that he trembled every time she looked at him with her
full pure peaceful eyes

Thus hard bestead, he reached his chamber the first night,
and gave vent to his heart in that soliloquy with which we
began   But to explain this sufficiently, to show how the
violence of such an emphatic speech agrees with what we know
of him already, another little statement will be necessary

Lucidor was of a deep character, and for most part had
something else in his mind than what the present scene
required   hence talk and social conversation would never
prosper rightly with him, he felt this, and was wont to continue silent, except when the topic happened to be particular,
on some department which he had completely studied, and of
which whatever he needed was at all times ready   Besides
this, in his early years at school, and later at the university,
he had been deceived in friends, and had wasted the effusions
of his heart unhappily, hence every communication of his
feelings seemed to him a doubtful step, and doubting destroys
all such communication   With his father he was used to
speak only in unison, therefore his full heart poured itself out
in monologues, so soon as he was by himself

Next morning he had summoned up his resolution, and
yet he almost lost heart and composure again, when Julia met
him with still more friendliness, gaiety and frankness than
ever   She had much to ask, about his journeys by land and
journeys by water, how, when a student, with his knapsack
on his back, he had roamed and climbed through Switzerland,
nay, crossed the Alps the selves   And now of those fair

islands on the gieat Southein Lake she had much to say, and
then backwards, the Rhine must be accompanied from his
primaiy origin, at first, through most undelicious regions, and
so downwards through many an alteination, till at length,
between Maynz and Coblenz, you find it still worth while
respectfully to dismiss the old River from his last confine ent,
into the wide world, into the sea.

Lucidor, in the course of this recital, felt himself much
lightened in heait, he nariated willingly and well, so that
Julia at last exclaimed in rapture. "It is thus that our othei
self should be!" At which phiase Lucidor again felt startled
and frightened, thinking he saw in it an allusion to their
future pilgrimage in common through life

From his narrative duty, however, he was soon relieved for
the stiangei, Antoni, very speedily oveishadowed all mountain
streams, and rocky banks, and rivers whether hemmed in or
left at liberty Under his guidance you now went forward to
Genoa, Livorno lay at no great distance, whatever was most
interesting in the country you took with you as fair spoil;
Naples, too, was a place you should see before you died, and
then, in truth, iemained Constantinople, which also was by
no means to be neglected Antoni's descriptions of the wide
woild carried the imagination of eveiy hearer along with him,
though Antoni himself intioduced little fire into the subject
Julia, quite enraptured, was still nowise satisfied · she longed
foi Alexandria, Caiio, and above all, for the Pyramids, of
which, by the lessons of her intended father-in-law, she had
gained some moderate knowledge

Lucidor next night (he had scarcely shut his door, the
candle he had not put down) exclaimed "Now bethink thee,
then it is growing seiious! Thou hast studied and meditated
many serious things what avails thy law-leaining, if thou
canst not act like a man of law? View thyself as a delegate,
forget thy own feelings, and do what it would behove thee to
do for another It thickens and closes round me horribly!
The strangei is plainly co e for the sake of Lucinda, she

shows him the fairest, noblest social and hospitable attentions
that little fool would run through the world with any one for
anything or nothing   Besides, she is a wag , her interest
in cities and countries is a farce, by which she keeps us in
silence   But why do I look at the affair so perplexedly, so
narrowly ? Is not the Oberamtmann himself the most judicious,
the clearest, the kindest mediator ? Thou wilt tell him how
thou feelest and thinkest , and he will think with thee, if not
likewise feel   With thy father he has all influence   And is
not the one as well as the other his daughter ? What would
this Antoni the Traveller with Lucinda, who is born for
home, to be happy and to make happy ? Let the wavering
quicksilver fasten itself to the Wandering Jew   that will be a
right match "

Next morning Lucidor came down, with the firm purpose
of speaking with the father , and waiting on him expressly
to that end, at the hour when he knew him to be disengaged
How great was his vexation, his perplexity, on learning that
the Oberamtmann had been called away on business, and was
not expected till the day after the morrow ! Julia, on this
occasion, seemed to be expressly in her travelling fit , she
kept by the world-wanderer, and, with some sportive hits at
domestic economy, gave up Lucidor to Lucinda   If our friend,
viewing this noble maiden from a certain distance, and under
one general impression, had already, with his whole heart,
loved her, he failed not now in this nearest nearness to discover
with double and treble vividness in detail, all that had before
as a whole attracted him

The good old friend of the family now brought himself
forward, in place of the absent father   he too had lived, and
loved , and was now, after many hard buffetings and bruises
of life, resting at last, refreshed and cheerful, beside the friend
of his youth   He enlivened the conversation , and especially
expatiated on perplexities in choice of wives , relating several
remarkable examples of explanations, both in time and too
late. Lucinda appeared in all her splendour. She admitted .

That accident, in all departments of life, and so likewise in the business of marriage, often produced the best result, yet that it was finer and prouder when one could say he owed his happiness to himself, to the silent calm conviction of his heart, to a noble purpose and a quick determination. Tears stood in Lucidor's eyes as he applauded this sentiment directly afterwards, the two ladies went out The old president liked well to deal in illustrative histories, and so the conversation expanded itself into details of pleasant instances, which, however, touched our hero so closely, that none but a youth of as delicate manners as his could have refrained from breaking out with his secret. He did break out, so soon as he was by himself

"I have constrained myself!" exclaimed he. "with such perplexities I will not vex y good father I have forborne to speak, for I see in this worthy old man the substitute of both fathers To him will I speak, to him disclose the whole he will surely bring it about, he has already almost spoken what I wish Will he censure in the individual case what he praises in general? Tomorrow I visit him I must give vent to this oppression "

At breakfast the old man was not present, last night he had spoken, it appeared, too much, had sat too long, and likewise drunk a drop or two of wine beyond his custo Much was said in his praise, many anecdotes were related; and precisely of such sayings and doings as brought Lucidor to despair for not having forthwith applied to him This unpleasant feeling was but aggravated, when he learned that in such attacks of disorder the good old man would often not make his re-appearance for a week

For social converse a country residence has any advantages, especially when the owners of it have, for a course of years, been induced, as thinking and feeling persons, to improve the natural capabilities of their environs Such had been the good fortune of this spot. The Oberamtmann, at first unwedded, then in a long happy marriage, himself a man

of foitune, and occupying a lucrative post, had, according to
his own judgment and perception, according to the taste of
his wife, nay, at last according to the wishes and whims of his
children, laid out and forwaided many larger and smaller
decorations, which by degrees being skilfully connected with
plantations and paths, afforded to the piomenader, a very
beautiful, continually varying, characteristic seiies of scenes
A pilgrimage through these, our young hosts now proposed to
theii guests, as in general we take pleasure in showing our
impiovements to a stranger, that so what has become habitual
in our eyes may appear with the charm of novelty in his, and
leave with him, in permanent remembrance, its first favourable
impression

The neaiest, as well as the most distant part of the grounds,
was peculiarly appropriate for modest decorations, and altogether rural individualities   Feitile hills alteinated with
well-watered meadows, so that the whole was visible from
time to time, without being flat, and if the land seemed
chiefly devoted to purposes of utility, the graceful, the attractive, was by no means excluded

To the dwelling and office-houses were united various
gardens, orchards and green spaces, out of which you imperceptibly passed into a little wood, with a broad, clear carriage-
road winding up and down through the midst of it   Here, in
a central spot, on the most considerable elevation, there had
been a hall erected, with side-chambers entering from it
On coming through the main door, you saw in a large mirror
the most favourable prospect which the country afforded,
and were sure to turn round that instant, to recover yourself
on the reality from the effect of this its unexpected image,
for the approach was artfully enough contrived, and all
that could excite surprise was carefully hid till the last
moment   No one entered but felt himself pleasurably
tempted to turn from the miiior to Nature, and from Nature
to the mirror

Once in   otion in this fairest, brightest, longest day, our party made a spiritual campaign of it, over and through the whole. Here the daughters pointed out the evening seat of their good mother, where a stately box-tree had kept clear space all round it   A little farther on, Lucinda's place of morning-prayer was half-roguishly exhibited by Julia   close to a little brook, between poplars and alders, with meadows sloping down from it, and fields stretching upwards   It was indescribably pretty   You thought you had seen such a spot everywhere, but nowhere so impressive and so perfect in its simplicity   In return for this, the young master, also half against Julia's will, pointed out the tiny groves and child's gardens, which, close by a snug-lying mill, were now scarcely discernible   they dated from a time when Julia, perhaps in her tenth year, had taken it into her head to become a milleress, intending, after the decease of the two old occupants, to assume the management herself, and choose some brave millman for her husband

" That was at a time," cried Julia, " when I knew nothing of towns lying on rivers, or even on the sea, nothing of Genoa, of Naples and the like   Your worthy father, Lucidor, has converted me, of late I come seldom hither "   She sat down with a roguish air, on a little bench, that was now scarcely large enough for her, under an elder-bough, which had bent deeply towards the ground · " Fie on this cowering ! " cried she, then started up, and ran off with her gay brother

The remaining pair kept up a rational conversation, and in these cases reason approaches close to the borders of feeling   Wandering over changeful, simple natural objects, to contemplate at leisure how cunning scheming man contrives to gain some profit from them, how his perception of what is laid before him, combining with the feeling of his wants, does wonders, first in rendering the world inhabitable, then in peopling it, and at last in overpeopling it. all this could here be talked of in detail   Lucinda gave account of everything, and, modest as she was, she could not hide that these pleasant and convenient combinations of distant parts by roads, had been her work, under the proposal, direction, or favour of her revered mother

But as the longest day at last bends down to evening, our party were at last forced to think of returning, and while devising some pleasant circuit, the merry brother proposed that they should take the short road, though it commanded no fine prospects, and was even in some places more difficult to get over   " For," cried he, " you have preached all day about your decorations and reparations, and how you have improved and beautified the scene for pictorial eyes and feeling hearts. let me also have my turn "

Accordingly they now set forth over ploughed grounds, by coarse paths, nay, sometimes picking their way by stepping-stones in boggy places, till at last they perceived, at some distance, a pile of machinery towering up in manifold combination   More closely examined, it turned out to be a large apparatus for sport and games, arranged not without judgment, and in a certain popular spirit   Here, fixed at suitable distances, stood a large swing-wheel, on which the ascending and the descending riders might still sit horizontally, and at their ease, other see-saws, swing-ropes, leaping-poles, bowling and nine-pins courses, and whatever can be fancied for variedly and equally employing and diverting a crowd of people gathered on a large common   " This," cried he, " is my invention, my decoration !   And though my father found the money, and a shrewd fellow the brain necessary for it, yet without me, whom you often call a person of no judgment, money and brain would not have come together "

In this cheerful mood, the whole four reached home by sunset   Antoni also joined them, but the little Julia, not yet satisfied with this unresting travel, ordered her coach, and set forth on a visit to a lady of her friends, in utter despair at not having seen her for two days   The party left behind began to feel embarrassed before they were aware, it was even mentioned in words that the father's absence distressed them. The conversation was about to stagnate, when all at once the madcap sprang from his seat, and in a few moments returned with a book, proposing to read to the company. Lucinda forbore not to inquire how this notion had occurred to him, no for the first time in a twelvemonth "Everything occurs to me," said he, "at the proper season this is ore than you can say for yourself" He read them a series of genuine Antique Tales such as lead man away from himself, flattering his wishes, and aking him forget all those restrictions, between which, even in the happiest moments, we are still hemmed in

"What shall I do now!" cried Lucidor, when at last he saw himself alone "The hour presses on. in Antoni I have no trust, he is an utter stranger, I know not who he is, how he comes to be here, nor what he wants, Lucinda seems to be his object, and if so, what can I expect of him? Nothing remains for me but applying to Lucinda herself she must know of it, she before all others This was my first feeling why do we stray into side-paths and subterfuges? My first thought shall be my last, and I hope to reach my aim"

On Saturday morning, Lucidor, dressed at an early hour, was walking to and fro in his chamber, thinking and conning over his projected address to Lucinda, when he heard a sort of jestful contention before his door, and the door itself directly afterwards opened The mad younker was shoving in a boy before him, with coffee and baked ware for the guest, he himself carried cold meats and wine "Go thou foremost," cried the younker · "for the guest must be first served, I am used to serve myself My friend, today I am entering somewhat early and tumultuously but let us take our breakfast in peace, then we shall see what is to be done, for of our company there is nothing to be hoped The little one is not yet back from her friend, they two have to pour out their hearts together every fortnight, otherwise the poor dear hearts would burst On Saturdays, Lucinda is good for nothing, she balances her household accounts for my father, she would have had me taking share in the concern, but Heaven forbid!

When I know the price of anything, no morsel of it can I relish Guests are expected tomorrow, the old man has not yet got refitted, Antoni is gone to hunt, we will do the same."

Guns, pouches, and dogs were ready, as our pair stept down into the court, and now they set forth over field and hill, shooting at best some leveret or so, and perhaps here and there a poor indifferent undeserving bird Meanwhile they kept talking of domestic affairs, of the household and company at present assembled in it Antoni was mentioned, and Lucidor failed not to inquire more narrowly about hi . The gay younker, with some self-complaisance, asserted, that strange as the man was, and uch mystery as he made about himself, he, the gay younker, had already seen through him and through him " Without doubt," continued he, " Antoni is the son of a rich mercantile family, whose large partnership concern fell to ruin at the very time when he, in the full vigour of youth, was preparing to take a cheerful and active hand in their great undertakings, and withal to share in their abundant profits Dashed down from the summit of his hopes, he gathered hi self together, and undertook to perform for strangers what he was no longer in a case to perform for his relatives And so he travelled through the world, became thoroughly acquainted with it and its mutual traffickings, in the mean while not forgetting his own advantage Unwearied diligence and tried fidelity obtained and secured for him un-bounded confidence from many Thus in all places he acquired connexions and friends, nay, it is easy to see that his fortune is as widely scattered abroad as his acquaintance, and accord-ingly his presence is from time to time required in all quarters of the world "

These things the merry younker told in a more circumstantial and simple style, introducing many farcical observations, as if he meant to spin out his story to full length

" How long, for instance," cried he, " has this Antoni been connected with my father ! They think I see nothing, because

I trouble myself about nothing , but for this very reason, I see
it better, as I take no interest in it To my father he has
intrusted large sums, who again has deposited them securely
and to advantage. It was but last night that he gave out old
dietetic friend a casket of jewels , a finer, simpler, costlier
piece of ware I never cast my eyes on, though I saw this only
with a single glance, for they make a secret of it Most
probably it is to be consigned to the bride for her pleasure,
satisfaction and future security Antoni has set his heart on
Lucinda ! Yet when I see them together, I cannot think it a
well-assorted match The hop-skip would have suited him
better , I believe, too, she would take him sooner than the
elder would Many a time I see her looking over to the old
cur udgeon, so gay and sympathetic, as if she could find in
her heart to spring into the coach with him, and fly off at full
gallop " Lucidor collected himself he knew not what to
answer , all that he heard obtained his internal approbation
The younker proceeded " All along the girl has had a per-
verted liking for old people I believe, of a truth, she would
have skipped away and wedded your father, as briskly as she
would his son "

Lucidor followed his companion, over stock and stone, as it
pleased the gay youth to lead him both forgot the chase,
which at any rate could not be productive They called at a
far -house, where, being hospitably received, the one friend
entertained himself with eating, drinking and tattling , the
other again plunged into meditations, and projects for turning
this new discovery to his own profit

From all these narrations and disclosures, Lucidor had
acquired so much confidence in Antoni, that immediately on
their return he asked for him, and hastened into the garden,
where he was said to be In vain ! No soul was to be seen
anywhere At last he entered the door of the great Hall ;
and strange enough, the setting sun, reflected from the mirror,
so dazzled him, that he could not recognise the two persons, who were sitting on the sofa, though he saw distinctly

that it was a lady and a man, which latter was that instant
warmly kissing the hand of his companion   How great,
accordingly, was Lucidor's astonishment, when, on recovering
his clearness of vision, he beheld Antoni sitting by Lucinda !
He was like to sink through the ground   he stood, however,
as if rooted to the spot, till Lucinda, in the kindest, most
unembarrassed manner, shifted a little to a side, and invited
him to take a seat on her right hand   Unconsciously he
obeyed her, and while she addressed him, inquiring after his
present day's history, asking pardon for her absence on domestic engagements, he could scarcely hear her voice   Antoni
rose, and took his leave   Lucinda, resting herself from her
toil, as the others were doing, invited Lucidor to a short stroll
Walking by her side, he was silent and embarrassed, she, too,
seemed ill at ease   and had he been in the slightest degree
self-collected, her deep-drawn breathing must have disclosed
to him that she had heartfelt sighs to suppress   She at last
took her leave, as they approached the house   he on the
other hand turned round at first slowly, then at a violent
pace to the open country   The park was too narrow for
him, he hastened through the fields, listening only to the
voice of his heart, and without eyes for the beauties of this
loveliest evening   When he found himself alone, and his
feelings were relieving their violence in a shower of tears, he
exclaimed

"Already in my life, but never with such fierceness, have I
felt the agony which now makes me altogether wretched   to
see the long-wished-for happiness at length reach me, hand-
in-hand and arm-in-arm unite with me, and at the same
moment announce its eternal departure !   I was sitting by her,
I was walking by her, her fluttering garment touched me, and
I have lost her !   Reckon it not over, torture not thy heart
with it, be silent, and determine !"

He laid a prohibition on his lips, he held his peace, and
planned and meditated, stepping over field and meadow and
bush, not always by the smoothest paths   Late at night, on

returning to his chamber, he gave voice to his thoughts for a moment, and cried . " Tomorrow morning I am gone , another such day I will not front "

And so, without undressing, he threw himself on the bed Happy, healthy season of youth ! He was already asleep the fatiguing otion of the day had earned for him the sweetest rest Out of bright morning dreams, however, the earliest sun awoke him this was the longest day in the year , and for hi it threatened to be too long If the grace of the peaceful evening-star had passed over hi unnoticed, he felt the awakening beauty of the morning only to despair. The world was lying here as glorious as ever , to his eyes it was still so ; but his soul contradicted it · all this belonged to him no longer; he had lost Lucinda

His travelling-bag was soon packed , this he was to leave behind him , he left no letter with it , a verbal message in excuse of absence from dinner, perhaps also fro supper, might be left with the groom, whom at any rate he must awaken The groom, however, was awake already Lucidor found hi in the yard, walking with large strides before the stable-door " You do not mean to ride ? " cried the usually good-natured man, with a tone of some spleen. " To you I may say it , but young master is growing worse and worse There was he driving about far and near yesterday , you might have thought he would thank God for a Sunday to rest in And see, if he does not come this orning before daybreak, rummages about in the stable, and while I am getting up, saddles and bridles your horse, flings hi self on it, and cries ' Do but consider the good work I am doing ! This beast keeps jogging on at a staid juridical trot, I must see and rouse him into a smart lively gallop ' He said something just so, and other strange speeches besides "

Lucidor was doubly and trebly vexed he liked the horse, as corresponding to his own character, his own mode of life , it grieved hi to figure his good sensible beast in the hands of a madcap His plan, too, was overturned , his purpose of flying

to a college friend, with whom he had lived in cheerful, cordial
union, and in this crisis seeking refuge beside him. His old
confidence had been awakened, the intervening miles were not
counted, he had fancied himself already at the side of his true-
hearted and judicious friend, finding counsel and assuagement
from his words and looks   This prospect was now cut off:
yet not entirely, if he could venture with the fresh pedestria
limbs, which still stood at his command, to set forth towards
the goal

First of all, accordingly, he struck through the park,   aking for the open country, and the road which was to lead him
to his friend   Of his direction he was not quite certain, when
looking to the left, his eye fell upon the Hermitage, which had
hitherto been kept secret from him, a strange edifice, rising
with grotesque joinery through bush and tree and here, to
his extreme astonishment, he observed the good old man, who
for some days had been considered sick, standing in the gallery
under the Chinese roof, and looking blithely through the soft
morning   The friendliest salutation, the most pressing entreaties to come up, Lucidor resisted with excuses and gestures
of haste   Nothing but sympathy with the good old man,
who, hastening down with infirm step, seemed every moment
in danger of falling to the bottom, could induce him to turn
thither, and then suffer himself to be conducted up   With
surprise he entered the pretty little hall it had only three
windows, turned towards the park, a most graceful prospect
the other sides were decorated, or rather covered, with hundreds
of portraits, copperplate or painted, which were fixed in a
certain order to the wall, and separated by coloured borders
and interstices

"I favour you, my friend, more than I do every one, this is
the sanctuary in which I peacefully spend my last days   Here
I recover myself from all the mistakes which society tempts
me to commit   here my dietetic errors are corrected, and my
old being is again restored to equilibrium"

Lucidor looked over the place, and being well read in

history, he easily observed that an historical taste had presided
in its arrangement

"Above, there, in the frieze," said the old virtuoso, "you
will find the names of distinguished men in the primitive ages,
then those of later antiquity, yet still only their names, for
how they looked would now be difficult to discover. But here,
in the ain field, comes my own life into play here are the
men whose names I used to hear mentioned in my boyhood
For so e fifty years or so, the name of a distinguished man
continues in the remembrance of the people, then it vanishes,
or becomes fabulous   Though of Ger an parentage, I was
born in Holland, and for me, William of Orange, Stadtholder,
and King of England, is the patriarch of all com on great
 en and heroes

"Now, close by William, you observe Louis Fourteenth as
the person who—" How gladly would Lucidor have cut short
the good old man, had it but been permitted him, as it is to
us the narrators for the whole late and latest history of the
world seemed impending, as from the portraits of Frederick
the Great and his generals, towards which he was glancing, was
but too clearly to be gathered

And though the kindly young an could not but respect
his old friend's lively sympathy in these things, or deny that
some individual features and views in this exhibitory discourse
might be interesting, yet at college he had heard the late and
latest history of Europe already, and what a man has once
heard, he fancies himself to know forever   Lucidor's thoughts
were wandering far away, he heard not, he scarcely saw. and
was just on the point, in spite of all politeness, of flinging
himself out, and tumbling down the long fatal stair, when a
loud clapping of hands was heard from below

While Lucidor restrained his movement, the old man looked
over through the window, and a well-known voice resounded
from beneath "Come down, for Heaven's sake, out of your
historic picture-gallery, old gentleman ! Conclude your fasts
and hu iliations, and help me to appease our young friend,

when he learns it. Lucidor's horse I have ridden somewhat hard , it has lost a shoe, and I was obliged to leave the beast behind me   What will he say ? He is too absurd, when one behaves absurdly "

"Come up !" said the old man, and turned in to Lucidor. "Now, what say you ?" Lucidor was silent, and the wild blade entered   The discussion of the business lasted long   at length it was determined to despatch the groom forthwith, that he might seek the horse and take charge of it

Leaving the old man, the two younkers hastened to the house , Lucidor, not quite unwillingly, submitting to this arrangement   Come of it what might, within these walls the sole wish of his heart was included   In such desperate cases, we are, at any rate, cut off from the assistance of our free will , and we feel ourselves relieved for a mo ent, when, from any quarter, direction and constraint takes hold of us   Yet, on entering his chamber, he found himself in the strangest mood , like a man who, having just left an apartment of an inn, is forced to return to it, by the breaking of an axle

The gay younker fell upon the travelling-bag, unpacking it all in due order, especially selecting every article of holyday apparel, which, though only on the travelling scale, was to be found there   He forced Lucidor to put on fresh shoes and stockings , he dressed for him his clustering brown locks, and decked him at all points with his best skill   Then stepping back, and surveying our friend and his own handiwork from head to foot, he exclaimed " Now, then, my good fellow, you do look like a man that has some pretensions to pretty damsels , and serious enough, moreover, to spy about you for a bride   Wait one moment ! You shall see how I too can produce myself, when the hour strikes   This knack I learned fro your military officers, the girls are always glancing at them , so I likewise have enrolled myself among a certain Soldiery , and now they look at me too, and look again, and no soul of them knows what to make of it.   And so, from this looking and relooking, from this surprise and attention, a pretty enough result now and then arises, which, though it were not lasting, is worth enjoying for the moment

"But, come along, y friend, and do the like service for me ! When you have seen e case myself by piecemeal in y equipment, you will not say that wit and invention have been denied me " He now led his friend through several long spacious passages of the old castle " I have quite nestled myself here," cried he " Though I care not for hiding, I like to be alone, you can do no good with other people "

They were passing by the office-rooms, just as a servant came out with a patriarchal writing-apparatus, black, massive and co plete, paper, too, was not forgotten

"I know what is to be blotted here again," cried the younker " go thy ways, and leave me the key Take a look of the place, Lucidor, it will amuse you till I am dressed To a friend of justice, such a spot is not odious, as to a tamer of horses " And with this, he pushed Lucidor into the hall of judg ent

Lucidor felt himself directly in a well-known and friendly element, he thought of the days when he, fixed down to business, had sat at such a table, and listening and writing, had trained himself to his art Nor did he fail to observe, that in this case an old stately domestic Chapel had, under the change of religious ideas, been converted to the service of Themis. In the repositories he found some titles and acts already familiar to him, in these very matters he had cooperated, while labouring in the Capital. Opening a bundle of papers, there came into his hands a rescript which he himself had dictated, another, of which he had been the originator Handwriting and paper, signet and president's signature, everything recalled to him that season of juridical effort, of youthful hope And here, when he looked round, and saw the Oberamtmann's chair, appointed and intended for himself, so fair a place, so dignified a circle of activity, which he was now like to cast away and utterly lose, all this oppressed

him doubly and trebly, as the form of Lucinda seemed to
retire from him at the same time

He turned to go out into the open air, but found himself a
prisoner   His gay friend, heedlessly or roguishly, had left the
door locked   Lucidor, however, did not long continue in this
durance   for the other returned, apologised for his oversight,
and really called forth good humour by his singular appearance   A certain audacity of colour and cut in his clothes was
softened by natural taste, as even to tattooed Indians we
refuse not a certain approbation   "Today," cried he, "the
tedium of bygone days shall be made good to us   Worthy
friends, merry friends are come, pretty girls, roguish and
fond, and my father to boot, and wonder on wonder ' your
father too   This will be a festival truly, they are all assembled
for breakfast in the parlour "

With Lucidor, at this piece of information, it was as if he
were looking into deep fog, all the figures, known and
unknown, which the words announced to him, assumed a
spectral aspect, yet his resolution, and the consciousness of a
pure heart, sustained him   and, in a few seconds, he felt
himself prepared for everything   He followed his hastening
friend with a steady step, firmly determined to await the issue,
be what it might, and explain his own purposes, come what
come might

And yet, at the very threshold of the hall, he was struck
with some alarm.   In a large half circle, ranged round by the
windows, he immediately descried his father with the Oberamtmann, both splendidly attired   The two sisters, Antoni,
and others known and unknown, he hurried over with a glance,
which was threatening to grow dim   Half wavering, he
approached his father, who bade him welcome with the
utmost kindness, yet in a certain style of formality which
scarcely invited any trustful application   Standing before so
many persons, he looked round to find a place among them for
a oment   he might have arranged himself beside Lucinda,
but Julia, contrary to the rigour of etiquette, made room for

him, so that he was forced to step to her side   A toni continued by Lucinda

At this important   oment, Lucidoi again felt as if he were a delegate, and, steeled by his whole juridical science, he called up in his own favour the fine maxim   That we should transact affairs delegated to us by a stranger, as if they were our own, why not our own, therefore, in the same spirit? Well practised in official oiations, he speedily ran over what he had to say   But the company, ranged in a formal semi-circle, seemed to out-flank him   The purport of his speech he knew well, the beginning of it he could not find.   At this crisis, he observed on a table, in the corner, the large ink-glass, and several clerks sitting round it · the Oberamt ann made a movement as if to solicit attention for a speech, Lucidor wished to anticipate him, and, at that veiy moment, Julia piessed his hand   This threw him out of all self-possession, convinced hi   that all was decided, all lost for him

With the whole of these negotiations, these family alliances, with social conventions and rules of good   anners, he had now nothing more to do   he snatched his hand fiom Julia's, and vanished so rapidly from the roo , that the company lost him unawaies, and he out of doors could not find himself again

Shrinking fro   the light of day, which shone down upon him in its highest splendour, avoiding the eyes of men, dreading search and pursuit, he hurried forwaids, and reached the large garden-hall   Here his knees were like to fail him, he rushed in, and threw himself, utterly comfortless, upon the sofa beneath the minor   A id the polished arrangements of society, to be caught in such unspeakable perplexity !   It dashed to and fro like waves about him and within him   His past existence was struggling with his present, it was a frightful   oment

And so he lay for a time, with his face hid in the cushion, on which last night Lucinda's arm had rested   Altogether

sunk in his sorrow, he had heard no footsteps approach,
feeling some one touch hi , he started up, and perceived
Lucinda standing by his side

Fancying they had sent her to bring him back, had commissioned her to lead him with fit sisterly words into the
assemblage to front his hated doom, he exclaimed "You
they should not have sent, Lucinda, for it was you that
drove e away I will not return Give me, if you are
capable of any pity, procure e convenience and means of
flight. Foi, that you yourself ay testify how 1 possible it
was to biing me back, listen to the explanation of my conduct,
which to you and all of them must seem insane Hear now
the oath which I have sworn in my soul, and which I
incessantly repeat in words with you only did I wish to live,
with you to enjoy, to employ my days, from youth to old
age, in true honourable union And let this be as fiim and
sure as aught ever sworn before the altar, this which I now
swear, now when I leave you, the most pitiable of all men "

He made a movement to glide past her, as she stood close
before him, but she caught hi softly in her arms "What
is this !" exclaimed he

"Lucidor !" cried she, "not pitiable as you think you
are mine, I a yours, I hold you in my arms, delay not to
thiow your arms about me Your father has agreed to all,
Antoni marries my sister "

In astonishment he recoiled from her "Can it be?"
Lucinda smiled and nodded, he drew back from her arms
"Let me view once more, at a distance, what is to be mine
so nearly, so inseparably?" He grasped her hands "Lucinda,
are you mine?"

She answered "Well, then, yes," the sweetest tears in the
truest eyes, he clasped her to his breast, and threw his head
behind hers, he hung like a shipwrecked marinei on the
cliffs of the coast, the ground still shook under him. And
now his enraptured eye, again opening, lighted on the mirror
He saw her there in his arms, himself clasped in hers, he

looked down, and again to the image   Such emotions accompany man throughout his life   In the mirror, also, he beheld the landscape, which last night had appeared to him so baleful and ominous, now lying fairer and brighter than ever; and himself in such a posture, on such a background ! Abundant recompense for all sorrows !

"We are not alone," said Lucinda, and scarcely had he recovered from his rapture, when, all decked and garlanded, a co pany of girls and boys came forward, carrying wreaths of flowers, and crowding the entrance of the Hall   "This is not the way," cried Lucinda   "how prettily it was arranged, and now it is all running into tumult !"   A gay march sounded from a distance, and the company were seen coming on by the large road in stately procession   Lucidor hesitated to advance towards them, only on her arm did he see certain of his steps   She stayed beside him, expecting from moment to moment the solemn scene of meeting, of thanks for pardon already given

But by the capricious gods it was otherwise determined. The gay clanging sound of a postillion's horn, from the opposite side, seemed to throw the whole ceremony into rout "Who can be coming?" cried Lucinda   The thought of a strange presence was frightful to Lucidor, and the carriage seemed entirely unknown to him   A double-seated, new, spick-and-span new, travelling chaise !   It rolled up to the hall   A well-dressed, handsome boy sprang down, opened the door, but no one dismounted, the chaise was empty. The boy stept into it, with a dextrous touch or two he threw back the tilts, and there, in a twinkling, stood the daintiest vehicle in readiness for the gayest drive, before the eyes of the whole party, who were now advancing to the spot Antoni, out-hastening the rest, led Julia to the carriage "Try if this machine," said he, "will please you, if you can sit in it, and over the smoothest roads, roll through the world beside me   I will lead you by no other but the smoothest, and when a strait comes, we shall know how to help ourselves   Over the mountains sumpters shall carry us, and our coach also "

"You are a dear creature!" cried Julia   The boy came forward, and with the quickness of a conjuror, exhibited all the conveniences, little advantages, comforts and celerities of the whole light edifice

"On Earth I have no thanks," cried Julia; "but from this little moving Heaven, from this cloud, into which you raise me, I will heartily thank you"   She had already bounded in, throwing him kind looks and a kiss of the hand   "For the present you come not hither, but there is another whom I mean to take along with me in this proof excursion, he himself has still a proof to undergo"   She called to Lucidor, who, just then occupied in   ute conversation with his father and father-in-law, willingly took refuge in the light vehicle, feeling an irresistible necessity to dissipate his thoughts in some way or other, though it were but for a moment.   He placed himself beside her, she directed the postillion where he was to drive.   Instantly they darted off, enveloped in a cloud of dust, and vanished from the eyes of the amazed spectators

Julia fixed herself in the corner as firmly and commodiously as she could wish   "Now do you shift into that one too, good brother, so that we may look each other rightly in the face "

Lucidor You feel my confusion, my embarrass   ent I a   still as if in a dream; help me out of it.

Julia Look at these gay peasants, how kindly they salute us!   You have never seen the Upper Hamlet yet, since you came hither   All good substantial people there, and all thoroughly devoted to me   No one of them so rich that you cannot, by a time, do a little kind service to him   This road, which we whirl along so smoothly, is my father's doing, another of his benefits to the community

Lucidor I believe it, and willingly admit it   but what have these external things to do with the perplexity of   y internal feelings?

Julia Patience a little ! I will show you the riches of this world and the glory thereof Here now we are at the top ! Do but look how clear the level country lies all round us leaning against the   ountains ! All these villages are much, much indebted to   y father ; to mother and daughters too. The grounds of yon little ha   let are the border

Lucidor Surely you are in a very strange mood. you do not see   to be saying what you meant to say

Julia But now look down to the left, how beautifully all this unfolds itself ! The Church, with its high lindens, the Amthaus, with its poplars, behind the village knoll ! Heie, too, are the garden and the park.

The postillion drove faster

Julia The Hall up yonder you know it looks almost as well here as this scene does from it.   Here, at the tree, we shall stop a moment now in this very spot our image is reflected in the large   irror. there they see us full well, but we cannot see ourselves —Go along, postillion ! There, some little while ago, two people, I believe, were reflected at a shortei distance, and, if I am not exceedingly mistaken, to theii great mutual satisfaction

Lucidor, in ill humour, answered nothing they went on for so e time in silence, driving very hard. "Here," said Julia, "the bad road begins a service left for you to do, some day Before we go lower, look down once more My mother's box-tiee rises with its royal summit over all the rest Thou wilt drive," continued she to the postillion, " down this rough road ; we shall take the footpath through the dale, and so be sooner at the other side than thou " In dismounting, she cried. " Well, now, you will confess, the Wandering Jew, this restless Antoni the Traveller, can arrange his pilgrimages prettily enough for himself and his companions it is a very beautiful and commodious carriage "

And with this she tripped away down hill Lucidor followed her, in deep thought , she was sitting on a pleasant seat, it was Lucinda's little spot She invited him to sit by her.

Julia So now we are sitting here, and one is nothing to the other Thus it was destined to be The little Quicksilver would not suit you Love it you could not, it was hateful to you

Lucidor's astonishment increased.

Julia But Lucinda, indeed! She is the paragon of all perfections, and the pretty sister was once for all cast out I see it, the question hovers on your lips who has told us all so accurately?

Lucidor There is treachery in it!

Julia Yes, truly! There has been a Traitor at work in the matter

Lucidor Name him

Julia He is soon unmasked You! You have the praiseworthy or blameworthy custom of talking to yourself and now, in the name of all, I must confess that in turn we have overheard you

Lucidor (starting up) A sorry piece of hospitality, to lay snares for a stranger in this way!

Julia. By no means! We thought not of watching you, ore than any other But, you know, your bed stands in the recess of the wall, on the opposite side is another alcove, commonly employed for laying up household articles Hither, some days before, we had shifted our old man's bed, being anxious about him in his remote Hermitage and here, the first night, you started some such passionate soliloquy, which he next morning took his opportunity of rehearsing

Lucidor had not the heart to interrupt her He withdrew.

Julia (rising and following him) What a service this discovery did us all! For I will confess, if you were not positively disagreeable, the situation which awaited me was not by any means to my mind To be Frau Oberamtmannin, what a dreadful state! To have a brave gallant husband, who is to pass judgment on the people, and, for sheer judgment, cannot get to justice! Who can please neither high nor low, and, what is worse, not even himself! I know what my poor mother

suffered from the incorruptibility, the inflexibility of   y father
At last, indeed, but not till her death, a certain meekness took
possession of him   he seemed to suit himself to the world, to
make a truce with those evils which, till then, he had vainly
striven to conquer

Lucidor (stopping short, extremely discontented with the
incident, vexed at this light mode of treating it) 'For the
sport of an evening this might pass, but to practise such a
disgracing mystification day and night against an unsuspicious
stranger, is not pardonable

Julia We are all equally deep in the crime, we all
hearkened you   yet I alone pay the penalty of eaves-
dropping

Lucidor All ! So   uch the   ore unpardonable ! And how
could you look at me, throughout the day, without blushing,
whom at night you were so contemptuously overreaching?
But I see clearly with a glance, that your arrangements by day
were planned to make mockery of me   A fine family ! And
where was your father's love of justice all this while !—And
Lucinda !—

Julia And Lucinda ! What a tone was that ! You
meant to say, did not you, How deeply it grieved your
heart to think ill of Lucinda, to rank her in a class with
the rest of us?

Lucidor I cannot understand Lucinda.

Julia In other words, this pure noble soul, this peacefully
composed nature, benevolence, goodness itself, this woman as
she should be, unites with a light-minded company, with a
freakish sister, a spoiled brother, and certain mysterious
persons ! That is incomprehensible !

Lucidor. Yes, indeed, it is incomprehensible

Julia Comprehend it then ! Lucinda, like the rest of us,
had her hands bound   Could you have seen her perplexity,
how fain she would have told you all, how often she was on the
very eve of doing it, you would now love her doubly and trebly,
if indeed true love were not always tenfold and hundredfold of

itself   I can assure you, moreover, that all of us at length
thought the joke too long

Lucidor   Why did you not end it, then ?

Julia   That, too, I must explain   No sooner had   y father
got intelligence of your first monologue, and seen, as was easy
to do, that none of his children would object to such an exchange, than he determined on visiting your father   The
i portance of the business gave him much anxiety   A father
alone can feel the respect which is due to a father. "He must
be informed of it in the first place," said mine, "that he   ay
not in the end, when we are all agreed, be reduced to give a
forced and displeased consent   I know him well, I know how
any thought, any wish, any purpose cleaves to him, and I have
  y own fears about the issue   Julia, his maps and pictures,
he has long viewed as one thing, he has it in his eye to transport all this hithe1, when the young pair a1e once settled here,
and his old pupil cannot change he1 abode so readily, on us
he is to bestow his holydays, and who knows what other kind
friendly things he has projected   He must forthwith be in-
for ed what a trick Nature has played us, while yet nothing is
declared, nothing is determined "   And with this, he exacted
from us all the most solemn promise that we should observe
you, and, come what might, retain you here till his return.
How this return has been protracted, what art, toil and perseverance it has cost to gain you1 father's consent, he himself
will info1m you.   In short, the business is adjusted. Lucinda
is yours

And thus had the two promenaders, sharply removing from
their first resting-place, then pausing by the way, then speaking and walking slowly through the green fields, at last reached
the height, where another well-levelled road received them
The carriage came whirling up   Julia in the mean while
turned her friend's attention to a strange sight   The whole
machine1y, of which her gay brother had bragged so much, was
now alive and in motion, the wheels were already heaving up
and down a multitude of people, the see-saws were flying;

may-poles had their climbers, and many a bold artful swing
and spring over the heads of an innumerable multitude you
might see ventured   The younker had set all a-going, that so
the guests, after dinner, might have a gay spectacle awaiting
the   "Thou wilt drive through the Nether Hamlet," cried
Julia, "the people wish me well, and they shall see how well
I am off"

The Hamlet was empty   the young people had all run to
the swings and see-saws, old men and women, roused by the
driver's horn, appeared at doors and windows, every one
  ave salutations and blessings, exclaiming "O what a lovely
pair !"

Julia There, do you hear? We should have suited well
enough together, after all, you may rue it yet

Lucidor But now, dear sister !

Julia Ha ! Now dear, when you are rid of me ?

Lucidor One single word ! On you rests a heavy accusa-
tion   what did you mean by that squeeze of the hand, when
you knew and felt my dreadful situation ? A thing so radically
wicked I have never met with in my life before

Julia Thank Heaven, we are now quits, now all is
pardoned   I had no mind for *you*, that is certain, but that
you had utterly and absolutely no mind for me, this was a
thing which no young woman could forgive, and the squeeze
of the hand, observe you, was for the rogue. I do confess, it
was almost too roguish, and I forgive myself, because I forgive
you, and so let all be forgotten and forgiven ! Here is my hand

He took it, she cried "Here we are again ! In our park
again, and so in a trice we whirl through the wide world, and
back too, we shall meet again "

They had reached the garden-hall, it seemed empty, the
company, tired of waiting, had gone out to walk   Antoni,
however, and Lucinda, came forth   Julia stepping from the
carriage flew to her friend, she thanked hi   in a cordial
embrace, and restrained not the most joyful tears   The brave
man's cheeks reddened, his features looked forth unfolded, his

eye glanced moist, and a fair imposing youth shone through the veil

And so both pairs moved off to join the company, with feelings which the finest dream could not have given the

CHAPTER LAST

"Thus, y friends," said Lenardo, after a short prea ble, "if we survey the most populous provinces and kingdoms of the firm Earth, we observe on all sides that wherever an available soil appears, it is cultivated, planted, shaped, beautified, and in the same proportion, coveted, taken into possession, fortified and defended   Hereby we bring home to our conceptions the high worth of pi operty in land , and are obliged to consider it as the first and best acquirement that can be allotted to man   And if on closer inspection we find parental and filial love, the union of countrymen and townsmen, and therefore the universal feeling of patiiotism, founded immediately on this same inteiest in the soil, we cannot but regard that seizing and retaining of Space, in the great or the small scale, as a thing still more important and venerable   Yes, Nature heiself has so ordered it!   A man born on the glebe comes by habit to belong to it, the two giow together, and the fairest ties aie spun from their union   Who is there, then, that would spitefully disturb this foundation-stone of all existence, that would blindly deny the worth and dignity of such precious and peculiar gifts of Heaven?

"And yet we may assert, that if what man possesses is of great worth, what he does and accomplishes must be of still greater   In a wide view of things, therefore, we must look on property in land as one small part of the possessions that have been given us   Of these the greatest and the most precious part consists especially in what is movable, and in what is gained by a moving life

"Towards this quarter, we younger men are peculiarly con-

strained to turn, for though we had inherited from our fathers
the desire of abiding and continuing, we find ourselves called
by a thousand causes nowise to shut our eyes against a wider
outlook and survey   Let us hasten, then, to the shore of the
Ocean, and convince ourselves what boundless spaces are still
lying open to activity, and confess that, by the bare thought
of this, we are roused to new vigour

"Yet, not to lose ourselves in these vast expanses, let us
direct our attention to the long and large surface of so many
countries and kingdoms, combined together on the face of the
Earth   Here we behold great tracts of land tenanted by
Nomades, whose towns are movable, whose life-supporting
household goods can be transferred from place to place   We
see them in the middle of the deserts, on wide green pasturages,
lying as it were at anchor in their desired haven   Such movement, such wandering, becomes a habit with them, a necessity,
in the end they grow to regard the surface of the world as if
it were not bulwarked by mountains, were not cut asunder by
streams   Have we not seen the North-east flow towards the
South-west, one people driving another before it, and lordship
and property altogether changed ?

"From over-populous countries, a similar calamity may
again, in the great circle of vicissitudes, occur more than
once   What we have to dread fio   foreigners, it may be
difficult to say, but it is curious enough, that by our own
over-population, we ourselves are thronging one another in
our own domains, and without waiting to be driven, are
driving one another forth, passing sentence of banishment
each against his fellow.

"Here now is the place and season for giving scope in our
bosoms, without spleen or anger, to a love of movement, for
unfettering that impatient wish which excites us to change our
abode   Yet, whatever we may purpose and intend, let it be
accomplished not from passion, or from any other influence
of force, but from a conviction corresponding to the wisest
judgment and deliberation

"It has been said, and over again said Where I am well, is my country ! But this consolatory saw were bettei worded . Where I am useful, is my country ! At home, you ay be useless, and the fact not instantly observed, abroad in the world, the useless man is speedily convicted And now, if I say . Let each endeavour everywhere to be of use to himself and others,—this is not a piecept, or a counsel, but the utterance of life itself

"Cast a glance over the terrestrial ball, and for the present leave the ocean out of sight, let not its hurrying fleets distract your thoughts, but fix your eye on the firm earth, and be amazed to see how it is oveiflowed with a swarming ant-tribe, jostling and crossing, and running to and fro forever ! So was it ordained of the Lord himself, when, obstructing the Tower of Babel, he scattered the human iace abroad into all the world Let us praise his name on this account, for the blessing has extended to all generations

"Observe now, and cheerfully, how the young, on every side, instantly get into movement As instiuction is not offered them within doors, and knocks not at their gates, they hasten forthwith to those countries and cities whither the call of science and wisdom allures them Here, no sooner have they gained a rapid and scanty training, than they feel themselves impelled to look round in the world, whether here and there some profitable experience, applicable to their objects, may not be met with and appropriated Let these try their fortune ! We turn from them to those completed and distinguished men, those noble inquireis into Nature, who wittingly encounter every difficulty, every peiil, that to the world they may lay the world open, and, through the   ost Impassable, pave easy roads

"But observe also, on beaten highways, how dust on dust, in long cloudy trains, mounts up, betokening the track of commodious top-laden carriages, in which the rich, the noble, and so many others, are whirled along , whose varying purposes and dispositions Yoiick has most daintily explained to us.

"These the stout craftsman, on foot, may cheerily gaze after, for whom his country has made it a duty to appropriate foreign skill, and not till this has been accomplished, to revisit his paternal hearth In still greater numbers do traffickers and dealers meet us on our road, the little trader ust not neglect, from time to time, to forsake his shop, that he may visit fairs and markets, may approach the great merchant, and increase his own small profit, by example and participation of the boundless But yet more restlessly do we descry cruising on horseback, singly, on all high and by ways, that multitude of persons whose business it is, in lawful wise, to ake forcible pretension to our purses Samples of all sorts, prize-catalogues, invitations to purchase, pursue us into town-houses and country-houses, and wherever we may seek refuge: diligently they assault us and surprise us, themselves offering the opportunity, which it would have entered no man's mind to seek And what shall I say of that People which, before all others, arrogates to itself the blessing of perpetual wandering, and by its movable activity contrives to overreach the resting, and to overstep the walking? Of them we ust say neither ill nor good, no good, because our League stands on its guard against them, no ill, because the wanderer, mindful of reciprocal advantage, is bound to treat with friendliness whomsoever he may meet

" ut now, above all, we must mention with peculiar affection, the whole race of artists, for they, too, are thoroughly involved in this universal movement Does not the painter wander, with pallet and easel, from face to face, and are not his kindred labourers summoned, now this way, now that, because in all places there is something to be built and to be fashioned? More briskly, however, paces the musician on his way, for he peculiarly it is that for a new ear has provided new surprise, for a fresh mind fresh astonishment Players, too, though they now despise the cart of Thespis, still rove about in little choirs, and their oving world, wherever they appear, is speedily enough built up. So likewise, individually,

renouncing serious profitable engagements, these men delight
to change place with place, according as rising talents, combined with rising wants, furnish pretext and occasion For
this success they commonly prepare themselves, by leaving no
important stage in their native land untrodden

"Nor let us forget to cast a glance over the professorial
class these, too, you find in continual motion, occupying and
forsaking one chair after the other, to scatter richly abroad
on every side the seeds of a hasty culture More assiduous,
however, and of wider aim, are those pious souls who disperse
themselves through all quarters of the world, to bring salvation
to their brethren Others, on the contrary, are pilgriming
to seek salvation for themselves they march in hosts to consecrated, wonder-working places, there to ask and receive what
was denied their souls at home

"And if all these sorts of men surprise us less by their
wandering, as for most part, without wandering, the business
of their life were impossible, of those again who dedicate their
diligence to the soil, we should certainly expect that they, at
least, were fixed By no means! Even without possession,
occupation is conceivable, and we behold the eager farmer
forsaking the ground which for years has yielded him profit
and enjoyment , impatiently he searches after similar or greater
profit, be it far or near Nay, the owner himself will abandon
his new-grubbed clearage so soon as, by his cultivation, he has
rendered it commodious for a less enterprising husbandman
once more he presses into the wilderness, again makes space
for himself in the forests , in recompense of that first toiling,
a double and treble space , on which also, it may be, he thinks
not to continue

"There we shall leave him, bickering with bears and other
monsters, and turn back into the polished world, where we
find the state of things no whit more stationary Do but view
any great and regulated kingdom, the ablest man is also the
man who oves the oftenest , at the beck of his prince, at the

ordei of his ministei, the Serviceable is transferred from place
to place To him also our precept will apply Everywhere
endeavour to be useful, everywhere you are at home   Yet if
we observe important statesmen leaving, though reluctantly,
their high stations, we have reason to deplore their fate , for
we can neither recognise them as e igrators nor as migrators
not as emigrators, because they forego a covetable situation
without any prospect of a better even seeming to open , not as
migiators, because to be useful in other places is a fortune
seldom granted them

"For the soldier, again, a life of peculiar wandeiing is
appointed , even in peace, now this, now that post is intrusted
to him, to fight, at hand or afar off for his native country,
he must keep himself perpetually in motion or readiness to
move , and not for immediate defence alone, but also to fulfil
the remote purposes of nations and rulers, he turns his steps
towaids all quarters of the world , and to few of his craft is
it given to find any resting-place And as, in the soldiei,
courage is his fiist and highest quality, so this must always be
considered as united with fidelity , and accoidingly we find
certain nations, famous for trustwoithiness, called forth from
their home, and serving spiritual or temporal regents as
body-guards

"Another class of persons indispensable to governments,
and also of extreme mobility, we see in those negotiators,
who, despatched from court to court, beleaguer princes and
ministeis, and overnet the whole inhabited world with theii
invisible threads   Of these men also, no one is certain of his
place for a moment   In peace, the ablest of them are sent
from country to country, in wai, they march behind the army
when victorious, piepare the way foi it when fugitive, and
thus aie they appointed still to be changing place for place,
on which account, indeed, they at all times caiiy with them a
stock of farewell cards

"If hitherto at every step we have contiived to do ourselves

so e honour, declai ing as we have done the   ost distinguished
portion of active men to be our   ates and fellows in destiny,
thei e now remains for you, my beloved friends, by way of
termination, a glory higher than all the rest, seeing you find
youi selves united in brotheihood with princes, kings and
emperors   Think first, with blessings and revei ence, of the
imperial wandei er Hadii an, who on foot, at the head of his
army, paced out the circle of the woi ld which was subject to
him, and thus in vei y deed took possession of it   Think then
with horror of the Conqueror, that armed Wanderer, against
who   no resistance availed, no wall or bulwark could shelter
armed nations   In fine, accompany with honest sympathy
those hapless exiled princes, who, descending from the summit
of the height, cannot even be received into the modest guild
of active wandei ei s

"And now while we call forth and illustrate all this to one
another, no narrow despondency, no passionate perversion can
rule over us   The time is past when people i ushed forth at
random into the wide world   by the labout s of scientific
travellers describing wisely and copying like artists, we have
become sufficiently acquainted with the Earth, to know
moderately well what is to be looked for everywhere

"Yet foi obtaining perfect information an individual will
not suffice   Our Society is founded on the principle that each
in his degree, for his purposes, be thoroughly informed   Has
any one of us some country in his eye, towai ds which his
wishes are tending, we endeavour to make clear to him, in
special detail, what was hovering befoi e his imagination as a
whole   to afford each other a survey of the inhabited and
inhabitable world, is a most pleasant and most profitable kind
of conversation

"Under this aspect, we can look upon oui selves as   embers
of a Union belonging to the world   Simple and grand is the
thought , easy is its execution by understanding and strength
Unity is all-powei ful , no division, therefore, no contention

among us! Let a man learn, we say, to figure himself as without per anent external relation, let him seek consistency and sequence not in circumstances but in himself, there will he find it, there let hi cherish and nourish it He who devotes hi self to the ost needful will in all cases advance to his purpose with greatest certainty otheis again, aiming at the higher, the more delicate, require greater prudence even in the choice of their path But let a man be attempting or treating what he will, he is not, as an individual, sufficient foi himself, and to an honest mind, society iemains the highest want. All seiviceable persons ought to be related with each other, as the building proprietor looks out for an architect, and the architect for masons and carpenters

"How and on what principle this Union of ouis has been fixed and founded, is known to all Theie is no man among us, who at any moment could not to pioper purpose employ his faculty of action, who is not assuied that in all places, whither chance, inclination, or even passion may conduct hi , he will be received, employed, assisted, nay, in adverse accidents, as far as possible, iefitted and indemnified

"Two duties we have most rigorously undertaken first, to honour every species of religious woiship, for all of them are comprehended ore or less directly in the Creed secondly, in like anner to respect all forms of government, and since every one of them induces and promotes a calculated activity, to laboui according to the wish and will of constituted authori-ties, in whatevei place it may be oui lot to sojourn, and foi whatever time Finally, we ieckon it oui duty, without pedantry oi rigour, to piactise and forwaid decorum of manners and morals, as requiicd by that Reverence for Our-selves, which aiises from the Thiee Reverences, whereto we univeisally piofess oui adheience, having all had the joy and good fortune, some of us from youth upwaids, to be initiated likewise in the highci geneial Wisdom taught in ceitain cases by those venerable men. All this, in the solemn hour of paiting, we have thought good once   ore to recount, to unfold, to hear and acknowledge, as also to seal with a trustful Farewell

> Keep not standing fix'd and rooted,
>   Briskly venture, briskly roam !
> Head and hand, where'ei thou foot it,
>   And stout heait are still at home
> In each land the sun does visit
>   We are gay whate'er betide ,
> To give space foi wand'ring is it
>   That the world was made so wide '